THIS IS TOTALLY NORMAL

STORIES

TIM MEYER

ALSO BY TIM MEYER

Novels & Novellas:

In the House of Mirrors

Less Than Human

The Thin Veil

Sharkwater Beach

Primal Terra

Lords of the Deep (with Patrick Lacey)

Limbs

Kill Hill Carnage

Paradise Club

The Switch House

69

Dead Daughters

Pteranodon Canyon

Malignant Summer

The Sea, the Stars

Rainbow Filth

Lacuna's Point

Wormwood (with Chad Lutzke)

DEMON BLOOD: SERIES

Enlightenment

Gateways

Defiance

COLLECTIONS:

Worlds Between My Teeth

Black Star Constellations

This Is Totally Normal

CONTENTS

TRUNKS

1979

1.

The heat was so intense that the roadkill before him smelled like grilled burger meat.

Officer Nick Santiago scraped the poor sucker off the road with the shovel he kept in his trunk, then heaved the remains at the central New Mexico flatlands, leaving them for the coyotes. He wiped off the sticky, smooshed jack rabbit residue in the dirt, then placed the shovel back in the trunk. He prayed next year's county budget would allow the board to expand the maintenance department so he wouldn't get stuck spending most of his shift unsticking dead animals from the hot-tar highways. There were so many other things Santiago imagined himself doing at that moment, like kicking his feet up on the desk back at the station, drinking unhealthy amounts of coffee, and combing through the local rags.

Instead, he was out here searching the highway for kills.

Glorious.

He ambled back to his cruiser, wiping the midmorning sweat from his brow. It was a June scorcher, and he was starting to really resent the New Mexico summers. Six years since he moved down this way from Idaho, and he'd regretted relocating ever since. Of course, he'd packed up everything he owned and left his hometown behind for only one reason—a girl. But that hadn't panned out, and now he was kinda stuck here.

Stuck.

Like the rabbit he'd peeled off the highway, he was waiting for someone to come along and scrape *him* up.

Then again, he wasn't truly stuck—he was well aware he could move back home any time he pleased, just peel himself away from this place. But that was a hassle he didn't feel like dealing with. Packing, moving, finding a new job, essentially starting over again where he'd been born. A rebirth of sorts. Plus, he had friends here now, a few really good ones, other officers, guys he liked to hang out with at the bar on Sundays come autumn, watching Roger and the Boys march toward the next Super Bowl. He wouldn't trade those Sundays for anything. The beers, the laughs, the incessant cheering. Nothing compared.

No, he was a New Mexico boy now, whether he wanted to admit it or not.

Santiago packed himself into the cruiser and cranked the engine to life. Before he shifted into gear, a blur sped past him. He didn't get a chance to clock it—no time to fire up the radar gun—but his intuition pegged the bastard at a hundred-plus miles per hour. A solid forty-five over the speed limit, a major moving violation, one he couldn't simply ignore.

Santiago sped off after the driver, light rack flashing, siren blaring. He pushed the cruiser to a buck-twenty and still had trouble catching up with the offender. But within half a mile, the speedster began to realize he'd been caught and started to slow, veering their orange Dodge Challenger onto the shoulder.

"Dispatch, this is car four, over," Santiago said into the radio.

"Hear you loud and clear, car four," Heather said.

"Hey, Heather. Can you run a plate for me? Thinking this one might have some heat on it."

"Sure thing, Nick."

"Appreciate it, darling." He read off the Texas plate, and she came back a minute later to tell him the car was as clean as a new whistle. "Well, I'll be damned."

"Registered to a Ross Reeves," Heather relayed.

"Thanks, darling. Hey, how about you and me go out tonight and paint the town all shades of red?"

He imagined her rolling her eyes as she said sing-song-like, "Goodbye, Officer Santiago."

Unable to keep himself from smiling, he climbed out of the car, fixed his hat, and took off for the Challenger, his drawing hand resting above his holster. He didn't know why the thought of needing his weapon suddenly overpowered him. After all, he had never approached a vehicle that way before, but this…this felt different. Dangerous? Maybe. He couldn't articulate the exact aura this orange Challenger gave off, only that he was oddly suspicious of it. A silly image of him knocking on the window only to discover no driver inside had his imagination running wild.

Silly.

The dumbest notion, really, but he couldn't unstick the thought from his mind. The rabbit had been easier to remove than this whacky idea.

Of course, when Santiago arrived at the window, he found himself staring at his own reflection. Tinted windows weren't illegal, but Santiago wished they were. He couldn't tell what the hell was waiting for him on the other side of the glass. For all he knew, he was staring into the black, soulless eyes of a double-barreled shotgun.

He rapped his knuckles on the roof, wondering what was taking the driver so long to show his face. "Window, please," he said promptly.

A hesitation. He almost couldn't believe it. Maybe the driver was contemplating a smooth getaway. Wait until the copper got nice and close, and then—*zoom!* Spin the tires on the asphalt, let the world fill with smoke and flecks of rubber dust, and make for the horizon. He'd never witnessed such a thing, but he'd heard stories.

"Come on now, we ain't got all day."

Finally, the window descended, revealing a man in his mid-to-late-thirties, sporting a thick mustache and a Big Texas cowboy hat that Santiago immediately wished he'd owned. The accessory would have gone great with his Dallas-blue Roger Staubach jersey. Santiago couldn't see the man's eyes behind the pair of gold aviators, and that didn't sit too well with him. Then again, nothing about this routine stop sat particularly easy.

"License and registration, please," he asked the driver.

Ross Reeves (presumably) handed over the information. "I'm so sorry, officer," the man said, adjusting the collar of his black duster.

Before looking at the two pieces of identification, Santiago stole a quick glance at what he could see of the front seat, the dashboard, and the backseat. Nothing concerning, nothing in the least. No apparent weapons. No partially concealed drugs. But why the guy wore a duster on a hundred-twenty-degree day in mid-June was something he'd never understand, even if Tex here was somehow able to manufacture a decent explanation.

"I didn't mean to speed," Reeves added.

"Didn't mean to?" Santiago looked over the information—everything matched what Heather had told him. "In a hurry, Mr. Reeves?"

"Yes, actually. My sister is pregnant. She lives in San Diego. The baby is due any day now, and I hoped to make up some time on these empty highways. You have my deepest apologies for causing you any inconvenience."

Santiago's instincts kicked in. He knew the slimy bastard was lying. "Flying's faster."

"Oh, it is!" Reeves laughed. Something between a giggle and a guffaw. "But I can't afford a ticket."

Santiago ran his eyes along the length of the car, admiring the beautiful, pristine coating. The cop wagered that, even with the aid of a magnifying glass, he wouldn't find a single scratch. Not the faintest mark. "But you can afford this delicious hunk of metal?"

"Times have been hard on all of us lately, huh? Besides…t'was a gift from my father."

"Your father couldn't have flown you to California?"

This question seemed to tie the man's tongue, and Santiago celebrated the victory with a smile of his own. "Please, officer. I really must be on my way. I understand I was speeding. Please issue my ticket and allow me to continue. I'll slow it down. Promise. Hand to God."

Santiago gazed at the man, deliberately taking his time as if the drawn-out scrutiny would encourage the bastard to admit the truth.

Plus, Santiago had never been rich. Grew up poor all his life and stopped living paycheck to paycheck only a couple of years ago. Holding up this punk from getting to his destination seemed reasonable payback for the shitty hand life had dealt Nicholas Santiago.

"Please," the man pleaded, showing his teeth.

Santiago didn't know if the man was trying to display a sensitive side or if he was about to growl at him. The man's teeth were slightly sharper than an ordinary set, but Santiago didn't get a good look at them. The man's lips tightened around them as if he needed to hide this fact. Could have been the desert heat that made them look pointed, distorted them in some way. Either way, Santiago wasn't dwelling on it.

"Okay, listen here, Tex. I gotta good mind to—"

Something moved. He heard a knock, a small movement, like a raccoon caught in an attic grate trying to nudge its way out. Not quite frantic but calculated. Then…silence. Santiago followed his ear to where he thought the noise had originated.

"What was that?" Santiago asked, checking the backseat.

"What was what?" Reeves shot back.

"You messing with me?"

Reeves took an innocent approach, raising his hands, wholly visible, and grimaced at the cop. "Didn't hear a darn thing, officer."

"Was that your…trunk?" Santiago moved down the car, bypassing the backseat and going straight for the rear. He examined the surface of the trunk cautiously, preparing for something to jack-in-the-box out at him.

Reeves was out of the driver's seat faster than a slingshot. "Officer," he said, offering up a pleading hand. "Please. You really don't want to do that."

Drugs, Santiago thought. *The sonofabitch is hauling grass. Something harder? Lucy or heroin?* Santiago couldn't smell anything save for the hot, softened asphalt. His cop's nose was blind to any other smell. *Damn this heatwave.*

But drugs didn't explain the bump. What else was he hauling back there?

Santiago put a hand on the trunk, tapping his fingers on the surprisingly cool metal. He didn't think much of it at first, but the surface of the car's exterior shouldn't have been that cold, not out here beneath the blazing desert sun. "Open it."

Reeves froze, then stood up straight, a defiant flex. "No."

"Not gonna ask you again, partner. Open the goddamn trunk."

Reeves looked away, making eyes with the flatlands as if they might provide a death-defying escape. Reading the man's mind, Santiago almost laughed. Trying to run now, out here in the flats, was dumber than trying to pet a pack of coyotes with a sausage in your pocket. Clear space that stretched to the horizon flanked the road; nowhere to run, nowhere to hide. Reeves wouldn't get twenty yards before Santiago could call on his revolver and sink a thirty-eight into one of his legs.

Santiago's hand went to the holster again. He dropped the two ID cards on the asphalt, doubting their authenticity anyway.

"I'm begging you, officer," Reeves said, "do not open that fuckin' trunk."

Another bump. Something inside. *Someone?*

"Who's in there?"

"Not a who," Reeves said, "but a *what*."

"Huh?" The strangeness of this answer didn't register. "Stop dicking around. Pop the trunk."

Reeves eyed him one last time, and then his pleading face broke, and he smiled. "Okay, sir. Have it your way. Don't say I didn't warn you."

The driver ducked back inside the driver's seat and pulled the lever near the floor pedals. The release popped with a metallic *click* followed by a *thud*, freeing the trunk from its locked position. Santiago's heart rate spiked as the trunk lifted, the hinges squeaking as it crept upward. Why he was scared, he didn't know. But he suddenly had a very bad feeling about this, the sinking sensation in the pit of his stomach worsening with each passing moment. Before he could even think about heading back to the squad car and calling for backup, he found himself gripping the bottom of the trunk and raising it, only a few inches at first. Thin tendrils of smoke poured through the opening like a ghostly spill, and Santiago retracted his hand at once, jumping back a few feet as a frozen bolt traveled through his fingers, up his arms, and into the four chambers of his heart.

"Oh, goddammit!" he said, shaking his hand as if a hungry barracuda had suddenly latched on. He examined the damage immediately and saw white flakes of frost had stuck to his fingers. *Frost? In New Mexico? In summertime?*

It was the craziest damn thing he'd ever seen.

"You have thirty seconds," Reeves said, and his face was no longer one of a man trying to convey innocence or smooth-talk his way out of a ticket. He was proud, overly confident, and very much enjoying this interaction and the turn it had taken. "And then there will be nothing left of you."

Santiago gritted his teeth, then went for his gun. He didn't know exactly what he would do with the weapon once it was free, but he knew he'd need it for whatever was next. Pointing the revolver at Reeves, he squinted down the barrel. Somewhere in the distance, the desert buzzards screeched as if staking a claim on whoever might be left standing.

"Ten seconds," Reeves said, his confidence not faltering even after the weapon's introduction. "Five."

Santiago's eyes returned to the trunk, the cool, misty vapor pouring out like a waterfall's ghost. To his horror, the trunk's cover rose, unfolding like the maw of some great beast. On its own, the trunk opened until it couldn't anymore. Santiago stared in disbelief, then flicked his eyes back on the driver, who stood a solid five feet from the driver's seat. There was no clear way he was responsible for opening the trunk.

It's a trick. A mind trick. That's all. Rigged some way, like those fancy Vegas magic shows.

As Santiago tried to convince himself that this was an elaborate hoax, the cold vapor began to change color, a myriad display of blues and yellows, reds and greens. They flashed like nightclub strobes, and Santiago felt himself lured in by its peculiar appeal. *Hypnotized* wasn't the best word for what he felt—but it was close. His eyes became heavy, his limbs languid, devoid of any fight. He wanted to climb inside and sleep forever. Inside that trunk, that colorful womb. The unknown called to him—whatever horror lived within the unusual spectacle.

As he continued to stare at the light show before him, his feet began to shuffle forward. Toward the trunk, toward the smoke, toward the flashing lights within. An ambient noise filled his ears, an incessant buzzing, and he no longer heard the engine of his cruiser running in the background. The screeching of hungry buzzards had been silenced. Santiago dropped his gun on the asphalt, not caring if the impact would accidentally cause the trigger to send off a rogue shot. He moseyed forth, concentrating solely on the mysterious presence inside that trunk. The frigid temperatures welcomed him, sang him songs of comfort, and promised him reprieve. From the heat. From his life. From all that ailed him, which wasn't all that much these days. But the promises of a new, better life were too hard to ignore.

As the smoke cleared and Santiago's sight was swallowed by the trunk's endless depths, some indeterminable thing climbed out of its frigid chamber. He suddenly wished he hadn't dropped the revolver. Wished he'd called for backup when he'd had the chance. There was no opportunity now. Nowhere to go. No way to avoid what was coming for him.

Santiago screamed, and the desert listened to the harsh sounds of his bones breaking one by one.

2.

THE SODA MACHINE in the far right-hand corner of the Twilight Motel was tucked behind the stairwell like a secret hideaway that few knew about. Surprise, surprise, it was out of order again. Emilio Reyes knew not only the machine's secluded location but also the special trick to get it working again. Tap the Sprite two times, the Diet Coke once, the Dr. Pepper *three* times, punch the wooden-paneled belly six times with a little force and flex, and out would pop a random refreshment. Today, the machine was gracious enough to spit out a can of regular Coke. The kid cracked the top so quickly that he almost ripped open his thumb on the metal mouth. He took a sip, audibly sighed, and then left the safety of the stairwell, wandering back out beneath the late-morning sun.

The rising temperature in Valencia, New Mexico, was way above average that day, but Emilio was used to the summer heat. The heat didn't bother him. It was the cold winter nights he'd never get used to.

He rounded the back of the motel, continuing to chug the soda. He wondered how long it would take for Mr. Moats—the Twilight Motel's big cheese—to realize he'd been pilfering soft drinks. A part of him figured the man was far too busy dealing with drunks and financially delinquent lodgers to worry about some missing cans of cola. But to ensure he wouldn't get caught, Emilio used the secret method sparingly, once every few days, to keep himself safe. He also made sure the time of day was just right. Moats was always tucked away in his office mid-morning, keeping track of the books. At eleven years old, Emilio didn't exactly know what *keeping track of the books* entailed, but he figured it had to do with money.

Everything grownups did had to do with money.

Everything.

As he returned to the room his mother was renting, the one they'd been stuck in for the last several months (since before the previous school year ended), he noticed an orange car pulling into the parking lot. He couldn't remember ever seeing an orange vehicle before, let alone one that looked like ripe clementines. Maybe a few brownish ones that could pass for orange under the right light, but not like this. The cars he was used to seeing had rust-eaten sides and dented hoods, not gleaming exteriors as if they'd just left the car wash, a sun-kissed sheen sparkling across the entire surface. In other words, this looked like it belonged to someone with money.

A drug dealer?

He'd hung out at the Twilight Motel long enough to know about drugs. Adult things. Nasty things. Bad things that bad people did. His mother never preached to him about the dangers of drugs, but the topic had come up in school last quarter. One student had found a hypodermic needle sticking out of the playground sand and had brought the discovery to the attention of the lunch-period chaperones. The school was forced to schedule an assembly later that afternoon. A forty-five-minute lecture on needles and the harmful effects of drugs on the human body commenced, and even though it was a bit over Emilio Reyes' head, he got the gist. Drugs were bad; stay away from them. Okay?

But Eric Latoya, one of his schoolmates and best friends, told him his cousin Johnny used to *sell* drugs and that he'd gotten rich from it. *Drives the fanciest car. All from slinging a little grass.*

It sounded no bueno, and Emilio had enough smarts to determine that Eric's cousin was—in all probability—not a nice dude. But the way Eric spoke about him was marked by admiration, as though he wanted to sign up for a route at his druggy delivery service.

The orange car that reminded him of the Challenger he'd seen on the library's popular car calendar definitely belonged to a drug dealer, or so Emilio convinced himself. He toyed with the idea of heading over there, talking to the driver, seeing if he could get a little information. Maybe he could play detective, interview the man, learn more about him and his intentions at the Twilight Motel, and then take the information to Mr. Moats himself. Maybe if he tattled and helped keep this criminal element away from the Twilight, Mr. Moats would give him free Cokes every day. Then he wouldn't have to worry about getting caught. It sure would ease his conscience some.

But he was too scared to go over there. Instead, he watched from a safe distance as the man parked the orange Challenger outside Moats's office, stepped into the lot, and headed for the door. As he did, the man caught him staring. He tipped his big Texas cowboy hat and smiled. He couldn't see the man's eyes behind his gold-rimmed aviators, but Emilio was fairly certain the man had winked at him.

Despite the heat, a horrible chill coiled around his spine, casting a layer of frost around the crown of his skull. As soon as the man disappeared into the office, Emilio ran all the way back to his room. Back to his mother, where it was safe.

3.

"Mom, Mommy, Mom-Mom," he said, trying to shake her awake. "I think I saw a bad man."

His mother didn't move. She was so wrapped up in the white sheets that she looked like a mummy. Moaning, she turned over, away from him. An empty bottle of some forbidden adult beverage rested on the nightstand next to her. The room smelled like an acid bath.

"*Mom,*" he complained, shaking her once more.

She muttered something in Spanish.

Instead of giving up, he rounded the bed to the side she was facing. He leaned over the mattress and reached for her face. With both thumbs, he pried open her right eye.

"Mom!"

She launched herself awake, face twisted with fury, cursing at him in Spanish, words he knew not to repeat. *Ever.* Then she asked, "What the hell is wrong with you, O?"

O. Her nickname for him. She didn't like his full name and never called him by it, not even when she was pissed. She always hated *Emilio* because his father had insisted on naming him that. It had been *his* father's name, and he had refused to listen to any alternatives. And now that the son of a bitch was gone, far removed from the picture by his own choosing, she was stuck with this little boy whose name she hated. She'd never admit that to him, of course, but Emilio wasn't dumb—he could see it in her eyes and hear it in the way she spoke to him. It was as though she had no time for anything he had to say, or maybe she simply didn't care. That was okay, though. At least she spoke to him. He had friends whose parents yelled and screamed and beat them unmercifully all the time. Sandy Cortez-Reyes never laid a finger on her son. Not even at her angriest.

After a few seconds of sticking her motherly glare on him, she rolled her eyes and collapsed on the mattress. Emilio had backed himself into the wall, wondering if she'd finally break, finally lay a palm across his cheek. But she hadn't. Her anger seemed to abate, and the two were left staring at each other in the dimness provided by the blackout shades.

"Damn it, O," she said, hiking up the sheets to cover her bare shoulders. "You can't wake me like that."

"Sorry," he said, "but there's a drug dealer here. *In the Twilight!*"

This news didn't surprise her. She didn't even blink. "What are you talking about, niñito?"

"I saw a man," he said, pointing at the curtain-covered window. "He was driving an orange car."

Mom couldn't help but giggle. "And that automatically makes him a drug dealer?"

"No, it was… I think it was an expensive car."

"Oh," she said, covering her mouth, feigning surprise. "Oh my.

We should alert the authorities at once. Get the FBI down here to investigate immediately." With her head dipping to the side, she smiled. "Should we call the President of the United States while we're at it?"

He didn't think it was that funny, but she sure did. She laughed into her pillow. Giggling school-girlishly.

"I'm serious," he said.

"You have an active imagination, my sweets." She rolled over, taking the sheets with her, wrapping herself like a wedding-dress burrito. "Let mommy rest. She's very tired."

"You're always tired."

This caught her attention. She glanced at him over her shoulder. Not liking the tone and the accusations it carried, she glared at him. "I have to work later."

"Yeah," he said.

"What's 'yeah?' You know I have to work. You like sleeping in a bed at night, right? You like food in your belly?"

He looked over to the "bed" she mentioned. It was a mattress on wheels, the kind they rolled in and out at a guest's request. Sometimes, his mother let him sleep on the regular bed, the queen, but that was once a week if he was lucky.

"Things could be worse, you know," she reminded him, and certainly not for the first time, though every time she did, it sounded like it would be the last. Like, maybe things would turn around. Get better. And soon.

"I know," he said, now staring at his dirty shoelaces. If he said anything about how dirty they were, his mother would tell him, *At least you have shoelaces.* So on and so forth. That was how these conversations went, and when you were eleven, there was nothing you could say or do to change the outcome of these circumstances. Things just…*were.*

Mom sighed as if everything they'd talked about stole what remained of her energy. "Go play while I sleep for another hour or two."

"There's nothing to do."

"There's *plenty* to do. What about your friend Robbie? The boy from room 213?"

He didn't care for Robbie too much, but he was the only other kid at the motel close to his age. He'd moved in with his parents last month. "I guess…"

"Go. It's going to be a late night for me."

With that, she went back to bed and was snoring almost immediately.

4.

ON THE WAY TO knock on the door of room 213 to see if Robbie was home, Emilio noticed the orange car parked in the big lot where the other tenants and one-night guests kept their vehicles. He must have finished his business with Moats, booked himself a room, and began his residency amongst the Twilight's community. Whether here for the long-term or just a night was yet to be determined, but with a car like that, Emilio doubted the man was sticking around. He probably had a Santa Fe mansion to go home to, surrounded by sycamores and tall fences too high to climb over. Most likely, the man was in town for business, but what business he had in Valencia… Who knew?

Drugs?

Definitely drugs.

The car grabbed his attention again. This time, the smooth, gleaming paint job didn't let go. Something about the way the Challenger sat there unnerved him. He couldn't tell what exactly, but only that it called to him. Which was stupid. It was just a car, a *silent* car, and it didn't have the ability to *call* to him. Yet, for some reason, that's exactly what it felt like. For one, he had trouble taking his eyes off the powerful machine, as if doing so would cause damage, like staring at the sun too long—only the opposite. *Look anywhere else, kid, and your retinas will burn*, that cool orange finish said. Those headlights were like eyes themselves, always leering.

His curiosity was firing on all cylinders. Like he knew there was magic inside those two doors, magic that wanted to get out. And how could a boy pass on such a magical experience?

Go ahead, the car urged. *Come over. Have a peek inside. I certainly won't hurt you.*

He stopped walking and turned his left shoulder toward the parking lot. A heat bow arched over the row of cars, distorting the horizon beyond them. The sun baked his flesh, and the warmth of the late-morning hour brought a toasty comfort to his cold insides. Taking in the motel's sights, he saw vacant porches, not a single soul of any kind, and empty windows like zombie eyes. Also missing was the gangly neighborhood cat that often patrolled the parking lot and begged for food with those gorgeous green eyes. The rattling from the window air units droned on, working their hardest to keep things cool in the hellish environment.

The car demanded his attention, though. His presence. The lure of that special vehicle could not be ignored, and Emilio felt himself slinking across the lot toward the four-wheeled beast. Seconds later, he found himself standing next to it, peeping back and surveying the windows of the rooms, making sure no one had crept over and was now spying on him. Not that he was doing anything wrong—admiring such a thing of beauty was certainly no crime. But maybe he wanted to touch it, run his fingers along the machine's brilliant armor, and maybe that was going too far. Momma always told him never to touch anything that didn't belong to him, and her lessons occasionally echoed in the catacombs of his mind when he neared the precipice of any wrongdoing. But this time... This time, he was able to cast her motherly hand-me-down advice to the side and continue with the thing he knew he shouldn't do.

He moved along the length of the Challenger, examining its shell and smooth paint job. Not a speck of rust. Not a dent. No imperfections of any kind. Not that he expected any. But a dent or a scratch was almost a given in this place. He was concerned for the safety of this majestic machine. Parked here amongst so many other cars, cars belonging to careless owners, a scratch or a dent was almost a sure bet.

His heart fluttered when his fingers grazed the surface. The smooth coating electrified his fingertips, imbuing a sense of power within. He wondered what it would be like to sit in the front seat or, better yet, position himself behind the steering wheel and press his foot against the pedal. Hear the roar of the engine block, the power of the V12 thrumming through him. If he closed his eyes and concentrated hard enough, he could almost feel and hear it.

The faint smell of gasoline brought him back to reality. Down the line, a few cars away, one of the tenants—a Twilight lifer who went by the name of Bobby Bricks—had brought his car to life, gunning the gas, filling the air behind him with dirty, noxious exhaust. He stuck his head out the window and fixed Emilio with a hard, suspicious gaze. A look that made the kid want to shrink and hide. "Hey, kid. You screwing around?"

Emilio shook his head, *Nope.*

Bobby didn't say another thing. Just shot him another dirty look, more threatening this time, and went on his way. Kids got no respect from their elders in the Twilight, no sir.

Emilio automatically hated the guy for interrupting his daydream. As Bobby peeled off in his rusted Chevy, Emilio's attention returned to the Challenger. The orangeness. The perfection. The magic. He drifted around to the driver's side, and his eyes fell on the door—which was *open.*

Open?

It couldn't be, but it was. Not *wide* open, not enough for the casual pedestrian strolling by to notice. But from the rear, he could see the lip of the door sticking out about an inch. As if the owner had weakly pushed it shut and assumed it had closed all the way. He walked over to the door, figuring it was shut enough for the lock to catch. But when he pulled on the door handle, the door clicked and opened, offering him a clear view inside.

What the…

He stared at the empty front seat and detected the smell of hot leather wafting out, merging with the faint scent of sticky tar that always seemed to permeate the motel grounds. He stole a glance at the motel windows. Still nothing. No one was watching. All was clear for him to make some bad decisions. He'd forgotten his mother's request—to go see what Robbie was up to. He'd forgotten his mother completely. The only thing that filled his head now was how cool it would be to sit inside the Challenger—and not just any ol' Challenger, but a nifty orange one, orange like wildfire, orange like plump Florida tangerines.

He decided to do it. Real quick. Even if he got caught, he had a good excuse. He was just a kid; he didn't know any better. Didn't know it wasn't cool to go around and sit in other people's cars. He knew kids could get away with a lot, and his mother wasn't the best at disciplining him, so he could get away with more than most kids his age. She couldn't really take anything away because there wasn't anything *to* take away. Couldn't send him to his room because the motel was his room, and he rarely left anyway. He supposed she could lock him in the bathroom for a day, but there were worse punishments to suffer, and he decided a seat in this machine was well worth it.

The leather was plush; the material felt like it had the unnatural ability to absorb him. He twisted the dials on the radio even though there was no power. He pulled on the sun visor to block the invading brightness. The wheel was locked in place, but he pretended to make full revolutions, imagining the wheels squealing on the hot surface below. With his deepest voice, he mimicked the roar of this power-house of an engine. He even made the gear changes along with each pantomimed shift.

Then he saw *him*. The owner. Walking toward him with an *I-mean-business* gait, like nothing in the world could throw him from that direct path.

Emilio's heart raced, the spike of fear so jolting he thought he'd died instantly. In the moments that followed, he acted on pure instinct, driven by a terror so untapped he couldn't even process his own thoughts. The door was sealed shut, and escaping wasn't an option. If he opened the door, he'd make too much noise, and the man would notice him immediately. He'd get a good look at him, too. No, he did the only thing that made sense at the time: he turned and dove into the back, curling himself into a ball behind the driver's seat.

Knees tucked to his chest, he waited for the door to open, the man to reach inside and grab him by his hair, haul him out like a cat stuck in a washing machine. But that didn't happen. The door opened, yes. The man got inside, sure. Closed the door behind him. But instead of reaching back and grabbing Emilio by his shaggy head of hair, the man cranked the engine to life and shifted into gear.

As the car rolled out of the parking lot, the thought of being locked in the bathroom for a day suddenly wasn't the worst punishment he could imagine.

5.

CHIEF MICHAEL TAVARES got the call around noon and headed out to the spot where Heather had said Santiago called in that Texas license plate. When he and Officer Tim Kendall arrived on the scene, Tavares knew he was in for a nightmare of an afternoon. Hell, a nightmare of a *week* if they couldn't locate their missing deputy.

They found the cruiser empty, the driver's side door wide open. Santiago's revolver was on the pavement, every round in the chamber accounted for.

"Shit," Tavares said first. Then he followed that up with, "Get everyone down here that you possibly can. We have a missing officer, and he may have been abducted." *Dead by now*, he wanted to add, but he wasn't ordering funeral flowers until they had the body.

Kendall went back to his car and got on the horn. Tavares hustled back to his, hoping to grab a quick smoke and clear his head, but when he arrived, he heard Heather's voice coming through the radio.

"Chief?" she said, sounding alerted.

"Go ahead, Heather." He lit his smoke. "Tell me you got good news. They found Santiago hiding out in Mexico. It's all a big prank or something."

"Not quite," she said, sounding disappointed. "We got a call from a worried mother in Valencia. Says her son went to play with a friend but never showed up. He's been missing for about two hours now."

A migraine settled in. He tried to smoke it away, even though the cigarettes usually made them worse. He rubbed his temples, pressing hard enough to conjure white blinking stars in front of him. "Where at?"

"Twilight Motel."

"Twilight Motel," Tavares repeated as if he might have visited the place decades earlier and suddenly remembered it existed. "The one out on nineteen that's owned by that ol' weasel…what's his face?"

"Manny Moats," Heather said.

"That's the son of a bitch. Busted him for running tricks out of that place once or twice, if I remember correctly."

"Man's been clean for a decade, according to the reports."

"Clean, yeah," Tavares said with a chuckle. "Well, that may be."

"I can send someone else on it," Heather said.

Tavares's instincts kicked in, and he got the good sense that this was something he should investigate himself. "I'll check it out, interview the mother. Just give me the details."

Heather recited what she'd scrawled down.

"Appreciate it," he said once he had the woman's contact information, including her room number at the motel. "I'll head over there just as soon as we get more uniforms down here."

He put the radio back on the cradle and headed back to Tim Kendall. His officer crouched about twenty feet from where Santiago had abandoned his ride, staring at the pavement with a focused gaze. Then he brought two fingers to his eyes, looking at them dubiously.

Whatever he was staring at, Tavares immediately hated it. "What you got there, Timmy?"

Kendall cringed away from whatever had grabbed his attention, then showed his boss what he'd sampled from the road. Tavares saw the red smears immediately, and the migraine's band ratcheted around his forehead, squeezing his temples into submission.

The white stars returned on their own accord this time.

"Blood," Kendall confirmed. "It's definitely blood."

6.

THE CAR HAD BEEN in motion for at least twenty minutes, but Emilio thought it could have been an hour, maybe two. He'd begun to sweat profusely. A crippling bout of nausea swept through him, and he had to close his eyes to balance himself out and keep down what his stomach wanted to lift up. He paid careful attention to his body, ensuring his stillness. His silence. He even took short, shallow breaths through his nose so the driver wouldn't hear him. Through the window, he watched the clouds speed past as the Challenger cruised along the interstate toward an unknown destination, farther and farther from home.

The more miles they tallied, the more Emilio realized he was dead meat. That he was never coming back. That he was never going to see his mother again. That this situation would not resolve itself peacefully. Death is the last thing on an eleven-year-old kid's mind, but that was all Emilio Reyes could think of—a scene at the cemetery like in those afternoon movies that sometimes played on the television set, the priest holding a eulogy for the recently departed, his mother breaking down in tears and throwing herself over his closed, empty casket.

Empty because they'll never find me, he thought.

His mind was beginning to turn on him, the bad outcomes seeping in. It had been two years since his mother forced him to visit church on a Sunday morning, and he hadn't wasted a single thought on God or prayer since. But now, he silently recited every prayer he'd committed to memory (the *Our Father* and a few lines from the *Hail Mary*), begging the Lord to forgive his sins and spare his life just this once. He'd be a good boy for his mother from here on out. He promised he'd never do anything bad whatsoever as long as he lived, which was hopefully a pretty long time.

He shut his eyes, trying to block the coming tears. He put a hand over his mouth because the waterworks were on the way. No matter how hard he tried to cage his emotions, he couldn't control the overwhelming stress of the situation. The *trouble* he'd created for himself. He begged God to grant him the power to travel back in time, to when he was faced with the decision to knock on 213's door or get a closer look at the orange Challenger.

God did not listen, though. And so Emilio was stuck here, forced to deal with the consequences of his reckless pursuit of an interesting afternoon.

Suddenly, the car veered off the road and slowed. Emilio thought he'd failed in his effort to conceal his hiding place. Maybe the driver had heard him crying over the intermittent static of the radio as it searched for a station to lock onto. But the car trundled to a stop, and the driver popped the door open without skipping a beat.

"About time," he heard a man—not the driver— say before the driver closed the door. The ensuing conversation was muffled, the closed door providing a near-silent vacuum.

Emilio poked his head up, timidly glancing over the back seat, hoping to sneak a peek through the rear window. He tested the movement, creeping up slowly, making damn sure not to rock the car as he dropped his knees on the leather. Then he lifted his eyes over the backrest and stared out. He saw two men conversing near another car, one far inferior to the Challenger in every way. To put it bluntly: it was a "heap of crap" (his mother's slogan), the kind of ride his mother *might* have been able to afford. The tan paint job was chipped and peeling in various places, the chrome bumper rusted and dented all over, looking more like a demolition derby battering ram rather than a daily workhorse that would get you from point A to B without breaking down.

The man in the cowboy hat, the Challenger's owner, was listening to the other man, a short, round guy in his mid-forties. He wore a Hawaiian shirt and aviators with gold rims and blackout lenses and spoke with his hands a lot. His bald top reflected the sun, a patch of lightning-white, and as he went into his animated explanation of whatever the two were discussing, a black, braided ponytail—attached to the back of his head, near his neck—whipped side to side like a tassel.

Emilio listened.

"You gotta believe me," the semi-bald man explained. "I didn't do anything."

Cowboy Hat crossed his arms while arching his back.

"Seriously?" Baldy asked. "You think I stole the money? Is that what you think?"

"Don't matter what I think," Cowboy Hat said calmly. "Only matters what the trunk thinks."

Emilio must not have heard him correctly. He thought he heard the man say *trunk*, but that couldn't be. Trunks don't think. Was it someone's name? Someone who went by *Trunk*?

"The trunk?" Baldy seemed just as confused. His lips shriveled like decomposing grapes. "Fuck you talkin' about, man?"

Cowboy Hat flashed him an incredibly wide smile, showing teeth that weren't exactly designed for eating green veggies and orange carrots. No, they look like a carnivore's teeth, a *Tyrannosaurus*'s or something. Not quite as sharp, but close.

Emilio's mysterious chauffeur nodded in the Challenger's general direction. "The trunk has the ability to detect the truth."

"The trunk?" The man laughed incredulously. He bent forward and slapped his right knee, then erupted with more laughter, the annoying, barking kind. "Are you fucking putting me on, fella? Huh?"

"Not putting you on, buddy. Go ahead. Open it. Unless…you're lying to me."

"I'm…" The man's face went dead still, the laughter cutting off like someone had stabbed him in the gut. "Told you I ain't lying. Look, let me talk to Carmucci directly. I'll get this whole thing sorted out, and we can get back to business, okay? What's his phone number? Thought I saw a gas station some miles back; I'm sure they have a phone I can use."

"Carmucci isn't interested in direct contact." Another Big Texas grin, like he was selling oil and on the brink of closing some lucrative deal. "That's why he sent me."

"Well, I don't like the look of you, the feeling I get when I talk to you. You…you don't seem like a reasonable fella to me."

"Sorry, but that doesn't mean a dick's worth of spit to me." He stepped aside and welcomed the other man forward with a horizontal sweep of his arm. "Open the trunk."

The man's feet remained rooted to the desert floor. "You going to kill me? Over what amounts to unpaid parking ticket fines compared to the kind of mula Carmucci's making? Stuff me in that trunk? Is that it?"

"Not if you're telling the truth."

"And the trunk knows?"

"Oh, yes. The trunk knows all things."

The man seemed to toss around the idea of leaving, running back to his car and trying to escape before Cowboy Hat could do anything to stop him. He glanced back at his crappy ride and must have concluded that whatever he was planning wasn't going to work. Then he stepped forward. Toward the trunk. Reluctance made him work for each step.

Emilio heard a hard, mechanical thud, and the whole car shook. The trunk rose a few inches. The man took a few hesitant steps forward, then stopped a couple of feet away.

"What's them lights?" Baldy asked Cowboy Hat, but Cowboy Hat just stood there, observing, not interested in questions and answers. "Hey, I said—"

The trunk's lid popped all the way open. A loud noise was released, like two cars barreling toward each other and slamming on the brakes to avoid a colossal impact. Squealing. Screaming. Emilio couldn't see what was happening just past the rear bumper, but he heard Baldy cry out a frantic scream that almost sounded wet, like the man was drowning and screaming at the same time. Then the car lurched violently. Emilio was displaced from his knees, the sudden movement knocking him back into the seats. In an instant, he dropped himself back to the floor, put his hands over his head, and waited out the seismic shift until it was over. The rumbling lasted fifteen seconds, then abruptly stopped. In the silent aftermath, Emilio peeked up, toward the trunk, wondering what had caused the world to shake.

Wondering what had happened to the bald man.

He rose, eyeing the top of the trunk, which continued to block his view outside. Then, suddenly, the trunk slammed shut, and Emilio found himself peering into Cowboy Hat's eyes, the bluest eyes he'd ever seen, and those eyes peered back into Emilio's.

At first, Emilio didn't know what to do. He wanted to move, to escape the car, but there was nowhere to go. The man would beat him to either door, his only egresses. Even if he managed to hurdle the front seats and slip out before the man could get there, the man was obviously bigger, stronger, and faster. Emilio was no slowpoke, but he doubted he could outrun an adult, especially one with such an athletic build. He looked strong and healthy, with lean legs that gave off the impression he could sprint long distances, even if he wasn't dressed for it. The man looked like his gym teacher, Mr. Venchini, who once played professional soccer in Europe. Cowboy Hat had muscles under that duster of his, a man who appeared very conscious of his physique.

But his physical traits weren't the most alarming quality. It was that…

He looks like a killer, Emilio thought.

The eyes convinced him. Those blue dime-sized orbs, like cold planets devoid of any lifeform whatsoever. While staring at them—an exchange that lasted far too long—Emilio's skin hardened. An arctic chill merged with the hot, pumping blood in his veins. And God, who could forget those teeth?

The man's head tilted sideways, obviously curious about the cargo he'd unknowingly transported there. Emilio distanced himself the best he could, resting his bottom on the armrest between the two front seats. Then he decided to go for it—to make for the door. To escape. He whipped around, reaching for the door handle. But before his fingers could even touch the surface, the door was yanked open, and Cowboy Hat's eyes were fixed on him.

"Well, well. Ain't you a curious sight," Cowboy Hat said, the words seeming to taste delicious to him. "Where'd you come from?"

"Please don't kill me!" Emilio shouted. "I won't tell anyone, I swear!"

The empty promise elicited a chuckle. "Tell anyone what?" He nodded back to where the incident with Baldy occurred. "What exactly do you think you saw, boy?"

"You…" Emilio hesitated. His active imagination painted the scene his eyes hadn't beheld. But it was the man's screams—his last—that would haunt him forever. "You killed him!"

Cowboy Hat shook his head. "Nah, son. You got it all wrong. I didn't kill him. Heck, I never killed anyone." The man's eyes shifted to the trunk. "It was the trunk."

The words barely seemed to register in Emilio's ears. The trunk? How could a trunk kill a man? It didn't make sense. But he couldn't explain that awful noise that had come from the Challenger's back end, that metallic screech and subsequent crunch. It had not been a mechanical noise. Nor had it been a human one. And because he couldn't make sense of it, the door to the impossible had been left ajar.

"Please don't kill me," Emilio said, his eyes dripping with warm tears.

The bad man sighed. "I'm not going to kill you. Come out of there."

"I don't trust you."

"Why not?"

Emilio didn't have to remind him of what had just taken place.

"That business you saw," the bad man told him, "was between me and that man."

"Are you a drug dealer?" An honest question that caused the man to smile again.

"Where would you get a silly idea like that?" Cowboy Hat scratched his scalp beneath the crown of his hat. "You've been watching too many of those midnight movies on the cable box, haven't you?"

Emilio almost confessed what he knew of Eric Latoya and his drug-dealing cousin but managed to keep the secret to himself.

"Okay, kid," the bad man said, reaching for him now. "Come on out of there."

Emilio recoiled from the stretching fingers.

"Don't make me rip you out."

"You can't make me," Emilio said. "You can't!"

"I beg to differ," Cowboy Hat said, his voice rough, tough, and scratchy. Then he gripped his paw around Emilio's skinny ankle and began to pull.

Emilio screamed. But out there in the desert, there was no one to answer his distressed calls for help, save the coyotes, and even they ran for cover when the boy's cries reached them.

7.

TAVARES WATCHED the woman break and begin sobbing into her hands, the kind of sorrowful crying you couldn't help but feel connected to. If you didn't feel for someone who cried like that, you weren't human. He fixed Timmy Kendall with a quick glance, and Kendall's focus was on the peeling wallpaper of this shit-splat motel room. How anyone could live in a place like this was beyond Tavares's comprehension, but he also supposed there were worse places to call home.

Like the streets. The back of a car.

After a few minutes, the woman's tears slowed some.

"Listen, Miss…Cortez-Reyes, was it?" He glanced at his notes and realized he hadn't taken any.

"Yes," she said, dotting the corners of her eyes with a napkin. "You can call me Sandy."

"Sandy," he repeated, testing the name on his tongue like some unique flavor he might want second helpings of. "Don't believe I've ever met a Sandy before. It's a nice name." The compliment was an attempt to put her at ease, but it hardly worked. She offered him an obligatory smile, but that was it. No *thank you*, no *that's very nice of you to say*. The silent fallout brought a spell of awkwardness, but he needed to continue, do his job, and get the hell out of there, if for no other reason than to be done with this uncomfortable interaction. Besides, there was work to do. In one day, in a town where not much happened, he'd lost an officer and an eleven-year-old kid. "So…your boy."

"O," she said. "Emilio. I call him O."

"Cute. You have any pictures of him?"

She dug through the nightstand and produced a solitary photograph, then handed it over to Kendall like it was her last dollar. "That was taken last year. We took a bus to the San Diego Zoo. That was when things were…better."

Kendall glanced at the picture for a beat, committed it to memory, and then gave it to his boss. Tavares stared at the image twice as long. Cute kid. Shaggy hair. Athletic-looking but small. An easy target for some pervert-weirdo kidnapper.

"Kid have a father?" Tavares rolled his eyes at his own question. "Stupid, I know. All kids have fathers, don't they? What I meant was —is O's father in his life?"

"No," she said in a tone that suggested she wasn't willing to elaborate on the subject.

"What do you do for a living, Sandy?"

"What does that… What does my job have to do with finding my son?"

"Just a question. We like to be thorough. Lots of times, kidnappings are committed by someone close to the victim. Sometimes they're random. But still, policework is a lot like gambling—you gotta play the odds."

Sandy's eyeline migrated to the bedspread. "I work at Tito's."

Tito's. Tavares nodded, knowing the place. Some of his co-workers referred to the joint as *Tit-O's.*

"You notice any change in the clientele there?" Tavares asked.

"What do you mean?"

"Like, you got any stalkers? Any of them boys gettin' extra handsy with you of late? Any incidents that might have gained you an enemy?"

"No," she said, and he believed her. "In fact, it's been slow lately. Too slow. Having trouble keeping up with the rent."

"I understand. Sorry to hear that. Sounds like you got yourself a difficult situation." He flipped the empty notebook closed, the pages dry. Made him wonder why he even opened it in the first place. "We will do our best to find your son. I promise you that."

"He's so small." The waterworks again. Slower this time but just as heart-wrenching. If it wasn't unprofessional, he might have hugged her. "He can't defend himself."

Tavares didn't have the heart to speak his mind; he believed the boy was either already dead or more than halfway to the border. "We will do our best, ma'am," was the best he could offer.

8.

ALL HE TASTED WAS the dusty sand. He could smell the heat coming up from the ground. The sun was hot on his skin, and he could sense tomorrow's sunburn a day early. The manilla rope around his wrists and ankles burned, too.

"You ain't gonna roll your way to freedom, are you?" asked Cowboy Hat as he stood over him, hands on his hips, proud of the knots he'd tied. "I could leave you in the car, but that'd be worse than being outside, believe you me. You'd bake like a potato."

"What will you do with me?" Emilio asked, the fate of his future his only concern. He was still alive and hadn't been thrown inside the trunk with Baldy, so he guessed he was in the clear…at least for a little while.

"That's the question, ain't it? I have half a mind to throw you inside the trunk of our friend's shit heap, leave you out in the desert until the coppers find you. But that'd be killing you, boy, and I already told you, I ain't no killer. Besides, there's my safety to consider. My freedom."

That wasn't the answer he was hoping for.

"I have to hide this here car, get it off the road, keep the pigs at bay, and give me some time to get to my next post. You're going to stay there for a few minutes. Can you handle that?"

Emilio remained silent and still.

"Rhetorical question," Cowboy Hat said. He snickered. "Know what that means?"

Emilio shook his head.

"Means you don't have to answer it. The answer is obvious to the both of us. Got it?"

Emilio did not *get it* but nodded anyway.

"Good. Smart kid. I think we're going to get along just fine."

With that, he walked away, back toward the dead man's shit heap. He climbed inside the cab, started the engine, and drove off into the desert until the heat-blurry horizon swallowed him whole.

9.

Tavares cruised down the highway in the direction Santiago had been wheeling prior to his mysterious disappearance. He felt he needed to get a feel for the path and drive by the scene again. Maybe that would give him some answers and point him in the right direction. Whoever had taken him (or murdered him, hid his body in the desert) was likely still traveling west, which meant the potential killer would have passed right by the Twilight Motel.

It couldn't have been a coincidence. Could it?

He wasn't sure. All he knew—that both events happening in such close proximity, not to mention how the timing worked out— suggested it was more than coincidence. It made a very good case for being *related.*

The more he thought about it, the more the theory worked. Santiago pulled over the killer/abductor for speeding. Santiago discovered something he had on him or was searching the vehicle due to suspicious activity. And the man killed him or stuffed him in the trunk or both. Then he sped off toward the west coast, stopped at the motel, and picked himself up a little boy along his path of chaos.

Motives weren't clear, but the chain of events made sense to him.

He drove past the spot where Santiago's patrol car had been parked. The scene was clear now; the boys had a local company tow the vehicle back to the station. Besides the droplets of blood high-lighted by yellow evidence markers, the area was as it had been. There was nothing that signaled anything bad had happened. Just desert and rock and road. And that bright bastard of a sun shining over them all.

How this had happened in broad daylight, Tavares didn't quite know. It wasn't like the highway wasn't traveled—it was a main road that saw its fair share of wheels throughout the day. Then again, the incident occurred long after the nine-to-fivers had arrived at their workplaces. The suspect had been lucky in that regard.

Damn lucky.

Tavares set his sights on the western horizon. He zipped past the Twilight Motel, determined to follow the road until it led him to any clues regarding his deputy's whereabouts and the missing kid with a stripper mom whose soul was crushed under the weight of this tragic day.

10.

EMILIO DIDN'T THINK the man would ever return, and after an hour of lying there, waiting, baking beneath the rising temps the hot sun brought with its ascent, Emilio thought he was going to fry there. But an hour—maybe two—later, he saw a shadow appear on the desert's distorted horizon, a shadow that lengthened as it moved closer. The shape of the man's hat became distinct. His abductor returned a few minutes later, sweaty and silent but acting like he still had enough energy to complete another journey across the flatlands.

He walked right over to Emilio, untied the rope around his ankles, and hoisted the boy to his feet. Emilio was marched back to the car. He protested by digging his heels into the ground, but the man was way too strong and dragged him along with ease. Emilio kicked at the man's shins, but he avoided those quick toes by skipping to the side.

"Aggressive," Cowboy Hat said. "I like it."

Emilio screamed and kicked at the man one more time, aiming for the spot he knew would hurt more than any other place—the sensitive pouch between the upper thighs.

Cowboy Hat blocked the kick with his knee and retaliated by driving the heel of his palm into the bridge of Emilio's nose. The forceful impact drove the kid's head backward, forcing his chin up towards the sky. Emilio's vision darkened with a dizzying wave that messed with his equilibrium. He collapsed to the ground like the sack of dirty clothes his mother always made him lug to the laundromat. Pain blossomed in his nasal passages, then traveled to other parts of his head. A dull throb grew in his temples. He felt something wet trickle down his upper lip, and he knew it was blood.

"Don't do that again, boy," the bad man warned. "Jesus Christ, I'm trying to save your life here."

Emilio needed a reminder of how that was exactly, but no clarification seemed forthcoming.

The man clapped a hand on his neck, directed him to the car, and forced him into the back, pushing him over the lowered front seat.

Cowboy Hat knelt so he could look him in the eye. Those cool-blue flecks inside the man's irises seemed to move like the jelly inside a lava lamp. His chiseled face kept its stony façade. "You play nice, boy, and you might just live to see your mommy and daddy again," the bad man told him.

He didn't have the heart to tell the man he'd never see his daddy again. Not ever.

The bad man got into the driver's seat and cranked the massive engine to life. The seats vibrated with a power that almost seemed unearthly. Apocalyptic. The world shook, rattling Emilio's bones. But this wasn't as terrifying as when the trunk opened and…

What? *Swallowed* that man?

Ate him?

Emilio didn't know. In any case, he was certain he never wanted to experience *that* again.

But he would. And he knew it. Knew he'd see the trunk open again like the ravenous jaws of some terrible beast.

11.

JoJo Farmer put his elbow on the door jamb, sipped from his bottled lager, and stared past the four gas pumps, the only things that stood between him and the desert flats. The afternoon was getting older, true—but it was never *not* the right time to crack open a cold one. The best thing about owning his own business was that he couldn't get fired, so JoJo liked to drink on the job. In fact, getting sauced made him more amiable when it came to dealing with customers. Helped him focus while handling cash transactions, too.

He scratched his beard scruff and then ducked inside the store, wondering how much slower today could get. He had all but two customers so far, and that was during the "busy" hour before the normal workday began. Since then, it was as dead as a midnight graveyard out here.

He polished off what remained in the bottle, tossed the empty in the trashcan behind the counter, then ambled over to the cooler in the corner for seconds. He'd come to realize that second beers were almost better than the first. And let's face it—you could never stop at just *one*.

JoJo lifted the cap with the bottle opener on his key chain. Took a swig. Swished the lager around his mouth, let the foam build, and then swallowed. Burped, enjoying the sour aftertaste. Then he turned his ear to the road. The mechanical roar of a pristine machine purred in the distance. It was headed his way.

He knew that engine. The recognition supplied his arms with an icy tickle.

He went back for the front door, had himself a look-see. In about ten seconds, his instincts proved him right, and he saw the orange blur of that familiar four-wheeled box.

Shit, he thought, and immediately went back inside to hide the beer. Then he grabbed a breath mint, tucked his hair beneath his hat, and headed back outside into the sun. He watched the Challenger brake to a stop, a brume of desert dust swirling all around the impressive machine.

The driver got out and leaned on the open door. The bad son of a bitch flashed his pearly whites, and his teeth sparkled as though Mr. Clean himself had bleached them. Sharp bastards. Not quite like daggers, but shit—JoJo never had seen any like them. They almost looked like fakes.

"Afternoon, JoJo," the driver said.

"R-Rudy," JoJo said nervously, unable to shake that harsh scratch in his throat. "To what do I owe the pleasure of this visit?"

"Oh, you know. I was in the neighborhood."

"Oh?" JoJo had lived long enough and earned enough tenure in the business to know that men like Rudy Ramone (if that was the bastard's true name) didn't just drop by to say "hi." His appearance was always purposeful. Not the kind of visit you ever *wanted* to have. "Well, want a beer?"

"I don't drink and drive," he said. "And I got plenty of driving to do today."

"You're always driving," JoJo said with a chuckle, meaning to lighten the dark mood the man's appearance had cast over them. But Rudy didn't seem to find anything humorous about their unexpected conference. "Guess you don't drink then."

Rudy's mute response seemed to confirm this theory.

"Seriously. I'm all paid up with Carmucci. Don't owe that guinea fuck a dime. So what's with the visit? He trying to get me to throw bread at him? He can fuck himself sideways all Sunday long if that's what he's thinking."

Rudy sighed like he was finally allowed to reveal the secret he'd been holding in. "Can't say exactly. Don't know all the details—being honest, one-hundred percent truthful. Don't know what the big man has in his head, only I got a list, and—"

"List?" JoJo's nose wrinkled like used, wet towels. "What kinda list you talking about?"

Rudy shot him a warning stare, the kind that said, *You're treading in hazardous waters, friend-o. Questions are not welcome here.* "I reckon Carmucci has a list of acquaintances he doesn't trust very much. Look, I don't want to get involved one way or the other. Not my business. I'm told to do a job, so I do it, no questions asked, you understand? The less I know, the better off I'll be."

JoJo glared at the car. For some reason, he feared it. Every aspect, including the shiny orange coating that never seemed to dull, no matter how many years passed. Could have been the rumors, too. Could have been Rudy Ramone's status in Carmucci's *business*—not quite a hitman per se, but something close to it. The guy who made problems disappear. Guess *fixer* was the most fitting word for what he was.

Then, of course, there was the gossip of Rudy himself. What he *was.* Some swore the bastard wasn't even human. A devil in human skin, maybe. But not human. JoJo couldn't buy into those whispers; he had never been the kind to believe in the supernatural. Rudy was just a man who'd built himself a mysterious reputation, that was all. And hell, JoJo respected him for that. It wasn't easy to scare bad men, to be considered the baddest of the bad, but Rudy had accomplished just that. JoJo feared the man like hell, but his respect for Rudy's position in Carmucci's food chain was off the charts.

But the man and his mysterious ways aside, it was the car that unnerved JoJo the most. He couldn't properly pinpoint what it was that drove spikes of dread through his chest; he only got the vague sense that the vehicle—that orange Challenger—was the real enemy here. Then he saw the kid in the backseat peering at him through eyes as big as hockey pucks.

"What's with the kid?" JoJo asked. "He yours?"

"Ain't mine. That's a…a long story, friend-o. *Long* story. But we ain't got time for all that. See, what I need from you right now, JoJo Farmer—I need you to step to the trunk."

"The trunk?" What the hell the trunk had to do with any of this was quite baffling. JoJo went with it, though. It was best not to piss off the man who worked for Carmucci in this capacity. *Bad* man. *Real* bad. *The fucking baddest.* "What's the trunk have to do with anything, Mr. Rudy?"

"The trunk has the uncanny ability to know when a person is lying." Rudy flashed him that southern grin that sagged from ear to ear.

The trunk was a…a lie detector test? That was about the most batshit thing he'd heard in a while, and JoJo followed the news—batshit stuff was happening all the time. Just last week, some lady in Albuquerque was struck by lightning five times in a row and lived to tell about it. On Tuesday, a man caught his pecker in his fly, ripped the foreskin clean off, put the shredded remains on ice, and the doctors were able to patch him back up using all the same skin. *A miracle*, they called it. See? Weird stuff was always happening out there, but this? JoJo couldn't wrap his head around it. Plus, the weird stuff never happened to him. It happened to other people out there in the world. But JoJo's life was simple. He worked. He let Carmucci come by and stash a few packages where no one would suspect to find said packages. Then he turned a blind eye when some other bad men came to pick them up. Sure, there was cash exchanged at these transactions, cash he'd then hand over to Carmucci's financial *team* (if you could call them such a thing). And, of course, he'd keep a little change for himself. As was agreed upon, of course. He never skimmed a dime off the top, no sir. That would lead to trouble. That would lead to—

"Gonna need you to step on over to the trunk, sir," Rudy said, nodding his own way. It was an amiable enough offer, but the way he smiled, the kid in the backseat, the *fucking* trunk—none of this sounded like a good idea. But what other option did he have? He was no spring chicken, and there was nowhere to run, nowhere he could get safely without that orange beast tracking him down. "Please. Don't make *me* make *you*."

JoJo swallowed all the curses he wanted to mutter and then took the three steps leading to the dirt landing. Slow as he could, he shuffled over to the car. When he got there, Rudy dropped his arm across JoJo's broad shoulders, bringing him in for a friendly squeeze. Then, Rudy laughed as he assisted the man over to the rear of the car.

The kid inside pleaded with his eyes. Begged. His soft, delicate boy eyes filled with water. Something was wrong with this situation.

"Do you owe anything to Carmucci, JoJo?" Rudy asked, thrusting the key into the slot above the license plate. "Any funds you may not have reported receiving? Keep in mind—his bookkeepers are deadly accurate. A lie here will not help your cause."

JoJo swallowed. "If I come clean..." he said, unable to finish that thought. The fear of admitting such a thing tied his throat in a wicked knot.

"All will be forgiven," Rudy confirmed.

JoJo nodded. This was it. The end. He'd done all he could to live his best life, but when Carmucci's offer came through, and the drug business boomed—shit, the money that came pouring through here, stacks of dollars he'd only seen in gangster movies...hell, it was too good to pass up. He hadn't stolen much. A couple of bucks here and there, *beer money* practically.

Well, I do drink a lot of beer, he thought, continuing to nod as his eyes brimmed with weighty tears.

"It's okay," Rudy said, twisting the key to free the trunk. "The trunk will bring you peace."

JoJo waited for a gunshot to his temple that never came. The trunk swung open with an obnoxious screech, sounding like a hungry vulture attempting to fend off others from its claim. JoJo's brain couldn't process what he was seeing. An array of multi-colored lights came spilling out of the Challenger's rear, a heaping spread of fog like thick freezer mist leaking out onto the ground. The lights flashed so quickly that his head immediately began to throb. It dizzied him, making him want to pass out right there. He needed to sit, so he leaned back and—

He fell on his back. The clear desert sky blurred before him. He gathered enough strength to return his focus to the trunk, to see what he'd been looking at—partly out of curiosity, partly because he wanted to understand what kind of magic spell Rudy's Challenger had placed on him. He didn't receive any answers, nothing concrete, nothing he could make sense of. After the rainbow lights became an ordinary nuisance and no longer made him feel like his head was between a vice, something slithered out of the open trunk. He didn't know *what* at first, but it was cone-shaped, the open end rising out of the mist, narrowing as more was revealed. At first, he thought it was an animal of sorts. It had…*skin* was the best word for it. A vortex of dry flesh.

A worm. That was his initial and best guess as the thing emerged from the trunk and plopped onto the sandy ground below. In almost one movement, it started to slink toward him. Before JoJo could look over at Rudy and see the man's reaction to this insanity, sharp teeth grew around the monstrosity's convex rim, shark-like enamel that angled inward, designed to prevent prey from climbing out once trapped within. The worm, continuing to shimmy toward its target, snarled and gnashed its open gullet like a hooked fish gasping for breathable oxygen.

JoJo tried to turn, scoot back, move—but nothing, not one of his limbs seemed to work at that moment. And he attributed his personal malfunction to the bright lights working a hypnotic number on him. That peculiar daze continued to swim through his head, causing the world to feel topsy-turvy beneath him.

Within seconds, the worm's mouth was around his legs, chomping on his thighs, puncturing the muscle with those pointed teeth. He released a high-pitched scream, one that sounded girlish, before attempting to smack the beast on the top of its continuous mouth. His fists did nothing to free him, and the monster ignored the violence, continuing to eat. Gobble. Munch. JoJo watched his legs disappear in a fury of blood and teeth, and the thing's practiced, primal movements were efficient in their aim to cripple him. After a while, the blood made him sick, and JoJo couldn't bear to watch the mutilation of his lower half. He prayed to lose consciousness. Implored for God to end this intense suffering. He felt his brain go fuzzy, his vision grainy like the television at home sometimes went during a big storm.

A shadow fell over him, blocking out the sun. It was the bastard Rudy Ramone. He was grinning like the devil after a fruitful deal for delicious souls. Rudy tipped his hat. Winked at him.

Then the mouth that had devoured JoJo's legs dragged what was left of his body back to the trunk and hauled him inside. He was pitched into limitless depths, where the bright, multi-colored lights consumed him until a shockingly black abyss took him down forever.

12.

"You probably have questions," Cowboy Hat said, planting himself in the driver's seat. "I wish I had answers you could understand."

Emilio had tucked himself into a ball and was sitting in the back-seat, farthest away from the man he could get. His hands were still bound together. Sure, he had questions for the bad man, but they weren't worth asking. The only thing he wanted to know was if he'd live through this ordeal. Get to see his mother one last time. His school pals. Taste those delicious, stolen Cokes back at the Twilight.

The silent approach had kept him alive so far, so he figured, *Why stop now?*

"Don't matter," Cowboy Hat continued. "I have one more stop. One more. Then my business here is done. Can you believe it?"

Emilio was pretty sure this was another one of those *rhetorical* types of questions, the kind he didn't need to answer.

"You ever been to California, kid?" The bad man turned around and faced him. Emilio noticed a faded scar on his left cheek that he hadn't before. "You can answer this one."

Emilio opened his mouth to answer, but no sound came out. He resorted to shaking his head quickly as if trying to deter a fly from buzzing near his ear.

"Beautiful place. Maybe when we're done here, I'll take you there. See the ocean. You ever seen the Pacific?" Emilio's eyes relayed the message that he hadn't. They told the man that in his eleven years, he hadn't seen much of the world outside New Mexico's state lines, except when his mother took him to San Diego last year. *When things were better.*

"Yeah…always told myself if I had a son, I'd take him to see the ocean. Hell, I might buy a nice little place right on the beach. Something about the water that cools me down, you know? It's…serene. The desert…" He glanced out the window, observing the brown flatlands that swallowed up the view every which way. "The desert and the heat make me want to curl up and die."

Emilio wished the man would curl up and die, but he didn't say that. He kept that to himself, along with every other thought, pure and impure.

"Well, anyway," the bad man said, stomping on the gas, the throttle of the engine practically drowning his voice, "time to get moving. Places to go, people to interview." He paused, his lips spreading into a creamy-smooth smile. "A mouth to feed."

13.

Tavares stopped at a gas station many miles from Valencia, hit the pumps, and filled his tank. When he went inside to pay, he found the place empty, thinking that was a little peculiar. Then he figured the proprietor was probably in the back taking a shit or something. He waited ten minutes before deciding that wasn't the case, called out to the owner or whoever was working the cash register, and no one answered.

"Great," he said. He scraped together the change for a full tank and dumped the combination of dollar bills and coins onto the counter, piling them near the cash register. "It's here," he said to the empty store. He noticed the cigarettes and chew behind the counter and helped himself to some Skoal. Then he slapped two quarters on the Formica, adding to the sum.

After that, he noticed the camera behind the counter, one of those newish security devices that lots of places were getting nowadays, but out here in the middle of the desert, Tavares figured a place like this wouldn't have one. Then again, weren't places out in the middle of nowhere-ish always getting held up? With his lawman instincts at work, he moved around the counter to inspect the equipment. Once there, he ran his fingers along the back of the camera, tracing a wire that ran up the wall and disappeared behind the ceiling tiles. Next, he moved to the back of the store, over to a sign that read, "STOP! Employees Only."

"If you're back there, I'm coming in. This is Valencia Police Chief Michael Tavares, and I'm here on official business." He wasn't. Not really. In truth, he was fairly certain this place wasn't anywhere close to his jurisdiction, but it sounded like a nice warning, the most professional kind of announcement he could come up with. "Hello?"

He found a door that led to a small office. The barrier was open a smidge. Tavares pushed on it with his shoulder, the hinges protesting the movement with loud, rusty groans. The small room—no bigger than a bathroom stall—was empty. But the desk in front of him was cluttered with all types of trash: empty food and candy wrappers, along with a messy pile of nudie magazines, the real raunchy kind with all the devilish details of the big nasty exposed. Tavares shook his head in disappointment. As a good Christian, hoarding this filth was unforgivable in his book, but he couldn't arrest the guy (or lady, he supposed, but more likely a guy) for being a big ol' hornball. He could, however, get him for the marijuana roach that rested in the ashtray above the security monitor, placed above the VHS tape deck. Tavares picked up the leftover funny-smoke and sniffed the cauterized remains. Weak stuff. Hardly any skunk at all. Must have been smoked a long while ago. Either that or someone sold him weed-scented dirt. Not worth booking someone over, but if Tavares knew one thing—where there was smoke, there was almost certainly a four-alarm fire somewheres close, and if he spent all of ten minutes searching, he was positive he'd uncover more than just a leftover roach.

He dropped the funny-smoke back in the ashtray, turned his attention on the VCR, hit the rewind button, and watched the scene on screen squiggle with wavy lines and fuzzy static. The Tavareses didn't own a VCR yet—been putting it off despite the kids' pleas to get one from that new electronic store in the mall—but he knew how the machines operated. The station had one, though no one used it much, except for Heather, who occasionally ran community aerobics classes.

After about a minute of cruising backward through time, he

pressed the sideways triangle on the deck. The view from behind the cash register pointed directly outside, toward the pumps and a little beyond, which was good. Even though the picture was a bit fuzzy, he could make out enough to see if any cars dropped by for a pump. Any suspicious activity whatsoever.

In view, Tavares could see the proprietor hanging out in the store's doorway, watching the empty pumps. A minute later, a car slid into the square screen, pulling up next to the pumps but not *to* them. The light-colored Challenger—orange or yellow, he couldn't tell through the black-and-white scope—idled, the driver remaining seated for a few beats. The proprietor didn't move from his chosen spot, almost like he knew the person. Like this was a business dealing or something. *An exchange.*

His eyes fell back on the roach.

An uneasy current flowed through Tavares's belly.

The driver stepped out, revealing his wide-brimmed cowboy hat. The headwear's brim provided a nice shadow that, combined with the crummy picture, shielded the man's identity. Tavares didn't like how his eyes remained buried beneath that shadowy band. It gave him demonic vibes.

No eyes, no soul. All demon. Wasn't there a Bible verse about that? He wasn't sure exactly, but it sounded familiar. He was a good Christian all right and went to church more often than not, but he wasn't one of those remember-specific-passages-from-the-Good-Book types. Still, the Book did speak of demons, and looking at the man wearing the Cowboy Hat, Tavares couldn't help but think he'd just found one.

On camera, the two men exchanged words. Finally, the proprietor stepped away from the door and headed over to the car, the rear, just slightly out of the camera's reach. Tavares saw something moving in the backseat, something…

He leaned in for a closer look. There was a passenger back there; he was certain of it.

Then the car jolted like someone blew the tires out, took a shotgun to them or something. The body rocked back and forth with brute force. There was no audio to accompany what he was seeing, nothing else to help piece together exactly what was happening, but he saw

Cowboy Hat standing watch—the shadows could not conceal his grin. The man wore it proudly.

In a few seconds, Cowboy Hat raised his arm, looking like he was about to close something, and then Tavares pieced together that the trunk had been opened at some point during the exchange, off camera. Whatever had happened to the other man…it was over. The proprietor was nowhere to be seen.

Had he put him in the trunk?

Must have. But how? The man was not in a position to do such a thing. He was in the camera's eye almost the entire time. Unless something was in the trunk and had come out and grabbed the proprietor, but that…that wasn't likely. Was it? He refused to believe the proprietor had jumped in there willingly. Even if he had, that wouldn't explain the sudden jerky movements of the Challenger.

Next, Cowboy Hat got in the car and drove away.

As the car peeled out of the lot, Tavares glanced at the back seat. The face in the window.

He hit the pause button so fast he nearly broke his damn thumbnail and, possibly, the button itself. He rewound the footage, just a few frames. Pressed play. Froze the moment the face was directly in the window, facing him.

It was him.

The missing boy.

It was little Emilio Reyes.

14.

EMILIO HAD no idea where the madman with a monster in his trunk was taking him, but he sure hoped it wasn't California. California was so far. Impossibly far. Might as well tuck him in a rocket ship and blast him off to another planet. His mother would never find him in Cali. Cali meant being lost forever like those little faces on milk cartons are lost forever—no one ever found those faces, right? And he wondered—would he be one? Would his mother put him on a milk carton? His little face with the phrase, **HAVE YOU SEEN ME?** written in bold above whatever photograph his mother could scrounge up for the milk carton people. He always wondered how a thing like that could happen—how people could get lost.

Now he knew.

Stupid! This is my fault!

He continued to mentally abuse himself even when he realized it wasn't helping him escape. If anything, the self-reprimanding further grounded him in the situation. Imprisoned him, inside and out.

Okay, think. What would Shazam do? Well, if that show were real, Billy Batson would Wiz-out and go all superhero all over the madman's ass, but that wasn't possible because that was just a goddamn show, and goddamn shows are not reality. At eleven years old, Emilio knew the difference between reality and fantasy. But he wanted to believe there was a way out, a *superhero way out*. And thinking like that just made him realize how much he was stuck here. Just a stuck boy destined to die at the hands of this maniac and his pet trunk-monster.

"What is it?" Emilio asked, coming to terms with his fate. If he was to be fed to the beast within the ride, he'd at least like to know *what* would be snacking on his insides. Crushing his bones up like a garbage truck. "The thing in the trunk."

Cowboy Hat glanced at him in the rearview. "Just a thing. Don't worry yer purty head none about that."

"Are you going to let it eat me too?"

At this, the bad man balked. "Haven't decided yet. Should I?"

"No."

"No? Why not?"

"Because…"

"Because ain't an answer, son."

Emilio swallowed. "Because…I'm good."

"Good? Since when does that ever determine who should live and die?"

"I don't know."

"Never concerned no one. Certainly not God. You believe in God, son?"

Emilio didn't know how to answer that, not simply. So, he said, "I don't know."

"You don't know a lot, do you?" The bad man ran his tongue

between his lips as though the moment was a delicious one. "Know you don't want to die, though. Right?"

"No, sir."

"*Sir*. Very polite of you. Guess that's that good-boy persona shinin' through." He showed his teeth—meant to be a smile, Emilio supposed, but it looked too wolf-like to be a gesture of kindness. "Good is an interesting word. Good, bad. Irrelevant when you think about it, really. What's good to some is bad to others, no? For instance, take ol' JoJo back there. You might think what happened to that man was bad. Because he died, right? Death is bad. Am I correct to assume that you believe killing someone, prematurely taking their life from them, to be a negative thing?"

Emilio thought he was supposed to answer, "Yes." So he did.

"Very well. What if I were to tell you that he was a bad man, an incorrigible sinner whose soul was so corrupt that the devil himself doesn't sleep a wink knowing of his very existence? Would you consider the murder of a man like that good…or bad?"

When put like that, Emilio had no choice but to respond, "Good."

"Exactly. Thus, we enter this moral dilemma of deciding what's good and what's bad, and who's good and who's bad. We all have different standards, mind you. I'm sure our friend JoJo saw zero faults in his character and actions. In his mind, he was the good guy. Understand?"

Emilio thought so, confirming this with a nod.

"We're all the heroes of our own stories, son. Nobody paints themselves as the villain. Get it?"

Again, Emilio hurried to agree.

"So don't tell me you're all good." The bad man snorted. "You're gray like the rest of us." With that, he stomped on the gas pedal and crossed over into Arizona, speeding toward the final destination.

15.

TOOK several rounds of phone calls and escalation requests, but Tavares finally got the Arizona State Police to accept his story for what it was. Furthermore, he got them to dispatch units to the main highway, the exact coordinates Tavares could pinpoint on the map.

Took some arithmetic, but he was confident when he added the time from the tape and the mileage that the boys in blue would need to catch up with this child-abducting piece of shit (before he could get far enough into 'Zona, before they lost him along the desert roads), that his estimations were correct. Then Tavares picked up his numero uno deputy, Timmy Kendall, and hit the road. He turned on the lights, let the siren blare across the desert, and drove with his pedal to the floor until he crossed the state border.

"I'm coming for you, pal," he said to the little boy who could not hear him. "Coming to bring you home to your momma."

16.

SHE THOUGHT she'd eventually run out of tears, but that hadn't happened yet. The salty sting of fresh sadness drooled from both eyes in constant streams. Maybe there was no end to the sadness of losing your kid.

"Didn't lose him," Sandy Cortez-Reyes quietly uttered before the mirror that showed her fractured reflection. She had punched the glass in a fit of rage after the coppers left, something she'd have to pay for out of her own pocket, which meant she'd have to pick up some extra shifts at Tito's, which meant she'd have to—

It was too much to think about right now.

Didn't lose him, she thought, reminding herself again. *He was taken. Taken because you weren't watching. Taken because you were sleeping one off. How could you leave him alone like that?*

She felt like punching herself in the face, breaking that instead of the mirror again.

But what was a single mother to do? Smother her kid? Not let him out of her sight? Ever? Impossible. Emilio had walked around the premises of the motel plenty of times since moving in. He knew the rules. Never stray too far from the room, and if you see anyone or anything suspicious, you book your ass back here faster than a coyote on carrion.

He knew the rules.

Had he disobeyed them?

He was a kid—kids were apt to bend the rules a bit, occasionally break them. It was the normal kid thing to do. How could she be upset at him for living life according to his nature? Plus, she hadn't exactly treated him fairly this morning, had she? He'd come barreling into the room, running his mouth about drug dealers in the Twilight, and what had she done? She'd poked fun at him a little. Gotten on his case. It was no wonder he'd wanted to investigate the situation himself. She had practically forced him to.

She cried again. Slapped herself. Banged her head into the wall… hard enough for black and white stars to dance in front of her vision like fairy-tale pixies.

This wasn't O's fault. It was *hers*.

She decided that if he did come back to her, she wouldn't scream. Would not yell. Would not do anything except hug him, kiss him, and tell him how much his mommy loves him. That was it. All she'd do. No punishments of any kind, even if he admitted to breaking the rules.

The phone rang. The jarring sound freed her from the imprisonment of her thoughts. She hoped this was it, the phone call from that police chief—nice man, even if he had been a bit down to business—telling her that her son had been found safe, that she could collect him from the local station or, if she couldn't, they would bring him home.

She picked up the phone, wanting to say "Hello," but she could neither find her breath nor untangle her tongue.

Didn't matter. The man on the other line must have heard her failed response, the little puff of air her lungs managed to squeeze out. "Miss Reyes," the man said, and she did not recognize the voice. "I'm sorry, Miss *Cortez*-Reyes?"

"Y-yes," she managed, the hardest one-syllable word she'd ever spoken.

"Howdy," the man said, his voice rough and rugged but brimming with confidence. "I'm just reaching out 'cause, well… I got myself a pickle here and don't know which way to bend it. See, I have your son, *Emilio* he says his name is…"

Her heart tore itself in half. Another shuddering sob racked her body. "O…"

"That's right, ma'am. I'm just reaching out because I want to tell you personally that I am not a bad man. Your son happened to be in the wrong place at the wrong time, and he accidentally found himself in my company, you see. The hows and whys are not important. The only thing that currently matters is how this is going to end."

She couldn't wrap her splintered mind around what she was hearing. *O. Alive. Kidnapped.* "I…I don't understand."

"I have your son, lady. He's right here next to me, and he's okay. But the thing is…I can't exactly return him to your company. He's seen and heard way too much of my business, and my business relies on certain secrets being kept. And although he's a good boy—a fine lad you raised, I must say—I can't risk the chance of him speaking to anyone about my business. You see? You see the pickle, ma'am? An unbendable situation if I've ever seen one."

"He…" She shook her head, clearing the cobwebs. A finger dashed across both sets of eyelashes, wiping away the loose tears. "He won't say anything. You have my word."

"I know, I know. I know he won't say anything. He's a good boy, like I said. *Buuuuuut*…there's always a chance he *will* say something to someone because boys are boys and kids are kids. And if I've learned one thing in my three-hundred-and-nine years, it's that kids are of an unpredictable nature. Like…little loose cannons. Never know when they're gonna go off."

Three-hundred-and-nine years? Had he actually just said that? It was the least important thing he'd imparted since she'd picked up the phone, but she couldn't get past it. Maybe he had misspoken, or she'd misheard. Either way, it wasn't important.

O. O is all that matters.

"Please," she said, whimpering. "Please, let him go. I promise…he won't say a word about anything."

"I want to believe that, ma'am. I do. But…" The bad man clicked his tongue. "I just can't take that chance. So here's what I want to do because, like I said, I'm a good man—I want to give you the opportunity to say goodbye. Right here, right now. A lot of mothers who lose their kids never get that opportunity, and because I'm a good man, a righteous soul in this fucked up society built up all around us—I'm going to let you say goodbye."

Every ounce of strength ran out of her, and her body tingled with numbing needles that pricked every single one of her bodily nerves. "Oh god," she said, clapping a hand over her mouth.

There was a clicking noise in her ear, the static that came with the phone exchanging hands.

"Mom?" a small voice said.

He'd been crying. She could tell. And it wasn't the sound of his voice that relayed this; it was her motherly instinct kicking in. It was the same instinct that told her the awful truth: *this is the last time you'll ever speak to your son again.*

17.

WHEN TAVARES WAS five years old, he hid in the cabinet where his mother kept the pots and pans and stayed there for exactly forty-five minutes, giggling silently while his mother lost her goddamn mind worrying about where her son had gone off to. It was a cruel joke, but he hadn't realized that then. Now, almost forty years later, he reflected on what a little shit move that had been. She'd beaten his ass raw when she found out about the ruse, that he'd put one over her on purpose. He could still recall the lasting sting of that beating. And he'd been mad about it at the time, couldn't understand what the big deal was (*just a goshdarn joke*), but later—when he had children of his own—he understood with crystal clarity. Understood what his mother felt at that moment, the absolute meltdown that came with thinking your kid was lost, never coming back. Some things you can't know until you experience them yourself.

So he knew what Miss Cortez-Reyes was going through. Well, not exactly. For all she knew, her son was halfway to Mexico or there already. Tavares's mother had known her kid was still in the house because their home wasn't all that large, and she hadn't heard the front door open. She admitted later that she'd almost convinced herself Michael had sneakily slipped out a window or something. Still, she would have heard that noise, too. So, she'd remained committed to the fact that her boy was somewhere in the house, that he'd been playing around somewhere and had experienced a medical emergency.

Tavares didn't think Miss Cortez-Reyes was going to put a whooping on her son in this instance. She'd be grateful if they found him alive. The boy's only punishment would be never being allowed to leave her sight again.

He almost thought about calling the mother, letting her know what he'd found on the security footage, but knew instantly what a bad idea that was. He'd much rather have that conversation later... after he brought the kid home.

I will bring you home, he promised.

The car had been heading west, so he didn't think the driver was headed to Mexico. He supposed he could be. Maybe he wanted to get further west before crossing the border. But Tavares's instinct told him that wasn't right. That the driver wasn't headed south at all but west, continuing along his mission—whatever that was exactly. Kidnapping? Random people? The kid had no connection to the man who'd been stuffed in the trunk at the gas station—at least none anyone could piece together over the last twenty minutes. The gas station owner had been in and out of trouble with the law—had amassed a collection of drug charges over the years—so Tavares suspected the hit was drug, cartel, or gang-related.

Tavares couldn't shake the notion that the kid's abduction was accidental.

Wrong place, wrong time.

The static from the radio crackled. Heather's voice bled through the audible fuzz. "Hey, Chief?"

Tavares kept his eyes on the road but gave Kendall permission to answer the call with a quick twirl of his fingers.

"Hey, Heather. It's Tim. Go ahead."

"Hey, Timmy Town," she said, and there was something off about her voice. Grave. Like she was calling with bad news.

Christ, Tavares thought, *they found the kid on the side of the road. Dead.*

"Just got a call from the Arizona staties," she said. "They said they found him."

"Shit," Tavares said, hanging his head. "Fuck."

"The kid?" Kendall asked, sadness thickening his voice.

"Yeah," Heather said, "and, well—the driver of the Challenger."

"What?" Kendall's eyes shifted to his boss's. "Where?"

"Apparently, from what they're saying, there's a standoff at some roadside attraction on route seventy-one. They have him pinned."

Tavares grabbed the radio from his deputy's hands, not caring how rough he was with the transition. "Damn it, Heather, why didn't you just come out and say so? I need the details, STAT. Is the kid alive? And shoot me the coordinates."

"They didn't say much about the kid or whatever…but I have the coordinates."

"Well, we're waiting, darling."

Heather relayed the directions. Kendall traced his finger along the map. And Tavares punched the gas.

<h2 style="text-align:center">18.</h2>

EMILIO TRIED NOT to cry when speaking with his mother. Tried but failed. The waterworks started after she said, "I want you to know how much I love you," for like the third time. He couldn't help it. The bad man had said this was the last time he'd speak with his momma, and Emilio believed him.

"Where are you?" she asked after they had finished expressing their love for each other and apologizing for past wrongs. Wasn't a long list. Took all of twenty seconds each. Emilio sensed little time remained on the bad man's internal countdown.

"I don't know," he answered.

"Okay," the bad man said, walking toward him. "Three seconds left. Tell Mommy goodnight."

"Some place called—" he shouted, but by the time his eyes found the roadside attraction's sign with the name on it, the phone was plucked from his hands and slammed back on the cradle.

"Nuff of that," Cowboy Hat said, grabbing Emilio by the neck and directing him away from the payphone. He walked him over to the Challenger parked behind Willy's Wax Museum.

Willy, the owner of this fine establishment, had been on the bad man's list, and the bad man had already introduced him to the trunk. Emilio noticed the man's arm had fallen off during the feeding (which he had not been permitted to see) and lay on the dusty earth a few feet from the blood-spattered bumper that had once been a fine, sparkling chrome.

Cowboy Hat pushed him along. "Come on, son. I don't like this any more than you do, bet your bottom dollar on it." The bad man noticed the severed arm, said, "Aw, shit," and then bent to collect it. He surveyed the area as if looking for a place to toss the thing, like it was a fast-food wrapper and not someone's fucking arm, and then decided the roof of the wax museum would make the best hiding spot. Swinging the arm with both hands, he heaved the detached limb onto the structure's roof. Then he put his hands on his hips, nodding at the accomplishment. "There," he said proudly.

Emilio felt impossibly cold despite the heat of the day. Cowboy Hat rotated toward him, holding out both hands like a magician ready to unveil the final act of his mind-bending performance. "You ready, son?"

Emilio looked past the museum, the infinite stretch of desert, the mountainous rust-colored rock sitting on the horizon like Martian formations. He shook his head at the man.

"I know this is hard, buddy. Hate that it's come to this..." He reached out, grabbed the boy by the wrist, and then led him to the trunk. With his one free hand, he reached with the key toward the empty slot, slipped the metal inside, and turned.

Emilio screamed. Dug his heels in the earth and tried to break free from the man's grip. A useless waste of energy. The trunk opened like a mouth, releasing the sickening strobe lights. Mist poured out as if from a witch's cauldron. Emilio cried, begging for someone to help him.

But there was no one out here save for the buzzards that circled above, invited here by the terrified screams of the future dead. It was like they recognized that noise and came soaring right over. Out here, a scream was as good as a dinner bell. Emilio wondered if anything would be left for them once the trunk was finished. Or would the monster within leave a piece of him behind like it had Willy? Was the leftover limb intentional or accidental? Did the trunk even think about such things?

"C'mere, boy!" Cowboy Hat said, trying to curb the resistance.

Just then, the two of them stopped their scuffle. Something played in the distance, and they turned their ears to the desert, rapt with anticipation.

That sound...

Emilio recognized it. He'd heard it on TV. Maybe on *CHiPs*.

Sirens.

The police were on the way. He was saved.

Or so he thought. That was before the trunk began to rumble, groaning like the hungry belly of some massive dragon.

19.

WHEN THE PHONE went dead in her ear, Sandy thought a piece of her had died. Well, not a piece. More than a piece. A half? Three-quarters? Her whole? The latter seemed more accurate. It felt like the world below her had developed a mouth and was swallowing her whole, bit by bit. Like someone had torn out her heart in front of her, put it in a suitcase, a *trunk*, smiled, waved, and walked away. She felt as though she were the one who was missing despite having never left the room.

She collapsed on the bed and began screaming, hollering like someone was sitting on her chest and stabbing her repeatedly. She screamed until her throat hurt, ached, and felt like she'd yakked up huge shards of glass.

Five minutes later, when Mr. Moats charged through the front door, his face wiped with worry, she was still belting out the painful moans and piercing screams. When he came over to console her, see if there was *anything* he could do to help, she punched, kicked, and screamed at him. Cussed. Said things she'd never say if the grief wasn't so unbearable. Things she'd never repeat again in her whole life.

None of this made her feel any better.

She was lost.

She was dead.

She would never live again, and she was so sure that was true.

20.

WHEN TAVARES and Kendall arrived on the scene, the Arizona staties were in position, weapons drawn, using their collection of cop cars as shields. Near the back of the wax museum, Tavares spotted the orange Challenger, the criminal, and the kid. The man in the cowboy hat had the kid around the throat, holding what Tavares perceived to be a short knife, dangerous enough to stick the kid to death. The man had dropped to his knees so he could hide behind his captive, using the Reyes kid as a human riot shield.

"Son of a bitch," Tavares said, skidding to a stop and exiting the vehicle as soon as he popped the emergency brake. His weapon was out and pointed at the desired target faster than he could say "potato salad."

Kendall wasn't too far behind.

A trooper with a megaphone barked orders at Cowboy Hat, telling him to drop the knife, move away from the kid, and end this thing peacefully. But Cowboy Hat wasn't having any of it. He kept shaking his head and telling the coppers to back away or things would end grisly. That the boy would die. That he would ensure it.

Tavares's eyes were then drawn to the back of the Challenger, the trunk. A thick smoke poured out of the rear like a stoner had hotboxed in the thing. He waited for Jerry Garcia to pop out, spreading a goofy grin inside that trademarked beard of his while waving at the calvary, letting them all know this was just a huge joke, a grave misunderstanding. But that never happened. Instead, a prismatic collection of lights began to fire off like sparkling fireworks, exploding in the air and showering the ground with electric sparks. Something else appeared in the shallow depths of the smoke, and, at first, Tavares couldn't tell exactly what it was. He only knew that his eyes were playing tricks on him. It looked like...

A worm? A slug?

He couldn't tell for sure, but the moving lifeform revealed its cylindrical shape inches at a time. As the thing exposed more of itself, Tavares's potty brain thought the creature was quite phallic-looking. He immediately cleared the image of a giant johnson emerging from this weirdo's trunk and concentrated on the boy, the clusterfuck this hostage situation had become. He didn't have a clear shot at the abductor's head—no one did—and this standoff could drag on for hours...unless the staties were already positioning a sharpshooter to flank the bastard. He hoped they had. Time was running short, and the bad man would soon figure out this standoff was nothing more than a holding tactic, a way of keeping him distracted while all the pieces fell into place.

He had to know this.

Tavares sensed their time to save the boy was rapidly expiring. The man would soon decide to dig that knife into the boy's soft neck meat and vent his throat from ear to ear. If he was going out, he was taking the boy with him—so Tavares had decided.

He couldn't allow this to happen, so he crept around the car, moving to Kendall's side.

"What are you doing?" Kendall whispered, his words low enough so no one could hear him over the one-sided conversation transpiring through the megaphone.

Tavares didn't have time to explain, so he continued to drift toward the empty, flat space the desert offered to his right. His plan: Get an angle where he could line up a decent shot. He had never fired his weapon in a real-time situation before, but no one could match his accuracy on the range. It seemed all those hours of target practice and training were finally about to pay off.

But everything changed when the thing in the trunk elongated, stretching like a piece of chewing gum. A wave of gasps fell over the dozen present staties, and some of them recoiled from the sight of this monstrosity. Like a giant anaconda, the worm slithered across the desert floor, moving toward its target.

The boy.

"Back up!" Cowboy Hat shouted. "Drop yer weapons right the fuck now!"

Not one of the troopers accommodated the man's request. They kept their weapons on him, their fingers trembling against the triggers ever-so-lightly. Tavares guided his vision back to the thing from the trunk as it squirmed closer to the boy and the bad man.

Then it lunged and opened its mouth (the best word for it, in Tavares's opinion), revealing a circular row of sharp, ivory pegs. Tavares suddenly remembered what the creature resembled, though he'd only seen one in a textbook, never in real life. A *lamprey*, a kind of eel-type fish with a jawless, funnel-like mouth. It was heading right for the boy, only a few feet away. Then, like a cobra striking its prey, it launched itself from the ground, snapping like a fishing line as it extended toward the flinching kid. Its toothy maw collapsed around the boy's thigh, yanking him out of Cowboy Hat's grip. The Reyes boy went to the ground screaming, a combination of unfiltered fear and instant agony. In one forceful tug, the creature dragged him halfway back to the trunk.

Everyone was eerily still. The troopers. Kendall. Even Cowboy Hat, who seemed surprised by his pet's aggressive nature. Then the man realized how exposed he was. With his human shield now gone, there was nothing to protect him from a barrage of incoming bullets. He scrambled to find somewhere to hide before everyone else caught up to speed.

But there was nowhere to run that would save him.

Noticing the opportunity before anyone else reacted, Tavares didn't hesitate. He fired his weapon, aiming for the bad man's temple but catching his left eye instead. A splash of blood and juicy brain sauce squirted out the back of his skull as the spent round made its messy exit. The man stayed on his feet for all of five seconds, glancing at each of the troopers, seeming to wonder where the shot had come from, as if this knowledge was somehow more important than the result itself. Then he collapsed like a tall building during a quick demolition. When his head hit the ground, it bounced like a springy ball. A generous spill of thick blood wept from the back of his opened head, wetting the dusty earth below.

Tavares didn't have time to celebrate. He darted forward, sprinting toward the boy who was now only a few feet away from the Challenger's trunk, that awful void of sparkling light rushing to meet him. The good chief aimed his gun, hoping to get a clear shot. But the creature was undulating in a serpentine fashion much too quickly to instill any confidence of hitting the body while missing the boy.

"Fuck," Tavares cussed, still speeding toward the Reyes kid. Frightened and frantic, the boy tried to turn onto his belly, digging his fingers into the earth, but the sheer strength of the creature was no match for his attempt to delay the inevitable, and he was dragged until his feet touched the blood-stained bumper. "Dear Christ," Tavares said, stopping as the boy was hoisted over the bumper and hauled into the trunk.

Christ couldn't help him now.

No one could.

21.

THE PAIN WAS GREAT. It came in swells, and at one point, Emilio thought the monster might bite right through him and leave him in two pieces. As he felt himself ascend, he made one last attempt to hold onto something, to prevent his entire body from disappearing inside the trunk. He knew one thing—once he was inside, there was no getting out. And whatever mysteries awaited him inside, he did not want to know them.

Even though his hands managed a pretty good grip on the Challenger's bumper, the monster's force overmatched him, and his fingers slipped as if slick with grease.

The thing that happened next happened all in one moment, and in that moment, he saw his entire life flash before his eyes, one amalgamated image of everything he'd ever done and everyone he'd ever known. A life lived, compressed into one mental photograph.

And then he was inside. The trunk. Colors swirled around him in smoky wisps that blinked and brightened, sporadic and hectic. The monster continued to bite down, and he felt his organs band together. However, the further he tumbled through this bottomless world, the more the pressure eased up. Seconds later, there was no pressure. His body had found the foggy bottom of this place, this trunk, this other world inside the '71 Challenger. Smoke continued to swirl all around him, and a spot to his left cleared just enough that he could see the remains of the last victim, the owner of the wax museum. His head was all chewed up, riddled with deep marks caused by the monster's pin-nail teeth. His body lay motionless, his legs snapped and grotesquely mangled, unnaturally twisted. His remaining arm was bent backward at the elbow, sticking straight up. He looked like an action figure birthed from an assembly line accident.

Emilio squeaked out a scream and backed up. Above him, in the sky of the worm's domain, the monster whipped around the air like a firehouse hose left unattended and bleeding at full pressure. The kid's eyes had trouble keeping up with the movement. He wondered what it was doing, why it was moving that way. He expected an attack, for the monster to come slashing down from its airy loft, but nothing came. In fact, the thing seemed almost irritated, distracted by something else.

Emilio heard voices. Soft at first. But then they grew louder. Nearer. Men. Shouting now. It was coming from above. The smoke cleared, and the monster stretched above the thinning spread of clouds, disappearing from Emilio's sight.

What in the...

He couldn't finish that thought. The lights of this lair began to blink so rapidly that he became sick and dizzy. Shutting his eyes, he tried to steady his equilibrium, solely focusing on the dark tomb his closed eyes provided. Then he felt something on him. Pressure on his shoulders, his stomach, his legs. Hard. Something that ratcheted around his bones, something that told him that whatever was grabbing him wasn't willing to let go so easily. That it would fight for control over his body.

He thought this was it. The monster had come back for him and was ready to hand him over to his maker.

But then he heard a man shout, *"I got him!"*

Then Emilio was zipping through the air, no clear destination available, not in the voluntary darkness.

22.

Tavares heard the trooper shout, *"I got him!"* And a second later, the man's arms emerged from the trunk, one hand gripped around Emilio's ankle, the other around his upper arm. The rest of the crew joined in, helping to hoist the boy up and over the trunk's would-be gumline, if the rear were indeed a mouth.

Not having time to enjoy the moment, Tavares breathed a short sigh of relief and reacted to the next task at hand. The worm-like entity had pushed through the trunk's smoky barrier to violently whip its elongated form back and forth like a skewered snake trying to free itself. But there was nowhere for the creature to go, or so it seemed, as its tail appeared hitched to something inside the trunk. The swirling layer of mist, the kind that belonged hovering over the ground of some creepy graveyard, hid proof that the thing was tethered. But that didn't stop Tavares from believing it could escape. He watched as the *sucker* end zeroed in on one of the troopers, attaching its funnel of a mouth onto the man's side, latching onto the section of meat just above his hip. A hard crunch hit the airwaves, followed by the trooper's high-pitched scream. In a blink, the trooper was stolen from the earth and taken into the sky. The mouth flung the partially chewed body into the air like a child having a meltdown over an unwanted toy. The trooper's body hit the surface some thirty feet away and ragdoll-rolled another five. His motionless body lay still, actively bleeding from the puncture wounds the trunk-worm had left in him.

Tavares backed up when the monster turned its attention to the other lawmen. A part of him wanted to bolt, head for the cruiser and get the fuck out of there, but he glanced over and saw the boy, the troopers holding him up, trying to wake the unconscious kid and bring him back to life.

He'd come too far to run away now.

I'm bringing you home, buddy. Just like I promised.

Then the monster struck again. This time, it zeroed in on Tim Kendall, and before the deputy could get his weapon aimed, the mouth came down over his head, clamping around his shoulders. The grown man's childlike screams were muffled, swallowed up by the depths of the trunk-worm's seemingly endless throat. The worm pulled him into the air, stiffened its form into a straight line that angled toward the sky. Opening its throat, it created the perfect decline for Kendall to slide on down.

Tavares watched his deputy's entire body disappear into the fleshy tunnel. Then, before it could come and claim another life, the chief readied his weapon. He aimed at the monster and pulled the trigger. The shots displaced patches of flesh on the monster's body, but they hardly seemed to affect it. The trunk-worm continued its onslaught, picking the next available human shape, one of the men who'd hauled Emilio out of the trunk. Emilio had been laid on the ground about fifteen yards from the car's deadly end, which clearly wasn't far enough—Tavares figured the monstrosity could extend much farther than that. For some reason, though he had no official proof, he thought the trunk-worm's length was endless, could stretch beyond what any earthborn creature could or should.

This thing was clearly from somewhere else.

Alien, he thought. Something from science fiction novels and movies, something that was reshaping his view of the world, what he considered plausible in the reality.

But the time to assess reality would come later. Now, he needed to save all the men he could along with the boy he'd tracked all this way. He didn't travel this distance to watch the kid die horribly, get swallowed up by this unearthly beast.

He continued to unload shots into the monster, stripping away small flaps of its flesh. Blood trickled from the bullet wounds but not much, and Tavares was gaining a sense that his gun and the thirty-eight caliber rounds were ineffectual. He decided to holster his weapon for the moment while trying to work out a different method to fell this massive creature.

The trunk-worm dipped down for another feeding. Tavares thought it was heading directly for Emilio, and he even shouted at the monster, trying to attract its attention so it wouldn't head that way, but his cries were ignored, and the monster zeroed in on the smaller, easier target. One of the men jumped in front of the kid, blocking the monster's clear path to its intended victim. The trooper had his gun raised and began firing into the incoming mouth, pumping every shot he could before the awful orifice with the pin-nail teeth closed around his midsection, biting with unstoppable force. The man's legs came right off as the trunk-worm chewed through his middle. A slop of bloody organs fell from the body's open cavity, landing next to the severed legs, a pile of human parts that Tavares wished he could unsee.

But there was no unseeing this, *any* of this—these were images he'd carry with him always, memories he could never delete.

There was no coming back from the trauma this day would go on to cause.

Tavares sprinted back to the cruiser as fast as he could. He ripped open the door, ducked inside, and grabbed the double-barreled shotgun from between the seats. In a split second, he was running back toward the madness, slipping two shells into the barrels. When he arrived back on the scene, he barked commands at the other lawmen, instructing them to get out whatever weapons they had and start concentrating their firepower on the worm. They fumbled around like they had no idea what Tavares was talking about, like he was speaking in some unfamiliar language. Then Tavares got louder and more authoritative, and that got the staties moving. Some ran back to their cars to grab shotguns, while others stood where they were and released their revolvers from their hip holsters. Together, they stood in a row and aimed at the giant trunk-worm, concentrating their shots, blowing holes along its massive length. Pockets of flesh were ripped from the body, ejecting blood and muscle in wet bursts. The thing let out an ear-splitting screech, sounding like a tortured bird. It whipped around wildly, trying to dodge the incoming attacks, but the men's combined assault landed true. After a few minutes of the lawmen hitting the trunk-worm with everything they had, the creature weakened. Its movements became languid, as if the fight had fled its muscles, like everything was shutting down. With a thunderous groan, the thing crashed back to the desert floor.

The world shook on impact.

The trunk-worm lay still for a movement, but there were still sounds rolling out of its semi-open mouth, a low, incessant grumbling that let Tavares and the rest of the soldiers know it still lived to some degree. How much longer it would remain living was to be determined, but if Tavares were to place some chips on the outcome, he'd wager the thing had a few minutes left.

Tavares thought he'd help get the thing to its eternal destination a wee bit quicker. He strolled over to the trunk-worm, mindful that it could snap back to life, that, in a blink, carnage and bloodshed could easily replace this peaceful moment. Looking at its fallen form, he examined its body, the gooey surface of its wrinkled skin, the mouth that lay halfway open, revealing pointed, ivory teeth covered in human red and rags of flesh. After he stood over it for a solid minute, he realized this thing was truly dying, that they had won. The fight had vacated its body, and here it would lie eternally, baking in the desert sun until its slimy exterior dried out and became a flaky, shriveled carcass.

Unless they took care of it before that could happen.

He nodded at the thing, acknowledging the fight it had given them, the lives it had taken. Then he raised his revolver to where he assumed the monster's brain was located…if it even had one. Pulled the trigger. The single report echoed over the lands, alerting the buzzards that the time to feed was almost here.

One of the staties approached from behind, a timid appearance.

One by one, they approached a scene no one else on this planet would believe had happened and glanced at the now still creature.

"What should we do with it?" one of them asked.

Tavares exhaled a long, deep breath. "Get some gasoline. And a match."

"But..." another one said, the youngest of the squad. "Shouldn't we, like, keep it? For scientific research or something?"

"Yeah, we could be famous for discovering a new species," another added.

Tavares shook his head. "Gasoline. No one should ever know about this."

"What about the dead?" one of the staties asked, and an uncomfortable silence dropped over them. "What will we tell their families?"

Tavares stared at the dead man in the middle of the desert, Cowboy Hat, though he hardly looked like a man now. In death, his face had transformed. His flesh looked waxy, like a candle that had melted and then dried again. More like a Halloween mask than a human face, distorted and burnt.

The sun hadn't caused this.

Whatever this man was, Tavares thought, *this image is closer to his true form.*

The thought turned Tavares's veins into icy-cool streams.

"That man," he said, not liking the way *man* felt on his tongue. Like there was a better, more accurate word to use. *Monster. Beast. Creature.* "He killed them. Hid their bodies. We never found them."

"Are people going to believe that?" responded the man who'd started this line of questioning in the first place.

"Son," Tavares said, turning to them. "We are the police. People will believe whatever we tell them."

And it was true. Mostly, the general public and the families of the fallen went on to believe just that. Nothing unnatural, nothing outside the usual confines of reality, took place that afternoon just over the Arizonian border. Mostly, they believed the yarn Tavares and the other lawmen had spun for them.

Except those who knew the truth.

Like—

23.

EMILIO WOKE up several hours later in a hospital bed. His first waking thought was, *I dreamed the whole thing. The Challenger, the man, the trunk-worm.* He'd convinced himself that he had gotten sick, come down with a fever, and hallucinated the whole thing. But the second he saw the cops outside the room, the truth *wormed* its way back into his thoughts.

None of it truly felt like a dream. And the pain in his leg, the bandages wrapped around his thigh, brought it all back.

One of the cops came into the room after he woke up. A doctor accompanied him, but the doc left after a quick examination, making sure Emilio's vitals were tip-top—surprisingly, everything checked out. The doctor told him he'd be released in no time, and he said so with a comforting smile. He also told Emilio the wounds on his leg would heal just fine.

After the doctor left, the cop turned to him. "Emilio Reyes," he said, grinning.

"Yes?" Emilio wanted to cry. "Am I...in trouble?"

The cop shook with laughter, the kind that came right up from the belly. "No, son. You're not in trouble. You're safe."

"I bet I'd be in trouble if you knew what I did," he said, almost regretting saying it but also not really regretting it at all. He felt like he needed to confess what he'd done, as if doing so would absolve him of the sins he committed. Not just getting into the Challenger. But *everything*. The soda machine trick included.

"And what *did* you do?" asked the cop whose nameplate pin read *TAVARES*.

"I shouldn't have gotten inside that man's car," Emilio admitted.

"Did he lure you in? With...candy or something? Toys?" Tavares wasn't smiling anymore.

"No." Emilio shifted in bed. Every muscle felt like someone had taken a hammer to them. "I just saw the car and...I wanted to sit in it."

"You got in when it was empty?"

Emilio nodded. "The man—the bad man—came back when I was inside. I didn't know what to do...so I hid in the back. He didn't notice me until...well, much later."

"I see," Tavares said. "Well, kids will be kids."

"What's that mean?"

"Nothing. You'll know later in life, I'm sure of it."

O gulped. "Are you sure I'm not in trouble?"

"Fairly certain. I wouldn't haul you off to jail for being a curious kid, but...if I may offer a piece of advice...maybe don't go crawling into stranger's cars ever again."

Emilio swallowed. He wanted to ask the cop a question, the most important question he'd asked in all his life.

"Did you want to say something, Emilio?" Tavares asked as if he knew. Not only knew he wanted to ask a question but knew exactly what question he wanted to ask. "Now's the time. Before your mother gets here."

"She's coming?"

"Of course. I have a deputy bringing her over as we speak." He checked his watch. "Should be here in about twenty minutes."

Emilio felt himself fill with something heavenly. For the first time in what felt like forever, he felt safe. Like nothing could get him again. Not the bad man, not the—

Trunk-worm.

"So..." Tavares said, looking up from the time. "Did you want to ask me something?"

Emilio thought about it. Honestly, now that he'd given it some time to ruminate, the events from the past few hours felt awfully dream-like...

"No," Emilio said. "No, I don't really remember anything that happened after that."

Tavares nodded. "Best that you don't." Then the cop came over and patted him on the shoulder. "You're going to be all right, kid. For the rest of your life, you're going to be okay."

Emilio believed him.

24.

But Emilio did remember what happened after that. It came back to him sometimes when he was awake, sometimes when he was dreaming (especially when he was dreaming). That awful road trip with the bad man, the vehicle's trunk, and the strange thing he'd kept locked inside. The deaths of those other bad men and those police officers that had saved his life. Five months had passed, and Emilio was still thinking about it. At times, it was all he *could* think about.

Tavares had warned him to keep quiet about the events of that day, never to speak a word of it to anyone, especially his mother, but Emilio had trouble keeping a secret that big locked inside his own trunk—the trunk of his mind. He thought something that big should be let out, shared with everyone, not kept hidden from the world. But how could he do that and still keep his promise to the police chief? No one would believe him even if he did speak up. They'd call him names like *crazy* and *psycho* and would probably have him committed to a psychiatric facility, just like momma's Aunt Lucy. She had told crazy stories, too, accounts about being abducted by Martians and being tracked by the government for trying to break into Area 51. Now she lived inside some facility where they pumped her full of drugs and fed her intravenously. A place where they kept people in straitjackets and locked them away in padded cells.

Yes, if Emilio had told his mother or anyone else about the things that happened that day, *the truth*, he'd end up there too. Maybe Aunt Lucy and he could share a padded cell. Then momma could save a trip by visiting them both at the same time.

But what if there was a way to tell them what happened without telling them what happened? What if there was a way he could exorcise these demons within, let them out of his *trunk*, and not be judged or labeled or sent to the loony bin?

What if he wrote a story?

The idea came to him one afternoon at school, in English class. Mrs. Jetts was teaching them about stories and fables from different cultures. She explained how the tall tales were designed to entertain but also to interpret feelings and fears and explore certain topics through artistic means by burying the truth beneath a fictional playground.

So that was it. He needed to write a story. *His* story. That way, he could open the trunk and let the truth out, and no one would call him crazy or lock him away because it wouldn't be real. Just a story. Fiction. A thing he invented. He'd leave out certain details, of course. He'd change names, settings, and events. But the main idea would remain—an innocent eleven-year-old accidentally found himself in the backseat of a dangerous killer's car, forced to ride shotgun while the bad man went on a murder spree across the American southwest. It would be perfect. He would change the monster in the trunk, too. Make it more unbelievable. Make it scarier. The story had to be more frightening and less grounded in reality—that was the point. He needed to *bury* that truth deep so no one could dig it up.

So…he wrote it. Took him several weeks, but he worked on it every day after school, post-homework and pre-dinner. Sometimes, he even worked on it after dinner. Saturdays and Sundays, instead of leaving the room and knocking on 213 to see if Robbie wanted to toss rocks at empty soda cans, Emilio would sharpen his pencils, put graphite to loose-leaf paper, and write his little heart out.

When finished, the story was nearly fifty pages. More than he'd set out to write, but stories were funny that way—they had a habit of taking on a life of their own, sometimes surprising even the mind behind the words.

"What's this, O?" Momma said.

He'd handed her the handwritten manuscript with high hopes she'd read it. Even if she were the only soul to read it, it would make the whole experience worth it.

"I wrote a story."

"Oh," she said, casually flipping through the pages. "This is…this is a lot. Is this what you've been working on these last few weeks?"

He nodded.

She cozied up and rested her back against the headboard. She went to pour herself a drink, but the bottle was empty save for a few drops of backwash. "And here I thought you were doing homework."

He had been doing his homework, but he didn't tell her that. Didn't need to. His grades would do the talking for him on the next report card.

"Will you read it?" he asked. He wasn't begging, not exactly, but he knew the look he was giving her. It was a look she'd have an impossible time saying "no" to.

"Oh, I don't know, O. I'm not much of a reader." She put the manuscript down on the comforter. Leaned her head back and closed her eyes. It was only six o'clock, and she was ready for bed. Four hours until she had to leave for the night. For work.

"Please," he said, and now he *was* begging. "Please, it's important. I really want you to."

She couldn't say "no." Could she? Could she break his heart like that? After everything they'd been through over the past five months? The nights spent waking up from nightmares. Consoling each other. Dealing with their separate traumas derived from the same event.

"Okay, O," she said, but not without pausing for a beat. She was probably searching for another excuse to say "no" to him. But in the end, she agreed. "Okay, I'll read it."

And she did. She started that night, reading right up until the moment she had to leave for work. Took breaks to microwave dinner and go to the bathroom, of course. But she put a decent dent in the page count, getting a little over halfway.

"What do you think?" he asked, eager for her opinion. He hoped she had one. Preferably something positive. But he'd accept criticisms, too, as long as she wasn't mean about it. Not that he expected her to be. "Do you like it?"

She was quiet at first. Not a good sign. Then she said, "This…this is what happened to you? What that man did? What you saw?"

He gulped. The story he'd told her while still in the hospital, the one Tavares had corroborated, had been radically different. He'd told her he hadn't seen much of the bad man's "business"—despite what the bad man had told her on the phone—and that he'd mostly kept himself hidden in the backseat. Never mentioned a thing about witnessing at least one murder firsthand and enough of the others for his imagination to fill in the blanks. He never divulged that he'd heard the screams of those men almost every night, echoing in the catacombs of his most dismal dreams.

Slowly, he nodded.

"Oh, O," she said, dropping to her knees in front of him. She wrapped her arms around his neck and pulled him close. Squeezed him. Not too hard. It was the motherly comfort he coveted. They'd shared many similar hugs over the last five months, but none had felt this good. "I'm so sorry." She pulled back. "And the mother in the story…that's…that's me, isn't it?"

This was the painful part, the part he knew he was taking a chance on. But sometimes, the painful parts were necessary. You can't close a wound without suffering through the pain first.

"Yes," he said, hanging his head, knowing her disappointment could wreck him.

To his surprise, she lifted his head by raising his chin. "The mom in the story is addicted to medicine. Pills. Right?"

"Yes."

It was like she wanted to ask him about how he knew about those things, knew that pill addiction was a thing. He'd never told her about the hypodermic needle on the playground and the school assembly that followed. And he doubted like heck she ever read the letters the principal sent home.

"I can quit drinking, O," she said, and tears burst forth from her eyes, a whole damn flood. She began sobbing into his shoulder, his shirt instantly soaking in his mother's sadness, her regrets. It was his turn to hug her, so he did. Wrapped his arms around her neck and pulled her close. "Oh, God, I'm terrible, aren't I?"

He gripped her cheeks and stared into her eyes. "No, Mom. I love you."

This crushed her even more, and she continued to bawl for another minute or two—time was getting weird here, and the conversation that seemed like it would only take a second passed on for maybe an hour or more.

"I don't want to live here anymore. I don't want to work at that— excuse me—that *goddamn* place anymore." Anger and sadness bled together. She wiped her nose on her sleeve. "Tomorrow I'll find a new job, O. Something better. That place…it's not good for me. My boss, he steals from me. From *us*, I guess. He…he…he's a bad man. Like the men in your story. I can't work there anymore, O. You deserve better. A better mother, a better life."

He sniffled. Shook his head. Began to cry.

They held each other like that—minutes, hours. Didn't matter. Every second was painful and necessary.

CLOSING THE TRUNK

A few months later, things changed for Sandy Cortez-Reyes and her son. She ended up quitting Tito's by telling Tito to go fuck his own face right in front of the other girls, and didn't even care when the son of a bitch backhanded her, then had his security team literally throw her out on her ass. It was the best pain she'd experienced in her life, possibly second behind reading the words her son had handwritten on some loose-leaf paper.

The story.

What a wild one it was. A story about an ancient warlock who drove around New Mexico and collected the souls of the wicked. How did this inhuman fiend do such a thing? Well, he fed them to a giant monster that lived in a trunk. Something that looked like a dinosaur, a *T. rex*.

Wild stuff.

It was fiction, sure. Yet Sandy couldn't help but see the truth, the lines between the lines. It was O's way of dealing with what had happened, and a few other things that had clearly been bothering him. How he felt about living in this dump of a motel with his alcoholic mother. It was painful, but she knew it was necessary pain. Like the road rash from when she went tumbling across Tito's parking lot at the hands of his cronies.

Now, she had a new job. The day after she left Tito's for good, she called up Chief Michael Tavares and explained how she'd quit, detailing the violence that followed. He was all set to help her file charges, maybe pay the bastards a visit himself, but she stopped him from doing all that. She was done with that life and didn't want to drag it out any longer. Instead, she asked him for a job, one where seventy percent of her "paycheck" wasn't withheld because of mysterious "taxes" and "fees."

"Well," Tavares said on the phone, "just so happens Heather got a job working the books for her husband's new construction company, so we're looking for someone to work the phones at the station."

"Really?" Sandy asked, almost crying, trying to keep at bay that painful sadness in the throat that somehow connected to the emergence of tears. "Really, you mean it?"

"Sure. Of course. How about you come on down to the station tomorrow, and we'll have ourselves an *official* interview."

She told him that was great, and a few days later, she started that job.

A month later, they had enough money to move out of the

Twilight, enough to rent an actual apartment somewhere. It was one of the happiest days of her adult life.

She wanted to surprise Emilio with something special. Telling him about finally getting out of the Twilight was probably enough, but she wanted to do something extra. Something he would appreciate, something he definitely deserved. For sticking by her. For writing that story and telling her the truth. Funny how a work of fiction—inspired by a traumatic truth—could change their lives so drastically, but here they were.

"I have something for you," she said, sitting him down on the end of the bed.

"For me?"

She nodded and smiled. "Yes, sir. Two somethings, actually. One is a present." She presented the bag on the nightstand. It had a bow on it. "The other is some news. Which one do you want first?"

She could have predicted his answer but allowed him to say it anyway. "The present!"

"Thought you might choose that one." She grabbed the bag and handed it to him.

His eyes blew up at the sight of what was sitting inside. "No...way."

"Way," she repeated with a giggle in her voice.

He grabbed the item. Nearly had trouble lifting it out. She helped steady the bag while he scooped up the object and put it on the bed.

She loved the way his face beamed as he looked at the teal Corona typewriter. "I figured you could use this since you're such a good storyteller."

"Mom...it's...how did you afford this?"

"Don't worry about that, mister. Things are looking up for us." She punched him lightly on the shoulder and smacked her lips together to make a popping sound. Just then, she thought about having a victory drink, a shot of bourbon to celebrate their new fortunes, and then remembered she would soon be late for her next AA meeting. She was ninety days dry tonight. She *had* to be on time. "I have to get going for my meeting, but...I also have news."

"What is it?"

"We're moving."

His jaw dropped. "REALLY?"

"Really. Just put a deposit on a nice apartment in Pleasant Springs."

"That's where Collin Renlow's family lives."

"Oh, is he a friend from school?"

He nodded. "Yep. We draw comics and write stories together during recess."

"How cool is that?"

"Mom," he said, brushing back tears. "Thank you."

She shook her head. "No, thank you, O. It was you who saved us." She almost added, *You had to go missing in order for me to find myself again.* But that was something better left for her private thoughts. She'd maybe share it in the meeting tonight—*maybe.* Although, there were some trunks she'd rather not open in the presence of others.

"Why don't you get settled in," she said, grabbing her purse off the nightstand. "I'll order you a pizza. And you can spend the next couple of hours typing up *The Trunk.*"

He looked almost disappointed.

"What? You can't send that story to a major publisher all hand-written like that. I researched this thing, mister. They only accept typed manuscripts. Double-spaced."

"It's not that," he said. "I think...I don't want to tell that story anymore."

"Oh? Why not?"

He shrugged as if he had no particular reason. "I kind of like that it was just for us."

This brought a sting to her eyes. "I kind of like that, too." She checked her watch. If she didn't leave now, she would be late. "You have a new story in mind?"

"I think so."

"Good," she said. "Good. I'm going now. I'll be back soon."

Before she could turn for the door, O was jumping off the bed, his arms spread open, looking like he was going to bear tackle her. Instead, he wrapped her up for the sweetest hug.

Things were looking up indeed.

*

EMILIO WROTE INTO THE NIGHT, long after his mother returned from her meeting. He wrote about flying saucers and dinosaurs, worlds that existed beyond the stretches of ordinary imagination. He had fun pounding on the keys, allowing the letters to become words, words to become sentences, sentences to become paragraphs. When he finished, he had not just one story but several.

He took the manuscript for *The Trunk* and placed it in the bottom of his suitcase, where he figured it would sit for a long time. Maybe forever. Until he was ready to pull it out of the bottom of the trunk and revisit that particular pain.

But the trunk would remain locked for now, and he was happy to forget where he had left the key.

THE END

STREAMING LIVE FROM THE BOTTOM OF THE WORLD

1.

The number went up by ten, and Glenn Martin felt his heart flutter, the magic of the moment supplying his body with an electric rush. Ten in two minutes was pretty good. Not great. Nothing shattering. Certainly not enough. But it was a start, a good beginning, the one Glenn needed if he was to pull this off.

He glanced down at the semi-unconscious man, the dark crown of dried blood circling his hairless dome of sweaty, greasy flesh. Glenn held up his camera, the one he illegally borrowed—*stole*, to be more accurate—from a small pawnshop in a sketchy section of the Outskirts. If his numbers had been better, he might have hit a place in Mid-City, but Glenn Martin had nowhere near the number of followers required to access the next level. Nope, he was an Outskirts boy through and through. And he'd always been content with that.

Until recently.

Until he discovered the truth.

The man's eyes blinked, preparing the mind to inject itself back into the real world.

"Wake up," Glenn said to the camera and everyone watching live on the Stream. On his wristwatch, he saw his followers rise by another ten. At this rate, he might make it. *Might.* There were no guarantees the plan would work, but he was desperate enough to try. "Wake up, asshole."

The man glanced around his dark surroundings, squinting through the shadows of the abandoned warehouse. He slowly touched his forehead, sensing something wrong with it. And there was. The flesh had split where Glenn had knocked him out with a hammer, another accessory provided by the shop. There were many *borrowed* items around, and they were spread out before Glenn's guest on a mechanic's cart.

"What is this?" the man asked, his fingers hovering over the ripped, ruined flesh below his fading hairline. He was clearly afraid to probe the damage, afraid to seek the knowledge the hard lump and separated skin would divulge. "What have you done to me?"

Glenn smiled as he focused the camera's light on the broken man's face. He made sure to illuminate the splotches of red that stained his white dress shirt and silver tie. He thought that particular imagery might be of interest to his invested audience.

The meter rose by another twenty followers. One hundred in under ten minutes of going live. This was going perfectly. And once they recognized the man—oh, boy!—the numbers would skyrocket. Leave the stratosphere. Coast across the stars. Orbit distant suns. He'd have more than enough followers to sit atop Heaven's Tower in High-City, where only the biggest names in City Stream were allowed. That exclusive sliver of paradise reserved for those with qualifying numbers, that divine place that served the most succulent meals, supplied the finest amenities, and where every dream became a reality.

He was giddy with the potential.

"I..." the broken man croaked. "I asked you a question."

Glenn looked up from the camera, the footage he was capturing. "Oh, I heard you."

"Who are you? You're not from High-City."

Glenn only giggled, as he obviously wasn't dressed for luxury. Maybe the knock he'd given him had done more damage to his brain than previously thought. "You're funny, Mr. Mars."

Mars nodded, the grim reality of the situation settling in. "So... you know who I am."

Glenn snorted. "Doesn't everyone? Not a household in this world that doesn't know who Tommy Mars is. Oh, man. I used to love watching your streams. I used to *follow* you. In the early days—before you sold out—when it was extreme stunts and pranks. Before the cooking videos and interviews with celebrities that one gives a shit about."

"Well, I appreciate your support." Mars examined his environment a little closer. "This place...we're in the Outskirts, aren't we?"

Glenn pushed the camera in Mars's face, wanting to capture the moment of desperate realization—the moment the man knew he was out of his element and thoroughly fucked. "You're not in Kansas anymore, if that's what you're asking."

"You kidnapped me."

"You're perceptive."

"How?" He shook his head, trying to clear the cobwebs so he could focus on how he had ended up here. So he could make sense of this. "How did you do it? I don't...remember."

"It's because I know your secrets."

"My secrets?" Those words didn't seem to mean a thing to him.

"In due time. First..." The numbers spiked. Another hundred. "First, we're gonna have a little fun."

Glenn put the camera on the cart, making sure the feed was still concentrated on Tommy Mars. Once settled, Glenn picked up two items: a pair of pliers and a tube cutter.

"What are you doing with those?"

Glenn flashed him a dark grin. "It's funny. You probably don't even know what these tools are used for. Probably forgotten what it's like to be a working man."

Mars sneered. "Of course I haven't. Hey, I lived in the Outskirts, too, buddy. I haven't forgotten what it's like to get my hands dirty."

"That was so long ago, though. The riches and dreams of High-City have polluted you. Your soul."

"No, I know who I am. I haven't forgotten my roots."

"Oh, you don't know how funny that sounds to me."

He shook his head. "This is insane."

"Is it?"

"Yes, it is. My people will come looking for me. The Makers will send bots. I'm assuming you're streaming this little stunt so you can grab a few followers? Right? So you can accumulate enough in a short amount of time and get out of the Outskirts? Gonna make a run at getting into Mid-City or..." Mars put a hand over his mouth and gasped, feigning utter surprise. "Gosh, you're gonna gain enough to get into the big city? You gonna be a High-City boy after all of this? Huh? Is that your grand scheme?"

Glenn lost some enthusiasm for his plan, and it showed. His stomach revolted with the pressure of a thousand escaping butterflies. "It's a solid plan."

Mars laughed at this. Hard. Enough to shake his entire body. "There's a reason no one has kidnapped a Gold-Level Streamer before. Because it's fucking stupid. My people are gonna find out where I am. They're gonna bust down that door. And they're gonna take you the fuck out." Mars's smile lacked zero confidence. "You're pathetic. And you didn't think this through, did you? You're what— gonna torture me on the Stream? People will follow *you* only because of *me*. You get that, right? They won't be *true* followers. They're fakes. It's a cheap attempt to imitate something great. I worked hard for my followers. I *earned* that shit."

"Shut up."

"No, you shut up. And listen to me. Before this goes too far and there's no going back."

There was already no going back, and Glenn knew it. "I'm done listening to you. I'm done following you. I've been following you my entire life, and it's your turn to follow me." Glenn stepped in front of the camera, blocking his audience's view of High-City's brightest star. "Listen to me. He's the fake. Tommy Mars is a phony, and he's got all of you fooled. And tonight, I'll prove it."

"You're a psycho!" Mars called out from behind him.

Glenn's cheeks flushed. "I said shut up."

"What are you going to do? Any second, those doors will bust open and—"

"Shut up!" Glenn dropped the pliers on the ground, walked over to Mars, and prepped the tube cutter for work. Mars's eyes puffed with alarm, realizing he had no place to go. His arms were chained above him, and his feet were secured with an iron loop attached to the ground. There was no wiggle room. Glenn knew that. He'd at least thought that much ahead. "You deserve this."

Glenn placed the mouth of the tube cutter around Mars's left forefinger. Mars wrestled with the kid's grip, but it was no use. His movements had limitations, and he was only delaying the inevitable. Plus, Glenn knew he was stronger than Mars even though the man was almost three times his age. Glenn, after all, had worked in the Outskirts since he was twelve and deemed old enough and fit enough for manual labor. He'd worked on his strength for the past seven years, while Mars had worked on his sweet tooth and beer gut for the last twenty.

The empty hole slipped around the prominent man's finger, and Glenn squeezed the handles together, bringing out the blade like a sideways guillotine. Mars's forefinger came off like the charred dead end of a retired cigar and fell to the ground. There was screaming and bleeding, and Glenn enjoyed bits of both.

Mars watched the scarlet squirt from the finger's stump. "You…" He turned his attention away from the bursts of red and looked up at Glenn, his eyes wet and pleading for this madness to stop. "You can't do this…"

"I already am."

Another finger came off with a hard, crunchy snip.

Screams followed. So did viewers. They tuned in by the thousands, hundreds of thousands, from the Outskirts to the High-City, and everywhere in between.

2.

Glenn watched the numbers surpass his expectations. It was like Christmas, and even though his Christmases were nothing like those experienced in Mid-City or High-City, they were still special to him. His mother could only afford to give him one present each year. Still, that overwhelming rush of shredding through the newspaper wrapping, revealing what probably cost his mom a month's worth of tricks, was the best feeling in the world. That same feeling comforted him now and filled his bones with a cozy warmth.

"You're never gonna survive this," Mars said, his fingerless left hand trembling and dripping. Somehow, the man was still conscious. Glenn assumed he would have passed out on the dirty ground after watching the second or third finger come off. He was a little impressed by how the megastar was handling this. "They'll kill you. The Council. They won't let you get away with this."

"They can't refuse me. I'll have the most followers in the world. Of all time."

"You're a fake. You cheated."

This pissed him off—these accusations of playing unfairly and navigating outside the designated rules set forth by the Council of High-City. He knew streamers lived different lives, free from the shackles of a normal society. You could rob a bank and get sent to trial, earn yourself a conviction, and spend the rest of your miserable life locked away on some island prison. But if you streamed the entire robbery and had enough followers to back it up, accumulated numbers high enough to generate a heavy flow of revenue for the Makers in High-City, the owners and operators of the Stream, arguably more important and influential than the Council of Three themselves—well, then all was forgiven. "There are no rules for streamers. You know that."

Not many attempted to stream illegal activities. Most were shut down before they could gain traction with followers, before they could garner the monetary rewards. Others simply got buried in the overabundance of streams, pushed too far down in the program's algorithms, and most of those who streamed criminal activities had no follower base to begin with. Very few attempts were successful, but they did happen from time to time.

But no one had ever kidnapped and tortured a high-profile celebrity, one of the biggest names in the game. It was ludicrous to even try. And impossible. Mostly because big security teams followed them almost everywhere, especially in public settings. Also, no celebrity would be caught dead anywhere near the Outskirts, much less inside of them.

Except for the bleeding man sitting before Glenn Martin.

"I'll kill you," Mars said through his teeth, and the display of pearly whites inspired Glenn to pick up the pliers. "You finish what you started here, boy, because I won't stop until I kill you."

Glenn wondered how hard it would be to rip out each tooth and if his followers would enjoy that kind of thing. The finger-snipping bit had scored very high, and those tuning in were hungry for more. He could see their comments beneath the rising number of followers. Not all of them were good comments. Some of them were pleading for Mars's life. Some of them were very derogatory, calling Glenn all types of horrible names, things he would dare not repeat. Some of them called him a "cheater," and that hurt worse than anything because he wasn't cheating. This was the game, and he was playing by the rules.

Some started using the hashtag *#FreeMars*. It was already trending across the three levels on every major social media site.

Maybe his followers weren't really followers at all. Maybe they were turning against him. Maybe society wasn't comprised of the bloodthirsty animals he had expected. The comments were slowly sliding in Mars's favor. Some said they only *followed* to chime in and drop the *#FreeMars* hashtag, instantly unfollowing afterward. His numbers dipped, rose, then dipped again.

Mars must have noticed something was amiss. "What's the matter? Plan not going well?"

Glenn's knuckles blanched as he squeezed his tablet. He held back in fear that he might break the cheap model.

Mars tried to hide a laugh behind his knowing grin. "Thought everyone would jump on your side, huh? Thought they would all tune into the violence? You think society is this sick group of blood-thirsty savages made up of people who are constantly searching for something miserable to enjoy? A traffic accident? A man jumping off a bridge? A tortured celebrity? Well, you've underestimated them. And you should be ashamed of yourself."

Glenn watched the numbers fall off rapidly. Cold dread alighted on his shoulders. He still had his core audience, but the threat of falling out of range for Mid-City access was real. At this point, the delusions of passing under the golden arches of High-City were fading fast.

Glenn's jaw quivered. *I just haven't done enough,* he thought. *Fingers weren't enough. I need to kick it up a notch.* He grabbed the pliers.

"What are you doing?" Mars's eyes shot wide. "Stop. You've lost. Just admit it. There's no need to—"

"I've dreamed of this moment for so long." Glenn put his face in front of the camera. "Oh yes. Are you ready, followers? Are you ready for the big reveal? The moment we've all been waiting for?" He turned to Mars and shoved the camera in his face. "Go ahead. Tell them. Tell our followers. *My* followers."

Mars's expression was wiped clean. "What are you talking about?"

"Tell them what you were doing here. In the Outskirts. Tell them your secrets."

Mars swallowed. "I don't know what you're getting at. But I was kidnapped and—"

"Liar!" Glenn bellowed. He placed the camera aside and readied the pliers. Mars screamed and tried to turn his head, but Glenn was already forcing the metal inside, pushing past his lips and clamping the jaws around one of his molars. Mars issued a few strange sounds Glenn had never heard any human make—piggish squeals and gagging cries. Glenn applied strength to the cause, and after a few minutes of wiggling the pliers back and forth, the tooth lifted from its root and came out, a swell of blood following its exit.

Mars closed his eyes and howled at the roof. His sounds actually hurt Glenn's ears, causing him to cringe. Glenn examined the bloody tooth and the damage done. He held the crimson nugget before the camera for all to see.

But it did nothing to boost his numbers. They were stagnant. And after a few seconds, greater digits dropped off.

"No," Glenn said, throwing the pliers and the extracted tooth on the mobile cart. "No, stop. This…this isn't right. There must be something wrong."

A red smile crossed Mars's face. "You idiot," he said, spitting blood. "You really thought this would work. That just proves one thing—celebrities hold the true power of this world. We run it. We are the blood that courses through the veins of our cities. We are everything. And you, the common folk, are just here to worship us. Give us our strength. Feed our godlike powers. That's it. Our followers are loyal, and they would never let you win. Morbid curiosity is out. True entertainment is in. We are gods, and you can't kill a god."

"Impossible." Glenn closed his eyes, breathed deeply, and mentally ran through his bag of tricks. There had to be a way to kick-start the numbers again. There *had* to be. "Fine. If that's the way they want it. Then that's the way they'll get it."

He reached under the cart and grabbed his gun.

"Oh fuck."

"That's right." Glenn marched over to Mars and pressed the barrel against his temple. He turned back to the camera. "This is it, High-City! This is your last chance. Say goodbye to your shining star."

"Don't do this."

"Or what? What are you going to do?"

"You don't *want* to do this."

"Oh, I really think I do." He leaned in and whispered in Mars's ear, "I've been waiting for this moment, *Dad.*"

Mars glanced up at him, confusion marking his face with a series of rough ripples. "What?"

"That's right." Glenn beamed with his unspoken knowledge. A thick vein pulsed beneath the flesh of his forehead like a worm rising from its earthly bed. "I know your secrets."

The number of followers jumped up to a respectable total.

3.

MARS DIDN'T WANT to believe it, but he knew the second he opened his eyes that this psychopath was the product of an early mistake. Back in the day, as his status on the Stream rose, Tommy Mars had a thing for whores. Cheaper the better. It wasn't a big deal. Lots of people had their vices, their addictions, things that came along with the quick capital flow. He'd been living in Mid-City at the time, and he used to visit the Outskirts at least twice a week to indulge. He would rent an apartment in the shittiest section under the pseudonym "Chester Banks" and score a couple of prostitutes for the night. Sometimes mistakes happened. Sometimes, they got pregnant. Most of them *dealt* with it. Some of them didn't. So it goes.

Anna Martin hadn't dealt with their problem. She'd had the child, and that child grew up to be the shining sack of shit in front of him, holding a gun against his temple and threatening to blow his brains out the back of his skull for all to see. Mars cursed himself for allowing her to keep it. But things were different in those days. He didn't have the pull he had now. He was a C-level celebrity, and it took him ten years to reach the pinnacle of his Stream career, where he could do anything and get away with everything. Where he became untouchable, a cash cow for the Makers and the Council of Three.

"I know your secrets," Glenn repeated to him and the camera. "You secretly visit my mother once a month. You give her money—hush dollars for keeping her mouth shut about me. About your other indiscretions."

It was true, all of it. How the kid found out, he didn't know. Maybe he had been too sloppy, too careless. It didn't matter now. The only thing that mattered was how he might escape this mess. "Yes. You're right. Absolutely."

Glenn's eyes expanded, clearly not expecting an admission to come so easily. "You admit it?"

"Yes."

Glenn's smile widened when he saw the numbers increase. They wouldn't stay there for long. Besides, Mars was already coming up with lies to tell his followers, how he could take back the truth. Hide it again. Bury it. Deep.

I just told him those things so he'd let me go, he recited. *Glenn Martin was a deranged young man. He just needed some help. Someone to love him. And I had to lie to give him the comfort he needed.*

"Son," Mars said, the word tasting burnt and acidic on his tongue. It turned his stomach. The fact that he'd had a hand at making this monster sickened him to the core. "Put the gun down. I can help you. You can come live with me in High-City. Isn't that what you want? There's no need for *this*."

Glenn looked at the camera, the unseen sets of eyes that stared back through their tablets and monitors and television projectors. The counter ticked up, and Mars caught a glimpse of a very high total, one that almost couldn't be real.

But it was.

The kid was doing it now.

He was gaining followers. Lots of them. True fans.

Maybe.

Come on, damn you, Mars thought, wondering where his rescue was. Surely, the kid hadn't covered his tracks *that* well. He was an amateur, after all. A rat that scurried the streets of the Outskirts. The son of a cheap whore. *Save me already. I deserve it. My followers will demand it.*

"Become a god with me," Mars said, hoping to play on the boy's dreams. "You're so much better than this life."

"You're full of lies, *Dad*." He shook his head. "You're just being nice to me because you want me to let you go. Then what? You'll kill me. Like you said, right?"

Mars felt his world unravel, come apart at the seams. "Fuck you, you little shit!"

Glenn knocked his own head with the butt of the gun as if there were voices within that wouldn't keep quiet. Whispers that spoke further untruths. He closed his eyes and screamed at the roof.

"You crazy bastard. I should have had you and your mother killed." It was true—he should have. It wouldn't have been hard. With his godlike powers over the three cities, it wouldn't have been harder than any other chore. One phone call—that's all it would have taken. "But no, I guess I have a weakness. Compassion. And now that weakness is going to kill me."

"Goodnight, Dad," Glenn said, raising the gun level with Mars's head.

Pulled the trigger.

A loud electric zip exploded throughout the warehouse. Mars closed his eyes and waited for the end to come, for that fabled oblivion to claim him. He expected to open his eyes and witness a city in the clouds and choirs of singing angels.

But he opened them to something else instead.

The half-missing head of Glenn Martin. Most of the kid's skull and brain matter had been blown out and now decorated Mars's shirt. He felt the gel spatter sticking to his neck and cheeks. A chunky spray speckled his right arm.

Mars blinked. Glenn was still standing as if he were alive. But he couldn't be. Vital components of his body were now gone, reduced to jelly.

It took several seconds for him to collapse and crumble to a heap on the floor.

In rolled several killbots. They wheeled around the warehouse, beeping and chirping, their laser eyes directed at the fallen kid.

Mars growled at them. "What the fuck took you assholes so long?"

The bots trilled in response.

"Bullshit. Get me out of here."

One of the bots made its way over to Mars. Using the tools at its disposal, it freed him from the chains that confined him to the floor. Once that was done, the chains around his wrist were cut.

He was free.

He rubbed the painful marks the chains had dug into his skin. Scratched them.

Glancing at Glenn's tablet, he saw the number of followers increase. The high total. Impossibly high.

More than I have. More than I've ever had.

Mars stormed over to the camera and smashed it on the ground, killing the feed and severing the connection to the Stream.

He turned back to the bots. All four were facing him.

"What?"

No answer. They just peered at him with their laser eyes.

He shifted uncomfortably.

"What is it?"

Not a single chirp.

"Oh." He understood what this was, what needed to happen. "Oh, you were...I see. The Council doesn't want to deal with the embarrassment, do they? I get it." He stood up straight, tilted his head back, and waited for the end to come.

He wondered what Heaven would actually look like, if it would resemble the top of the tower in High-City.

"We're not here to kill you, Mr. Mars," said one of the machines. He wasn't sure which one relayed the message. "We're here to bring you home."

Tommy Mars gulped, nodded, and almost cried.

He was a god, after all.

OCEANS SWALLOW OUR SHORES

The curvature of the Ferris wheel's apex was visible in the ocean murk, some thirty yards below the surface. It rested on the shelf beneath the swirling clouds of sand and unknown cosmic substances that floated like dandelion spores through the iridescent waters. Squinting, looking down, Mona could barely make out the rest of the pier, the shops that had sold saltwater taffy, the merry-go-round, and the rollercoaster they used to call "The Shoulderbreaker" because of the rough way it slammed you into the cart's sidewalls with each jerky turn. It was all lost down there, the whole boardwalk that held so many childhood memories.

Mona extended her fingers toward the glistening water, leaning forward out of the small rowboat. Within an inch of making contact, a hand gripped her shoulder.

She turned to see Kieran's worried face. He must have known how nervous he looked because his puckered lips quickly smoothed into a relaxed smile.

"Wouldn't do that," he said, as if she didn't already know better.

She chewed her tongue.

"I know you're anxious," he said, glancing back toward the shore where the rest of the team awaited their return. One of the men in hazmat suits—Banderson, Mona thought—gave them a curt wave. No one on the shoreline looked like they could stand still; they were twisting, turning, looking around for something to fixate on other than the mission ahead of them. Kieran waved back, letting them know all was okay.

So far.

"But please don't make me regret letting you do this," Kieran said, not even trying to hide the pleading in his voice. He might as well have punctuated this by getting down on both knees and clasping his hands together. "Thirty minutes down there. Not a second longer."

Mona nodded, barely hearing him. Something about the way the tide moved ensnared her focus.

"Are you listening?" he asked.

She guided her vision away from the water, finding Kieran's eyes. "Yes, I heard you."

"I want Kate back, too." He nodded as if trying to convince himself it was true. "I do. But I don't want to lose you either."

"You won't," she said, running through protocols in her mind, how these things were supposed to go down. Sure, they were breaking the rules, but then again, were there any rules for something like this? *When the unknown enters the hotel, all preconceived notions and logic must check out.* One of her father's philosophies, one of the many bestowed upon them while he'd been alive. Mona wondered what he'd say about this "rescue" mission. Would he have supported the dive? Would he have risked losing two daughters to this…whatever this was?

"Environmental conundrum," was how the president of the United States put it, but Mona and the rest of her colleagues knew it was much worse than that. *Environmental disaster* was more accurate, but good on the pres's writers for leaving the incident's aftermath vague and relatively benign-sounding. They were only a few days past the Atlantic swallowing up the pier and some of the east coast, and the Department of Oceanic Research had already lost one whole crew— five divers—to the new sea.

"Your sister's team had sixty minutes before they went dark. You're getting half that. Observe and report, that's all. This isn't a rescue mission. I *need* you to understand that, Mona. Or I'm pulling the plug right now."

Mona felt a sharp pain on the tip of her tongue before realizing she was biting it. "I said I heard you."

Kieran huffed loudly, then wiped his nose with his thumb. He gave her one last hard look as if his stare could make her give up on the idea of going after Kate. But she wouldn't budge. She was going down there with or without his blessing.

At long last, Kieran nodded and swirled his forefinger in the air as if to say *let's get this show on the road.* "Get her suited," he said, then turned to the shore, slumping his shoulders with immediate regret.

*

THE TWO ASSISTANTS in hazmat suits had gotten her suited for the dive, and she put the last touches on her gear, placing the airtight goggles over her eyes. Then came the helmet, some state-of-the-art apparatus that would allow her to breathe underwater while talking to the crew on the surface. To Mona, it looked like the glass housing of some outdoor light fixture. In fact, the base threaded into the neck of her diving jacket like a lightbulb. She looked more suited for a landing on Mars than a dive to the bottom of the continental shelf.

She gave Kieran two thumbs up. Face like a stone, he returned the gesture with two thumbs of his own, but their height showed a lack of confidence, a sense of doom. These were "goodbye forever" thumbs, thumbs that wished you luck in the next life. Because they were thumbs you'd never see again.

Mona didn't feel that way, though. It didn't feel like she was jumping into a watery tomb.

Thirty minutes. I will find you, Kate.

She turned her back to the crew, took a deep, calming breath, and dove into the icy waters, the weird ocean swelling all around her.

*

THE WATER just off the coast of the Jersey shore was clearer than ever. Whatever unknown event had caused all of this, what people around social media and national news outlets had dubbed "The Dragging"—due to the way the coast had been *dragged* into the ocean—was keeping the typically turbid waters somewhat limpid. The deeper she descended, the clearer it became. She could see a few feet in front of her, and the more depths she swam through, the more crystalline her path transformed. Not iridescent like the surface had been.

She slowed as she entered a field of floating orb-like lights no bigger than marbles. She imagined this was what astronauts felt while floating through space and being amongst a sea of stars. Taking a moment to absorb this experience, she observed the star-like substances with a child-like gaze, marveling over the smoothness of its slow movements through the tide. She held up her hand as one of the balls of light drifted past her, afraid to put her gloved fingers on the surface of the foreign material.

What would Kate have done? What did *she do?*

Kate had always been the more curious sister. Mona remembered her parents taking them on a trip to a local environmental and nature center, where, in the lobby, they had these big boxes with window cutouts and black vinyl flaps to conceal what was inside. The object of the "game" was to stick your hands inside, blindly feel the object within, and try to guess what it was. Sometimes, it was an animal bone or an arrowhead fossil. Never anything particularly sharp or dangerous. Nothing *alive*. Still, Kate never had a problem feeling around these dark cubbies; she just stuck her hands in them without a care in the world, without second-guessing or hesitation. Mona had never voiced her concerns about the activity but would secretly let her sister go first. That way, when Mona stuck her hands in, she knew for a fact whatever was inside did not have teeth and would not bite her.

She thought it was funny—in a non-humorous way—that Kate had beat her out here, signing herself up for the first dive to check out the most devastating environmental disaster to hit the East Coast since Hurricane Sandy.

Mona stretched her fingers toward the small ball of light, wishing she was brave enough to touch it. Knowing that Kate had done exactly that. She had probably touched all these floating particles, experimenting with how they moved against the pressure she applied to them. Kate probably would have tasted the light if she had been able to remove her helmet.

Curious Kate, Mona thought in her mother's voice.

The light grazed Mona's fingers just then, zapping her like a doorknob stealing a few extra electrons. She retracted her hand and shook it in the water, trying to rid herself of the lasting vibration that settled in her fingers and was now running up her arm, rattling her bones. She panicked as if she'd been bitten by something at the nature center's feel-and-guess game.

The lights did something amazing then. They began to glow, pulsating at different times, reminding Mona of the holiday house lights that took turns showcasing different areas of the house. The well-coordinated blinking kicked her heart rate up a few beats per second, and she thought hard about swimming away from them, abandoning this "recon" mission and heading back to the surface.

But then the lights went out, the orbs deactivating their lanterns, and she was left in the dark, the only light coming from the flashlight she had brought from the surface. She whipped that beam through the dark water, trying to locate what she'd seen, those small electric charges, but was unsuccessful in detecting them.

She gathered her breath. Waited. Then decided to soldier on. Because that's what Kate would have done if the roles were reversed…if she were looking for her.

Right?

She would have, Mona surmised.

Even if she knew what you did, Mona? Mom's voice. Again. She turned it off, angled herself toward the bottom of the shelf, and darted deeper into the Atlantic, focusing on the shrouded outline of the Ferris Wheel and the rest of what the ocean had dragged down.

*

"The ocean doesn't just swallow up the shore, Mona," Kate had said to her no less than twenty-four hours before she went missing in these strange waters. Those words haunted her because…well, she was right. Scientifically speaking, what had happened along the Jersey Shore four days ago just wasn't possible. It wasn't beach erosion. It wasn't a construction issue—the girders holding up the pier, the entire boardwalk, failing and sending everything tumbling into the ocean. This was something else.

Some were saying an asteroid struck the pier the night it all went down, but there was no evidence to support that. Local astronomers and reports from NASA pretty much ended such speculation. The running theory—the one that had made the most sense, the one Kate had believed in—was that the Dragging had taken place below the surface, inside some deep pocket along the shelf. A scan of the ocean floor had presented evidence of a massive divot not far from the coast. The underwater drone they had sent out before Kate's team's mission never came back; Mona was told "electrical issues and heavy signal interference" had been the culprit. After her run-in with those floating bulbs of light, she could theorize why the drone had failed.

But she wasn't down here to recover lost drones or government-funded equipment; she was here for Kate. To find her body. Bring her back to the shore. Give her the proper funeral she deserved. For her mother's sake.

The deeper she plunged into the cloudy abyss, the less control she felt over her sadness, and her heart began to ache. *I'm so sorry, Kate. It should have been me down here. You deserved to live.*

You were always the good sister.

The self-pity party ceased when she reached the apex of the Ferris wheel. She gripped the sides of the top cart and peeked across the ocean floor, the debris and wreckage from the boardwalk resting at the bottom. It all looked much more intact than she had envisioned. The taffy joint sat as it once had on the pier, the painted cartoon mascot of a giant piece of candy not displaying a single crack or scratch. The "Shoulderbreaker" coaster rested in the sand, completely unscathed, not a single rung on the track out of place or damaged. A casino arcade had taken quite a tumble along the shelf, and it was busted up, spilling video games and Skee-Ball machines across the sandy bottom like guts from a sliced belly. It was the most normal representation of a disaster down here. Everything else looked unnaturally staged as if the seaside attractions and establishments were collectibles the ocean had stolen from the shore and kept on display for all who wandered down here.

Mona cruised farther down, leaving the top of the Ferris wheel and kicking herself toward the "Shoulderbreaker." Gripping the tracks, she climbed along the railing like a ladder, recalling all the times she rode it as a kid. Memories flooded back to her, which got her thinking of Kate again. The two of them never went on a ride or entered the funhouse without each other, without holding each other's hands upon entry.

You can do this, Mona, she coached herself, leaving the tracks and gliding toward the ocean floor, where the sunken pier waited for her. She landed on top of the funhouse, planting her feet on the bulbous plastic mold of a giant clown head. On summer nights, when the boardwalk had been alive, the clown's eyes had lit up an evil electric red, which had always given her the chills. Even now, her bones were arctic, recalling those vivid memories.

She remained there for a moment, glancing left and right, trying to choose between heading toward the ruins of the arcade or swimming north to visit the more adult-oriented section of the boards, where the strip of bars and restaurants was located. She eyed the arcade's wreckage and figured if she was going to start anywhere, it'd have to be there. It was where Kate would have gone, the Skee-Ball junkie she'd been.

Mona checked her watch. Only fifteen minutes left. It was at least a five-minute swim to the surface. She had to hurry.

She kicked the clown right in the nose and propelled herself toward the derelict remains of her childhood.

*

SOMETHING CHANGED as soon as she reached what was left of the arcade. It was like the shadow of some ancient behemoth moved over her, blocking out the light from above. But when she glanced up, seeing the smattering of glittery light hitting the water and the hull of the boat that had transported her out here, she knew nothing enormous occupied these waters. Nothing visible, anyway. No, this was an *invisible* behemoth, one of the mind. And right now, it was swimming fast, above and all around.

She took a deep breath. Then she almost jumped when a voice blared in her right ear. *"Mona? Come in? You {static}?"*

After she stopped her heart from punching through her chest, she sighed, then said, "Yeah, Kieran, I can hear you. Jesus, you almost killed me."

"{static} sorry. Have y{static}{static}{static}?" A brief silence followed the crackling and crinkling. She tapped the glass globe that contained her head, the way she used to hit the old television set at her parents' house when the picture went out. *"You there? Mona? I can't {static}{static}{static}."*

"It's hard to hear you, Kieran," she said, moon-jumping along the sandy bottom of this ocean realm. "I'm almost finished with my assessment. Be back soon."

She didn't know how to turn off the link, so she listened to thirty more seconds of Kieran attempting to make contact, the intermittent static too much to cut through. He finally gave up, and the ensuing silence welcomed her, and she embraced the momentary stillness.

Then she got to work, pushing over the toppled wreckage, dislodging pieces of the collapsed roof—what she could—while wondering if Kate's body was trapped underneath somewhere. Some of the pieces were too heavy to move, especially near the bottoms of the piles. The huge splinters of broken clapboard siding went floating, sky-bound fragments of what used to be the arcade and surrounding gift shops. Wrapped candies and t-shirts with humorous expressions came loose from the collapsed building materials and began spilling past Mona. She ignored them, hoping to dig a little deeper before giving up, hoping—no, praying—Kate's body was inside waiting for her. Really, though, she'd settle for any part of her sister's crew. Just something to confirm everyone's worst suspicions about what had happened down here.

Because *not* finding them—that would be infinitely worse. Because the unknown would give way to wild speculation and rumor.

Mona blinked and screamed into her globe of a helmet, a frustrated cry that would have stirred any sea creatures out of hiding... had any signs of life been present. She pounded her fists against the remaining piles of detritus, directed her rage at the limitless ocean beyond the shelf, and shouted obscenities until her throat went hoarse and her voice was rendered useless.

Bright lanterns again. Those floating electric orbs returned, shining like lightning bugs at dusk. So many hovered around her that she had to shield her eyes from their collective glow. She waited for the darkness and light to balance themselves. Then she glanced up and saw a whole swarm of jellyfish migrating away from the coast, heading out to sea. Hundreds of them pushing with their tentacles. Like a flock of birds evading a bad storm. What were these creatures fleeing from? And why *away* from the shore?

When Mona faced the pile of junked arcade games again, an amalgamated hill of classic joystick-centric beat-'em-ups and claw-game machines, cheap prizes and tendrils of tickets all flooding out of them, a familiar face peered back at her. Eyes open but cloudy-white, like drowning had erased her sight. Her hair was wild, an undulating frill of brown-black strands bouncing in the buoyant tide. Seaweed wrapped itself around her wrists and ankles like green manacles, keeping her rooted in place. A thick, slimy band of seaweed curled around her bloated throat. The restraints didn't matter, though. Even if she were free to leave, she wasn't going anywhere. Kate was dead.

Mona gasped, and that subtle sound hurt while coming up. Warm trickles of tears streamed from her eyes. Instinctively, she reached to wipe them away, but her hand struck the glass bulb around her head.

Oh, Kate, she thought, collapsing to her knees.

"*Helloooooo, sister,*" a voice said, but it couldn't have come from Kate. Her midnight-blue lips hadn't moved.

"What?" Mona rasped, jumping back to her feet and glancing around in every direction to see where the voice had come from. But there was no one else here. She tapped her helmet, wondering if someone had hijacked her communications system and was playing a despicable prank on her. "Hello? Hello?" she spoke rapidly into the helmet, but no one responded. "Kieran? Can you hear me?"

"*No one can hear youuuuuu,*" the voice said again, clearly belonging to Kate…if Kate had been gargling a mouthful of dead worms as she spoke. "*You are alonnnnnnne.*"

"Stop this," Mona pleaded, fighting against the scratches in her throat. "This isn't real."

"But it is. It's all happening." Kate floated there in front of her, and even though Mona couldn't see her eyes, she knew her sister's corpse was looking right at her.

No, not at me.

Through me.

Into me.

"I can hear your thoughts," Dead Kate said, her monotone voice coming through her comms better than Kieran had. *"I can see what you did."*

That one got her, sent a chill down her spine like a lightning bolt, frying every nerve. "Wha–" she said, breathless now.

"Do you love him?"

The tears spilled more steadily now; her face was a wet canvas of petrified flesh.

"Do you love him?" she asked again. The seaweed seemed to move her, control her. Like the environment down here was possessing her. It pushed her closer to Mona, who unknowingly drifted a few feet from her original stopping point. *"Do you love my husband?"*

Mona sobbed, a barking cry, and it felt like her chest was cracking in two. "Oh god."

It was only one time, Mona wanted to say but couldn't bring herself to utter those meaningless words.

"One time," Dead Kate repeated her thought aloud, and Mona swore she saw the ends of her dead sister's lips curl up. Like a Dr. Seuss character smirking. *"Do you love my husband? Do you love my Kieran?"*

Mona shook her head. "What are you?"

At this, Dead Kate lost her smirk, and her face went blank again, imitating the dead so perfectly well. *"I am your sister."*

"You're not my sister; you're dead and–"

Before she could finish that thought, several more bodies floated into view, drifting up from the pier's wreckage around her. It was Kate's crew, the rest of the divers who had followed her into this unknown world below the surface. Seaweed was wrapped around their extremities as well, controlling their movements like marionette strings. Mona didn't have the slightest who pulled them, but she understood sticking around to find out was a bad idea.

Her alarm went off, the surface calling her back.

"You can't run from us," Kate said, and it wasn't just Kate's voice this time—the whole crew sang this threat like a chorus. And they all sounded the same, dead and languid. Very little of their true voices remained, replaced by something else, something that was *trying* to sound human but just missed the mark. *"We will swallow your oceans. We will swallow your shores."*

Mona peddled her way toward the surface and did not look back. She waited for the seaweed to curl around her feet and drag her back down to the shelf floor, where she would remain rooted there with her sister. Forever.

But that didn't happen.

*

WHEN SHE BROKE THE SURFACE, she unscrewed the helmet from her neck attachment and took the biggest gulp of fresh air she could, letting the salty atmosphere fill her. The rowboat was overturned, with no signs of the three other men who occupied it. She shouted Kieran's name but received no reply. She swam closer to the shore, stopping when she spotted the entire team she'd come with. They were lying in the sand, not moving. Their hazmat suits had not protected them from whatever happened here.

She spotted three bodies in the water, not far from the shore. One of them was Kieran. She could tell from his shape, size, and what he'd been wearing when she'd last seen him.

She almost swam to him but stopped when movement in the distance caught her eye. On the dunes beyond the shoreline, a figure stood tall underneath the pale gray skies. Mona squinted, seeing her sister.

It was Kate.

And she still looked dead. She was shedding her seaweed restraints. When she was free of them, she turned and disappeared down the dunes toward land.

The ocean had swallowed the shore, but it hadn't swallowed her.

WOLVES IN THE DIAMOND

1.

Summer is for baseball and beaches, but we didn't have any beaches near Prescott Valley while growing up, though we did have a lot of sand. Not beach sand, but like desert sand, the hard, compact stuff that scrapes up your knees when you slide too carelessly. And we did slide a lot in those days, especially that summer. And we were careless. Care*free* and careless. That was us. *The Werewolves.*

2.

Yep, not a June passes without me thinking back to the summer of '93. It was a special time in my life when I was twelve, living for the moment, one day at a time, and thinking a lot about baseball. When school let out that June, the first thing we did—the *eight* of us—was head to the vacant parking lot on the border of Prescott Valley and Sandstrom, a sandy flatland that used to be fairgrounds, but since no fair had come strolling through those parts in decades, we commandeered the property and made it *our* baseball field. Collectively, the whole crew saved up weeks' worth of allowances for chalk to mark out the baselines and the batter's box, bags for the bases, and a small collection of balls in case we lost some over the fence.

The fence.

Before I go any further, I should probably mention the fence and what was on the other side of it. It'll make sense later, I promise, but know this: the fence was the only thing separating our makeshift field from the town junkyard. Through a sparse gathering of trees, you could see stacks of compressed cars and trucks, towers of metal that looked pretty cool, and you could sometimes hear the harsh grinding of metal-on-metal as the workers placed the totaled vehicles in the crushers and ran the machines. We became used to those sounds, but the one sound that always got to us—or *me*, really—was the aggressive yipping and barking that came and went throughout our games. The junkyard dogs patrolled the grounds, keeping their territory free and safe from intruders and outlanders of any kind. This was one of the few reasons we brought extra balls—hopping over the fence was dangerous business. And it wasn't like we were cranking them out regularly, either. Of the eight who played, only two of us could smash a homer. And I wasn't one of them.

Peter Strand was the best of us, the most complete player. He could field. He could run. He could hit for bases or knock a grand salami far past the trees, farther than we could see. The latter he did often, and the rest of us had to suffer through his celebratory jog around the base paths. Pete wasn't smug about too many things, but baseball was one of them. He was good, and he knew it, and he had a bright future ahead of him. The rest of us envisioned him playing in the majors—although, when you're twelve, playing professional sports seems like an almost obtainable goal. It's not until later in life that you realize how delusional that dream is.

Pete was also my best friend. He and I hung out *all* the time, went everywhere together, and rarely a day went by that we didn't see one another.

That summer was the best and worst of my life. It was the summer I made a lot of good friends, and it was the summer I lost most of them.

3.

IT ALL STARTED toward the end of June. I remember being up to bat, pointing my aluminum slugger toward the fence, envisioning myself connecting on the next pitch and launching a home run for the ages, one that would be talked about until September rolled around. But the next pitch Aaron Horowitz threw was a dagger, and I whiffed, *hard*, so hard that everyone playing the infield let go of a few stomach-holding chuckles. Before I could brush off the embarrassment, Trent Pitino came flying onto the field on his Huffy (the one he'd outgrown but had to use because his parents refused to buy a new one until Christmas), breathing heavily with this panicky look etched into his face. He ditched the bike between first and second.

"You guys!" Trent said, breathlessly sprinting. "There's been a murder!"

Everyone looked at him for about three seconds, then shrugged and refocused on the game at hand. I'd lost count of the balls and strikes, but I'm fairly certain I was behind. Before Aaron could toss me another zinger, Trent screamed, "It was a kid! Mark Schuman! Pete, you know him! He's in our class!"

Pete took a mild interest in this new announcement, but the next bit of info really caught our attention.

"Guys…" Trent edged his way toward the pitcher's mound, and the deflated sound of his voice drew everyone in from the outfield. We crowded around him as he said, "They found him in pieces."

"Nuh-uh," someone said, and I'm sure it was Davy Renner. He never believed anything until the evidence was in front of him, and Trent hadn't brought a limb to the field for proof. "You're lying, dude."

"Am not! It's in the papers! They found him near Sparrow Point or…shit, what was left of him."

Sparrow Point was a popular park near downtown Prescott Valley, and what was left of Mark Schuman (according to the news article I'd read later) was nothing but a torso and a few scattered limbs. The boy's head was found several days later, wedged in a sewer grate.

Everyone went silent after Trent's story. Pete was the one to rally us back, telling us all it was a one-off, just a thing that happens sometimes, that happens in every town across America sooner or later, just we never hear about them, these grisly murders. Pete's *facts* felt like a lie, and I could sense everyone deduced that much from his tone alone. Still, we carried on with the rest of the afternoon and played baseball. The game lost its fun, and we played what some competitive coach might call "lazy ball." We didn't chase pop flies or dive for grounders heading for the gaps; we just took what amounted to batting practice, and even when we swung the bat, there was just no *oomph.*

When we left the field that evening, so close to sundown, we heard a dog howling at the coming moon. At least, I thought it was a dog at the time.

Now I'm not so sure.

4.

NO MURDERS HAPPENED over the next two weeks, and the town—not a big town, but not a small town either—somewhat returned to normal. Our parents were less worried about sending us out to play unsupervised. They never caught the person who murdered poor Mark Schuman, savaged his body, and left his parts scattered around like some heinous game of human fifty-two card pickup. Everyone assumed the killer was just a drifter, someone passing through the park that day. No one considered someone who lived here. A teacher. A policeman. The guy who packed your groceries at the supermarket. The bank teller who cashed your weekly paycheck. Maybe because that made it too real. It was better to believe the killer had moved on, that the town was safe. It's funny how people lie to themselves so they can cling to normalcy.

We played baseball a lot during those weeks. Took us a few days to get back into the swing of things (no pun intended), but once we did, man, it felt amazing. We laughed. We hollered. We endlessly argued about every tag at the plate. And we watched Pete up his batting average to somewhere in the seven hundreds. The time spent on those abandoned fairgrounds over that post-murder period was a much-needed break from reality.

Still, something out there howled beneath the bright moons, a noise that carried on the wind, a warning that everyone seemed to ignore. Even us.

5.

IN THE SECOND week of July, on a real scorcher, the kind of day that makes you sweat just standing there, we were back on the diamond, getting our daily baseball on. Despite the heat, Pete was having a hell of a day. He was four for five and had already smacked two dingers. Patrick Kemp hit two himself, which left us with one extra ball.

I was in left field when Aaron served Pete a fastball on a platter. I mean, it was right in his hot zone, down and inside, and Pete turned on the pitch and cranked it high. Just from the pop of the bat, I knew it was gone. We'd never see that red-stitched orb again. As it sailed over my head, Pete victoriously flipped his bat and skipped toward first. He always took pleasure in running the bases after a moonshot like that. Not that he had to; we never kept score (just individual stats) and never played for anything but fun. Pete would try out (and play) for the middle school team next spring, but during the summers, he was ours. On our team. *The Werewolves.*

You're probably wondering how we arrived at that name for our little…club, for lack of a better term. Well, as it happened, we got that name on that hot-ass July day. See, once the ball cleared the fence—and the trees behind it—we were out of balls, and it wasn't even noon yet. Half the squad wanted to go home to their air-conditioned homes and play Sega, but the other half wanted at least another hour of game time.

Pete decided for us. He nodded at me and said, "You're up, Branson."

I scoffed. "Up for what?"

"You're in left," he said, hands on his hips as he strolled toward the outfield. "You need to find us a ball."

I looked at the wooden fence, average in height and climbable, but the dogs on the other side—quiet as they had been that day—made me shake my head like a horse ridding itself of a few pesky flies.

I tried to get out of it and pleaded with Pete, pulling the *I'm your best friend* card, *so don't make me do it*. But he was having none of it. Rules were rules. When we were out of balls, the man (boy) in left field had to be the one who climbed into that forbidden territory. The Junkyard.

This was also the first time it happened. I'm not proud to admit it, but I was petrified. Even if all went well and the junkyard dogs didn't rip me to shreds, I was worried about falling off the fence, landing funny on my foot, and snapping my ankle. My mom and dad would kill me, and there would be no more baseball for me that summer.

But I did it. I climbed the fence, getting a little shove up from the others, and hopped over to the other side. I landed on a pile of branches and twigs that snapped on impact. At least it wasn't my ankle. I surveyed the area, looking for the closest baseball, but couldn't see any. The tree's foliage drooped down, providing an obscured look into the junkyard. In the distance, I saw a dirt road flanked by stacks of vehicles that hadn't met the crusher yet, along with loose tires and rusted auto parts. I snuck through the branches and leaves, hoping I was quiet enough, waiting to hear the monstrous growling of some guard dog. I made sure my feet landed softly on the patches of packed dirt and collections of fallen sticks. All while scanning the area, trying to find a damn baseball.

"Any luck, Branson?" I heard someone say, and I guess it was Pete. He was usually the only one who called me by my last name.

"*No,*" I whispered back. In retrospect, I should have said nothing. Because I think that's when *he* heard me.

Inching my way to the clearing ahead, I crouched so the branches wouldn't scratch my face. Still no ball in sight, and even though we hadn't hit a ton of home runs, I still expected to see one by now. Most of us batted righty, so the balls should have been in that area…unless they rolled down the small incline that started to dip about forty feet from the fence. I hoped they didn't, that I'd peek down that incline and see a baseball staring back up at me within grabbing distance. But, of course, a boy couldn't be that lucky.

A scared boy.

When I did look down that incline, I spotted a ball about halfway down the hill. It had gotten caught on an overgrown root, and most of the white was now brown with dirt and mud. What a relief. At least I wouldn't have to go all the way down and risk being spotted by the dogs or the junkyard employees. I scrambled down, grabbed the ball, then turned to come back up. I went to speed up the hill, wanting to reach the fence as quickly as I could, but something stopped me.

Movement in my periphery. Fast. Like a room shadow moving when you're all alone after midnight.

I spun, expecting to see one of the dogs with its mouth open, drool and frothy slobber dangling from its sharp canines. But it wasn't a dog.

It was a man.

"Hey there," he said in a croaky voice as though he had a bad cold or something. "Didn't mean to startle you."

I froze, unable to work my legs and my mouth. My brain immediately went to Mark Schuman, his boy parts scattered around the park like concession stand litter after a music festival. I knew the second I laid eyes on this man that he was the killer—he had murdered Mark Schuman. His shirt was torn all over the place, like he'd run it through a shredder before putting it on, and his jeans weren't any cleaner—they too had rips and tears only a bear claw could make. His long black hair dangled over his face, so I couldn't see him too well, but there was also something familiar about him, like I'd met him before. Had a conversation with him? Maybe. The hint of familiarity lingered and got stronger when he stepped forward.

I shrunk back.

"I'm not going to hurt you," he promised, a promise I knew he'd break if I let my guard down.

"Stay away," I said.

"I'm here to help you, Branson."

Shit. He knew my name. The killer knew my fucking name.

It knocked the breath out of me.

"Calm down," the man said, pumping his hand like that would help. "I can—" He stopped mid-sentence and grabbed his stomach with both hands, taking an *I-ate-something-bad* bow. "I'm here to help," he said, weakly now.

Then I saw his eyes. They weren't like any I'd ever seen before. They were glowing. Two luminous moon-donuts: silvery circles with dark, endless centers. As he hunched over, he growled. I stepped forward, two quick shuffles that rustled the long-dead leaves. I could see his face a little better; it looked…*off.* I guess that's the best way to put it. Misshapen. *Huge* where the forehead was concerned, yet smaller everywhere else.

"*You're all…*" he tried to muscle out, and then: "*…in grave danger.*"

Then he stretched like a contortionist, his limbs undulating and snapping in ways they shouldn't have, bending at the joints in opposite directions—like, his elbow bent backward the other way with a wicked crunch.

That got me moving.

I hustled up the hill and tossed the ball over the fence. Not sure why. I was on the verge of being killed by this man (*monster*), and the last thing that should have concerned me was whether my friends would get to continue their game. But after releasing the ball, I was climbing that fence, though faster in my mind than my body would allow. Luckily, on this side, the fence had cross boards where the pickets were nailed, and I used them for leverage to elevate myself. I was up and over faster than a six-four-three double play.

Once I was over and back on solid earth again, I encountered a collection of worried faces. They must have heard the killer talking to me, must have heard the whole exchange.

"What's the matter, squirt?" Billy Steadman asked, taking off his glove and tucking it under his arm. Of all the kids in the group, Billy was perhaps the biggest *dick* of them all. Called everyone *squirt* or *shrimp*, undoubtedly terms he inherited from his asshole father.

"I saw a man," I said, realizing I was shaking now. "At least I think he was a man. He looked like a…" *Wolf* was the word on my mind, and I don't know why, other than the lingering memory of watching the Lon Chaney Jr. classic at Pete's house last Halloween. For some reason, the man reminded me very much of that film, the transformation scenes in particular. "I think he was the killer."

Everyone gaped at me. Then they burst out laughing. Some of them bent over and slapped their knees. Others howled at the sun like day werewolves themselves. Everyone save for Pete, who just stared at me like…well, like he believed me.

"Quiet," Pete said, and everyone listened, the laughter tapering off. "You really saw someone over there?"

I nodded.

"Okay," Pete said. And I realized where I recognized the man's face from, though I wasn't going to say it. Not then. Maybe not ever. "Let me see. Boost me up," he told the group.

They did as he said. Pete glanced over the fence, but he couldn't locate any killer. The junkyard Dobermans came rushing up the hill, barking and growling at Pete as he made his presence known. God, if I'd been a few minutes slower getting back over…

"No killer," Pete said once his feet were back on the dirt. "Maybe your eyes were playing tricks on you."

"He looked like a wolf," I said. And to this day, I'm not sure why I said it. It was something meant for my thoughts that just kind of came out. But once it was out, I couldn't take it back.

The others teased me. But Pete could see I wasn't jerking around, that I was serious, and he got them to stop.

"Like a…werewolf?" Pete asked.

I had no choice but to follow through with my instincts. "Yeah. He had weird eyes. And his face was messed up. Clothes all torn. Like he just changed back into a human."

"Nuh-uh," Davy Renner said in his whiny voice. "You're lying. Trying to scare us."

I stood my ground. "I think he killed Mark Schuman."

Silence. Everyone absorbed the information I just dropped on them.

Pete said, "I believe you." After that, everyone else did too. "Look," he said, addressing the group, "Werewolves aren't real. But child killers are. And if Branson says he saw the killer, then I believe him."

"So…" Aaron said, looking at the infield dirt. "Should we stop playing baseball? Until he's caught."

Pete shook his head. "No. No, there are eight of us and only one of him. We stick together. He can't hurt us that way. Besides…" There was a glimmer in his eye. Moonlight. Maybe my mind *was* playing tricks on me—I couldn't get the man's eyes out of my head, their silvery reflections. "In the diamond, we're the wolves."

6.

WE ARE *the wolves* kind of stuck. Over the next week, we started calling ourselves the Wolves as a team name…even though we weren't really a team. Then we became The Werewolves (Pete's suggestion). We were so fond of the name that we were gonna have Trent Pitino's dad

—who owned a printing shop—make us jerseys with WEREWOLVES branded across the chest, and we'd each choose a number and have our names on the back. We'd have to save up the rest of our summer allowance for that, though. Maybe fall allowance, too.

But it never got that far.

Because a week later, we stopped playing altogether. Because that's when another murder happened.

And this time, it was one of our own.

7.

BILLY STEADMAN WAS FOUND about thirty feet from his bike near Floral Park, maybe a mile from his parents' house. His body was ripped in two. The papers said whoever did it must have been a giant because crime scene investigators revealed that he came apart with such ease —"like tissue paper." They could tell by the condition of the torn flesh —straight, not ragged.

Even though Billy was a dick, I cried at his funeral. The others did, too.

8.

FOUR DAYS LATER, someone broke into the Renner's house through Davy's window just after midnight. Just came crashing through like a wrecking ball. Davy's father was up like a lightning strike in reverse and came barreling into Davy's room, ready to greet the criminal with his shotgun, but he was too late. Davy's body was on the bed. Well, *some* of it was. The rest was on the wall. Some on his desk. Some of him on the floor. Splattered across his closet door...

9.

AARON HOROWITZ WENT to put the garbage out for his mother and never came back. They found him three days later in the woods behind his house. He was in a tree. The claw marks dug into his face made it hard for his mother to identify the body.

10.

PATRICK KEMP REFUSED to leave his house with all the killings going on. But it didn't save him. Hiding in his basement, underneath a blanket on the couch, he heard movement upstairs. Troubled movement. But his parents were upstairs, and they had been drinking wine. So maybe they were getting a little frisky, about to *do it* on the kitchen table *(gosh, it wouldn't be the first time)*.

When he checked on them (after a long spell of silence), he opened the kitchen door and found a total massacre. He couldn't distinguish which bloody part belonged to his father and which belonged to his mother. He almost fell down the stairs. And when he heard the beast in the corner next to the stove, growling and feasting, he *did* fall down the stairs. But that pain was only temporary. The beast standing in the stairwell doorway looked down at him. Patrick blinked. And then it was over, his life, short as it was.

11.

MY PARENTS WERE GETTING ready to move us out of Prescott Valley. I suspect if we'd had money, we would have gone sooner, after the second or third killing. But we didn't. So they had to "make arrangements."

It was August, nearing the end of the summer of '93, and we were set to move the first week of September. Someplace in Oklahoma. I begged my parents not to, but they weren't having any of it. It was too dangerous here. And the cops—they had no leads.

But I did, and I had kept it secret, and now I was hating myself, feeling responsible for the deaths of my friends. I don't know how things would have turned out had I told the adults what I'd seen on the other side of the fence, but maybe it would have made a difference.

Pete called me the night I found out we were moving. We talked about it. He was sad; I was sadder. After he said it would be all right, that we could still write each other, his tone got serious.

"Was it him?" he asked. The question came from left field.

"Who?"

"My stepfather." Pete's stepfather had been kicked out of his house a few years back, but I never heard about him after that. Only saw him once or twice, and I think he was drunk both times. Pete never talked about it, but I assumed things were bad. The cops were often involved in the Strand's family affairs.

"Yes," I told him. "It looked like him."

Pete cussed. Cried.

I tried to calm him down. "We can tell the cops."

"No." The cops, he said, did not know how to handle the situation. But apparently…he did. "I have a plan." He told me when and where to meet him.

"I'll have to sneak out."

"Right on. And Branson?"

"Yeah?"

"Bring your bat."

12.

I DON'T KNOW why I agreed to it. Sneaking out past midnight was something I'd never even considered, but times were desperate. I mean, the way I figured it (in my twelve-year-old brain) was if we could take down Pete's stepfather and turn him over to the cops, then the killer would be caught, and we wouldn't have to move to Oklahoma. It was worth sneaking out and dying for. So I figured at the time. Guess I'd come a long way from that kid who was too scared to climb the fence to fetch a ball.

There weren't many of us left. Pete invited the remaining *Werewolves*, but only I showed up. He was disappointed but also *got it*.

"He wants me, Branson," Pete said as we stood near the mound, the moonlight shining down on us. "He's killing my friends to get to me."

It didn't make sense even at the time. Why didn't he just go after Pete and be done with it? Why kill us all? Why drag it out?

"Because he's a sick man, and he wants me to suffer," Pete told me. Then he pointed his bat at the fence and shouted, "I know you're out there, Forest! Show yourself."

Forest Tilly didn't show himself. Not at first. But a few minutes later, two long arms stretched over the fence, pulling a body over onto the other side.

Forest looked much like I'd remembered. Only his clothes weren't torn up. *Yet.*

"You need to stop, Pete," he said. "This ends tonight."

"Damn right it does," Pete told him. "I'm going to kill you."

Forest looked at me, those silvery eyes glowing. "You should run." And when I didn't: *"Now."*

"We can take him, Branson."

Forest stopped walking. Looked at his stepson. Then to me. Then back to Pete. "Jesus," he said, shaking his head. "You don't even know."

"Know what?" Pete asked. "Know *what?*"

"God, this is all my fault. Your mother…she didn't understand. I tried to explain it, but…she didn't *want* to understand. She just kicked me out."

"What are you talking about?" Pete was crying, his tears glistening beneath the full moon.

Then, grabbing his stomach, Pete lurched forward. He cried out like someone had run a sword through his six-pack.

"It was you, Pete," Forest said. "You killed them, your friends."

On cue, Pete started to change. Hair grew on his arms and neck, his face, a thicket of coarse animal fur. His jaw became almost unhinged, sharp teeth crowding his mouth. A sound escaped him, bubbling up from somewhere deep in his throat, one that couldn't have been produced by a normal kid on the cusp of thirteen. This was no puberty glitch. It was the beginning of a howl, and the moon had brought it out of him.

I backed away.

"You really should run, Branson," Forest said again, and as he did, his face began to take its wolfish shape. Then he spun to his stepson. "I'm sorry I did this to you, boy. I was hoping to show you how to control it—the urge to kill—but I was too late. It has to end tonight. There's been enough killing, and—"

Pete—the beast he'd become—leaped at his stepfather, swiping a claw across his face. Raw red slashes opened on the man's transforming flesh. The two wrestled, locked in a powerful grapple, and that's when I decided to skedaddle. There was no use sticking around and seeing how this would play out. No matter who won, I'd be the grand loser.

I went for the fence and jumped for the top at full speed. Got my hands on the other side, and my desperate strength helped me pull myself up and over. I looked back at the scrap before disappearing on the other side, catching a glimmer of Pete's eyes before going down. There was no boy left in them—only the moonlit glow of the wolf inside.

My friend was gone.

13.

I CRIED myself to sleep and woke up the next morning in a junked car to the sound of a hundred different voices. When I sat up, I saw the whole junkyard crawling with cops and K-9s. They were looking for me, so I helped them out and climbed out of the rusted vehicle, waving my hands and crying for help. They rushed over to me, telling me I was going to be all right, even though I really wasn't.

They marched me back up the hill and around the diamond's outskirts, threw a towel over my head, and told me not to look. But telling a kid not to look at something potentially horrific is like telling a horse not to graze on the green stuff. So, I peeked around the towel to see two bodies lying in the center of the diamond. Two *human* bodies. One was Forest Tilly's, and the other belonged to Peter Strand. Their eyes were open, but they no longer carried that luminous glow—they were all human. And dead.

I didn't realize I'd stopped walking. The cops tried to move me along, tearing me away from the scene as if I was crazy enough to have a closer look. They assured me some animals got to them, said I should think about what I saw that night because later they'd want the whole story. But I never gave it to them, not the truth. They had a story made up already, that Forest Tilly was the one killing the children, that he took us to the baseball field to complete his ritualistic spree. And I'm ashamed to say I went along with that tale, told them that was exactly how it went down. Then I told them we were attacked by wolves, and that was good enough for them.

The killings stopped after that.

We still moved to Oklahoma, and I never saw that baseball field again.

But sometimes, on a still night during the full moon, I can still hear that howling. I can still hear my friend Pete.

GULLS

The sea vultures circled above, attracted by the spoiling meat and bold scent of blood. Of the flock, the daring ones began to test their meals, swooping down and getting just close enough to the potential feast before leveling off and climbing back up the vast blue expanse. Few clouds traveled the boundless, cerulean stretch. The sun reached its zenith, casting a shimmering glow across the ever-flat ocean.

The safety-cone-orange emergency raft floated atop gentle waves, pushing toward an endless horizon. Lucy Mitchell rested her chin on the inflatable wall, watching the haze that lined the distance as far as she could see, and waited for someone, another ship of any kind or a passing plane, to come and rescue them.

But there was no one. No activity (save for the gulls) for almost six hours.

"We're gonna die out here," Vincent said, lifting his head. He'd used his T-shirt as a barrier between his exposed face and the sun's deadly rays. Lucy could already feel the burn ruining her flesh, but that was the least of her concerns. Getting rescued was all that mattered.

They'd played out this conversation twice since the cruise ship went down and they found themselves lost at sea.

"They'll be looking for us, I already told you. A luxury charter like that—they'll come looking. We're probably already all over the news.

Trending on Facebook, Twitter… Our faces are probably on every television screen in the United States."

Vincent shook his head. "No, no. We drifted too far from the crash site."

"How would you know?" she asked, abandoning her view of the bleak unknown and turning to him. "Are you a captain? A sailor? Are you Ponce De Le-fucking-ón?"

Vincent laughed off her snappy tone, a howl that echoed over the endless waters.

"No," she barked. "You're not. You're a fucking cook."

"Yeah, well. A *good* cook. I make the best Swedish meatballs you've ever tasted in your entire life, sweetheart."

Disgusted, she turned back to the quiet sea. There was something serene about the way the waves moved. Even though the situation was dire, and even though she was fearful and fully aware they *could* very well die out here, the reality of death marching toward them, the rhythm of the sea brought her tranquility. It wouldn't last, certainly wouldn't. But for now, she would bask in it. As much as she could. Before Vincent started his mouth again.

"We should throw him overboard," Vincent said, not more than a few minutes later. The gulls above seemed to hear and understand his suggestion, and they squawked in shrill delight.

Lucy slowly turned her head, her lower lip quivering. "You will not *touch* him."

Vincent wrapped his shirt around his head and lifted his hands in surrender. "Just a suggestion. Sooner or later," he said, his eyes finding the sky, "those birds are gonna get hungry. Real hungry. Sooner or later, they'll have no choice."

Lucy ignored him, even though she knew it wouldn't stop him.

"See those movements," he said, pointing up, his forefinger circling along with the flock's pattern. She gave in and followed his gaze, watching one of the gulls descend and pull up when it got about twenty feet from the raft. The gull rejoined the circle, falling in line with its winged companions. "They're testing the waters, so to speak. Won't be long before they go in. Guarantee if we don't move or talk for a while, they'll come gunning for us."

"Delightful."

"You may think not having food or drinkable water is our biggest problem." Vincent shook his head adamantly. "It's those birds. Never underestimate a hungry animal."

She looked to her husband, whose battered corpse lay on the other side of the raft, sprawled out in a gingerbread man pose.

"Telling you," Vincent said, "we should toss him. Carrion is only gonna attract the birds."

"He's my husband. I'm not leaving him."

Vincent cackled. "Oh, sweetheart. You don't know how funny that is to my ears."

Lucy growled. "Listen, asshole. Whatever you think you know about me, about my husband—you don't know shit."

A wide smile traveled across Vincent's face. "Oh, but I do. I know things. Where were you when the ship went down? Huh? What were you doing, love?"

"What are you talking about?"

"I saw you," he said, winking. "I saw what you were up to."

"I..." She shook her head and swallowed. "I was looking for Daryl." Her softened gaze fell on the corpse, the so-purple-it's-black contusions, the open cuts that had crusted over, blistered and crisped. "He was in the casino."

"Uh-huh." That knowing smile never left the cook's face. Never moved. "Before that."

She glared at him, her eyes narrowing. Pinching her lower lip between her teeth, Lucy said, "You don't know the first thing about me."

"I know many things about you..." Another vicious laugh escaped his mouth. "I know what you were doing."

A part of her wanted to lunge at the man, grab his throat, and strangle him to death. Leave *him* for the birds. *He* should have died, not her husband. Daryl didn't deserve it. It was bad luck how he'd fallen, how he'd smacked his head on the flotsam, which knocked him into a dream he could never wake from. Could have happened to someone else. *Should have.* Someone who deserved it.

"Were you spying on me?" Lucy asked. "You were, weren't you?"

Vincent waved off the claim. "Please. I happened to be in the right place at the right time. Well, right for me. Wrong for you." A giggle, almost child-like. "Oh, I saw you. *All* of you." His wink made her skin crawl.

"You sick bastard."

"You're the sick one." His eyebrows arched, which would have been comical under normal circumstances. "Remember—I've seen what you can do with that tongue of yours."

Anger flashed through her, an uncontrollable surge of sheer rage. She launched herself from her side of the raft, at Vincent, who reacted immediately, drawing the knife he'd been sitting on. The long blade had been lifted from the ship's culinary department. Its long metal body caught the sunlight just right and momentarily blinded her.

She backed down but was unsuccessful in tempering her emotions.

"No, no," Vincent said. "None of that."

She paced back and forth, a caged lioness ready to spring at her observer despite the thick sheet of indestructible glass between them. In this case, the knife was the barrier. A big one. Sharp.

"A good cook always keeps his favorite knife handy, yeah?" His taunt came with another burst of laughter, and Lucy sneered. "Come now. It's all in good fun, yeah?" He nodded at the corpse. "Why are you so angry? Your husband is gone. Judging from your... hmm, how shall I say—*extracurricular* activities aboard the cruise ship—one would think you'd be glad to be rid of him. No?"

She eyed him, wondering how she could disarm him, take the knife, and slip the blade gracefully into his throat, how she could overpower him. He knew his way around a knife, sure, but did he know how to kill? She doubted it. Then she realized she didn't know how to kill either. She'd let her instincts take over. His versus hers.

What are you talking about? This is crazy. You can't kill another person just because you don't like his accusations.

Accusations?

Truths?

It was strange how quickly she was falling apart. Six hours lost at sea and she was ready to murder someone over a few words. Back in the real world, in normal society, where there were structure, laws, and consequences for acts of violence, she would have ignored these churlish remarks. But here... now...

Now, she wanted blood.

As she struggled with her terrible thoughts, a gull dove and landed on Daryl's chest. It squawked a warning cry and then pecked at the cold flesh of Daryl's cheeks, pinching and peeling away a layer of skin to reveal the pink softness beneath.

"NO!" Lucy shrieked, hurling herself at the bird. Before she reached her husband's corpse, the bird took flight, its fleshy prize dangling from its beak.

"Told you," Vincent said. "Should just donate him to the gulls and get it over with. They won't stop. Not now that they've had a taste."

"Shut up!" She ran her fingers along the damage, whimpering. Her fingers grazed his hard, cold skin. "Jesus..."

Vincent sat up, resting his elbows on his knees. "Look—I'm not some heartless bastard, yeah? I know he's your husband. I know you loved him—at some point, anyway. Maybe not today, but at some point—"

"WILL YOU SHUT UP?" Spittle hung from her lip. She bit down so hard that her jaw began to ache. "Seriously. Shut. Up."

"Those gulls will come back. They'll keep coming. Do you see how many of them there are?"

She glanced up, humoring him. If she was being honest, the fact that the gull had actually stolen from Daryl's corpse frightened her. She didn't really think they'd go for it. She convinced herself Vincent was just being a dick, trying to frighten her.

The gulls were accumulating numbers. Doubled since her last audit. A few more dove down but stopped about ten feet from the raft, then rose slowly, watching how Lucy and Vincent reacted.

"Telling you," Vincent said. "It's gonna get worse. They will come, and we won't be able to defend ourselves if they all come at once."

"What do you want me to do? Throw my husband overboard? Just let them... those *beasts... eat him?*"

Vincent's head lolled back and forth as if he were playing ping-pong with the notion. "Yes."

She huffed.

Vincent hung his head. "I know it's not an easy thing to do. But look—you throw him over, and they eat, and maybe they leave us alone until rescue comes, yeah?"

"You said rescue wasn't coming." Glowering at him, she turned from her husband. "Which is it?"

"No, I said we're gonna die out here. Especially if you keep that fucking corpse aboard." He pointed the knife in her direction. "You know, your husband wouldn't be the first to have an empty casket funeral. Pretty sure you'll get a good deal from the funeral home. Burying an empty is probably a lot cheaper, I would imagine."

"I don't appreciate your humor."

"Not joking—*literally* cheaper."

"If you weren't holding that knife right now, I'd kill you."

He studied her. "Interesting." Twirling the knife in the air, he winked at her. "You're an interesting woman, Lucy Mitchell."

She swallowed. "How do you know my name?"

He smirked like a kid who'd gotten caught with his hand in the cookie jar. "I looked you up. On social media. After you know—I saw you and Roberto in the—"

"SHUT UP." She growled a guard-dog's tune. Then she glanced over her shoulder as if Daryl were listening, hearing things he shouldn't be hearing. Her secrets. Her very bad secret.

"What are you looking at him for, doll? He's dead. He can't hear us."

"You don't know me. You can judge me, sure, but you don't know a damned thing about me, about my life."

He grinned. "Roberto was a busboy. Setting the bar pretty low, huh?" At this, he tittered. "This wasn't the first time, was it? Tell me it wasn't. Oh please, tell me."

She closed her eyes. Fresh tears squirted down her face.

"Ah, it wasn't." Vincent nodded, nodded like he understood, understood everything. Everything about her, about her life, about her past—about what she was doing on that fucking cruise in the first place. "You were gonna leave him, weren't you?"

She sobbed. Ugly cries. After thirty seconds of this, she screamed, a rage-filled outburst that frightened even the bravest gulls. The circle above actually broke off, and some of the birds went their own way.

"Weren't you?" he repeated.

She nodded. "When we got home."

"You fucked Roberto because you wanted him to catch you."

She didn't answer, but her silence was confirmation enough.

"But he didn't catch you. Because he wasn't interested in finding you on that cruise ship. He was off doing other things. Gambling. Drinking. Hitting on other women, maybe?"

Taking a deep breath, Lucy collected herself. Straightened her posture. Opened her eyes. "Yes. Okay, yes. All of it is true. Is that what you want from me? Is that it?"

Vincent shrugged. "If we're gonna survive this thing, I just thought we should get to know each other better. Know each other's secrets. No secrets amongst survivors. That's the rule of the open sea."

"What about you? What's your secret?"

Sunlight glimmered in his eyes. "I'm just a cook, Lucy. Just a cook. A good cook. My biggest secret is that my medium steaks come out a little too pink, yeah?"

She didn't know why, but at that moment, she knew Vincent deserved to die. More so than Daryl, even if he had been a shitty husband.

Vincent opened his mouth to speak, but a white glob rained down on him, splashing the left half of his face and splattering his shoulder. Slowly, he touched the heavenly substance, realizing it wasn't so heavenly.

"Holy shit," Lucy said, giggling. This was the best she'd felt all day. Well, second best. "You got shit on."

Vincent chuckled. Lucy burst into laughter, a deranged display that hurt her ribs. Before they knew it, the two of them were in stitches, rolling around the inflated floor, unable to control their hysterics.

It stopped when a gull swooped down, alighting on Lucy's head. It pecked at her face, going right for her eyes. She batted the thing, smacking it, sending it back into the air.

"What the fuck?" she screamed at the fleeing bird. She kept her eyes glued on its dark silhouette as it sailed back into the blue heavens. "What the fuck?"

"Told you," Vincent said. "They are hungry." He held out his knife, waiting for one of them to dive on him. Shielding his eyes against the day's brightness, he crouched down. He never bothered to wash the bird shit out of his hair. "Come on, fuckers. Come on!"

The next brave gull plummeted, landing on Daryl. Its beak went right for the dead man's eye. Before Lucy could react, the gull plucked the eyeball clean from its socket. The second the eye ripped free, the sinewy muscle stretching and snapping, the bird was off into the sky, heading back to its friends to share the trophy.

Lucy screamed. She dropped to her knees and put her hands on the sides of her husband's ruined face. "No, goddammit. No!"

"Come on!"

She turned in time to see a bird strike Vincent. His knife slashed through the air, connecting with the aggressive gull. Loose plumage exploded like a busted pillow during a slumber party free-for-all. With savage intent, Vincent stabbed the bird over and over again. Blood arced into the air as the gull squawked and hissed. Once it stopped flapping, Vincent dropped his knife on the raft, took a wing in each hand, and tore the bird in two. Bathed in bird blood from his hair on down, he stood there, catching his breath.

Lucy looked on, barely able to believe what she'd just seen.

"Fuckers, man," Vincent said, examining the surprising amount of blood that had come from the thing. "At least we have food if—"

The next attack came full force and much too fast for anyone to prepare. A cluster of gulls stormed down on him, pecking at his head, screeching angrily, tearing flesh from the cook's face. Stripes of blood opened around his features as the birds led with their beaks. Vincent covered his face with his arms, protecting his eyes, but then the flock turned their attention to the exposed flesh on his back. Lucy watched one of the birds dig its beak so far into Vincent's muscle that it nearly disappeared.

Vincent screamed out, then began flailing around, doing whatever he could to scatter the birds from their delicious feast. The raft began to rock, too much for Lucy's liking. She didn't know that much movement could capsize them, but she didn't know it *couldn't* either. As Vincent fought off the sea vultures, she turned and saw three birds digging into Daryl's face. Most of the flesh was gone, his attractive features now replaced by a glistening red mask.

She screamed, her worst nightmare suddenly coming to life. Waving her arms, she screamed at the birds that continued to feed despite her antics. She swatted one of them, which didn't do much except anger the damned thing. Ruffling its grayish-white feathers, it lunged at her face, though she leaned back in time, the beak missing her nose by inches.

She cowered, giving up, not willing to risk her face for her husband's corpse. The birds feasted on his opened flesh. One of them had poked a hole in his abdomen to worm out a strand of meat that looked like the end of an intestine.

Lucy crawled into a ball in the corner of the raft. She watched Vincent fend off the vultures as they continued their pursuit of his eyes. He blindly felt around the ground for his knife. After a few attempts, he got his fingers around the handle, grabbed hold, and began slashing at his feathery foes. One reckless swipe connected with a gull's neck, nearly severing it in one blow. The gull's head hung sideways as a crimson geyser spouted out of the fresh opening. He continued to fight, but Lucy could tell he was overwhelmed. The gull shit that stained his shoulder, apparently, had not brought him good fortunes.

Eight gulls swarmed him, pecking at his head, shoulders, and neck. He screamed in frustration, knowing he was overwhelmed, knowing they'd get to him eventually. It was only a matter of time before he ran out of gas, before they wore him down to nothing. Lazily, he cut at them, swipes that connected with nothing but the salty air.

One last defeated outburst and Vincent kicked his energy into high gear, slashing and rotating, rotating and slashing. The birds' ability to dodge the attacks surprised Lucy, and she marveled over their deft wing-work.

As if the sea vultures could communicate—and maybe they did, silently, on some level of collected consciousness—they dove in for the kill. With help from others above, all eight of them descended on Vincent, pecking and striking at his face, honing in on the cook's eyes. Lucy couldn't even see his face anymore—his upper half was a frenzy of feathers and blood.

Vincent lost his footing, stumbled sideways, and flipped over the raft's side. Lucy looked just in time to see him fall beneath the dark ocean waters. He came up for air a second later, and the gulls were on him. One of them had gotten his eye halfway out of the socket, and with help from a feathered friend, it severed the attached sinew with one bite. A squirt of scarlet shot out of the open cavity, splashing the side of the raft. Vincent cried out for help as he treaded water.

Lucy only watched as the raft floated away from his body. When he was about twenty feet away, she spotted a fin gliding across the water toward Vincent, where the man was now thrashing, continuing his futile fight against the vultures. She couldn't turn away from what was to come. The shark opened its jaws and clamped around Vincent's body. In a blink, he was pulled beneath the surface, leaving Lucy with no clue that he'd ever be seen again. All that remained of him was a blood-orange stain in the center of the endless blue and what bits the gulls had pilfered. Nothing else.

She turned back to Daryl. She didn't want to admit it, but the cook had been right. They wouldn't stop. They never would.

She had no choice.

Using what strength remained, she crawled over to Daryl, forcing herself to look away from his cratered face. She gathered him in her arms and hoisted his body, which weighed about three times as much as she imagined he would. Using her legs, she got him off the floor and over the side of the raft. With a magnificent splash, it was done.

Lucy fell on the plastic surface and looked up at the sky. The birds continued to form a perfect circle. She wondered how they did it, how they accomplished such a thing. She supposed she would never know, even if she were rescued. If someone came and saved her right now, whisked her away from this nightmare vacation, and took her back home, she would never know how birds flew and formed perfect patterns in the sky…because she would never look at another bird again, would never even want the word "bird" mentioned in her presence. Not again, not ever.

She closed her eyes and ignored the sounds of the gulls feasting on her husband's flesh, the stripping of skin as it peeled back from the muscle and bone.

In the distance, she thought she heard a motor.

She thought she heard freedom calling her name.

BETTOR'S EDGE

The living room reeked of water damage and old money, but Dylan McGraw hardly cared. The first thing he did upon entering the sizable luxury suite was check the bathroom, specifically the toilet, to make sure it was operational. He flushed and was relieved when the water circled the bowl and disappeared. Next, he turned on the shower head and stuck his hand in the stream to test the pressure and temperature. For the water to warm, it took longer than expected, but the pressure was fine.

Next, he moved into the bedroom and inspected the power. The lights came on, the lamp next to the bed blinked to life, and, more importantly, the television started without delay. HBO was readily available, just as the placard on the nightstand declared.

"At least I'll have *Game of Thrones* to get me through this," he said, dropping himself on the king-sized mattress. Tucking his hands behind his head, Dylan closed his eyes and tried his best to shut off his brain, but his thoughts were running a thousand miles a minute, in all different directions, and he couldn't catch up.

"Dammit," he said, lifting himself up. He swung his feet off the bed, lowering them onto the plush carpet. He'd kicked off his shoes and removed his socks, leaving them at the front door—an old habit —and now enjoyed the way the fluffy threads felt against his bare feet. He curled his toes, allowing his nerves to experience every fiber, the sensation traveling to his arches, past his heels, and up his ankles.

He could have done that for hours, but he wanted to explore more of the suite, gain a sense of what was to come.

If anything.

"This place doesn't look haunted," he said as he walked out of the bedroom, into the living area, and headed for the windows, floor-to-wall sheets of crystal-clear glass that overlooked Atlantic City, New Jersey. Outside was dark.

The hour past dusk had suffocated the sun, and the city stood weary, a lost, nearly-forgotten metropolis looking as if its last days were hiding just around the corner. A few neon signs promoting the names of other casinos glowed with a fuzzy brightness, but the rest of the strip looked dim and left for dead. Dylan remembered how alive the city had been in his youth, remembered when his parents and grandparents drove him down the shore to walk the boards and eat at fancy restaurants. Hell, even ten years ago, when he'd first turned twenty-one and had gotten the taste for the betting life, a flavor he'd developed an addiction to, the place had been lively and full of lights and sounds, and… well… *people*.

Yes, plenty of those.

But now, the streets and bars and strip joints—hell, the casinos—were pretty empty, even on weekends.

The city wasn't what it had been, yet it still clung to its charm, at least through Dylan McGraw's eyes. From the window, he could pinpoint the location of every backdoor poker game in progress, every underground prop betting ring front, and every chicken and dogfight currently being held. Dylan kept away from the latter because animal abuse was bullshit, but any other type of bet he could get action on…well, Dylan didn't say "no" too often. Even when the odds were stacked against him.

And, surprisingly, he'd done all right. Survived the last ten years on prop betting alone and never once had trouble paying the bill of the sleazy motel where he hung his hat that week. Nor had he ever gone to sleep hungry.

Until recently, that is. Until a spell of shit luck.

A few weeks of ill-advised bets had put him in the hole, about twenty grand, which was all he had in savings. *Stupid shit luck*, he thought, thinking back to the local high school basketball game that only put ninety total points on the board when the over (ninety-three) had been all but guaranteed. That was an anomaly, he thought, though that one anomaly had robbed him of six grand. Then there were the more *unconventional* bets. Sports betting was fun and all, made up the bulk of his winnings, but the stranger bets were what really cranked Dylan's engines and drove him deeper into the world of gambling degeneracy. This past week, he'd lost bets on how many inches of rainfall were reported during last Tuesday's storm, lost big when he took the under on how much Disney's latest movie would gross at the box office on opening weekend, and lost *bigger* when his favorite porn site failed to reach ninety-million views last Friday. It was a rough week made rougher when his buddy, Mitch Yates, told him about a peculiar bet he and his cohorts had assembled.

Mitch had pitched it like this: *"We found a one-legged stripper and bet her she couldn't climb to the top of the Ram's Head water tower in under thirty seconds."*

Dylan hadn't given the bet much thought and told his friend he was in, no questions asked. It was one of those wagers that didn't come around often. But when it did, you didn't pass on it.

After meeting with the stripper and determining she was in no way fit enough to reach the top—*let alone in thirty seconds*—he'd placed five grand on her failing.

But the woman had scaled the thing in under twenty-seven, forcing Dylan to cough up every last penny he had to his name.

The soul-crushing replays of the past week dispersed when something moved behind him, flickering in the reflection of the suite's window.

He spun, his throat ratcheting down, making it hard to breathe.

There was no one behind him.

Nothing.

Jesus, he thought, *been here for five minutes, and I'm already jumpy.*

He pressed his back against the window, placed his hands on his knees, and sucked in a deep breath. His heart pounded in his ears. When he realized he was being an idiot and that this was the easiest fifty-grand he'd ever make, he chortled.

Then the phone rang, which startled him more than it should have.

"Stop being a jackass," he coached himself, making his way over to the nightstand in the bedroom. He took the phone off the cradle and said, "McGraw here. Make it snappy. I have premium cable television to watch."

"Mr. McGraw," spoke the familiar voice. "Glad to see you've settled into your room. Enjoying your stay thus far?"

The bettor.

The man who'd approached him two days ago with this crazy proposition. A man he'd never met before. A man who pulled up to him on the street while Dylan was in line at the local hotdog truck. He'd stepped out of the back of a nondescript black sedan with the windows tinted. Dylan had spotted him immediately, then saw him approach with another man following closely behind. At first, he'd thought the man was a detective or maybe a government official, and Dylan had begun to wonder what he'd done. Nothing he was aware of, he'd been sure of it.

Next thing he knew, he'd found himself in the back of the sedan, drinking a dirty martini and listening to the man's pitch.

One night in the haunted suite atop the Sugarstone Casino. Fifty grand.

"Enjoying it just fine," Dylan said, his eyes searching the room for more moving shadows. "A little dated, but cozier than I imagined."

"It's one of the finest suites in all of A.C."

"Just haunted, that's all. Right?"

There was a pause, and Dylan thought the call had dropped.

"You still there?" he asked, his eyes still bouncing between the room's dreary décor. Old peeling wallpaper, abstract paintings that inspired nothing, and lamps that wore an inch of dust on their exteriors. It was clear no one rented this room. Ever.

"Yes, still here, Mr. McGraw. Still here."

Dylan chuckled. "I have to say, man. Fifty grand for one night seems like a poor bet on your part. I mean, we both know there's no such thing as ghosts. So, come on. Come clean. What's the catch? You a guy who gets off on this sort of thing? I'm half expecting you to show up in a gimp suit and a sex swing. I mean, I'm broke, but I ain't *that* broke, so if that's the gig, man—I'm out."

Another wave of silence. "I assure you, Mr. McGraw, this is nothing like that."

"You got cameras in here?" He looked to the corners of the room, where the ceilings met the walls. "You spying on me?" He didn't see anything, but that didn't mean they weren't there. Built into the walls.

The television. Hell, they could have hidden a camera in the smoke detector or the Keurig. "You are, aren't you? You want to watch… whatever this is."

"You're mistaken." His voice was humorless. He sounded bored by Dylan's accusations, as if this were something he'd expected.

Or he's heard it before.

A shiver scattered across his network of nerves. "Then what is it? You have to admit, man—I agreed to this on some pretty shady details. Now that I'm here and committed, I think you should give me a little more info. Shit, I don't remember you telling me your name."

He swore he heard the man titter, but he wasn't positive. The man's voice, when he spoke, gave no inclination that he found any of this amusing. Even when they had spoken in person, the man gave no hints that this was simply a game to him.

"That's because I didn't, Mr. McGraw. You were so swept away by my offer that you never bothered to ask."

That sounded like an untruth to Dylan's ears. Surely, he hadn't been *so* blinded by the offer that he hadn't asked for the man's name or credentials. He didn't know anything about the guy on the phone, not a single thing other than he had a brown paper bag containing fifty grand and was willing to part with it in exchange for a night in a haunted casino suite. To McGraw's ears, that had sounded like easy money.

But now, he wasn't so sure.

"Who are you?" Dylan asked, feeling his heart rate spike. There was still time to back out. He could build back his bankroll some other way. He knew a few sharks with low rates. He could borrow ten, maybe fifteen grand, and double it within a week. Local basketball games or grinding it out in Texas hold 'em—it could be done.

He didn't need *this*, whatever *this* was.

"Does the name Miranda Hoskins mean anything to you?" the man asked, and the very mention of the girl's name drove an invisible stake through Dylan's heart.

He opened his mouth to reply, but the words wouldn't come; it was like someone had closed their fist around his larynx.

"I'll take your silence as confirmation of the truth." The man didn't speak again, not right away.

"I didn't do anything," Dylan blurted almost involuntarily.

The bettor made an amused noise, the first time that night he'd deviated from his tough persona. *This was fun for him now.*

"Didn't you?" he asked.

Dylan glanced around the room nervously, waiting for the door to bust in, waiting for the trap to spring.

"I didn't do anything, man. This is a mistake. You've… you've got the wrong guy."

The bettor clicked his tongue. "No need to make excuses, Mr. McGraw. Own your past. Your mistakes. Your misguided decisions."

"I don't know who you are and what you think you know, but that girl… wasn't my fault. I didn't have anything to do with it."

"Hmm. That's weird. I don't believe you."

"Jesus Christ," he said before slamming the phone on the cradle.

Dylan marched across the bedroom, into the living room, and grabbed his jacket, throwing it over his shoulder. Next, he went straight for the door, charging like a bull through Pamplona. He cursed himself the whole way there, thinking how stupid he was and how smart he'd been in the past when placing bets with strangers. Being flat broke probably played a part in his foolishness. Still, that wasn't a good excuse. Being smart had kept his head above water all these years, kept him from needing to get a real job.

Kept him alive.

When he reached the door and turned the knob, he found it locked from the outside.

"What the fuck?"

He tried the knob again, turning harder, but the lock didn't budge.

"No. What? This…"

The phone rang again. Dylan turned to find himself staring at the far wall's window and the reflection it cast. In it stood the shadow from earlier, only it wasn't a shadow anymore.

It was a girl.

Seventeen. Maybe eighteen. Her skin ashen, grayed from death's eternal touch. Dark rings circled her lifeless eyes. Her blouse was as dirty as the day she died, the printed flowery depictions stained with earthy strokes of mud and grime. A trickle of blood leaked from her nose. Rainwater soaked her head, her hair endlessly wet and curly. Her colorless lips moved, twitching like the wings of a butterfly in the throes of eventual death. A perpetual chill sliced through her, and her body trembled.

"Oh, fuck that," Dylan said and scrambled into the bedroom, slamming the door behind him.

The phone continued to ring. He waited for the girl's spirit to come knocking on the door. Then he realized it was a ghost, and, to the best of his knowledge, ghosts didn't knock.

They enter at their own will.

He locked the door anyway. The phone never stopped ringing, and he figured it wouldn't unless he answered or ripped the power cord out of the wall.

"What the fuck is this?" was how he answered the call.

"It is what I said it was," the bettor replied, sounding fuller of himself now. Happier. *The fucker* is *enjoying this.* "One night. Fifty grand. *If* you survive."

"Survive?" He punched the wall, nearly breaking his fist. "You said nothing about surviving."

"Didn't I? I believe I did. I also believe you were so fixated on the fifty grand that you didn't understand what you signed up for."

"I didn't—I didn't think…"

"No, you didn't *think*. And I expected so much more from you, a man who's *survived* the last ten years on *thinking* alone."

"That girl, the one you mentioned?"

"Miranda Hoskins. You know her name. Don't act like you don't."

Dylan knew her, all right. He'd never forget her.

"Yes. *Her.* She's here."

"Of course she is."

"How? I mean…how is that possible?"

"I told you. The Sugarstone Casino is a special place."

"It's haunted? For real?"

"Not quite."

"Jesus, man. Just tell me."

"There are some places in this world that are…let's use the word *thin.*" He clicked his tongue, and the sound carried like a shotgun blast directly into Dylan's ear. "Yes, *thin* is best. It's a thin place, a place where two worlds meet, merge, cross over—the land of the living and the land of the dead."

"Jesus fucking Christ."

"But it's a funny place because the spirits wandering those halls and the casino floor—they're not tethered there. Sugarstone's not a haunted place, per se. No, places are rarely haunted. Usually, people are."

"What are you saying? She... she followed me here?"

"Miranda Hoskins..." His voice stumbled a little when he spoke her name, a stutter that hadn't been there before. "...has been following you for a long time, Mr. McGraw. She haunts you. Because of what you did to her."

"I didn't..." He wiped sweat from his forehead. Perspiration dripped from every pore. "I didn't... fucking... kill her, man. I didn't. I swear to God. I didn't touch a hair on her head."

"No..." The bettor sniffled. "No, maybe not. But you didn't save her."

Dylan couldn't hold his emotions any longer. His mind broke, and tears sluiced down his cheeks. "How do you know these things?"

"Because... I've been in that very room where you now stand. Because I've seen her with my own eyes. And I've listened to every word she had to say."

"Who—Who are you, man? Tell me."

A deep breath in Dylan's ear. A silent spell.

"My name is Morton Hoskins, and Miranda was my daughter, you sick son of a bitch."

Before Dylan could fathom a response, the lights cut out, sinking the suite into the deepest darkness he'd ever known.

***

"You never overplay Jacks, man. Everybody knows that."

Mitch Yates was a cocky prick but a hell of a card player, and Dylan respected him for both. He didn't exactly admire him because, after all, Mitch wasn't the kind of guy you'd follow into battle. He walked on the wild side, made crazy bets when opportunities emerged, and treated women like total garbage. Dylan respected him but never wanted to grow up and become him.

Still, he acted like the big brother Dylan never had. Took him under his wing. Showed him the streets, how to play cards, and where to find backroom games; every penny Dylan would eventually earn was all because of Mitch and his "blueprints," his self-proclaimed method of winning.

"Queens. Kings. Aces. Play the heck out of them. But you overplay Jacks, and you're gonna get burned. Not all the time, but enough to leave a couple scars. Especially in the casinos where you're playing against noobs who watch this shit on TV and think they're gonna be the next World Series of Poker Champion. They'll overplay their Queen-Kings , and the next thing you know, you're in a coin flip for your entire bankroll."

They hustled down the street, trying to make the next game. It was six blocks over at a strip club Mitch frequented. They passed dark alleys that Dylan was scared to look down. This wasn't the best of neighborhoods, and sometimes, stopping to tie your shoe or taking a minute to examine spent hypodermic needles in the gutter tripled your chances of getting robbed. It was the kind of neighborhood where, if you heard a newspaper rustling as it scraped along the sidewalk behind you, you ran like hell.

But for some reason, Dylan did look down the next dark alleyway. Curiosity, maybe. Perhaps the universe was working its magic, and the attraction to that particular alley was magnetic. Maybe he couldn't avoid the impending disaster, even if he tried.

The visible darkness allowed a semi-obscured view to the end of the alley, where Dylan spotted a moving heap, a shadow that undulated from its position on the ground. It flopped around, almost gracefully, like a carefully planned dance routine, the artsy kind, something interpretive, the kind Dylan could never understand. What he knew from dancing came from strip clubs and sleazy bar scenes.

He stopped following his mentor.

"What are you doing?" Mitch asked.

He didn't respond. Instead, he moved into the mouth of the alley, inspecting the shadow, its frolic with the dark. Something that felt like cold fingers brushed against his bones, but he ignored it, shifting his focus to the dim mess ahead.

"Dylan?"

Again, no response. He inched further into the alley, and it felt like floating.

The shadow faced him, and as it did, he realized it wasn't a shadow. It was a woman with pale skin and huge dark circles around her eyes. Her nose was bleeding. White foam bubbled on her lips and at the corners of her mouth. She spotted Dylan approaching and began crawling toward him like the dead girl at the end of The Ring, *the part where she climbed out of the goddamn television.*

"Holy shit," Dylan muttered, backing up once the dark lines in her face became visible. Her blouse was ripped and torn, revealing bruised, dirty flesh beneath. Dylan's eyes didn't have to wander far to spot the reason she was out here—no more than a few feet from her, a spent syringe glimmered in the frail moonlight. The needle dripped its last droplets of poison.

"Pleath," the woman rasped, reaching for him. "Bad...drug...bad..."

A hand fell upon Dylan's shoulder. He almost screamed.

"What is this?" Mitch asked, amused. "Well, shit. Looks like we got ourselves a junky." His eyes drifted from the woman to the weapon she'd chosen to brutalize herself with. "Oh shit, looks like she's overdone it."

"We have to help her," Dylan said, reaching into his pocket for his phone. Before he could grip onto it, take it out, flip it open, and punch those three famous numbers, Mitch stopped him.

"Let's wait this out," he said with the devil in his eye.

"What?" Dylan shook his head. "Man, if we don't call nine-one-one right now, she's gonna die."

"Wanna bet on it?"

He treated Mitch's words like a sucker punch and backed away.

"What the fuck are you talking about, man?"

"I'm talking about a bet, you idiot. You said she's gonna die. I say she's gonna soldier up and live this one through." He glanced at the girl and smiled. "She's a fighter. I can tell."

"I'm... I'm not betting on..."

"A grand."

Dylan whipped his head back and forth. "No... That's...that's so fucked up."

"Two?" Mitch took one predatory step toward him. "Twenty-five hundred? I know you're good for it, Dill. We cleaned up pretty well these last few weeks. The poker gods have been kind."

"I'm saving that money."

"For what?"

"College?"

Mitch sneered. "Who needs college when you've got the edge, man? When you play the odds over a lifetime, you'll always win. Remember that."

Dylan thought about running, screaming for someone to help while he called the paramedics, but something kept him rooted to the dark alleyway.

"Five grand. That's my final offer. Take it or leave it, but you have to hurry up." He nodded at the crawling woman. Her pace had slowed. She was fading fast, either dying or heading into a coma from which she may never wake.

Dylan cleared his throat, unable to speak the words his brain told him to. Finally, he squeaked out one lonely word: "Okay."

They turned toward the woman. She glanced up at them, her eyes pleading, filling with tears. Her body didn't move. After a few moments, she closed her eyes and never opened them again.

Fifteen minutes later, Mitch felt her wrist for a pulse and then turned to his protégé.

"Guess you're five grand richer, kid," he said as Dylan turned and purged what he'd eaten for dinner onto the sidewalk.

***

WHEN THE LIGHTS came back on, Dylan rushed into the living room, immediately arming himself with the lamp next to the door. He ripped the cord from the outlet and tied it around his arm, doubting the lamp would protect him from the woman's vengeful spirit. But it was better than nothing.

When he faced the living room, however, defending himself from an angry specter immediately fled his thoughts.

"M-Mitch?"

Mitch was in the center of the living room, hanging from the ornate chandelier by a rope. The noose was pulled taut around his noticeably raw throat. His head hung awkwardly to the side as if someone had buried an axe three-quarters of the way into his neck. An eerie stillness held his body hostage.

"Jesus Christ," Dylan said, stumbling into the center of the room. He landed on his knees a few feet from where his friend had hanged himself.

Or… *where someone had done it for him.*

Mitch's eyes suddenly flickered with life. His body began to contort, spasm, vibrate spastically. Strangled sounds emanated from his mouth as he wriggled like a suffering worm. Dylan crab-walked away from the center of the room. After another few seconds of squirming, the rope tethering Mitch finally broke, sending him plummeting to the floor. Mitch landed feet first but had no strength to support himself and went sprawling to the ground.

"Holy shit!" Dylan shouted, immediately rushing to Mitch's side.

Mitch gasped for air, struggling against the noose. Dylan helped loosen the knot. Once free, Mitch inhaled greedily, desperately.

"Are you…how…are you alive?" The angle of Mitch's neck didn't make much sense; his vertebrae were clearly broken, having snapped during the hanging. By all counts, Mitch shouldn't be breathing. Yet here he was. Alive. *Very* alive.

"She's…she's…here."

No shit, Dylan thought, examining more of his friend's injuries. His pallid skin was deeply bruised with purple and yellow marks that ran down his arms and neck. It looked like he'd been beaten with a baseball bat. But not recently. Maybe several days ago.

Then it clicked.

He's not real. He's…

Dylan blinked, and his friend was gone. His breath left him just as quickly. Spinning in a circle, he looked for any actual evidence that Mitch *had* been here, something he could use to disprove the notion that he was going crazy. No longer swaying, the chandelier was as still as it had been when he first got there.

He looked so real.

But there was no evidence, not a single hint.

Then he looked to the window, the mirrored reflection, and saw *her*.

Miranda Hoskins.

She was nearing him. He whipped around and faced her, the woman he'd once watched die in an empty alleyway. She hadn't overdosed like Mitch had suspected. Dylan had read the story in the paper a week after it happened. Her dealer had given her poison, cut her fix with ricin. If he'd dialed 911 when he first arrived, they might have had a shot at saving her. Mitch always told him that there was nothing they could have done, that she would have died anyway, but Dylan never believed him.

And now she was here.

In the same room.

Dead. But not.

She approached him. His eyes fell to the open wound on her arm, where she'd injected the poison that killed her. The hole, about the size of a quarter, was black with rot and ruin and unearthly decay. And there were...*things* sticking out of it. Little obsidian ribbons undulated from the fluid surface, like rippling blades of grass on a windy day. The things seemed to get bigger with each step Miranda took, stretching.

Dylan found his back against the window, and he stole a glance at the streets of Atlantic City. It was a far drop, and he was worried. If the specter wished, she could shove him to his death.

If she can touch me.

By his estimation, she *was* a ghost, and traditionally, ghosts were transparent. Using his knowledge of the supernatural, which he had gathered through endless hours of phony ghost-hunting programs, he doubted she could hurt him. Of course, he knew nothing of the real thing. The truth of the beyond was a mystery to him.

Dylan pictured himself barreling through her, racing toward the door, down the hallway, and into the elevator. But the second he went to put his plan into motion, those black *somethings* exploded forth from Miranda's arm. They reached out and stretched like taffy, three in total, grabbing him and lifting him off the soft, shaggy carpet. One went for his throat, corkscrewing around his flesh like the tentacle of some deep-sea monster around an unsuspecting galleon, and choked him. The two others gripped him underneath his arms. They pushed him against the window, holding him there.

"Please!" he shouted just before the black vine tightened around his throat. Having swelled to three times its size since escaping the wound, the ghost's peculiar extension was now as thick as an elevator cable. "I wanted to save you!"

The apparition did not speak. Miranda only smiled knowingly, her lips curling at one end. Her dark eyes stared as she paced back and forth, as if she were contemplating what to do with him.

Then, the vine released his throat. She continued to hold him in place while he pled for his life.

He followed the fluid motion of the black vine, watching it scoop an object off the ground, a tiny something that looked like a...

A needle.

Shit.

"No, please. I… I don't deserve this."

The ghost looked like it wanted to laugh, but a wry smile fixed her lips instead. Before Dylan could protest once again, the needle was already entering the softest spot in the crook of his right arm, sinking the contents of the syringe into his veins, flooding his system with…

…*poison.*

He fought against it, squirming, trying to wriggle his way to freedom, but it was no use. Every effort to break free failed. She picked up another needle and stuck him again. Then a third. He had no idea where they were coming from, but by the fifth stick, he felt lightheaded, woozy, and nauseous. By the seventh stick, his world had grayed at the edges. By the tenth, he was lost behind a blurry veil from which he would never again emerge.

The last thing he saw before fading out was the crooked smile of the woman he could have saved, the woman who'd won him a cool five grand and pushed him down this path of moral decay.

If he wasn't so numb, he would have screamed.

***

"Sorry to bother you, Chief Hoskins," the young detective said, pacing the living room of the Sugarstone suite. "But since the room is under your name, I thought you might be able to ID the kid. Paint us a better picture of what happened here."

Morton Hoskins walked over to the wall of windows and peered down at the corpse. The deceased's flesh had already taken on a dark hue, deep gray patches that resembled gathering storm clouds. Morton's eyes bounced from the dead kid to the dead girl in the window's reflection. She placed a gentle finger over her smiling lips. The black extensions slithered and twisted from her arm as if begging to be fed again.

Christ, Morton thought to himself. *I thought this would end it.*

He'd already delivered her the two fuckwads who'd watched her die, who'd placed bets on her survival. He thought that would make her go away, release her from this existence. But the way she looked at him, the way her eyes glimmered with the need to feed, the way the black tongues growing out of her arm licked the air with an eternal hunger—that told him his work wasn't done.

"Morton?" the detective said, snapping him out of it.

"Yes?"

"The kid? You recognize him?"

It took a moment to deliver the lie. "No, never seen him before."

"Hmm. Just another junkie that broke into your room, wrecked the place, and then overdosed?"

"Yes."

The detective eyed him as if he could smell the deceit. "Well, that would explain the broken door frame. And the…mess."

Morton nodded.

The detective closed his notepad. "I guess that's it then. Sorry for bringing you out here like this, but, you know, protocol and all. Wouldn't want to deviate from the rules just because you're the boss."

"I appreciate your due diligence."

The detective smiled. "At least that's another scumbag junkie off the streets."

Morton's face went rigid, lost some color.

The detective's smile immediately went missing. "Oh shit. Sorry, boss. I totally forgot about Miranda."

"It's…all right."

"I didn't mean it like that. I—"

"I said it's all right, detective."

"Miranda, man. She was…different."

Morton nodded. "Why don't you get out of here. I'll finish up."

"Are you sure?"

"Yeah."

"I'll stay if—"

"I'd like to tidy up a few things, alone, if you don't mind."

"Yeah…" The detective looked like he knew leaving him was wrong, especially with so much evidence that could be contaminated. Plus, the coroner hadn't even shown up yet. "I don't have to tell you not to trespass the yellow tape, do I?"

Morton laughed. "No. No, I'm not going to muck up a crime scene."

The detective laughed nervously as Morton showed him to the door, thanked him, and wished him goodnight.

Once he was gone, down the hall and into the elevator, Morton returned to the center of the room. Facing the window and the shadowy outline that stared back at him, he held his arms out in surrender.

"How many more?" he asked, almost out of breath. He felt like crying. In his eyes, tears were born. "How many?"

"Just one," a frail, raspy voice whispered in his ear.

Before he could react and defend himself in any way, a long black vine rose from the floor, possessing a syringe.

His final scream was cut short by the needle slamming into his voice box.

FEASTING ON THE FRUITS OF FOREVER

When she dreamt the first dream, Debbie Liu found herself strolling through a massive garden filled with lush vegetation and exotic flowers. The latter bloomed wild myriad colors—tropical blues and fiery reds, pumpkin oranges and sea-glass greens. The air was heavy, laden with a thickening mist that clung to her bare arms and face like spider silk in the dark. No sky could be seen beyond the cloudy veil, even though the heavens were of little concern to her. She was too busy taking in the magic of this new dreamworld. Passing an apricot tree that had grown fat fruits the size of gym-class softballs, she wondered how these toothsome treats would taste if she were to bite into the plump offerings. Were they offerings, though? Were they edible? In dreams, it sometimes seemed like everything was possible. But here—inside this one—it felt different.

She took the path down a ways, and when she rounded the bend, passing more vibrant veggies and bountiful snacks, she saw a woman standing in the center of the path, blocking her travel should she test the dream's length and go that far. The woman wore what Debbie's fifth-grade teacher might call "olden clothes." A frumpy blouse stained the color of earwax, sporting a sizable vertical gash up her midsection. It appeared as though something inside the clothing had escaped hastily, without regard for the clothing or the garbed party.

The woman had black hair like raven feathers and lips that seemed too blue to belong to a living person. She stared through eyes that changed color each time Debbie viewed them from a different angle. First, they were dark; now they were almost copper, like the pipes on the ceiling of her mother's basement. She was hesitant to continue. But there was something comforting about this place, too.

"Hi, little one," rasped the figure in a hushed *I-have-secrets* voice. "Come here."

Debbie moved toward the woman, suddenly realizing this was not one of those dreams she could control. Her legs moved without permission, and each step brought her closer to the end of the line. The closer she got, the more she could see the dream ended there. The heavy mist shrouded everything behind the woman. The peculiar orchard disappeared into that hanging, wet curtain. Dirt smears, she could now see, marred the woman's skin all over, a marble pattern of filth that covered her arms and face. Smudges of brownish-black on the fabric of her blouse—evidence of a dry attempt to wipe the material clean.

"Come," she said.

"Who are you?" Debbie did not expect a straight answer because dreams rarely provided such. Dreams, she found, were like bad riddles—incomprehensible and annoying to solve.

But the woman replied softly, gracefully: "I am the Mother of All Things That Must Grow."

Great. Another riddle. Debbie detested them, but Dream Debbie seemed enamored, smitten with the Mother's grotesque charm.

"Come," Mother said, and she came. Mother plucked a juicy plum off a nearby branch. Droplets of moisture bubbled on the plum's skin, and Debbie's mouth watered with anticipation. "Bite into it. It's okay. Let the nectar escape into you."

She accepted the snack. Sunk her teeth into the plump handout, allowing the sweet and tart flavor to conquer her tastebuds. Juice slid down her throat, and she worked the pulpy mouthful around with her tongue before swallowing.

"Good girl," Mother said, patting her head, her eyes glowing with that intense copper light. "You'll like it here in the Garden of Dead Dreamers." Her voice changed, becoming deeper and raspier, like someone trying to tell a spooky ghost story around a campfire. "You'll like it here, Debbie. You'll eat from my gardens and drink from my rivers, and you will grow big and strong."

Debbie felt the urge to flee but couldn't. And when Mother smiled, crawling bugs flooded out in a great, endless swarm. The girl identified them as *wood ticks*.

*

"DEBBIE!" her mother shouted in her face. And when Debbie snapped her eyes open, she was screaming too. Screaming so loud her throat burned.

Then she realized she was in her room with the light on. She felt cold and hot all at once, with a warm, wet layer beneath her. When she ran her fingers along the bedsheets, she couldn't tell if she had sweated through them or peed herself.

"You had a bad dream, honey," her *(real)* mother said. "That's all it was."

But she couldn't remember having one. Not at all. Which was weird, considering she always remembered her dreams in great detail.

"I'm sorry," Debbie said.

"No need to be sorry." Her mother kissed her forehead. "What was it? A scary monster?"

"I don't know."

Her mother smirked in a way that let her daughter know she understood. "Okay, well, was it a tickle monster!?" Her mother dug her fingers into Debbie's hips—the weak spot that always got her giggling—and began working them in a way that wasn't torturous in the least.

Debbie howled with laughter and begged her mother to stop, even though she didn't want her to.

Once Mom let up, she stood and made her way to the doorway, threatening to shut off the light and place Debbie back in that darkness.

"Mom?" Debbie asked. "Why won't you let Daddy come back?"

At this, her mother swallowed what looked like an entire hard-boiled egg. "That's a complicated answer, sweetheart. One not suitable for three a.m., okay?"

Debbie thought it was as good a time as any but only nodded.

"We'll chat tomorrow," her mother said, then switched off the light.

Debbie didn't dream again. Not that night.

*

IN SCHOOL THE NEXT DAY, she daydreamed about an odd orchard in the clouds. It was clear in her mind, this image, and she couldn't remember where she'd seen the mental photograph before.

"Debbie?"

Debbie glanced up to see Mrs. Ryerson glaring at her, holding a chalk nugget against the board, mid-mathematic equation.

"Debbie, what did you say?"

Debbie hadn't said anything. Had she?

Had I?

"Nothing, Mrs. Ryerson," she answered politely.

"Okay." Mrs. Ryerson placed the chalk back on the ledge and turned her back to the lesson.

"She said something about the *Children of Hooperstown*," Billy Jackson said, snickering. Billy was the kind whose snickering was contagious, and others in his inner circle snickered right along with him.

But Debbie wasn't snickering. She was confused.

"Who are the *Children of Hooperstown?*" asked Kendall Burnett.

At this, Mrs. Ryerson let go of a gusty sigh. "That's…a story for another time, perhaps. Maybe ask your parents about it. They can tell you. Or…you know, Google it. With their permission, of course."

Debbie raised her hand, though it seemed she was the only one who still followed such classroom etiquette.

"Yes, Debbie," Mrs. Ryerson said, her eyes growing soft as if she immediately regretted giving the girl permission to speak.

"Does this have to do with the old chemical plant? The one that's shut down?" Debbie didn't know where this knowledge came from, only that it was inside of her.

"What happened then happened almost twenty-five years ago, kids," Mrs. Ryerson said. "It's in the past. Like I said, if you want to ask your par—"

"There's an orchard there now," Debbie continued. "And the woman that lives there…she speaks to me."

Everyone went dead quiet. But seconds later, Billy was hooting into his right hand. Peppered laughter came from different corners of the room, and Debbie couldn't pinpoint the culprits. If she could, she'd pull each one aside during lunch and tell them this was no laughing matter.

This was serious.

"Debbie," Mrs. Ryerson said, stepping down the aisle toward her. "Debbie, that's not true. No one's been inside of that chemical plant in years. So many years. I assure you."

Debbie shook her head. Again, the little voice inside spoke for her, "That's not true. She's there now, tending to her gardens."

No one laughed at this. A coldness came about the room, sweeping over the children like someone had left the window open on a wintry afternoon. Debbie's arms came alive with cold bumps.

"Debbie, I'm going to have to stop you now. Let's get back to our math—"

"But it's true!" she shouted, and she'd never raised her voice like that before, not to any adult. Not even to her mother. Or her father. Before her mother *kicked him to the curb* (her best friend Beth's words).

"Debbie."

"Mrs. Ryerson, I'm not making it up. I…I *see* her." And she did. Clear as day. The woman in the cloudy orchard—she picked pears from pretzeled branches, collecting them in bushels.

"What are you doing?" Mrs. Ryerson asked.

At first, she didn't know what her teacher meant. But then she followed her gaze and saw that Mrs. Ryerson was focused on her desk. She glanced down and saw her hand, armed with a pencil, sweeping back and forth rapidly over a blank sheet of notebook paper. She couldn't stop herself even if she wanted to—and let's face it, she *didn't* want to. Curiosity had bested her, and she was more interested in whatever she was now capable of than the consequences of her discourteous classroom behavior.

Mrs. Ryerson looked down at Debbie's thirty-second doodle. When Debbie finished, she removed her hand, revealing the sketch everyone in class was suddenly so interested in. Pretty much everyone had left their seats and meandered over, leaning over each other's shoulders to glimpse what the peculiar girl had drawn.

Debbie stared down in awe of her creation. There were two figures —one small, one tall—joined at the hands, and the tall one had great big eyes that seemed to glow, if only just for her.

*

Do you miss your Dad?

Do you?

He wasn't a good man. He did bad things, Debbie Liu. Bad, bad things. He hurt people. Your mom mostly, but other people too. Stole things from them. Robbed them. Beat them. How many lips have been split on your old man's knuckles? Too many to count. Too many.

You miss him?

You do?

That's a shame, but I know that feeling, that emptiness that rests in the center of your soul, like a piece of you has broken off and floated out to sea, past the horizon, never to return. He's still your father, after all, flesh and blood. And even if he isn't good, he still loves you. There's love in his heart, my sweet child. And you still love him so much; I can see the adoration in your eyes now. It's hard to turn your back on your own blood. Shun them. Walk away. Pretend like they never existed. I will never shun you, sweet one. You are mine. Eat my fruit. Drink my rivers.

Dream with me.

Here. Now. Eternity.

Your mother hates your father. She will never let him back. Never. You know that. She'll do anything to protect you, like all mothers should. But protection from that which cannot hurt you? Your own father, your own flesh and blood, he who helped create you?

I would never do that, my sweet.

Meet me in the gardens of dreams, and you will see your daddy once again. The three of us can dance in the orchard. And together, we will feast on the fruits of forever.

I will be your mother now. You will need no other than me.

*

A MOTHER KISSED her daughter's forehead. "Promise me, no more acting out in class."

A week and a few meetings with the school counselor later, everything seemed to trend in the right direction. Annie Liu didn't put much stock in what the school staff told her. So what? The kid drew a spooky sketch (thank you, Babysitter Becka, horror movie aficionado) and rambled on about some local kids who got sick twenty-five years ago (thank you, Google). It didn't mean anything. Well, it meant something. But not what the teachers, counselors, and principal suggested.

Deborah Liu did not need *professional help.*

She needed to deal with her father being forcibly removed from their family. Over time. In her own way. And Annie knew she had to be the one to help her. She just didn't know *how* yet.

We're all figuring this stuff out as we go along, she thought, pulling together the flaps of her daughter's jacket and zipping her up.

"I promise, Mommy," Debbie said, sporting a mischievous grin that could mean she intended to keep that promise sacred or that she intended to break that promise the moment she stepped past the front door.

Annie narrowed her eyes. "You'll be the death of me, kiddo." She planted one last kiss on Debbie's forehead before ushering her out the door, seeing her off to the end of the street where the bus would pick her up for school.

*

ON THE WAY to the bus stop, Debbie's attention was lured by a strange object in the center of the street. She recognized the object at once—it just didn't belong *there.*

Feast on the fruits of forever…

Questioning her state of consciousness, she rubbed her eyes. When she was finished and the dark stars bursting before her began to fade, she focused on the street, the thing left behind for her and no one else. It was still there, resting on the road, in danger of getting run over by some careless idiot behind the wheel. She looked both ways, then left the safety of the sidewalk.

Running into the street, she locked her eyes on the bushel upon the twin solid yellow lines painted on the dark asphalt. She peered down and saw a mound of colorful fruits, some big, some small, the likes of which she'd never seen. Something that looked like a cherry-colored pineapple sat buried beneath the teal plums and royal-blue apples.

Hey, sweetheart, called a familiar voice.

She glanced up and spotted her father across the street, standing there and waving howdy to her. His smile stretched so wide she feared his cheeks might split.

"Daddy," she said fondly and dreamlike.

An odd smell found her nose, an unpleasant stench that triggered nausea. She almost lost her breakfast right there in the middle of the road. Then she looked down into the bushel, seeing that the fruit had rotted away. Clumps of brown, shriveled pulp sat in a mushy pile. A coating of fuzzy white mold had grown on the collective surface of these exotic fruits and now clung to the sides of their wooden container. Resting just beneath the surface, she saw something else, rounded but larger than the other items, something that wasn't a fruit left to wither and expire. It was much too hairy to have come from the earth.

Disgusted, she forced herself to reach down, curious about what the object could be. As she touched the slimy, hairy material, she looked away, across the street, at her father. Only her father was no longer there.

She was there.

Mother.

Her eyes glowed like the golden reflective candy wrappers on her favorite bite-sized caramel sweets.

Feast. Forever.

The object was surprisingly weighty, and she had trouble

extracting it from the pile of rotten fruits. But when she did, she screamed.

The glazed whites of her father's dead eyes rose to meet her.

Debbie screamed so loud that she didn't hear the car horn blare out in warning, the squealing of slammed brakes, or her mother screaming her name in the distance as the vehicle slid out of control and toward her.

ATTIC GIRL

Today, Jason Mettleberg killed himself.

Or tried to.

He had tied the rope around an attic truss and looped the noose perfectly, just like the Internet had instructed. There was a moment of doubt when he placed the noose over his head, letting the texture of the straw-rough material scrape against the flesh of his neck. While doing so, he recalled everything that had led to this moment, every single detail. Shouting matches with teachers and his parents. His younger brother and his douchebag friends going through his room, messing with his belongings, stealing his stuff, things like video games and collectible comic books. They would destroy his most prized possessions, some of which were irreplaceable. They'd call him names. Make fun of him. Endless taunts that echoed in the chambers of his dreams. Same with the kids at school, those ignorant tyrants who ridiculed him for wearing a shirt with Wonder Woman on it, who'd kick the back of his pants as he walked down the hall for seemingly no reason other than the fact that he was - maybe - a little bit different.

High school wasn't a walk in the park. Middle school, however, had been a breeze; he'd made so many friends there, enjoyed every moment of those three precious years. But high school, that goddamn place, was absolute hell. Worse than he could ever imagine. Finding new friends had been difficult, almost impossible. In those three years, he had found one person he got along with - George Betterson - but George, lately, hadn't had time for him, not now that he had a girlfriend. George's spare time was no longer spent on trivial things such as Mario Kart 64 tournaments, Halo 2 all-nighters, and epic games of Magic: The Gathering.

He thought of this and more, and suddenly, the noose around his neck felt good. Right. Just. Like it belonged there. For the first time in three miserable years, Jason Mettleberg felt a sense of proper direction, like fate had swooped in and guided him down this righteous path - and the title of that journey was Death.

He mounted the small stool and prepared to kick it out from under him. He wondered if it would hurt, the fall and the death. Maybe initially. He hoped his neck would break so he wouldn't suffer those brief moments of strangulation. But even if his vertebrae snapped, there was still a chance he'd stay conscious for the remainder of his slow demise.

But that was a chance he was willing to take. Besides, the moment would be temporary; the death and its impact on those who supposedly loved him…well, that stamp was eternal.

Before he could kick his plan into motion, a shadow crawled out from the attic's darkest corner. He hesitated again, watching the shadow take shape and form an outline. Within seconds, the shadows surrendered to the dim, hazy attic light, and the outline filled in.

It was a girl.

What the hell?

Long strands of black hair led the way. Her appearance made Jason think of *The Ring,* that iconic scene where the dead girl crawled out of the well and through the television.

"Hello?" he asked her, and in response, she looked up. Her eyes were sunken. No, her whole face was. She was more bone than skin, and not just in her face. She wore a tattered cream-colored dress, marred with strokes of dirt and grime, ripped in several places, the threads shredded throughout. Her arms were so skinny that her elbows looked as big as golf balls in comparison. Her wrists were delicate twigs. As she stood, her torn outfit revealed a portion of her midsection, and Jason could see every rib on her left side.

She was young. Twelve maybe. Freckles dotted her cheeks. Her eyebrows were dark to match her hair. Sparkling in the attic's darkness, her sapphire eyes almost pleaded with him. Begged for his help.

"Who…" he began to ask, but the rope constricted his vocal cords. Loosening the noose and slipping it over his head, he asked, "Who are you? Where did you come from?"

She put a finger over her mouth, silencing him. "Please. Don't tell anyone."

A secret. A juicy one at that. How long had this girl been up here? And where had she gotten that dreadful dress? It looked ancient, from another century. "I don't understand. Were you… how long have you been up here?"

"A pretty long time."

She looked underfed, rail-thin.

"I can get you help," he said, and suddenly, a rush of excitement entered him. Suddenly, he had a purpose again. A reason to exist.

At least for now.

"No." She shook her head as if help was the last thing she needed. "Please. Nobody can know I'm here."

"Why?"

"It's a long story… *complicated.*"

"I like long stories."

She shook her head again. "Not this one."

He could tell she wouldn't give. "Fine." A beat, an awkward pause. "Are you hungry?"

"God, yes."

"I can get you food."

"Please."

He threw the rope on the ground, postponing his last breath. "Okay. I'll be right back."

"Okay." She reached out as he walked by and gripped his arm. Her flesh was cold, freezing, a sub-zero sensation shooting up his bone. "And Jason," she pleaded, mostly with her scintillating eyes. "This is our secret. Tell no one about me. Or bad things will happen."

He nodded. "Okay."

While walking downstairs to fetch her some food, he wondered how she had known his name.

*

Two days later, Jason brought her more food. He set the leftover pork chops down in front of her. She looked at them as if she weren't all that hungry, which was odd, he had to admit. She'd eaten the other meals in the same fashion—taking her time with each bite and barely finishing what was on the plate. He thought a girl as hungry-looking as her would practically inhale whatever was set before her. But nope. She took her time.

She looked better, though. Not as famished. Some color had returned. The sickly gray-white complexion had faded some. Jason thought food and water had helped that cause and was proud that he'd been able to help someone in trouble.

What kind of trouble exactly, she still hadn't revealed. But she was here. Safe from whatever or whoever was after her. And for now, that was enough. The time would come when she'd feel comfortable enough to tell him her deepest, darkest secrets.

And he would be there to listen.

After she started biting into a pork chop, wincing like the meat held strange, inedible flavors, he turned for the attic stairs to leave her alone while she ate.

"Stay with me," she said, setting the pork chop down on the plate. He turned back to her to see she'd only nibbled at it, that she hadn't even eaten the hunk she had put in her mouth. The chewed bite rested on the corner of the plate.

"I can't. My mom's sick, and my dad is working overnight. Jeremy is sleeping over at a friend's house. I have to take care of mom."

"She'll be fine," the girl said, smiling. "Come. Sit."

It wasn't that he didn't want to, but his mother was calling to him, ringing the bell at her bedside, which meant she needed something. A glass of water. More fever-reducers. But… the allure of abandoning his mother and her needy demands was all too attractive. He flashed her a boyish grin. "Okay. Just for a minute."

The girl bounced on her heels.

He sat across from her, the untouched plate between them. He stared into her eyes and noticed they were more blue, bright cerulean seas of youthfulness. More alive than ever. The freckles on her cheeks really popped. Her dress was still ragged. He had offered to head to the thrift shop downtown and buy her some new threads, but she'd refused. More mystery she hadn't elaborated on.

"I just realized I don't even know your name."

"Beth," she bubbled. Her spirits were high, almost infectious. Around her, his negative vibes dissipated. Became nothing. He didn't waste a second of his thoughts on all the bullshit he had to endure between school and home. It was just her, her mystery, and his willingness to live and die another day.

"Beth," he repeated. "Nice."

"It's okay."

Her eyes beamed, and he felt that comforting warmth filling him, running freely through every channel his body offered.

They talked for an hour. Mostly about him, his past, his life at home and school. How it made him feel. How he sometimes wanted to hurt himself and others. It was therapeutic. It lifted him from a dark place. In the dimness of the attic, in the presence of the girl, he saw a light. The bell rang several times in that hour, but he ignored it. Every time. After a while, he became deaf to it.

Until he felt tired.

He yawned and stretched his arms.

"I better go," he said.

She pleaded with him, asking him to stay and tell more stories. But he couldn't. Mother was screaming now. Cursing. Calling him nasty names. Things she wouldn't ordinarily call him. *Cocksucker. Piece of shit.* It would be better if he just helped her.

She's just sick. Not acting right.

He said goodnight to the Attic Girl and left her with the plate of now-cold pork chops.

The next morning, the plate was still full. She hadn't taken a single bite. But she looked healthier than ever.

Mother had gotten worse.

Much worse.

*

A WEEK LATER, mother was transported to the hospital, where she was bunked in the Intensive Care Unit. Her lungs had filled with fluid;

she'd caught a touch of pneumonia. And when they'd taken some preliminary blood tests, they discovered her white cell count was low, which meant she also had some sort of infection.

"Dad is taking off from work to stay with her," he told Beth, setting down a peanut butter and jelly sandwich on the small antique nightstand that the Mettlebergs planned to unload at a future garage sale. Beth eyed the sandwich as though it had barked at her, but that was it. She didn't touch it.

Her appearance changed drastically over the last week. She looked better, livelier. Her color had returned to full strength, her cheeks blooming with a cherubic rosiness. Hair seemed healthier, not as greasy and grimy as previously noted. She moved around like she had energy, loads of it. She was healthy enough to go home, for sure, wherever that was. Jason had asked multiple times, but Beth had skillfully dodged the subject. She had turned the questions on him, asking about his life and his past, wanting to hear the stories of all the terrible things that had happened to him over the years. And surprisingly, her subterfuge worked, and he willingly, gleefully, told her everything she ever wanted to know.

"You should be with them," she said, touching his cheek. Her fingertips were warm, not the frigid toothpicks they'd been. "You should be with your family."

"No," he said, shaking his head. "I'd rather be here."

She giggled.

"Not hungry?" he asked.

She shook her head, looking elsewhere, avoiding his questioning gaze.

"Why not? Don't think I haven't noticed you not eating much. You've barely eaten anything over the last week, and yet you... you look a lot better."

She didn't speak a word, continuing to eye her dim surroundings.

"Can you help me make sense of it, Beth?"

No, she couldn't. Tight-lipped, she shrugged.

"You can't stay up here forever."

That caught her attention. "I know," she said, staring at him now. Her gaze locked on, filling him with a strange sense of bewilderment. He knew nothing about this girl. Even stranger, she looked as if she'd significantly aged since last week. She had looked twelve or so, but now she looked fourteen, fifteen. Almost as old as him. He was positive it was a trick of the attic's lackluster supply of light.

But still.

It was weird.

"Just a little longer," she said, "then I promise to leave. Find somewhere else to go."

"You could always go home."

Her cheerful face fell. "Who said I have one?"

*

A WEEK LATER, Dad was in the hospital. Things had gotten worse for Mother, too. She'd entered the ICU and never left. Dad wasn't as bad, but his lungs were seventy percent filled, and it was really hard for him to breathe. The day Jeremy started to feel a little woozy, Jason marched upstairs, dropped down the attic ladder, and climbed up with only one thing on his mind – who was this girl in the attic? This Beth?

He wasn't dumb. His family's sickness and her arrival couldn't be a sheer coincidence. Not to mention that she had barely touched the food he'd been sneaking her. And yet, she'd gained weight. Lots of it, actually. She'd swollen up like a tick feasting off the family dog. Her muscles were bulky. A layer of fat wrapped around her midsection like a belt. The once exposed ribs were now a doughy patch of skin. Her face looked puffy as if she was experiencing an allergic reaction to shellfish.

She was feeding on something, and he couldn't help but think it was him and his family that had given her sustenance.

It was ridiculous, of course.

But, also, it made sense.

As he moved through the attic, he heard Jeremy downstairs, hacking, coughing his head off. Jason knew it was only a matter of days before he'd end up like mother and father.

"I know what you're doing," Jason told the seemingly empty attic. "I know what you're doing to *them*."

The shadows seemed to bustle about the room. The trusses created long stretches of shaded areas extending in seemingly endless directions. The silence and stillness were most unsettling; Jason swore he heard cockroaches skittering within the boxes of junk, worthless items that should have been tossed a decade ago.

"Come out and look at me," Jason said. He noticed the rope hanging from one of the trusses, the noose at the end of it. It was an invitation, he thought. *I'm onto her, and she knows I can stop it, make it all go away.* "Face me," he said, gritting his teeth. *"Beth."*

Beth is death, his inner voice said. *Beth is death.*

Out of the shadows stepped a limb, long but meaty. It was almost too long to be human, the leg, and covered in globules of fatty flesh. Flabby pockets jiggled like gelatin as she planted a foot on the creaky attic board. More of her came bumbling into view, and he noticed she had swelled some since his last visit. She was portly now; her dress, the stitching, flexed to its maximum capacity, threatening to burst at every seam. Her face was rotund, her cheeks bloated with layers of blubber. Her eyes—less blue now. Dark. Almost blue-gray, like the summer sky merging with bad weather. She was older now, too. Taller. Mature-looking. As old as one of his youngest teachers. Mid-twenties probably.

"Geez," he said, backing away. The bulbous form standing before him caught him off-guard. A rush of fear seized him for a moment; otherwise, he would have turned and run, shut the attic door, and probably put a lock bolt over it, trapping the girl (*thing*) up there forever. "Christ… wha-what are you?"

She opened her mouth to respond, but strings of noxious juices filled her oral cavity. Foam soaped her lips, bubbling like a toxic stew. She stepped toward him, shaking the plywood platform beneath his feet. He felt his knees give a little, and for a second, he thought he was going down. They held, though, as did the rest of his body. Examining the fatty tumors, the softball-sized domes clinging to her arms and neck, he raised his hands as if to call a truce.

"What are you?" he asked again, almost breathless and unable to speak anything else.

The Girl-Thing opened her mouth to reply but instead croaked a long, drawn-out vocalization that chilled Jason's bones.

His paralysis broke, and he made for the attic ladder. In a blink, he found his footing on the landing's carpet, folding up the stairs, tucking them away before the monstrous thing could waddle its way to the only exit. The door slammed shut with an authoritative bang, and he listened as the thing above him stomped on the wood. The white square plywood that hid the drop-down stairs bounced as she pounded on it. Jason wondered if it would hold.

The loud knocks of pure frustration went on for a few minutes. He could hear the thing grunting, growling each time it attempted to break free. Slowly, he backed away. Soon, the period between attempts grew longer, and then, there were no periods - just a still and eerie silence.

He went downstairs and into the kitchen, where he found Jeremy hunched over the counter. His brother's face was ghostly white, his lips fresh out of their usual pink hue. He looked up from his phone at his brother.

"What is it?" Jason asked.

"It's Mom," he said. "She's… she died."

Beth is death, he thought again. *Beth is death.*

*

THE FUNERAL WAS POSTPONED. They put it off as long as they could. Dad's situation had worsened once again. He'd been placed in a medically induced coma, and the doctors didn't seem very optimistic about his recovery. Jason knew he had a day left, maybe two. His brother had refused to go to the hospital and had spent the last two days in bed, shivering, running a fever that hovered just over 104. Ibuprofen did nothing to bring the temperature down, and Jason knew why. It didn't matter what the Mettlebergs did to help their recovery—there *was* no recovery. For all of them, this path ended in death.

Or did it?

Jason knew there was only one way to stop it. All of this had started with him, and it had to end with him.

He marched upstairs. Pulled down the attic stairs. Climbed. Cleared his head on the way up, putting aside his negative feelings, his collection of obstructive emotions. He forgot about school, the hellish days spent surviving the hallways, the brutal names hurled his way when he passed by certain assholes. He didn't just forget, but he forgave them too. He had forgiven all of them. His parents, Jeremy, the bullies—none of that mattered in the grand scheme of life. They could do anything they wanted to him. They could call him names, poke fun at his hobbies, hell, they could even toss him around the gym locker room and kick him in the back of the shorts. But they could never take away what was inside of him—his happiness…or what remained of it.

He'd not only forgiven them, but he also pitied them. They were the broken ones, not him.

"I know what I have to do," he told the empty attic that truly wasn't empty. There was at least one other presence here, but there was something else—a non-physical resident. A powerful entity devoid of corporal assets. It flowed out of him, that magical source he could tap into. He wore it like a badge. It would protect him. He was sure of it.

From the shadowy corner, the Attic Girl emerged. She was bigger than ever, looking more like Jabba The Hutt than a human being. Her once-blue eyes had gone completely cloudy and gray. Dark, viscous fluids dribbled from her cave of a mouth. Her jaw hung at an awkward angle as if someone had broken it via a strong left hook. Her tumors had ballooned several sizes larger than Jason's last visit— massive mounds of malignant growth, practically covering every inch of her flesh. Her expanding bulk had split her dress in several areas, reducing the garment to rags; torn and tattered fabric clung to her, hiding portions of her form. The tumor-like tissue bulged through the uncovered areas, an unsightly mess of flesh and disease.

Jason forced himself to look, to take her in. "I know what must happen."

Her head tilted sideways like an animal that wished it spoke the common tongue.

Jason's vision found the rope. The noose hung there still, calling to him. His eyes watered and spilled tears. He walked over to the rope, his heart pounding against his chest, rattling like a badger in a trap box. The makeshift platform awaited, anxious for him to place his feet on its surface. The Attic Girl crawled forward like a snail, and in fact, a sheen of glistening moisture followed in her wake. What she was and where she'd come from—Jason would never know. But it sure didn't seem like this planet.

He stood on the platform and slipped the noose around his neck.

Her eyes fixed on him. He wasn't sure what he expected from her, what her reaction would be. Part of him thought she might protest, but there was no backlash. He thought maybe she wanted this. Wanted him to die. Wanted him to suffer in his final moments. Then again, maybe not. Maybe she needed him. Needed him so she could feed, siphon his negative emotions, the travesties in his life. Each story he'd given her, every tale he had told her about his abuse at home and school, the shitty things that had happened to him over the years—that was her food. Maybe that was why he hadn't caught whatever his family had. She was feeding on them differently. Theirs was negativity of a different source. *They* were broken, inherently destructive. They were the abusers, not the abused.

No, she needed him.

Needed Jason so she could get to the others, the source.

I am the source.

"I forgive them," he said to her, the rope scratching his neck.

She recoiled as if this were a sword through her stomach, one that pierced vital organs. The noise that emanated from within her distended throat sounded like the roar of hurricane-force gales mixed with a little demonic, record-scratching warble. Partial shadows swallowed some of her.

"I forgive them all." He was crying now, the tears falling unrestrained. With both hands, he pulled the noose tightly against his skin, just under his jawbone. The tighter it was, he had read, the better chance he had at a clean break. The less chance of suffering.

Boom, lights out, he was hoping.

"I forgive them, and they will no longer hurt me. And *you* will no longer hurt *them.*"

The Attic Girl shrieked as the shadows swept across her, stealing away the light.

"Goodbye," he said to everyone and everything.

He kicked the bucket from under him. Dropped. The rope snapped. No, that was his neck. His legs kicked, instinctually fighting, though the rest of him had discovered peace. Yes, in those moments, there was peace. But also regret. A sharp dose of it flooded him, needling his oxygen-deprived mind. In those last few moments, he was haunted, not by the past but by the future he'd never have.

Sure, life was shit sometimes, but there was also good out there. Ups and downs. Hills and valleys. So it goes. Life itself is a precious gift, something he had learned these last few weeks, and he was wasting it, sacrificing himself for people who didn't give two shits about him.

Maybe they'd learn from this. Maybe others would. Maybe his sacrifice would mean something after all.

Before Jason could close his eyes, the room bled away, delivering him to oblivion, that untapped space so very far away.

THE LAST GREAT HOT WING EATING CONTEST IN NORTHERN MISSISSIPPI

The last time Jed Cougar Metcalf won a hot wing competition, it was 2016. He was fifty pounds heavier and had a set of mutton chops that would have made Lemmy envious. Three years and one divorce later, intermittent dieting and discovering the benefits of a smooth face, Jed Cougar was ready to hop back onto the competitive food circuit. It was a passion that had never left, even though his new, healthier lifestyle had been for the better. He'd felt better, had more energy, and, mentally, he was in a *much* better space.

But goddamn, he wanted to be king again, champion of the best damn hot wing contest in northern Mississippi. It was a satisfying honor, and when Belinda had cleaned him out during the divorce, the only possession he was adamant about holding onto was that trophy from 2016. Three years later, and it was finally time. Time to compete again, time to win again, time to be crowned the King of the Buffalo Wings.

Not many people understand how much training goes into an eating competition. It's no different from training for a race or a weightlifting contest—you have to condition your body, prepare it for the ultimate punishment it's about to receive. Jed Cougar spent the last six weeks training, stuffing himself with as many buffalo wings as he could, averaging about seventy to eighty each night. He ate one-hundred-and-six when he won back in sixteen, and he knew he had some work ahead of him. Come the big day, he was ready, though.

He'd fasted for twenty-four hours before the competition, had eaten nothing and had only drunk a twelve-once glass of water every two hours. He was ready to push himself to the brink, go farther than he ever had in the past.

Now, on the dais, sitting before an audience of at least four hundred people, most of whom had come to the Evergreen County Fair specifically to witness the hot wings competition, Jed Cougar closed his eyes and recited his own personal mantra, something about being "one with the wing," and when he opened his eyes, Belinda was sitting across from him, looking like she hadn't aged a day since she up and left him two Augusts ago.

He wondered if she was really there or not. Glancing over at his competition, the six others who were fixing their bibs, waiting for the contest to kick-off, Jed Cougar realized Belinda wasn't actually there in front of him, that she was just an apparition, and she'd come here to throw him off his game. It was his mind's way of fucking with him. Hell, she'd always hated these eating competitions, and one of the reasons he gave up competing was because she'd told him to.

"You ain't nothing, J.C.," Belinda told him. "You ain't nothing but a worthless pile of gutter trash, and you'll always be gutter trash. Ain't no one gonna love you ever again, not the way I loved you, and winning this competition ain't gonna make anyone love you neither."

"Shut up," he whispered as the judge took the microphone and went over the contest's basic rules.

The man next to him, a big feller—not fat, just *big*—wearing a red bandana, looking like he climbed out of an episode of *Sons of Anarchy*, nudged him with his elbow. "Hey, buddy. You okay?"

Jed Cougar didn't say a word, but he nodded. He was what some folks might call "in the zone," despite the unwanted and unwarranted appearance of his ex. He locked onto the stainless steel bowl in front of him, the heaping pile of buffalo wings within. The afternoon sun glinted off the orange slathering of the county's best hot sauce. He was so focused, the judge's firearm sounding off, kicking the competition into action, barely registered.

When it did register, he was on. He tore through ten wings in about fifteen seconds, more than making up the ground he lost while stuck in the daydream. Around wing twenty-five, his lips started to burn from the sauce. It was a good sauce but not the hottest he'd ever eaten. There had been this place in Louisiana, about a mile outside of Baton Rouge, that had this flavor called Atomic Buzzsaw, and that had been the hottest sauce Jed Cougar ever tasted. This was nothing compared to that. This was good sauce, though. And although he didn't know the name of the flavor—he wasn't sure it had ever received a name—he enjoyed the hot burn on his lips.

"You ain't nothing but a piece of shit, Jed Cougar Metcalf," Belinda said. She was pacing the stage now, hands on her hips, barking insults. None of the others noticed her. The judge watched on, scratching his forehead where his ranger hat itched, a goofy smile plastered on his big dumb face.

Jed Cougar tried his best to ignore her, but he had to admit, she sure knew how to get under his skin.

She leaned in and spit in his face. "Fat fucking cow of a man. You ain't gonna ever become nothing. Nothing but a heap of cow shit. You limp-dick fucker. Got me a new man, one who can actually keep up with my sexual appetite."

"Shut up," he said between bites, and the two words cost him valuable seconds. "Shut up, shut up." He tried to blink her away, but she held her position, looking defiant as ever.

The clock continued to tick down. With five minutes left, the contest was more than half over. A representative brought him another bowl just as he picked clean the last wing and tossed it on the pile of bones. The rep took the bones away, over to another table where they'd be counted.

Jed Cougar wasted no time digging into the second bowl. Three wings in, he started feeling a little funny, funnier than before. He'd blamed the peculiar sensations on nerves and his ex's mirage, but now, he doubted both were the root cause of his trembling fingers and rapid heartbeat.

Someone in the audience screamed. He looked up from his wings to see a woman standing, pointing toward the trees surrounding the fairgrounds. Her mouth hung open in a giant O, and the sudden rush of fear had caused the veins in her neck to pop.

Jed Cougar followed her finger to the trees. From the woods' threshold, out stepped what appeared to be a six-foot chicken. At first, Jed thought this was a colossal prank, a funny man wearing a rubber chicken suit. But he knew how serious the county took the hot wings competition, and he knew no one in town would dare pull a stunt like this mid-contest. It had to be a kid, or someone from a rival county, come to ruin everything Evergreen County held sacred. But Jed Cougar began to doubt those theories when the giant chicken took off, darting across the fairgrounds. His mind wandered into stranger territories.

"The chickens are coming, Jed Cougar," Belinda told him, cackling like a witch. "Oh, buddy, the chickens are coming home to roost, y'all!'

The six-foot chicken plowed into the audience, sending bodies and collapsable chairs airborne. The chicken started pecking at its prey. It caught one man in the neck, and with its beak, the bird pulled back a strip of flesh and the chunky fillet of meat underneath. The man screamed, his hands immediately clasping down on the squirt of blood that jetted from the raw, ragged wound. Another chicken exploded from the tree line, streaking toward the frantic crowd of onlookers. Then another. About half a dozen chickens, some well over the six-foot mark, rushed the fairgrounds.

Sweat poured from Jed Cougar's hairline and down his face. None of the other competitors stopped and looked up from their wings. He'd fallen behind.

How could they not see this? How could they not care that we're under siege by a bunch of six-foot chickens?

It was because he'd imagined it, probably. That was the best he could offer. Belinda had been an illusion. The insufferable woman had walked straight out of his memories. And these chickens? Who was to say they hadn't leaped out of his imagination, too?

Again, his brain was railing against the idea of entering that hot-wing competition. This was all an elaborate way to get him to throw in the towel and return to his new, healthy lifestyle and safe, comfortable space. This was his brain's way of helping him.

And it was working. He'd stopped eating. The other competitors ate on, ignoring all distractions.

Jed Cougar decided he wouldn't let his brain get the better of him. Fuck the noise, everything that was happening around him. He grabbed a wing off the pile in front of him and bit into the savory, juicy meat.

* * *

THE BOY FED *the funnel with more green stuff, watching the tube suck it all up. He had no clue what the liquid was, only that Pawpaw told him it was "feedin' the chickens" and not to stop unless he said so.*

"We gonna grow ourselves the biggest chickens in Mississippi. Hell, the whole South! Gonna turn this whole operation around!"

The farm had been suffering as of late, and even though the boy was only eight years old, he knew the financial fuckery surrounding the family business. His folks had been fighting constantly, arguing and bickering about nearly every damn thing, and he and his two older brothers were taking bets on which would end first—the business or their marriage. The boy claimed their parents would last a lifetime and said so with a twinkle in his eye, and his brothers only laughed, told him he was young and delusional and that he needed to "read between the lines."

That had been a couple of weeks ago. Since then, Pawpaw had gained a new business partner and some hope. Also, he'd gained about twenty barrels of lime-green slime.

The chickens were swollen with the stuff. They looked like water balloons that had been overfilled, ready to burst. Pawpaw shut off the machine and climbed down from the platform where the controls were.

"Boy howdy! These chicks are good 'n' stuffed!"

The boy felt bad for the chickens. They didn't seem to like that they were being pumped full of the mystery serum. Their shrill cries hit the boy's ears like a rough ceramic mug dragged across glass. It wasn't the first time they'd been fed stuff, things to "enhance their meat," genetic alterations that would make them bigger and stronger and more profitable—but this was definitely the first time it had been done this way and with such... mystery.

The boy didn't like a thing about what he'd done, but he wasn't about to mention his concerns to Pawpaw. The old man was way too happy about the results, and happiness had come in small doses as of late. Who was he to rain on his father's parade?

"What's goin' to happen, Pawpaw?" the boy asked, hardly amused by

chickens' unnatural growth. They were getting larger by the minute. Almost doubled in size.

"They gonna get big, son. Big like... hell, big like Big Bird!" Pawpaw hee-hawed like the cowboy from his favorite western. "Gonna make us a goddamn fortune! Imagine that! Chicken wings the size of you!"

The boy didn't like the sound of that, not one bit. He'd seen way too many nature documentaries to know that humans shouldn't go around messing with things that don't come natural. It upsets the balance of things. Throws the whole world off-kilter-like. Naw, he didn't like it a damn bit.

But Pawpaw was happy. Best mood he'd seen in ages, at least the last month or so. The boy looked back to the chickens. They'd already doubled in size. The green ooze poured out of every orifice, looking for ways to escape the chickens' bodies. They had overfed them for sure. Too much, too fast. Even the boy had seen that. But Pawpaw? No, he was blind. All he saw were dollar signs, a way out of the money hole he'd dug for his family.

The boy backed away. The chickens showed no signs of stopping. Their growth only increased exponentially. They just kept getting bigger and bigger and...

Big as the moon, he thought. Big as the gosh-darn moon.

He felt an overwhelming rush of panic. Things felt wrong.

It was time to run. Before it was too late.

The chickens were on the move.

* * *

By the time Jed finished off the second bowl, most of the giant chickens had torn through the audience. What had been a fun and jovial environment was now a bloody, macabre battleground. The seemingly endless field, once a vibrant green plateau, was now slick with wet red. Limbs and chewed organs covered the grounds like trash after an outdoor carnival. The air was heavy with coppery stink.

Jed Cougar took his eyes off the bowl, waited for the third to be brought over, but none ever came. He looked to his right, where the assistant had stood ready to deliver the goods at a moment's notice, but she was gone. In her place was a small puddle of blood that leaked down the steps leading to the fairgrounds.

Jed Cougar glanced to his left, where he expected to find the other contestants, but their seats were now empty. Splotches of blood and hot sauce soaked the table cloth. Jed Cougar felt a bolt of panic spike through him, inducing a sharp pain in the center of his chest. He abruptly stood up, knocking over his chair.

His eyes locked onto two chickens fighting over the corpse of an Evergreen County resident, a man in his forties. One chicken pulled on the dead man's shoulder while the other ripped away at the man's leg. It looked like two puppies playing tug-of-war with a popular chew toy. Finally, after a few moments of the back-and-forth, the man tore in half, his gut bursting, his innards slopping onto the already blood-soaked ground. The super-sized chickens took their game and fled a few paces away from each other until sure they wouldn't be disturbed by one another. Then, they feasted. Jed watched with morbid fascination as they pecked at their meal, dipping their beaks into the red open cavity of the man's midsection, tearing away whatever was left of his bowels.

Jesus Christ, Jed Cougar thought. He surveyed the entire fairgrounds, the stage, and found that he was—currently—the only survivor. The chickens hadn't even noticed him. *Is this really happening?*

He ducked down, hiding behind the table. Two eyes stared back at him, causing him to leap backward.

"Holy fuck!" he shouted, staring at the skinny Asian girl who'd been sitting two seats away from him when the contest started. He had wondered how a girl her size could put down a hundred hot wings, but she was Evergreen County's defending champion, so it *was* possible. More than possible. Maria Kwon had done it.

She put a finger over her mouth, telling Jed to shut his trap.

Peeking over the table, Jed watched the herd of chickens stalking the grounds, hunting the fields like a pack of predators, each carrying a piece of something human between their beaks.

"We have to get out of here," he told Maria.

She shook her head, clearly not ready to move. Her entire body trembled. Tears dribbled down her cheeks.

"Yes. If we..." His voice cracked. Something moved on the other side of the table. The rank smell of the farm life, cow dung and pig filth, became increasingly bold. Neither Jed nor Maria moved a centimeter. They locked onto each other's eyes, each begging for the moment to pass, for their fates to be revealed.

A low peep and a wavering cluck sounded above them. *Just* over them. Jed closed his eyes. He wasn't under the table like Maria was. His position was exposed, his body visible at the right angle. All the monstrous chicken needed to do was lean over a little farther, and Jed'd be spotted. Jed prayed to as many gods as he could, hoping that would do the trick, that begging false deities was his last option, his only option of making it through this thing alive.

This thing.

This bizarre nightmare.

Nails clicked on the wooden boards that made up the stage's platform. The chicken was on the move. The thing crowed, and Jed heard the flapping of feathers. Next, he heard someone screaming. Jed peeked over the table again, slowly rising, partially expecting him to come face-to-face with the killer chicken's beak. But the beast had fled, jumped down, and took flight after another survivor. A woman was on the run, making for the woods. She got about halfway there before three chickens ran her down. They pinned her to the ground and ripped her arms off as easily as plucking a blade of grass from the soft soil. Like water from a fire hose, blood exploded from her mutilated shoulders, painting the picturesque green with more scarlet ruin.

Jed Cougar forced the rising bile back down and turned to Maria. "We can make it if we go now. We'll run around behind the stage, use it as cover."

Maria seemed hesitant, but she didn't protest this time. Instead, she grabbed Jed's hand.

"Where you going with that bitch?" Belinda said as soon as Jed and Maria took a stand.

Jed didn't answer. Instead, he guided Maria around the stage, down the stairs that led to the open field. There was a good quarter mile of open green, not a wild six-foot chicken in sight. He knew they had to run if they were going to make it; those fuckin' things moved fast, and Jed Cougar, in the best shape of his life since his younger years, still wasn't much of an athlete.

From the stage, Belinda called to him: "Fuckin' coward! Running off with another woman! Is that what you do, Jed Cougar? When the going gets tough? You run? Fuckin' always knew you were a coward."

He squeezed Maria's hand. "Ready?"

The ex-hot wing champion nodded.

"Let's run."

Behind them, something monstrous crooned.

* * *

THE RUN toward the woods was fueled by fear, the thoughts that they might not make it. That failing meant death, a terrible, brutal, agonizing way to go. Jed Cougar imagined his limbs torn away, one by one, still alive as he watched the genetically mutated birds feast on his exposed organs.

Genetically mutated?

What else could have done it, could have made those chickens so goddamn big? He'd heard rumors of old Bill Westwood's place, how the farm was failing, and that he'd taken extreme measures to secure a future in the chicken business. What that had been exactly? Jed Cougar hadn't the foggiest, but pumping his stock full of chemicals and genetically-enhanced substances had been mentioned, and Jed wouldn't put it past old Bill to attempt something so radical.

"Shit, J.C.," Belinda barked in his ear, "You ain't gonna make it. You're too fat, too slow. Even though you dropped a few pounds, so what? You still fat as shit. Ain't no one gonna love you even if you *do* make it out of this alive."

"Shut up, you bitch," Jed said, and Maria looked at him funny.

"What?" she asked, letting go of his grip. She drifted away from him, continuing to run parallel with him, keeping pace. "You just call me a bitch?"

"No," Jed said. "Was talking to myself."

She gave him a dirty look, and Jed knew he deserved at least that much. Belinda was inside his head, scrambling his brain the way he liked his eggs. He tried to keep pace with Maria, but the girl had gained a sizable lead on him.

Goddamn you, Bill Westwood, he thought. *I'll wring your neck if this is your fault.*

Behind them, something squawked. Jed stole a glance over his shoulder and saw three chickens sprinting after them, their beaks and breasts decorated with flecks of bright crimson.

"Run faster!" Maria said, spotting them too. She kicked it into high gear, leaving Jed to fall behind even more.

"See?" Belinda said, cackling in his ear. "Told you you ain't shit. Just a fatty, after all. Glad I left your stupid, big ass. Best decision I've ever made."

Jed ignored her, let his adrenaline funnel through his veins, and used it to pump his arms and legs faster. It was like he unlocked a gear he never knew he had. Within a few seconds, he'd caught up to Maria.

But the chickens were closing in.

They were gaining…and fast.

Then, a shotgun boomed.

Jed turned to see a chicken's head pop like a balloon, a bloody explosion taking its place. It kept running for a few feet, as the body hadn't caught up to the realization that its life had ended, and then fell flat on the grass, tumbling for a few seconds before it abruptly stopped. Two other chickens sped toward them, not seeming to care much about their future.

Jed saw Bill Westwood aim his shotgun and take another shot. Another six-foot chicken ate the metal slugs, its head splintering apart into fragments, a bloody flower that bloomed so elegantly in the glory of the midday. Like a drunk trying to find the exit before closing time, the headless chicken ran in all different directions before realizing it had died; then, it dropped to the earth.

Jed couldn't help but laugh a little; after all, he was saved. Bill Westwood, that son of a bitch, had come to his rescue. Jed wanted to punch the old coot on the shoulder, but he wasn't done yet with the shootin'. Another chicken sped toward them, hissing angrily. It opened its beak, displaying a thin row of sharp teeth, apparently sharp enough to turn human flesh into rags. But no matter. Bill West-wood pointed his boomstick, and with little effort, blew the creature's goddamn head clean off its neck. Jed watched the chicken give its final dance before succumbing to the notion of death, which included a graceless fall to the grass below.

"Lucky bastard," Belinda said, her smile wide and phony.

Jed turned to Bill. His boy was standing behind him, peeking around his father's big belly. The kid had been clearly scared by everything he'd witnessed today and with good reason.

"Shit, y'all," Bill said, hanging his head. "Tell me it ain't bad."

Maria backed away as if there were more of them chickens coming, then took off, sprinting into the woods, never to be heard from or seen again. Jed Cougar would never get to ask her how she stuffed all those chicken wings inside that small frame of hers.

"It's bad, buddy," Jed Cougar said, and for some strange reason, he could still taste the tang of the hot sauce on his lips. Even the bold smell of the carnage couldn't keep the flavor away. "It's real bad."

"Fuck you, Jed!" Belinda shouted in his face. "Fuck you for being a piece of shit!"

Belinda was a figment of his imagination, sure. But he wondered —just mused—if he could silence her for good.

"You're shit!" she said, "And I found a new man!"

"Can I borrow that shotgun," Jed Cougar asked Bill Westwood. The old man looked down at his weapon as if it were somewhat of a prized possession. "Well, sure, Jed. But I don't mind cleaning up my own mess. I know what I'd done is wrong, and I could put a fixin' to it."

"Sure thing, old buddy. But I gotta fix something first."

Bill handed the gun over.

Jed didn't waste any time—he pointed the gun at Belinda's mirage and pulled the trigger.

Thunder roared across the blood-stained fairgrounds.

* * *

BILL WESTWOOD PLACED his hand over his son's eyes.

"But... why?" the kid said frantically, seemingly unable to wrap his head around what had just happened.

"I don't know, son." That was the truth. What he'd just witnessed... he couldn't quite grasp it either. "I guess... well, I guess grief can change a person."

Bill looked down at Jed Cougar Metcalf's fragmented cranium. The man had turned his own neck into a bloody stump. His body lay motionless in the calm grass, bits of skull and brain sprinkled around him like wayward feed.

In the distance, they heard their chickens clucking, searching for a new source of nutrition. These chickens were hungry, and the world harbored plenty of food out yonder.

"Sometimes you eat the chickens," Bill said, signaling the Stations of the Cross and bending down to retrieve his shotgun, "and sometimes the chickens eat you." He flicked off bits of Jed Cougar from the shotgun's barrel, then slung it over his shoulder. "Come on, son," he said, marching toward the Evergreen County fairgrounds and the last great hot wings contest in Northern Mississippi. "We have a wrong to right, and that's that."

The kid followed, unable to keep his eyes off Jed Cougar's ruined head.

Boy howdy, what secrets that head had kept.

THE HAG ON THE FIFTH FLOOR

-1-

W hen Isabella Ruby Hobbs was born on July 5th at three-thirty in the morning, her father, Grant, wasn't in the room. He was sleeping in the car in the hospital's parking garage when the call from Kasey came through, snapping him out of some dream he instantly forgot.

"Hello?" he said, perking up, wiping away the blurry vision of the half-empty garage. "Kase? Everything all right?"

Before she spoke, he knew something was wrong. "Where are you?" Adrenaline flooded his veins the second her voice found his ear. "Grant?"

"I'm here." He fumbled in the dark for the door lock. "I'm outside, in the garage. Was trying to catch a nap before work." His neck hurt, and he ignored the stinger that shot down his arm. The pain wasn't as bad as the kind he suffered from falling asleep in the chair next to his wife's hospital bed.

"They're taking me in."

"Taking you in where?" He found the handle, pushed open the door. Planting his foot on the concrete pad, he stood up. The world wobbled. "Where are they taking you?"

She was crying now. In the background, he heard the nurses say it was time to go, that she needed to end the call.

"Kase, talk to me. What's happening? Are you all right? Is Isabella..." He choked back his next words, never thinking he'd have to *think* about asking a question like that, not in a million years. Bad stuff like this never happened to Grant Hobbs. He'd hardly ever been sick. Caught a cold once in a while, maybe every other year, but he'd been reasonably healthy throughout his life. Never broke a bone. Never got into a car accident. He used to joke around and say he was indestructible, like Bruce in that Shyamalan movie.

But, as he was slowly discovering, his first child wouldn't be so lucky. She was already off to a rough start. Luckily—if such a word could be used given the circumstance—the situation had been monitored since the whole thing started. At twenty-two weeks, baby Isabella had stopped growing inside her mother's womb. The doctors couldn't figure out the precise reason, only that she wasn't getting enough nutrients—something about the flow from the placenta being restricted—and she wasn't getting any bigger. Intrauterine Growth Restriction, they called it, IUGR for short.

Grant had hardly been interested in the science of it and only wanted to know the answer to one question: *Are my girls going to be all right?*

The doctors had seemed hopeful, but their optimism had come with a few caveats, challenges the newborn would face. Obstacles that carry on throughout childhood, perhaps even her adult life. They used phrases like "physical deformities" and "mental impairment," scary terms that made Grant want to cry, but in the end, the fact was this—he didn't care about those things as long as she was alive and healthy.

"Is Bella going to be okay?" he asked, finally, the words coming out in a squeak.

Grant was hardly surprised when she didn't answer. Instead, a new voice registered. "Mr. Hobbs, this is Dr. Hauer." His voice was calm and steady. In a different scenario, the tranquil nature of the doctor's tone would have soothed him. "We are taking your wife into the OR right this second. We've lost the baby's heartbeat and need to perform an emergency C-section. Do you understand what I've just told you?"

Shrouded in a dreamlike daze, Grant whispered, "Yes," into the phone. The concrete moved beneath him, the word tilting sideways.

"Get to the fourth floor, now. Your wife is going to need you."

And like that, the doctor was gone.

The wind blew through the parking garage, a light gust but strong enough to push Grant against the car, nearly strong enough to sweep him off his feet.

-2-

ONE WEEK LATER

THE NURSE CHANGED Isabella's diaper, which was smaller than Grant's fist. So tiny he couldn't believe such a size even existed.

"The diaper company makes them special for preemies," the nurse told them. "Only hospitals can get them."

Grant and Kasey looked down at their daughter through the clear plastic top of her incubator. Bella, her eyes wide, almost taking up the entire upper half of her head, glanced at them before searching the room. Grant couldn't help it. He leaned into Kasey's ear and whispered, "She still looks like an alien to me."

Kasey elbowed her husband but let out a brief laugh. "Idiot." She rolled her eyes and kept herself from laughing again.

"What? She does. Admit it."

"I will admit no such thing. My baby is beautiful."

"She is beautiful. Just like her mother."

Kasey kissed him on the lips. Genuine compliments came in small doses, and he knew he could always improve in that department.

I could improve in a lot of departments.

The nurse smiled, shut the incubator door, and tossed the soiled diaper into the hazmat container in the corner of the room. "I'll let you guys spend some time together. Feel free to let me know if you need anything."

Kasey smiled but then frowned as she looked down at Bella's face. "Oh, nurse?"

The woman stopped and spun on her heels. "Yes?"

"What's that black mark on her forehead?" Kasey asked.

Grant hadn't noticed it before, but now that Kasey pointed it out, it was obvious. A little black smudge that reminded him of Ash Wednesday. Faint. No bigger than one of her tiny thumbnails.

The nurse leaned over the clear capsule. "Oh yeah…didn't notice that earlier. We'll get it off during her next bath."

After the nurse winked and left, Grant couldn't help but stare at the odd mark. Considering how big the NICU was on sanitation, he was surprised they let this foreign substance anywhere near their baby.

It didn't sit right with him. The ashy stain bothered him, but who was he to tell the nurses how to do their job? Would they even listen if he demanded they scrub the thing off right this second?

"Don't worry about it, hon," Kasey said, rubbing his back. She must have seen the way it irked him, the way he glared at it. Obsessed over it. "The nurses here are amazing. Seriously. They've done such a good job."

"I feel like I should be here more."

"You have to work."

It was true. Grant had to bounce back and forth between his office job and the hospital, and sometimes, when he got home from the office, the energy to drive forty-five minutes north just wasn't there. On those days, he zonked out on the couch in front of the television, waking up with nothing but guilt.

"I know," he said. "But still."

"We need money. I don't even know what the bills will be like once we get out of here." Kasey was on leave from her job with three months' pay, but that wouldn't put a dent in the NICU fees. Sure, there were government grants and charity organizations that could help, but those things weren't guaranteed. Grant heard the total bill could be well over a million dollars. He'd freaked when he'd overheard another couple near the incubator diagonal from them discussing that very topic.

"I'll be here more. I can do it."

Kasey shot him a look. "Don't overburden yourself. We do the best we can, and that's all."

Kasey had fallen asleep in the chair, and Baby Bella had drifted off to dreamland shortly after. Grant slouched in another chair, watching them both. He had work in five hours but couldn't bring himself to leave. And he couldn't sleep either. Not here, not like this.

An hour later, his body protested the decision to stay. Bone-deep aches traversed his body, and his skin felt too tight around his muscles. His eyes felt like they'd been sucker punched a half dozen times. A rich fog fell over his thoughts. If he left now, he could catch a two, maybe three-hour nap before dragging himself into the office.

He decided to bail and kissed his wife on the forehead. Blowing his baby a kiss, he left for the exit.

But it was blocked. A woman was standing there—not a nurse. Her eyes looked like Grant's, heavy and dark. Her shoulders sagged. Her skin was pale, way too pale, clamshell white. Black, wavy hair fell at her shoulders, greasy and wiry. A funky odor that deodorant could easily mask tainted the air, filling his nostrils.

She didn't move when Grant raised his brow at her, making it very clear she was in the way. "Can I help you?" he asked. He couldn't stop a chilly claw from dragging down his spine. "Uh, hello?"

"I heard you earlier," she said, whispering. "About your baby. About the mark."

"Mark?"

The woman's head tilted to the side, and she touched the colorless skin between her eyes.

"Oh. Yeah, the ash thing."

"It's not ash," she said in a way that suggested she had also considered the Ash Wednesday analogy. "It's *her*."

"Who?"

"The woman. The hag."

Grant swallowed. There was something clearly off about this woman, and her sudden presence had him considering a personal day tomorrow. He didn't want to leave Kasey alone with this lunatic.

Grant searched the hallway behind her for a nurse, but he couldn't see any. "Hey, what's your name?"

Confused, the woman shook her head. "My name is Anastasia. But I don't see what that has to do with—"

"Cool name. Hey, listen. I don't mean to sound rude or, like, an asshole. But…are you all right?"

She stared, her expression blank.

Grant squinted. "Can I get you some help?"

"You don't know what's going on here, do you?"

"Uh, I know we're on the fifth floor of Center Street Hospital, inside the NICU. I know there are babies who are—"

"—In grave danger," she finished for him.

"Look, I don't know what your deal is, but it's late…or early, depending on how you look at it. I have to go to work. My wife, over there—she's sleeping. Please don't disturb her. Okay?"

"You need to listen to me. Your daughter—she has the black mark. She's been chosen."

"Okay, I'm trying to be nice here."

A nurse appeared from behind a curtain and asked, "Is everything okay here?"

"Everything's fine," Grant told her, not taking his eyes off the woman. "Anastasia here was just leaving. Weren't you?"

Anastasia glared at him, then smiled at the nurse. "Of course."

After she left and disappeared down the hallway, Grant turned to the nurse and asked, "What's up with her?"

The nurse sighed, letting go of a frustrated breath. "That woman— my heart breaks for her. But I'd be lying if I said I won't be glad to see her leave next week."

"She was going on about…" Grant didn't know exactly how to finish that sentence and not sound like a lunatic himself. "…she seemed disturbed."

"We can't talk about other patients and their situations, of course, but…I won't tell if you won't."

Grant nodded.

"Steer clear of Anastasia Wallace. Her baby has undergone some unfortunate setbacks and…well, her diagnosis is grim at best. She's not handling it well."

"Obviously. Thanks for the advice."

"Don't mention it." The nurse nodded over her shoulder. "Leaving for the night?"

"Yeah. Work. Duty calls."

The nurse flashed him a comforting smile, one that warmed him.

"You're doing a great job. You and your wife. Baby Bella will be just fine. You watch."

He didn't know why, but her niceties felt forced. Like a lie.

-4-

A WEEK LATER, Baby Bella was doing neither better nor worse, though the doctors and nurses remained optimistic. Baby Bella wasn't eating much, having trouble taking to the bottle, and the only real sustenance came from the feeding tube. She was growing but slowly. She would need to hit the five-pound mark before they sent her home, and in two weeks, she went from one-and-a-half to just over two.

Still a long way to go.

The week was hell on Grant Hobbs. The office needed him to stay late a few days—to fix the blunders of some other employees—and between the long hours, the hour drive, and spending the nights on the hospital's fifth floor, he was completely drained. His lack of sleep started to affect his mood, turning him rotten. He was having trouble maintaining his typical positive attitude—both at work and in front of his wife—and he found himself snapping at people, his temper shrinking with each hour of rest he was missing.

"You don't have to be such a dick," Kasey told him after he'd rolled his eyes and sighed and told her how much he *didn't* want to go down to the café and grab her a coffee. He *was* being a dick—and he noticed it immediately. Not like other times when it took him a few hours to realize the error of his ways.

"I'm sorry, babe. I'm just…whipped."

She blew out a frustrated gust and pulled herself out of the chair and onto her feet. "Fine. I'll go myself."

She was still recovering from surgery, and even though it had been a couple of weeks and the staples were out, she still complained of soreness.

"No," he said. "I'll get it. I'm sorry. You're right. I was being a total dick."

She sat back down and flashed him a peaceful smile. "Thank you. You're a superhero, you know."

"Don't feel like it. I feel like I got my ass kicked by one."

With that, he left, making his way across the hall, to the elevator, and down to the second floor where the café was open twenty-four-seven. He ordered two coffees, loaded them with cream and sugar, and then started for the elevator.

Someone screamed.

His heart thundered the second the screeching cry hit the airwaves. A small commotion followed, the shouting of several other anxious voices. Grant didn't know exactly how to react or how he should prepare for what was around the corner. It reminded him of when he used to hang out at seedy bars when fights broke out. The simultaneous sounds of scuffling and shouting, anger and shock rising together in an uproarious wave. But who would be brawling in a hospital at three in the morning? His mind turned to much darker thoughts.

Active shooter?

It wasn't outside of the realm of possibilities.

He froze up, waiting for the screamer to reveal themselves, and, hopefully, the reason for the shrill outburst.

Then he saw her.

Anastasia.

She was screaming, crying, and kicking her legs all at once. Two men in security guard outfits pull her through the lobby, one on each arm. She attempted to free her arms, but the men had gripped them tightly underneath the armpits, and she was no match for their strength.

Grant's first reaction was to go to her. He moved toward the struggle but quickly realized he had the coffee occupying both hands. He looked for a place to rest the two cups, but nothing was available. The floor was the only option, and he laid them by the elevator, out of the way, so no one would disturb them.

Then he ran.

He met up with Anastasia, the two guards, and a small throng composed of nurses, doctors, and nosey onlookers seeking a good story to tell their friends over lunch tomorrow. He went to move past the throng when one of the nurses stopped him, putting a hand on his shoulder and grabbing his coat.

"Don't," she said.

Grant recognized her. It was the same nurse who'd briefly told him about Anastasia, about the woman's baby and how it wasn't looking too good in terms of survival. Grant wanted to break free and go to her, handle the guards, tell them to get their greasy paws off her.

But he didn't.

Anastasia continued to yell: *"SHE KILLED HER! THE BITCH KILLED MY DAUGHTER!"*

Grant shuddered, recalling what she'd told him that night. About the black mark, about the woman who'd marked Baby Bella for…

…what exactly, he didn't know.

But maybe he did now.

-5-

WHEN GRANT CAME BACK with the coffees, Kasey was sleeping. He didn't wake her. Instead, he put her coffee on the radiator and watched Baby Bella sleep for the next hour. He examined her forehead.

The black mark was gone.

-6-

THAT NIGHT, he dreamed of the NICU. He knew it was a dream the second he fell into the illusionary world; rolling hordes of mist tumbled into the empty hallways, and an unsettling blue light illumi-nated the darkened corridors. He moved through it unevenly, the dreamworld skipping and pixelating. At the end of the hallway, his dream self came to a stop and paused to view the pods holding the incubators. One pod in particular called to him, glowing brighter with that intimidating blue light than the rest.

He drifted toward it.

Peeked inside.

A shrouded figure hovered over Baby Bella's incubator, elbows deep in the plastic encasement. Grant's first reaction was to ask the figure what was happening, why it had its hands in there. No one was supposed to access the incubators except for nurses, and the figure wasn't dressed like any nurse. Its all-black attire and dark, lacy veil that covered its face proved the figure was here with bad intentions. But Grant had no voice to speak; the dream did not allow it.

Baby Bella began to cry, and even though this was not real, Grant still felt his heart crack in half for his little girl.

The figure was taking her.

No, not taking her.

Crushing her.

Through the veil, the figure gritted their teeth, and Grant could make out the dark-stained white grimace through the material. Grant opened his mouth to scream, but Baby Bella's was the only voice he could hear. Her small but angry cries echoed against the walls of this illusive realm, and Grant moved to help her, moved to save his baby girl from the impending hands of doom.

The figure snapped its head up, staring directly at Grant. And Grant could see shimmering silvery tokens where ordinary eyes ought to have been. Bleached skin behind the veil, black tears running like cheap mascara.

"THIS IS MINE," the figure said, pressing its fingers into Baby Bella's skin. The snapping crunch of fragile bones quickly followed.

Grant woke up with a violent start.

-7-

GRANT WAS ten minutes late to work that morning. Surprisingly enough, in the last six weeks, this was his first occurrence. There had been a few close calls when he'd shown up one or two minutes past nine, but this was the first he'd gone over the allotted five-minute buffer before punching the clock. Not bad, and certainly no one would pull him into an office and talk to him about it. But inside, he felt a deep, surging shame and couldn't adequately articulate why. Just that he felt like he was letting someone down.

Himself.

The first couple of hours went by quickly. But after eleven, time started to drag, and his cubicle began to feel like an inescapable puzzle room rather than a workspace station. He hit the coffee bar for the third time that morning, and that was enough to propel him toward lunch.

Once the clock hit one, he was out of the office so fast that Lee Rodgers, his buddy three cubicles down, didn't have the chance to catch up and ask him if he wanted to hit the Chinese buffet. Grant hustled to his Accord in under five minutes.

And there was someone there, waiting for him.

Anastasia.

Grant froze and stared at the woman leaning against his door with her arms folded across her midsection as if he was late for something important. He didn't know what bothered him more— the fact she was stalking him at his workplace or that she was resting her body against his personal property so nonchalantly.

She stared back, her eyes cold and dark, like something inside them had broken off and died. A piece of her soul, maybe.

He swallowed a lump in his throat and pressed on, approaching the unstable woman cautiously, careful not to spook her.

"Can I help you?" he asked. "Anastasia, right?"

She didn't respond. Just stared. His neck burned from the awkward helplessness of this heavy moment.

"Look," he said, shrugging, "I'm not really sure what you want, but—"

"I came to warn you so it wouldn't happen to you, too."

"Hey, partner!" shouted Lee Rodgers. Grant turned just in time to catch his "friend" waving to him, a goofy grin plastered to his stupid face. "You wanna grab Chinese or—" He saw the woman blocking his way to the driver's seat. Her face. Her eyes desolate and glacial. "Oh. Didn't realize…" He danced on his heels, an awkward movement, as if caught perving or something. "I'll catch up with you later, man."

With that, the spineless shit left.

Grant felt his heart sink. Lee could have been his savior. Now, he was forced to deal with this situation alone.

Grant winced. "I'm so sorry about what happened to you. Your baby. But…"

"You don't know shit about it," she said. "And you don't know shit about me. So why are you sorry?"

"That's…" He hung his head, embarrassment burning up his cheeks. "That's just a thing people say. I'm sorry. I didn't mean anything by it. Just trying to be…nice."

Her steady gaze drilled deep into his, and just when he couldn't stand it anymore, just when he decided enough was enough and it was time to alert the authorities, she said, "I'm here because I want to help you."

"I'm okay," he said. "I appreciate your concern, I appreciate you coming down here to—"

Stalk me.

"—help me. But I'm good."

"You don't understand," she said, revealing something that was resting behind her—between the car and her back—the whole time. Something he couldn't see. Something shiny and metal, something he'd never had pointed at him in his entire boring life.

A gun.

"I wasn't asking," she said, motioning for him to get in the car.

-8-

GRANT DROVE WELL past his lunch break. Anastasia allowed him to pull over to call his boss and play sick for the rest of the afternoon to keep his employer from A.) getting suspicious and B.) disciplining Grant for leaving unexcused. *How considerate.* She had dialed the number for him and put the phone to his ear while keeping the gun trained on his gut. He was given a stern warning—try any funny business, and he'd be absorbing a round.

Grant didn't try any funny business. The call lasted all of ten seconds.

"What do we do now?" Grant asked.

"I want you to drive to Cedarborough Cemetery in Hooperstown, New Jersey."

Grant couldn't help it. He actually laughed in her face. "Hooperstown is damn near two hours away."

The barrel of the gun met his eyes in less than two seconds. He heard the click of the internal mechanism doing something dangerous. "Again, that wasn't a request."

Grant turned to the steering wheel, doing everything in his power not to explode, completely lose it, and start attacking this woman. Even though she was armed, he was pretty sure he could take her. Wrestle the weapon from her before she could pull the trigger. But did he want to chance it? Did he want to get himself shot or, worse, killed? Leave his newborn fatherless, his wife a widow?

Not worth the risk. Even though she had a gun, he didn't feel his life was in any danger. Far from it, actually. There was a part of him that felt safe with Anastasia here. A comforting presence that bundled in and around his bones, something born from mutual misery. However, if he reacted and forced her hand, he had no doubt she would turn on him, do exactly as she promised.

Pull that trigger.

"I need to call my wife," he said.

"No."

"Yes." His knuckles blanched as his fingers tightened around the wheel. "She'll think it's weird when I don't show up at the hospital directly after work. And there's no way I can make it there in time if we're going to fucking Hooperstown."

She hesitated, seeming to kick the idea around. Then she grunted. It was a noise a dog in the late stages of retirement might make after being asked to fetch a stick. "Fine."

Again, she made the call for him, shaking the gun in front of his face as if he could forget the consequences.

"Hey, babe," Kasey answered on the second ring. "How's work?"

"It's," he said, fighting the urge to shout, yell, tell her to hang up and call 911 immediately. "It's okay. Actually, that's a lie. It sucks today. Like, super busy. They want me to stay a few hours late."

"Oh," she said in that voice, the kind that made him feel like he crushed what little remained of her soul after the grueling last few months of their lives. "That does suck. Okay. Well, I'm still at the hospital with Baby Bella. They said her jaundice is getting better and we might get to hold her soon. Kangaroo Care."

A tear stung his eye. "I don't know what that means, but it sounds great."

"I'll see you soon?"

Choking on his own sadness, he bit his lip, suppressing the ugly cry that sought freedom from his throat. For the first time since he was hijacked by this crazy woman, he thought this might be the last time he'd ever speak with his wife. "Yeah, soon." A swallow that felt like a tennis ball going down. "I love you."

"Love you too."

They hung up.

Anastasia, emotionlessly, said one word: "Drive."

-9-

HE MADE GREAT TIME, reaching the shore area in under an hour and thirty-five minutes. Hooperstown in under two. Still, there was no way he was making it back to the Hospital (an hour away from where she wanted him to go) any time soon, and he was basing that off of nothing. She hadn't told him anything except to drive to the cemetery, which she plugged into his Maps App.

Grant pulled down Cedarborough Cemetery's main pathway—only wide enough for one car—and took the winding pavement through the center, observing the cracked, washed gravestones as they slowed by.

"This is an old place," she told him. "Also a bad place."

"It's just a cemetery," he told her. "Looks no different from any other I've been to."

"For some, it's just a cemetery." She pointed up ahead. "Take that left."

Grant did as she asked, careening the car onto the next extension.

"For me, this place is Hell."

"And what are we doing in Hell?"

She looked at him, and for the first time since he met her, she grinned. "We're going to meet the devil."

-10-

SHE DIRECTED him to the far back corner of the cemetery, a secluded place that didn't seem to have many visitors. The graves were older back here, looking centuries old, cracked and crumbling. When he neared the headstones, he saw the nineteenth-century dates chiseled into their pitted faces. The grass was taller here, and the trees overgrown, wily branches in desperate need of a good clipping. This neglected space was perfect for getting away with a crime, and Grant Hobbs was pretty sure he was about to witness one.

Or help commit one.

"Get out," she said, directing the barrel at his belly. "Let's go."

"What are we doing here?"

"No questions. Move."

Reluctantly, he dragged himself out of the car. There was a split second when he wondered how many guns this woman had fired and how accurate she would be if he took off running into the neighboring woods. Another part of him wondered if the gun was even loaded. These thoughts came and went, and he staved off these intrusive ideas by thinking of his precious newborn and her mother. He envisioned a future where the three of them huddled together on the couch, watching Disney movies until they passed out from too much popcorn and soda pop. A future where they attended all of life's greatest events—Christmas mornings, birthdays, high school graduation, college graduation, wedding day, anniversaries. He thought of these things, and that kept him from doing anything other than what the mad woman behind the gun told him to.

"Here," she said, waving him over to a large gravestone with a cross atop it. A shovel already rested at its base.

"What is this?" he asked, knowing where this was going but needing to hear the explanation anyway.

"Dig."

"I don't understand."

"I said, *Dig.*"

He picked up the shovel and began to dig. As he did, he read the gravestone, the name on the surface, the birth date and death date. As his eyes ran over the deceased's name, his heart jumped.

Anastasia Wallace.

Slowly, he rotated back to her, shooting her a glare that demanded answers.

"I was named after her, an ancestor." Anastasia wrinkled her nose as if something foul suddenly polluted the fresh air. "And it's her— the hag on the fifth floor."

An hour and a half later, Grant threw the final shovel of dirt over his shoulder. The wooden casket was finally revealed enough so that it could be opened.

Darkness crept its way across the sky, but there was still a half hour of good sunlight left.

Anastasia peered down into the hole with a vigilant gaze as if expecting the decomposed corpse inside to come bursting out with the ancient fury of some hellbent mummy. That didn't happen, of course, and Grant was left tired and drained from the impromptu excavation project the woman had bestowed upon him. He took a seat in the dirt pit, trying to catch his breath.

"You could have done this yourself," he told her.

"No," she said, "I couldn't have. She's already done with me and onto the next child—yours."

"Why? Why me?"

Anastasia's face melted with tears, an agony that Grant had never seen present in another person's expression before. Despite her actions, he felt for her. Her whole body began to shake, quivering as if a bone-cold chill had wormed its way into her center. The heavy sobs came next, which Grant relished. A part of him wanted her to hurt. Part of him thought maybe she deserved this, whatever happened to her. But that was just the anger speaking. He didn't mean that, and after a few seconds, he felt guilty for thinking such a thing.

No one deserved to lose a child.

No one.

"It's my fault," Anastasia said between the sobs. "Our family is cursed. By her. By what she did in life. A child killer. A cannibal. She was a midwife and specialized in stillborn births. Though, later in life, she developed a taste for living newborns. She would travel from town to town. Got away with it for years. When a town constable caught her, they found she kept the bones of all her victims tucked away in her effects as if trophies. They identified twenty-six different newborns but estimated there could have been well over forty."

"Jesus." Grant looked down at the casket. Earthworms inched their way across the near-rotten surface.

"They hung her for her crimes. Not too far from this spot. Buried her here. They shouldn't have done that. Her soul—it still lives. Her spirit is a maleficent one. Driven by her passion for death. Somehow, she's trespassed the spirit realm and entered ours once again." She took a breath and closed her eyes as if readying herself to admit some terrible knowledge. "I brought her to that hospital. And now she's after you. Your Bella."

Grant felt his rage surge inside him. "Shut up. Don't you mention her name."

"You must burn her bones," the woman said, calming herself, drying the tears on her shoulder, rubbing her eyes on the fabric. "Get out of there. Come with me."

Grant didn't move. He felt more rebellious now.

Anastasia held up her power play, directing the barrel at the center of his chest. "I don't want to hurt you, but I will if that's what it takes to end this. My family…they warned me about having children. The firstborn never makes it—that's what they told me. And they told me why, but I never believed it. Now I know. And she won't stop until the bones are burned. I'm sure of it." She stared at him hard. "I know you believe it too. I know you've seen her."

Grant grimaced.

"It's true. The curse is on you now. And once she has your Bella, once she breaks your sweet, innocent child in half and eats her bones, she'll move on to someone else's. And on and on, forever and ever. But…*you*…you can stop her. Right here and now."

Grant allowed his head to collapse in his hands. He couldn't believe he was buying into this nonsense. But he had seen something, hadn't he?

A dream.

That goddamn dream. It wasn't reality, though. *This* was reality, and he had never felt more lost and confused.

Grant glanced up from his palms. "If we do this, it's over, right? You'll let me go home? Back to the hospital? Let me and my family be?"

"I promise it," she said, her eyes still sparkling with receding tears.

"Okay," he said, "then let's burn this bitch."

Anastasia directed him to a small shed near the edge of the cemetery. There, he found a small red gas can and a book of matches—more staged materials. She'd clearly done some plotting, and Grant was rather impressed with how organized she was.

The crazy ones are, he mused, heading back to the dig site.

They'd been out here for hours, and no one had shown up to this section of the cemetery, not a single soul. He expected someone to come patrolling along, a caretaker or someone visiting an old relative, someone in the distance who spotted them, got curious, and decided to check out the commotion. But there was no one, and that made Grant equally terrified. For all he knew, after he carried out her insane plot, she would put two in his chest and bury him with her ancestor.

He thought of his family again. What their lives would be like without him in the picture. All of those wonderful life events sans a husband and a father. Or *worse*—with a second husband and a stepfather.

He couldn't leave them. He couldn't take that chance.

"Pour the gasoline," she told him. "Hurry. It's getting dark."

"Yes, ma'am," he said, dropping to his knees beside the shovel, gas can in hand. As he began to pour, a shadow appeared in his periphery. His gaze was drawn to it, and when he locked eyes on the source of the motion, he saw *her*.

The Hag.

It was the same woman from his dream, the one who'd stood over Baby Bella's incubator and cracked her fragile bones like a walnut shell. He could see her hooked nose and glimmering eyes through the dark, lacy veil over her face. Warts the size of plump maggots. Teeth stained with dark rot. He could hear her guttural laughter through her clenched smile.

"What are you waiting for?" Anastasia asked.

She couldn't see her. Only he could.

He reached for the shovel.

"What are you—"

He grabbed the handle and swung the metal spade at Anastasia's head all at once. Quicker than he ever imagined, he got the shovel in full swing before she could scream in protest. The flat side of the spade hit her squarely across her face, and the cracking of her skull hit his ears seconds before the gunshot went off. A burst of pain flared in his shoulder. The bullet punched through him, spinning him to the side.

Ignoring the agony that coursed through his shoulder and spread into his back and beyond, he turned. Anastasia was gone. Nowhere to be seen.

What the...

He peered into the grave to see the woman face-down and motionless in the disturbed dirt. A fissure had opened up near her hairline, and copious amounts of blood poured out in great rivulets.

Grant glanced up at the dark specter. The old woman's face contained unimaginable glee, her lips forming a dancing smile.

Grant knew what had to happen next. He jumped into the grave.

From Anastasia's throat, a sound emanated. An agonizing groan.

Grant knew that had to be the woman's last sound.

"I'm sorry," he said.

He brought the shovel over his head and slammed the spade down on her. Again. Again. Until her skull opened and the secrets within leaked out, lost forever.

-13-

Six weeks later, Baby Bella hit her weight goal, and it was time to send her home. It was an exciting day filled with congratulatory hugs from nurses, friends, and family. Grant had never seen Kasey happier, and although the road ahead was not free from obstruction, it was definitely clearer.

Baby Bella was going to be all right.

On the way out of the hospital, looking up from his tiny sweetheart nestled in the carrier and over to the plastic container she'd just spent the last few months in, Grant smiled.

Behind the incubator, the Fifth Floor Hag smiled back. Then she moved across the room, the phantom stalking that place now and forever.

WHITE WALPURGIS

BRIDAL PARTY

"All right, pretend like you're thinking," said Marla Quinn, snapping off a few photos while the bridesmaids hustled back and forth behind her.

The maid of honor changed something on the bride's IV, patted her shoulder, and kissed her forehead. The bride nodded, turning her head to look thoughtfully at the hotel room's far wall.

"But," Marla said, adjusting the flash, "like, think while smiling. Reflect on happy times, your life together so far, your *future*."

The maid of honor continued to play nurse, tapping a few pills into her palm. Abigail Pelton, the sick bride, did exactly as Marla asked. She posed, and she smiled, doing both without a hint of reluctance. Everything was going swimmingly, something Marla couldn't exactly say for all the weddings she photographed. You just never knew if you'd be shooting cooperative subjects or whiny brats who wanted nothing to do with pictures, but the Pelton bridal party had, so far, been superb.

Hope the guys are just as easy-going, she thought, cycling through the settings on her Canon Mark III.

"Nice. Perfect. You're a natural."

The maid of honor smiled.

Abigail smiled back.

Marla smiled because they were both smiling. And capturing her clients' special day was oh-so gratifying. Everyone was happy. Everything was perfect.

After she had grabbed the shots she needed, she asked the maid of honor what room the groomsmen were staying in.

"I'm sorry?"

"The groomsmen?" Marla said again. "Their… um… room?"

The maid of honor shook her head. "I'm sorry. Didn't Mr. Pelton brief you on…" She cleared her throat. "Didn't he tell you the details? Didn't your employer pass along that information?"

Marla shook her head. "No. No one told me anything." She pressed her palm against her forehead. "I'm sorry. I was told this wedding would be a bit unorthodox, but I just assumed it was the…" Her eyes drifted over to the bed. She nodded subtly at the monitoring equipment resting next to the bride.

"Oh," the maid of honor said, a hint of sadness bringing down her voice. "No, Abby's cancer has nothing to do with it."

Awkward City, Marla thought. *Can I make this any worse? At this rate, I'll never get another gig with Marvelous Creations.*

"So…" The maid of honor trailed off, staring at Marla as if maybe Marla would forget the whole thing, drop it, and go about her job. But Marla stood her ground, waiting for the maid of honor to divulge the juicy details of this odd wedding. "So, the thing is—there are no groomsmen."

"Oh. Oh, okay." She had never shot a wedding with no groomsmen before. Unorthodox, yes. But they were paying her double her normal rate, and, considering there was no other half of the bridal party, her workload was significantly less. She had nothing to complain about. "Just the groom, then."

"Yeah…about that…" The maid of honor cast her eyes to the suite's plush carpet, looking as if she didn't know how to break the bad news. "There isn't a groom, either. I mean, not really."

"Sooooo…who's getting married?" Marla's thoughts were suddenly all over the place. *A wedding with no groom and no parties. This isn't weird. Nope. Not at all.*

She reminded herself how much none of this mattered, that she was getting paid regardless, and that she'd be able to afford rent this month because of it. She reminded herself not to fucking worry.

Still, something about the ceremony's peculiar start unnerved her. A serpent of unease uncoiled in her guts.

"It's complicated. But you should talk to Mr. Pelton. He'll fill you in on the details."

"Perfect."

With that, Marla left the room in search of the father of the bride and some answers.

OPEN BAR

She found the bride's father at the bar, knocking back a martini. With the same hand, he slammed down the drink and ordered another.

"Oh, come on," Marla said, sidling up next to him. "Marrying off your daughter can't be *that* bad, can it?"

Elmer Pelton didn't find the humor in that joke, and his dry, searching eyes drifted across the bar to meet her smiling face.

Tough crowd, she thought.

"Yikes. Sorry. I was just kidding. Trying to lighten the mood." She scanned the bar and the wedding's other attendees as they drank and conversed, scattering secrets amongst themselves. No one seemed to be laughing or smiling. No one seemed to be enjoying themselves at all. *Am I shooting a funeral or a wedding?* Marla wondered, returning to Elmer Pelton. "Everyone seems so tense."

"So, your boss didn't tell you, I gather," Elmer said, sipping from another martini. His face was fixed in a bitter scowl, and the martini did nothing to help the cause.

Marla shook her head. "Nope. Not a thing." She forced another amiable smile. "But I'm starting to worry. Did I get mixed up in some voodoo cult scheme or what?" A quick glance around the room, honing in on the guests' odd choices in attire. "Seems like everyone is here for a funeral, not a wedding."

"Well, that may be because Abby's groom is…well, he's not with us."

Marla's lips wrinkled. "Yeah, the maid of honor clued me in on that." She swallowed, curiosity getting the better of her thoughts. "Sir, I can't help but ask—did something happen to the groom?"

"Something… happen…" His brain seemed to forget whatever he was going to say next, and his eyes found the ceiling. There was nothing above except ornate molding, dentil blocks, and marble plinths that held up the structural columns. A painting of an angel floating through heavenly clouds of white took up some of the ceiling as well. "No, Miss Quinn. No, nothing happened to him."

He offered her a defeated smile.

"Oh. Okay then. Look, you don't have to tell me—"

"Your employer promised my family and me that whatever you saw here today…it would be confidential. Hence the hefty payday."

Marla nodded. "Understood. Believe me. My lips are sealed. I just…weddings are supposed to be happy. A day of celebration. This…" She looked around the room once again, noticing she had drawn the attention of the other guests. Some eyes lingered on her, which disquieted her even more, making her feel like an intruder and less like a piece of this *supposed* joyous experience. "This is different."

Elmer Pelton put down another martini with ease. "Just, whatever you see here today—keep an open mind. And also, I'll need all the footage of what you capture before you leave."

"But I have to edit—"

"Uncle Horace will edit them for us." Elmer raised his empty glass in Uncle Horace's direction. Marla saw the man in the back corner of the room nod in response and give Elmer a toast of his cherry-topped drink. He looked less like a wedding guest and more like a man who dealt in shady business practices. Marla had never seen someone sit so comfortably in the shadows, with sunglasses on nonetheless.

"Okay. Uncle Horace it is," Marla said, realizing an argument with the father of the bride would get her nowhere. Besides, he was paying for the pictures. He could smash her SD card on the ground right in front of her, and she wouldn't care. Either way, she was getting paid.

New plan—fuck these people and their special day. Get in, get out, and try to forget you were even on this job.

"Thank you, Mrs. Quinn. Now, if I may bestow one more piece of advice on you this evening."

"Sure, man. Whatever."

"Whatever you see during the ceremony…whatever you witness… please, do your best to forget it ever happened."

Her throat suddenly felt six times smaller.

"And for the love of all that is unholy," he continued, "please don't scream."

A PHONE CALL

"Calm down, Marla. I can explain."

Marla paced the terrace, looking over her shoulder to make sure no one had followed her. "Explain? Explain? Jesus, Dom. You better do better than explain."

"I know you're angry."

"I'm not angry," she said, aware of her tone. "I'm not angry at all. I'm just freaked out. I mean—'don't scream?' What the hell is that, Dom? And don't tell me you have no clue."

Dom's heavy breathing caused static. "Marla, please. I don't know anything. Elmer Pelton didn't say anything about there not being a groom or what kind of wedding it would be. I knew the broad had cancer, and that was it."

"He didn't say? Because he seems to think he did."

"No. All he said was that there would be some uncomfortable sights, stuff about the cancer, and to send you."

"Me?"

"That's right, Marla. You. They requested you by name."

"You didn't tell me that."

"Would it have mattered? I get requests for you all the time. You're my best wedding photographer. *Word of mouth* is a big thing in this business."

She paused, enjoying the compliments, hoping there was more.

"Besides, you've shot strange weddings before."

"Not this strange."

"Remember that wedding you did last year? The one with the tarot card reader?"

"Yeah," she said, sticking a cigarette in her mouth and lighting up. "That was a hoot."

"That was strange, right?"

"Yeah, it was a little odd, and the lady was a kook. I mean, Jesus, she told me I'd start talking to my mother again, that we'd suddenly repair our relationship, and there is no way *that* is happening, not over my dead body."

"My point, Marla, is that you're the best. There's a reason why the Peltons asked for you." He sighed one more time, clearly growing bored of this explanation. She didn't care—it felt nice to be needed, and she was soaking in every compliment, basking in their soothing glory. "That's why they paid us extra."

She decided to take a gamble. "I don't know, man. I think I want more."

"More?" She heard him nearly fall out of his chair. At the very least, he knocked something off his desk. "More what?"

"More money, of course."

"Marla, no. You're being paid double your rate as it is, and that's more than enough."

"Not for this. I mean, must I reiterate the fact that I was told not to scream during the ceremony? I mean, what the fuck, Dom?"

Dom grunted in frustration. "Jesus fucking Christ, Marla. Fine. I'll throw you an extra hundred."

"Make it three."

"Three-hundred? No, no, Marla. No way. That's...that's, like, extortion or some shit."

"Maybe. But you'll pay it, or I'm outta here. And good luck finding someone to replace me in the next twenty minutes."

"Marla, you'll never work in photography ever again, least not in this state, if you walk off this job."

"I was thinking of starting my own business, anyway."

"Marla, please."

"So, three hundred is good then?" His silence meant he was thinking about it, and the longer he deliberated, the more Marla knew she had him. "PayPal me. To friends, so I don't have to claim it."

More silence. Eventually, he snarled: "All right. Fine. Three hundred. Headed your way. But don't think I won't forget this."

"I know you won't."

She hung up and waited for the money to come through. After the notification dropped down from her home bar and she saw herself three hundred dollars richer, she headed back inside, changing the lens on her camera as she went.

CEREMONY

"WE GATHER HERE TODAY," said the officiant, "to celebrate the joining of two special individuals as they prepare to spend their lives together in eternity. We welcome all of you on this special day, April the 30th, otherwise known in our hearts as Walpurgis Night."

Marla snapped a photo of the venue's banquet hall and the altar. The camera's flash went off, earning her dirty looks from the gathering, an odd collection of individuals that wore dark-colored clothing and hats with veils.

Funeral, she thought. *Funeral clothes.*

The robed man on stage stood beside the bride, holding up his arms, asking the congregation to "Please rise." He began humming some hymn Marla's ear didn't fully recognize. But she tried her best to ignore the strange happenings around her and concentrate on getting the shots she needed. The more she photographed, the more attention she received from the audience. It wasn't the first time she'd received dirty looks for doing her job; it happened quite frequently, and she'd gotten pretty good at ignoring them.

But these looks…they freaked her out. Those eyes didn't just relay displeasure; no, they were cast with hate.

Bunch of freaks.

Marla kept ignoring them, sticking to the job.

After the song was over, the robed man lowered his arms. The spectators continued to stand. Then they turned, facing the doors in the back of the hall.

Marla made her way to the front of the altar, getting a clear shot down the aisle. The bride was already on stage (unorthodox, yes) next to the beeping equipment that monitored her vitals and administered medicine. And everyone was awaiting the groom's arrival. *There is no groom,* she remembered the maid of honor stating, and Marla wondered who exactly might appear from behind those doors. Regardless, she was prepared, camera in hand, ready to capture the moment.

The doors swung open, and in walked a man, robed like the officiant, except he wasn't alone. He held a rope, and Marla followed the braided material to the floor, where beside the man walked a black goat.

The animal bleated. Its farm-stink filled the hall.

"Are you people *fucking* serious?" Marla said, standing up, letting the camera dangle from the strap around her neck.

Immediately, every eye in the room turned on her. Some were wide with horror as if Marla had committed some vile, atrocious crime. Some came at her with that familiar revulsion, their dark eyes burning with a sense of murderous intent.

"I mean, really?" she said again, holding out her arms, waiting for a reply. Something sane, something rational.

Before she could throw her arms up and storm out, walk off the job, a hand gripped her shoulder and tore her away from the stage.

"Ow!" she snapped. *"You're hurting me."*

The hand spun her around.

Elmer Pelton.

"You were told to keep an open mind. You were told not to make any noise."

No, she felt like saying. *No, I was told not to scream.*

"But this is ridic—"

He shushed her by putting a finger over her lips. Frozen by the inability to fully process what her eyes were seeing, she couldn't bring herself to remove his touch.

"You are being paid to act like a professional. *Act* like a professional. Do your job. Take your pictures. Capture our special celebration."

Marla glared at him but nodded.

Elmer headed back to his position on the stage. He stood next to his daughter, who looked down at the black goat fondly, the way a bride always looks upon her future husband.

I can't believe this is happening, Marla thought as she found herself snapping more photos. *Let's get this over with, shall we?*

The ceremony went on.

The robed man led the black goat on stage, across from Abagail Pelton. As the officiant commenced with the sacrament of holy matrimony, the maid of honor fiddled with the machinery and changed the bride's IV. Marla got lost in the man's words, the speech he spewed forth, the passages and phrases—spoken in some uncommon tongue —that the congregation gobbled up, the guests and their responses, their proud grins. Marla began to feel ill, the banquet hall spinning before her. She thought she might get sick, lose the sushi she'd chowed down during the cocktail hour. This was not right.

She needed to escape.

Turning back toward the emergency exit, she lost her grip on the camera. For a second, she forgot about the strap around her neck and expected the device to smash on the ground, shattering into small pieces. Music began to play, discordant plucking from an assembly of out-of-tune strings. The harsh melody only made the room more disorienting, and Marla's feet began to fail.

What the hell is happening to me?

She glanced up at the emergency exit and watched some robed figure step in front of her way out.

"Move," she said, swaying on her heels.

"Don't let her leave," said someone from behind her, and she recognized the voice of Elmer Pelton.

Marla drunkenly glanced over her shoulder, back toward the stage. Every eye was on her now, even those clad in shadows. She brought up her camera and began shooting the stage, focusing the flash directly into their staring eyes. Arms gripped her. She fought them off.

"C'mere," the robed guardian said, trying to corral her. He reached for the camera, but she dug deep for control over her body and kicked the man right in his ball bag. His head shot forward, and he groaned in considerable pain. As he hunched, she introduced his chin to her knee. With force. As much as she could generate.

The blow knocked the man on his back.

She continued to capture images of the stage, the flash flickering like an epileptic's worst nightmare. In the blinding bursts, Elmer's face twisted and contorted with the rage of some spiteful deity. He hopped off the stage, placed a hand in front of his eyes, and started toward Marla, teeth clenched, lips pulled back in a ferocious snarl.

The black goat bleated some more. Much to the chagrin of the audience, Marla carried on with her light show, and that, in turn, inspired the black goat to buck. The little guy kicked his legs in reverse, catching his robed escort right in the shin with bone-shattering force. The form lurched forward, dropped the rope, and grabbed the excruciating pain with both hands. He fell to the floor, out of sight, but not before the goat dropped a few heavy hooves on his face.

The black goat looked at Marla as if he wanted a reward for dispatching one of them. *I'll give all the hay in the world, little buddy, if you kick our way out. Hay or whatever you little fuckers eat.*

It was as if he heard her. The black goat lowered his head and charged off the stage, plowing into Elmer. Elmer flew into the first row of chairs, taking out seats and a few of the Peltons' guests. The crowd gasped; a few of them cursed. Some shouted for Marla to stop using her flash, for it was clearly riling up the groom. But that only motivated her to take more pictures. To document this whole clusterfuck. The strobe-like effect bounced around the room, the congregates acting like the light somehow melted their flesh.

The black goat resumed his reign of terror, kicking and ramming the fleeing members. He drove one of the robed guests through the drywall. Even when the man was down, the goat continued to grind his skull into him as if intending to pulverize the man to dust.

Keep going, little buddy. Keep kicking ass, my furry friend.

Through the chaos, Marla locked onto Abagail. The bride's eyes grinned at her. Spikes of dread penetrated Marla's flesh. A cold river ran through her veins, and she immediately thought she should get out of there since the room's attention had gone to the havoc-wreaking goat.

Don't worry, Marla, the bride's eyes said. *You'll be where you're supposed to go. Soon.*

Marla spun for the emergency exit. The guard was writhing on the ground, but he was starting to recharge his battery. He'd be up in a few seconds, and Marla would be his first destination.

She sprinted toward the door, barreled into it, and came out on the other side.

The other side.

A winter wonderland, an endless expanse of marshmallow hills beneath a colorless sheet of ever-stretching gray.

VISIONS

"COME SIT," said the girl in the wedding dress.

After glancing around at the pure-white scenery, Marla realized she was still at the venue, just three months earlier. It was January 30th, maybe. Definitely not April.

The bride sat on a small mound of snow next to the birdbath fountain that would spit intermittently under warmer conditions. She patted the powdery space beside her.

Marla, confused, still disoriented but not nearly as lightheaded as before, walked over and did as asked. The snow soaked through her pants, icing her bottom. As dreamlike as this sequence felt, the frigid burn was real enough.

"What is this?" Marla breathlessly asked the bride. "How come you're well enough to speak now? Are you not sick?"

Abagail Pelton smiled. "I'm still sick. Very sick."

"How—no, *what*—what is this?" She glanced at the sky and watched flurries descend from the ashen plain. "Where are we?"

"We're at the venue. Don't you recognize it?"

"Don't fuck with me. One second you're at the altar, looking woozy and fucking out of it, on the verge of passing out; the next, you're out here, fine and chipper. One second it's spring, wedding season, and now we're in the middle of a goddamn blizzard."

Abagail offered a squinty smile, one that said, *you're so cute.* "We aren't in a specific place," she said. "Meaning, I can make the world however you want to see it. But I scanned your thoughts, and I believe you prefer winter over warmer weather. You like snow. I don't know why that is." She glanced up as if this were a riddle that required all of her attention. "But it is."

"It's because I used to love snow days," Marla said around the knot in her throat. "No school on snow days. I hated school."

"Ah, yes. That makes sense." Abagail reached for Marla's hand.

Marla dodged her touch.

"Please," the bride said, her eyes soft and inviting. There was no malice behind them, not like there had been moments ago during the ceremony. The gaze that drove Marla out here was full of hate. Full of awful intent. "It is not my intention to hurt you."

"Then what is all of this?" She nodded back at the door, surprised that guests from the ceremony hadn't come out to look for her, wanting to smash her camera, her only defense against their psychotic tendencies, to pieces. "None of this makes any sense."

"It will."

Marla watched as Abagail extended her fingers once again. This time, she didn't retract her hand and allowed the bride to caress her skin. Abagail's fingers ran along Marla's knuckles, over her palm, down her wrist.

"You were chosen, Marla. By my family and me."

"What?"

"You have no family of your own. None that will care about your disappearance, anyway. Not after what you did to them."

"No, that's simply not true. I have a family. And of course they care about me."

"Oh?" Abagail's knowing, condescending smile widened. "Is that right? When's the last time you spoke with them? Any of them?"

(Her brother's face, his scowl, the twitch of his upper lip.)

(Mom, shaking her head in utter disappointment, the flare of her nostrils.)

(Her, running down the aisle, away from all of them, away from the church, down the street, into the distance, never looking back.)

"I..." She failed to produce a response, a *true* response.

"There's no need to lie, Marla. I know as well as you that it's been years since you communicated with them. And who could blame you? I can't. After all, you wasted their money, their time. You didn't just run away from your future but from them. And quite frankly, you embarrassed them."

"It wasn't what I wanted."

"How do you know what you want?" the bride asked with a giggle.

"Because it wasn't."

(Brian's face. His lower jaw dropping as he turned to watch her flee down the aisle.)

"But you were young."

"Exactly," Marla said. "I was young. Too young for...too young to commit."

"You would have been rich," Abagail said, a twinkle shimmering in her eyes despite her gray surroundings. She toyed with the curls in Marla's hair. "You would have had everything," she whispered.

"I know." Tears now. "I didn't love him. I didn't. I tried to, but… but… I just couldn't."

(Brian calling after her. Brian running down the aisle, promising her everything, promising her perfection, a life where dreams and desires fashioned realities.)

"Your family would have been rich too," the bride said, continuing to fill her head with statements she knew were true. "They would have had it all. Brian's family was beyond wealthy. *Beyond.* You have no idea how wealthy they were."

"Oh…I know."

"My family is wealthy. My family is as wealthy as Brian's. My father and his father—they work together."

Marla lifted her gaze to meet the bride's.

"Yes. We were well aware of your…*history*…before we hired you."

Marla nodded, putting the pieces together.

"Do you know what has to happen? Tonight, on the night of nights?"

Marla looked elsewhere, into the white drifts.

"It's Walpurgis Night. Do you know what that means to us?"

Marla shook her head.

"Named after Saint Walpurga, a woman who was very efficient at repelling witchcraft and defeating the dark magic. In Germany, covens would gather in the hills of the Harz Mountains to celebrate the thinning of the barriers between worlds, a holy night when the rising forces of evil were at their pinnacle. Townsfolk would hold feasts and fires, a celebration of their own, which they believed kept them safe and secure, prevented the terrors from the witches' sabbath from spreading down the mountainside and into their homes."

"Nice story. What does it have to do with me?"

"I've lived a long time, Marla. I've seen many sabbaths, many mountains, and participated in many celebrations."

Marla rotated to face her. "What are you…saying?"

"My spirit has been in the Pelton family for a long time. I am one of the originals. I was there for the first sabbath, and I will be there for the last." She squinted, looking down at her body, her hands feeling her chest, her stomach, and her legs as if making sure they were still solid, still there. "This body is failing me. It's the cancer. It's growing too fast, and I won't make it another six months—I won't see All Hallows' Eve, the next opportunity to carry out the ceremony. I need a new body, Marla, and I need one tonight. Specifically, I need yours."

Part of Marla wanted to run, but she couldn't find the strength. The camera was a weight, and she could barely keep her head up. "I…"

"Shhh," the bride said, putting a finger over her lips. "Don't say anything. Don't fight this. Fighting's useless, anyway. That sushi you helped yourself to…it was made with *Atropa belladonna.* So your fight's all but left you. There wasn't enough to knock you out, but enough to make you…*agreeable.*"

"Y-you…b-bitch."

The bride smiled. "I'm sorry, Marla. But you have a healthy body. And I need it. My family needs me. Yours…*doesn't.*"

The door to the venue creaked open, and even though her view was hazy, she could see inside. The dimly lit banquet hall remained as she had left it. She could see the Peltons gathered near the mouth of the venue. She could see the goat, and they had gotten the little beast under control.

"What's with the goat?" Marla asked, the only question left in her fading consciousness.

The bride squeaked with laughter. "Ohhhh… Every family needs a goat. You should know that by now."

(Her mother's scowl, the last words she said echoing across her thoughts, I HATE YOU I HATE I HATE YOU I HATE)

"Hmpf. Goat."

"Come on, Marla. Let's get you on your feet. They're waiting for us."

The bride helped Marla to the door.

Behind her, the wintry weather blew a cold gust across her shoulders, and even in the gray gloom of this false solstice, she felt sunshine blazing from within, a warmth she never knew.

VIRESCENT SKY

A bold green flash of lightning cracked the sky, and the world was never the same.

Some in the kingdom saw the heavens separate, the clouds drifting apart like magnetic opposites, the dark expanse splitting like a loose stitch, and witnessed something plummet from the Great Above, descend into the mountainous terrains of Boulder Ridge, the outskirt lands of the north. No one knew precisely what had fallen, but the olive blur couldn't have been anything short of a miracle, a message from the Almighty Himself. Some in the surrounding villages, like Townsend (the fishing community that lay to the northwesternmost edge of the Kingdom of Garrison), claimed the celestial object was buried in the mountains, that the fantastic emerald glow emanated from somewhere deep within the cliffs.

In response, King Elder Garrison IV, King Gary to most, sent his two sons, two of the kingdom's bravest knights, and one lonely scribe to document their discoveries.

I am that scribe.

This is that story.

The tale of five men who set out to investigate the source of the thing that changed the sky over Garrison forever.

That changed life itself.

1

"I was always father's favorite," John Henry Garrison said proudly from his saddle. His grin ate up most of his face.

"You keep wishing, brother," Bryce replied, calm like always.

"Eldest sons are the best sons. Plus, the throne will be mine once the old man kicks it. That has to account for something."

"Don't let your head swell with such grand delusions. You might float away like a jester's balloon."

John chuckled. So did Bryce. Even the knights, stony statues of men they were, cracked a smile.

"I love you, brother," John said. "Such a wit you are."

Bryce eyed the mountains. They were approaching the base of Boulder Ridge, and Bryce, the expert navigator of our quintet, searched for the cleanest way to the top, where the green light leaked upward and across the cosmos in a shimmering pool. The virescent beam bathed the entire mountainside in the alien glow, painting our flesh and armor with the same hue.

Everything was green.

Green was the color of God, or so the people in the villages now believed. Those who lived inside the castle grounds had different, more sensible opinions. The king was no fool. Any offering that came from The Great Above should be regarded with a cautious eye. After all, harsh storms came from above, sometimes resulting in lasting damages, destruction of property, and untimely deaths. But that was the way of life. Garrison dealt with it. Had always done so.

And they would deal with the mysterious glow now, today. Deal and conquer.

"Think we'll reach the top?" I asked Bryce as the man's eyes traced the route. "When's the last time a man climbed Boulder Ridge?"

"You ask too many questions, scribe."

"'Tis my job, my lord."

"Yes, I know." Bryce nodded at me, shining with confidence. "Aye. We'll make it. Good horses we have. Courageous beauties. Not more than a day, we'll reach the peak."

I wanted to tell him it wasn't the horses I worried about. That it was the men for whom I feared. Nothing felt right about the green flash, the aura that had brought forth peculiar changes to the town and its people. It was a feeling that crawled inside me, bringing me to question everything about the nature of our world and its potential fate. Was this our conclusion? That oft-advertised apocalypse? That prophetic end the men who came before us spoke about, the belief that The Almighty would one day descend from His throne to reap compensation for our sins? It sure felt that way. I was feeling first-hand the influence of these new skies. The unnatural quality regarding our task was starting to affect me in ways I dared not speak of to my company.

But the simple fact was—I started to hear things.

Whispers. Frail voices. Garbled, inarticulate syllables strung together, sounding like they were coming from perdition itself, the chorus of low devils, legions upon endless legions boasting of their future wicked accomplishments, and they sounded very angry with our pursuit of the knowledge these mountains now held.

2

THE WHISPERS FOLLOWED me up the mountain, fading in and out, intensifying depending on how close we were to the source's center. I did not dare speak of them to the others. Bryce and John Henry did all the talking, their conversations enough for ten men, let alone five. Half a day's ride up the rocky path, I started to feel weak. Not from lack of water or nourishment (we had a healthy supply of both), but from the light. Something about the glow got inside my head and cleared my thoughts. Dulled the activity between my ears.

"Are you okay?" Bryce asked me. I hadn't realized I'd drifted off. "Scribe?"

I was about ten gallops from them. The noblemen collected at the top of the path, me below them. I was confused. How long had I drifted? I did not know the answer, nor did I care to know. The possibilities left me with a haunted touch.

"We are almost to the top," John Henry announced. His face suggested he wanted to add, *Don't crack on us now, good boy!*

But he said nothing. Only stared.

I nodded, regaining my footing in the world I had so easily sailed from. An unfamiliar scent found my nose, and I caught myself wincing. "What is that odd smell?" I asked no one in particular.

"We don't know," Bryce said. "But we think it's coming from the source."

The source. That terrible lime color.

My doubts doubled.

"Shall we press on?" John Henry asked.

The group waited for me to answer. I wrestled with my conscience. Part of me wanted to turn my horse around, ride back to the king, and tell him that this was it, this was the end, make peace with your maker because oblivion was coming down around us all. Another part of me was curious to discover what secrets the voices kept, what green treasures awaited us atop the mountain. Riches beyond our wildest dreams? I hardly believed that. These were riches of a different kind, and we were not the beneficiaries.

"Yes, let's go," I said, though I believed those incoherent whispers were telling me to do quite the opposite—that they implored me to return to Garrison's castle, a ride back without setting eyes on the source of that heinous hue.

3

WHEN WE REACHED THE TOP, the horses were tired. We gave them drink while wetting our own tongues. The men were drained, too, and I was beyond exhausted. But we all wore the best masks we could. Men in our position were not permitted to show wear or sluggishness; we were heroes, mind you, protectors of the King's realm, and the King's realm had no room for false paragons. Somewhat of a celebrity myself, I couldn't risk my public image altered in any fashion should one of the men speak off-handedly of our adventure. An easily exhausted, unfit-for-duty scribe might get forgotten come the next quest, perhaps all future expeditions. And I couldn't risk that. My position in society granted me certain privileges, certain pleasures—wealth, fame, women. Things not easily obtained otherwise by a man of my undesirable looks and frail build. So I wore a tough mask, a shroud over my concern, and hoped the men would forget about that little incident on the mountain, my temporary spell of thoughtlessness. I dared not mention the increasing frequency of the dead whispers. Dared not mention them at all.

"It looks like it's coming from in there," John Henry said, nodding to a cavern's entrance ahead. The green light burned strongest there. It was hard to stare at it directly, but as we trespassed the opening and journeyed several steps inside, our eyes quickly adjusted.

We followed the tunnel to the source. The cavern eventually opened to a sprawling chamber bathed in the emerald glow of the earthbound object. At first, we stood before its magnificent existence for several minutes, memorized by its strange allure. In the center of the chamber, an egg about the size of a newborn foal rested, half-embedded in the cavern's soft rock. I glanced up at the vaulted ceiling, spotting the sizable hole where the egg had punctured through, where the light escaped and spilled across the sky, tainting our lands with that unearthly shine. The light flowed like a river, strange currents coursing from the source, spreading across the grand expanse above, a lid over our world.

"Good Lord," said John Henry, his eyes swimming in the light. "It's incredible."

"Yes," Bryce agreed. "But what is it?"

"Are you blind, brother? It's...it's an egg."

"I see it's an egg. But what *is* it? What's its nature? Where did it come from? And furthermore...what sleeps inside?"

Lord Bryce's last question iced my blood. An unsettling chill dashed across my shoulders and down my back. Teeth chattering, I tried to open my mouth, a failed attempt to beg our crew to abscond from the cave. Flee for our lives. Because whatever this was surely meant us harm. Whatever was in that egg, it would destroy us. The Kingdom of Garrison included. I was sure of it.

Still, the light held our intrigue. And the whispers *had* eased off. I was beginning to feel welcome here in the presence of the egg.

"We should move it," John Henry announced. "Bring it back to father. He'll want a look-see."

"I do not think that is the best idea, brother," Bryce said, moving away from our pack. He circled the landing site, inspecting the fallen treasure through narrowed eyes. "It might be evil."

"It doesn't feel evil."

I knew what John Henry meant. The longer we spent inside the chamber, the less the egg felt sinister. In the direct presence of the glow, my nerves were somewhat at peace. I wondered why that was. Surely, there was a good reason for it. I had felt on edge the entire journey, all the way up the mountain. Spells of panic had accompanied my every moment, but here, in the midst of this healthy, vibrant green, I was relieved from the stress.

Still, I had my doubts. It felt like a trap.

"Should we crack it open?" John Henry asked, stepping toward it, withdrawing his sword from the scabbard at his hip. "Maybe we should see what's inside? There could be presents in store for us. A gift from the Almighty Himself!" John Henry's brow curled like a snake tail, his lips following the same serpentine formation. "At the very least, we might be able to cook the world's biggest—and most delicious—omelet."

"Jest all you want, brother," Bryce said, approaching the egg with caution, "but I believe that would be a very unwise decision. I don't understand much of this strangeness, but I would speculate this egg contains nothing you'd want to throw down your gullet."

"Won't know unless we try," John Henry grumbled, still grinning. "The wife was stingy on the eggs and bacon this morning. My belly grumbles for a taste of this sky egg."

"I think we should leave it be." Bryce's hand hovered over the object. I saw the tremble in his fingers, the hesitancy of getting too close. I couldn't tell if the shell repelled his touch or if he was too frightened to set his flesh upon its surface. "I can almost feel something inside. Growing."

John Henry stepped to the egg, lifting his weapon. "I think we should end it. Right here and now. Not give it a chance to breathe, whatever's inside. That may be father's wish, after all. And I'm starting to feel differently toward it. Something about its presence sours my gut. I don't like the strangeness of it. What say you, brother?"

"No," Bryce said, putting out his hand as if that would stop the strike of John's sword. "There's something beautiful inside. Something...*pure.*"

"You're giving me the freaks, brother. A second ago, you thought this thing was evil."

"Never said it *was* evil. Said it *might be.* I can't explain it, but…I think whatever's inside means us no harm. Yes, I'm sure of it now."

Something changed in Lord Bryce's eyes at that moment. What exactly, I cannot describe with a stroke of my pen. He was just…*different.*

Altered.

John Henry communicated his disapproval with a wheezy sigh. "Father does not trust anything that comes from The Great Above. You know that. We should proceed with caution. Things are not always what they first seem. It's that way with people. And that's certainly true of things sent from the gods."

"No…"

I watched Bryce grow enamored with the egg. His fingers fell toward the surface of the leathery shell, threatening the object with his gentle touch. There was reluctance in Lord Bryce's movements as if, deep inside, he knew the idea was rotten. But still, he was going for it. I waited with bated breath to see if the egg would receive such human interaction.

"I'd think twice if I were you, brother," John Henry warned, but the advice went in one ear and out the other, and Bryce didn't so much as acknowledge it.

"It'll be okay," he replied, not really to John Henry. Not really to anyone. Maybe to himself. It was as if he were trying to convince the room, himself, the whole kingdom waiting back home, that this was the correct course of action—let the thing from the sky exist. Let it glow. Let it shine across the lands. Let it shine across us all.

I couldn't voice my apprehensions. Instead, I watched and scribbled down what I saw.

I blinked, and Bryce's hand was upon the egg, running his fingertips across the surface, petting the shell like a reliable mare. His eyes smiled.

And that was when the glow grew brighter, the cavern bellowed, and the entire world came undone.

4

BRYCE BACKED away when the sound erupted from some unknown source, sounding like an entire bog's worth of bullfrogs joining a hellish choir. The light intensified, nearly blinding us. I shielded my eyes from the emerald wash, hoping the terrible moment would soon end, hoping Bryce's curious fingers did not damn the entire kingdom for all eternity.

After the surge, the chamber returned to its original form, the glow present but tolerable. My head ached behind the eyes, but nothing unbearable.

Bryce uncovered his eyes, his stare immediately returning to the egg. "What the hell was that?"

"You pissed it off," John Henry said. "Don't do it again."

"I don't plan on it."

"Maybe we should leave it be," I suggested, ignoring my place. A scribe was hardly in the position to advise princes. In some corners of the world, this could earn the owner of the loose tongue a beheading. Luckily, Garrison was not one of those corners. "Maybe we should not disturb...*whatever* it is."

Both brothers looked at me as if my proposal were daft. It was probably best to keep my mouth shut, to keep the thoughts galloping across my brain inside, but I was on a roll. There was no stopping me.

"This thing..." I swallowed heavy air. "It's not...*right*. You see that, don't you? You see the green light that...that doesn't come from anywhere. I mean, do either of you see its source?"

The brothers examined the egg, as did the knights, and no one could come up with a proper answer. No, the light came from somewhere, but where, not an eye in the room could determine.

Invisible marionettes danced upon my shoulders, the *tap-tap* of their invisible feet shredding every active nerve.

"We should seal this place up," I continued. "Leave. Head back to your father's castle and report what we've seen. Tell him the thing that landed here is evil, something that should not be poked, prodded, studied, or attempted to be understood. We should leave, of that I am certain."

The brothers exchanged looks.

"Father entrusted us with the quest of taking care of the problem," Bryce said, stating the obvious but also seeming to remind himself of his current chore. "To return with no solution would make us look foolish, not only before the eye of our father but that of our kingdom."

"I agree, brother. Maybe not on much, but of that—aye."

"What would be foolish," I started, immediately regretting my audacity, "is to attempt to understand something that came from The Great Above. To assume that you can 'take care of it.' As if it's a thing so easily disposed."

Bryce pointed to the thing. "It's just an egg, scribe. A rather large egg, but an egg nonetheless."

"I still like the idea of an omelet," said John Henry, a grin appearing in the depths of his bushy beard. "An egg that size could feed the five of us. Even this big belly." He grabbed the pudge beneath his chainmail armor. "So full of tasty ales and Chef Calico's meals it is. Had I known it 'twas an egg we would discover here, I'd have brought the salt and pepper!"

Bryce ignored his brother's jest. He studied the egg once more, looking upon its surface, examining every inch. I waited for something bad to happen. It was only a matter of time. Since voicing my concerns, the whispers returned. Quieter than earlier but present. Like the friction of dead leaves farther on down the path. No articulation. Just noise that further fueled my dread.

"There's a crack," Bryce said after several moments.

John Henry went over for a better look. I did the same, though I kept my distance.

Sure enough, the egg had split. A syrupy substance the color of fresh sage leaked from the fissure.

Bryce leaned forward for closer inspection.

I opened my mouth to warn him but never released so much as a syllable.

The egg moved. It rocked back and forth at first, slowly, as if whatever was inside was just awakening. Then, it shook with force, the thing inside evidently seeking a rushed exit.

The knights jumped in front of Lord Bryce, unsheathing their swords and raising them for battle. Crouching, they waited for the birth of the unknown enemy.

Then it stopped. The egg lay still as if the thing inside had given up or returned to its slumber. Maybe it had died.

No. Though I wished for it, I did not believe those scenarios to be true. I believed the thing inside was playing dead, faking its demise, hoping for us to lower our guard.

And it worked.

The knights straightened their posture, slipping their weapons back into their scabbards.

"No…" I heard myself say. "Wait."

But as soon as the words left my mouth, it happened. The egg's shell divided into four separate pieces and split like the first bread of a fine feast. Green slop spewed forth, splashing the knights and Lord Bryce. One of the knights took some of the gunk to his face, and he began screaming as he attempted to scrub the stuff from his skin with his bare hands. It did nothing, and a fine smoke rose from the affected area. Even though the man was several paces away, I could see the damage the embryonic substance was inflicting.

It melted his skin and the muscle beneath. His flesh turned to soup, a scalding broth, and the more he tried to rid himself of the gross matter, the more he damaged his appearance, wiping away layers of his identity and reducing his image to leaky pus and skeletal offerings. It wasn't long before the man fell to the ground and began writhing on the cave's pitted surface. Then he stopped moving and lay dead.

Lord Bryce and the other nameless knight shed their armor with great haste as the acidic afterbirth began to burn away their outer layers. The material held on longer than the man's flesh had, but the chemical reaction would eventually have the same effect.

Once the men were safe, they reacted accordingly, meeting the fractured egg with a wave of their swords.

From the ruins of the egg, a snaking vine, thick as nautical rope, unfurled from the steamy pit of post-birth. Its head was a single eyeball, about the size of an ogre's fist. For several breaths, we watched the alien thing, unable to make the first move toward ridding our domain of it. The thing was an odd sight to behold, a terrible image we'd likely revisit with crystal clarity until the end of our lives, a ghastly gift sent from The Great Above.

What was it we were looking at? Some sort of…god?

The thing had no mouth to speak, so when John Henry asked a simple question—"What are you?"—the Eye gave no reply.

"What do you want?" Bryce followed, though talking was pointless.

The thing would not answer.

Only it did. To me. Silently. In the form of infinite mouths voicing their secrets.

"Do you hear that?" I asked, my pen trembling against my tablet. I hadn't realized my pen had run dry, and the tip of my utensil was scratching, tearing the surface of my paper. "Do you hear them whispering?"

Bryce and John Henry looked at me as if I'd grown several new heads.

"I hear them whispering," I admitted, "yet I know not what they say."

"Scribe," Bryce said. "Maybe you should try whispering back."

I closed my eyes, but it was of no use. I tried to communicate with the voices, asking them to quiet, to let only one speaker hold court at a time, but the effort was wasted. These speakers were designed to whisper, not to listen to the pleas of a celebrity scribe.

I shook my head.

"Damn the Above!" John Henry said, staring at the Eye. "I say we kill it then."

"Kill it?" Bryce said. "This is…this is a magnificent discovery, brother. Surely, Father will want to see it."

"Are you daft, boy? The thing is a murderous beast! It killed Wallace. Tore the flesh off his poor face. Look at him. There's hardly anything left to burn and kick out to sea!"

It was true. Wallace, the loyal knight, was now a melted skeleton from the neck up. Even the bones had begun to disintegrate.

"But, John," Bryce pleaded. "It's…it's a brilliant discovery. This will change the Kingdom. The entire realm!"

John Henry pointed his sword at his brother. "Brother, no. You are not thinking clearly. This thing is obviously a threat to our existence. It's come from the sky, true, but godly it is not. You can see that, can't you?"

For a moment, Bryce looked at the wandering Eye as it stretched around the immediate area. I couldn't see if the vine-like body had anything hiding beneath the rising smoke near its base, but the Eye appeared rooted in the ground like the stem of a flower.

"We will not harm it," Bryce announced. "It hasn't harmed us. What happened to Wallace was accidental."

"Pig shite!" John Henry said, and he moved toward the Eye with a determined step. Before he could get an inch farther, the Eye whipped around and turned its gaze on the sword-wielding prince, stopping John Henry like he'd hit an unseen wall.

The Eye was upon him. Blinking, the nightmarish observer scanned the being before it, taking its time to educate itself on human anatomy. Once the scan was complete, the vine lengthened, growing stiff.

"Nope," John Henry said, "don't like it." He swung his blade at the Eye's body, intending to sever the alien creature right where it sprouted. But his sword met another.

John Henry glanced up and found his brother's eyes. "Out of my way, fool."

Bryce shook his head. I could see something changing in his eyes, and that something was *green*. They glowed with that hideous color.

"I'm warning you, brother." John Henry grimaced. "Your sword is no match for mine."

"We shall see," Bryce said in a voice unlike his own. He freed his sword and swung for his brother's head, a heavy stroke as awkward as it was inaccurate.

John Henry ducked, the blade missing him by at least two heads.

"You trying to kill me, brother?" John Henry asked, crouching in a defensive pose. "Your own flesh and blood? Over this silly plant?"

Bryce glared at him with unbridled hatred. Personally, I had never seen a man look so hateful. His penetrating stare was that of fairy-tale villains, the evil-doers with no qualms about laying waste to an innocent village at the snap of two fingers. Lord Bryce Garrison was not the same man who had entered this chamber. He was changed. His head had been lost amongst the green shine of the place.

Bryce heaved his sword again, a lackluster attempt at removing his brother's head. John Henry backed away, grinning.

"This is not you, brother. You have become something else. *Someone else.*"

"*Shut up,*" Bryce growled, aiming his sword at John Henry's legs.

John Henry skipped over the swipe and then planted his foot on his brother's chest, kicking him backward.

The other knight, whose name I would never know, approached Bryce from behind, his sword down but arms out, looking like he wanted to bear hug the man. I opened my mouth to warn him, but it was too late. Bryce had heard (or sensed) him and spun, swinging with every ounce of muscle his body contained.

The motion looked effortless. The knight's head came clean off, and there was hardly any blood. At first, that is. There was a delay, a moment of stillness. Soon, my brain caught up to what my eyes had witnessed. I began to breathe again. Then, after the knight's head hit the cavern floor and rolled off into the shadows, the gaping hole between his shoulders squirted dark liquid like the exotic geysers in the lands west of the Maroni Desert. The headless body collapsed on the rocky terrain like a horse whose heart seized mid-gallop. The blood continued to stream from the smooth cut, spilling a puddle beneath the fallen knight.

"Lord in Heaven," John Henry said. And although he hid it well, I could tell the big man was frightened. Terrified that his brother was lost to this virescent influence. "Brother, what has become of you?"

"I can hear them," Bryce said, grinning, his head perceptibly unbalanced. "The whispering." His crooked lips faced me. "You hear them, scribe? Can you hear their beautiful hymns? Collective ballads from The Great Above?"

"You've lost what's inside your skull, brother," John Henry said, and then he poked at his brother's sword, attempting to disarm him while his gaze was elsewhere.

Lightning quick, Bryce parried the assault and ran his blade through his brother's midsection. The sword's tip pushed through him, skewering the big man's bowels, and came out the other side, bloody as a newborn babe.

John Henry choked on his surprise.

"Sleep now, brother. Your wounds will heal in The Great Above, that green abyss where all dead souls wander."

But John Henry didn't die. Not yet. Before he drifted off to whatever afterlife awaited him (maybe, indeed, the hell Lord Bryce had mentioned), he revealed a stunted knife and dragged its sharpest edge across Bryce's throat. Shades of cranberry poured like wine from a tipped goblet. John Henry's beard caught most of his brother's blood. As Bryce opened his mouth to scream, the cavern filled with primordial sounds, a collection of screams and whispers. Shadows scaled the walls, darkening the green glow of things. The Eye watched on, and although the cyclopean organism had no mouth with which to speak, no means of discernible expression, I could tell it was satisfied with the spilled blood, the ghastly murders that had resulted from its influence.

The two noblemen fell to the ground, the king's lineage severed in a single dark moment. The cavern's corrugated bottom channeled the royal blood, gravity spreading little rivers of red like webs of varicose veins.

The Eye turned to me, and I to it. There was a sudden connection, the creature working some hypnotic effect on my thoughts and actions. I tried to look away, *wanted* to avert my eyes from whatever terrible knowledge this organic oculus desired to bestow upon me— but there was no escape from its all-seeing eye. Universes unfolded before me, the infinite wisdom of the cosmos, the Great Above explained, eons and epochs of inconsequential information passing between my ears. It was too much. My head felt like it might explode, overloaded with every tiny detail of our long-spanning history, our endless future.

The Eye burned images into my brain, filling me with unearthly comprehension. I saw as The Eye saw, as Bryce had seen until his brother opened his throat.

And that vision will be shared.

Will be recorded.

Because I am a scribe and, therefore, that is what I must do.

As I exited the cavern, I glanced up at the shredded clouds tumbling across those virescent skies and over the hell-bound kingdom that would soon see what I saw—the glory of an untethered and ancient beyond that shall run the length of the lands, *all* lands, from here to eternity.

GRAYSON HOOK'S VAMPIRE MURDER MYSTERY DINNER

1.

"This is totally normal," he said, ringing the doorbell for the third time, only about fifteen seconds after the last one. "We couldn't—like—go to the movies or something? Like a normal couple? You had to sign us up for this?"

Marcia Wong eyed her fiancé as he impatiently jammed the bell's button a *fourth* time. This was going swimmingly well so far. And the drinking hadn't even started yet. "Hon, maybe relax? Ringing the doorbell a hundred times won't make them answer any quicker."

Chazz sneered. "I'm missing Thursday Night Football for this. Just so you know. Pats-Bills. Huge playoff implications."

"I'm sure you can watch the highlights when you get home. Or…" Marcia said, rolling her eyes, using the voice she reserved for lighting a match under his skin, "if you remembered to set the DVR like I told you, you could even watch the whole game."

His eyes turned to her and lingered. He projected that look. Yes, *that one*, the one that let her know this was going to be a night all right, the kind that would most likely lead to an old-fashioned shouting match on the drive home. And, if they were really lucky, they'd get to sleep separately tonight—her in the bedroom, he on the couch, and so it would go. She had half a mind to call the evening quits right then and there, but…

It was Katie's birthday. Katie was Marcia's best friend. And if she backed out now, headed back across that glorious Italian patio walkway that led to the car, Katie would never forgive her. Never. Never let it go. She'd likely bring it up on Marcia's wedding day, an event scheduled for next April unless something happened between now and then, something like one too many of the nights for which they were currently destined.

"This is bullshit," Chazz reminded her.

"It's Katie's birthday. Can you please act…I dunno…not like yourself tonight? Like, be normal? For one night?"

"Not like myself? What's that supposed to mean? Who the fuck else am I supposed to act like?"

She didn't want to answer that. Not now. "Just…please? You're cranked up to an eleven right now. Dial it back to a two."

"Pssh. I'll dial *you* back," he said jokingly, though she hardly found the childish comment anything but irritating. The look she shot him must have worked. His aggravation melted some, revealing some of the old Chazz she knew, the one who had stolen her heart and led them sprinting down this runway of love. "Sorry, babe," he said, dropping his aggressive tone and scratching the back of his neck. "Just…the game. And I'm antsy. You know how I do in social situations."

He was usually fine in social situations, the life of the party, unless the social situation was somewhere he didn't wish to be.

"Do you have any Xanax?" he asked.

"In the car. Maybe? I'm not sure now that you mentioned it."

"Shit. Should have grabbed some before we left." Chazz knuckled the doorbell one more time. "What. THE FUCK. Is taking so goddamn long to answer the fucking door?"

"It's a big house, babe," she said as if that might soothe him.

It was indeed a big house. A mansion—specifically—overlooking the bay but positioned far enough from the other mansions on Bay Loft Road's long, windy street to give off a hint of seclusion. The night was perfect for a murder mystery dinner—the sky provided an excellent dark backdrop. White caps crashed against the bluff's craggy bottoms. The delicate hissing of foamy water busting apart joined the chorus of nightly crickets. Above, the pale, luminous glow of the moon brightened the grounds, and, combined with the house's surplus of exterior landscape lighting, the shadows had no chance of overtaking the property on this whimsical twilight.

Chazz looked about ready to rip out some hair follicles, helping what his family genes had already started, when the door to the mansion swung open before him. The act allowed a considerable flow of golden, heavenly light to pour out onto the stoop. Facing them stood a man dressed in a black suit, a cardinal-red vest resting beneath the velvety material. The bespectacled man's face was long and gaunt, giving off a Jared-Leto-hundred-pounds-soaking-wet vibe. Or better yet—his appearance reminded Marica of Gary Oldman as Prince Vlad in Coppola's gothic masterpiece, top hat and all, which she guessed was the look he was striving for all along. He was older than them by about ten, fifteen years at the most.

"Welcome!" he said, channeling that Prince Vlad swagger, enunciating *Welcome!* as *Velcome!*

Chazz almost laughed. She saw the way his throat bobbed when the man appeared. He was undoubtedly trying to swallow some smart-ass comment while concealing a smile that held back a mob of childish giggles. Marcia refrained from punching his arm and telling him to knock it off.

"Hi," Marcia responded to the character in the doorway. "We're here for—"

"Grayson Hook's Vampire Murder Mystery Dinner," he finished for her, keeping up with the theatrics and suspending his forefinger in the air like this announcement was of great importance.

Marcia eyed her fiancé. She could see he was already scheming ways to trick the actor into breaking character, planning cracks only he thought were funny, hammering the poor fellow with annoying jokes until he was crying uncle and begging Chazz to leave the party.

She hoped to God he'd listen to her tonight, *actually* listen to her, and not be an asshole.

"Yes," she replied courteously. "Are you…Grayson Hook?"

The man flashed his teeth, revealing two extended canines. They were obviously fakes, good ones at that, not the cheap plastic inserts you'd find at the dollar store come Halloween time. They were the professional movie prop kind, the type that required a mold of your mouth to be properly fashioned.

"That is me, yes," he said, although "Yes" was pronounced "*Vyes,*" and it seemed like he was just putting Vs in front of random words instead of trying to nail the accent. But whatever—this was a relatively cheap date night compared to other murder mystery dinner theaters, so she couldn't really complain about the performances.

"Excellent."

"Please! Come in!" Grayson stepped back, ushering them in with a gentlemanly wave of his arm and a courteous bow.

The couple did as their vampiric host asked and entered the mansion.

2.

THEY FOLLOWED Hook through the long candlelit corridors lavishly decorated with paintings of nameless folks dressed in royal attire. During their stroll, their host was silent, lending an eerie vibe to the evening. Quiet was spooky, at least in Marcia's eyes. As she passed the paintings, those faces—hugely sinister, made even more so by the creeping shadows—leered at her as though her human form was disgusting, inferior to their vampiric nature. Each face displayed fangs sharp enough to tear through the toughest human tissue. She shuddered.

Never much of a horror fan—she appreciated some arthouse pictures and classics like *Jaws* and the aforementioned *Dracula*—she wondered if they would've been better off hitting a traditional murder mystery, the kind that *always* involves the mafia and a family celebration of sorts (a wedding, weddings are always involved) instead of this spooky adventure. Halloween had never been her favorite holiday, consistently placed behind Christmas and Thanksgiving in her top three. Hell, New Year's and St. Paddy's might have ranked higher had she given the list slightly more consideration.

The spooky stuff she could do without. Then again, tonight wasn't about her.

Once the hallway trek ended, she found herself in a long, rectangular dining room, a gorgeous feast placed on the table before her. A massive turkey, glistening with a thin layer of sweaty grease, sat at the center of the table. Dishes of meadow-green vegetables, buttery mashed potatoes, and steamy piles of stuffing were arranged down the line. Cups of creamy mushroom—she could smell it—were stationed at every place setting. A penguin-suited, white-gloved butler delivered hors d'oeuvres to each of the seated guests, bacon-wrapped scallops from the look of it.

After her eyes ran over the feast, Marcia spotted her very best friend in the entire world.

"Marcia!" Katie shouted, jumping from her seat the second she noticed she'd entered the room. She ran over and practically squeezed the life out of her, laying a hug on her that pushed all the air out of her lungs. "You made it!"

"Sorry we're late, hon," Marcia said, kissing her on the cheek. She could practically hear what Chazz was thinking behind her, all the jokes he was silently making, all the little jabs about their friendship, how he jokingly suspected they were lesbians or something.

After their embrace ended, Katie turned to Chazz. She raised her hand and gave her best friend's fiancé a cordial high-five. Chazz took the opportunity to slap her palm a bit on the hard side, letting that flesh-on-flesh slap really pop. Katie reacted like it was just another friendly exchange, treating the contact with a smile and bubbly laughter, but Marcia knew better.

There was a cruel undertone to that hard high-five. And it meant one thing: Chazz was jealous.

"Good to see you, buddy," Katie told him.

He took a beat to stare at her, and there was something menacing in those eyes that Marcia hated. It was quick, like a camera flash, and she was sure no one else noticed. Still, she'd let it go, as she did with most things when it came to Chazz and his sometimes inappropriate behavior.

"You as well," he replied with a cheesy grin. "Happy Birthday."

Katie thanked him, then spun back to the long dinner table, introducing her guest with both hands as if she planned on lifting the man from his seat. The guy wearing small reading glasses, whose name was Hugh or Howard or something with an H, stood and extended his hand for a manly shake, directing it at Chazz first and foremost.

"This is Hugo," Katie said. Chazz had never met him before, but Marcia had been introduced once at a work thing. "Hugo, this is Chazz."

Hugo and Chazz shook. Once moderately acquainted, Hugo rotated toward Marcia. "Good to see you again."

"Likewise," she replied.

The foursome placed their attention back on the table. For the first time, Marcia noticed they were not the only guests at Grayson Hook's dinner party. Another couple was seated at the table. They were in plain clothes—the man wearing jeans and a Nirvana T-shirt, and the woman black jeans and a gray T-shirt with the word *Invincible* printed in lovely cursive, something cute she probably spent thirty dollars on at the Paramus Mall. They were about the most normal couple she'd ever seen, but Marcia wondered if they were part of the show or just participants. Then she decided part of the fun was *not* knowing their status, just allowing the story to take her wherever.

"Please be seated," Grayson said, showing them to their seats.

Chazz sat and grabbed a biscuit from the woven basket in front of him. He dug in without waiting for permission to start...if any was required. There didn't seem to be, and since Chazz had dug in, so did the other couple, reaching for biscuits and helping themselves to the gravy and mashed potatoes.

"Please," Grayson said, his awkward Transylvanian accent thickening, "enjoy the human feast we've prepared for you. You'll want to save some room for dessert—it's...to *die* for." The vampire host laughed in that villainous *muhaha* tone that had Chazz obnoxiously guffawing. The other couple rolled their eyes, none-to-impressed with the corniness of it all. They whispered to each other, their eyes shifting from the host to their food, back to their host again. Like they were discussing the performance, grading it. Maybe they worked for a local rag and planned on writing a review. Food critics or something. Then again, maybe they were in cahoots with the acting company, actors disguised as guests.

While Grayson left them to eat in quiet, Katie turned to Marcia, touching her wrist and saying, "Oh my God, how's the wedding planning going?"

Marcia took a bite of the creamy mashed potatoes. "Oh, you know. It's a lot of work. We have the cake tasting next week."

"Really? Exciting!"

"Yeah. Hey, you should come."

"Me?"

"I mean…you're the maid of honor. And you love cake, so…"

"Well, I do love cake." She leaned forward, peeking over at Chazz, who was three biscuits deep and piling up a fat stack of sliced turkey breast onto his plate. "Hey, fiancé?"

"Mmm?" He stopped midchew and looked at her, arching his eyebrows as if waiting to hear about something he'd done wrong.

"You care if I crash the cake tasting?"

His eyes slimmed as he fixed his gaze on her. The thing with Chazz was you never knew what he would say next, and right now, Marcia felt that times a thousand. "I don't give a shit," he said, then popped a slab of juicy turkey meat into his mouth.

That was the best response Marcia could have hoped for. "Good," she said. "It's settled."

"Awesome. A threesome," Chazz added.

Marcia clicked her tongue, warning him. He shot back with a playboy smirk, the *aw-shucks* kind she couldn't convince herself she didn't love.

After they stuffed their bellies, Grayson Hook moseyed back into the room. He wore a cape now. With each step, the thin material rippled like hung laundry on a breezy afternoon. Wasting no time, he strode over to the table, put both hands on the empty seat at the head, leaned over, and said with almost no breath in his lungs, "There has been a *murder*."

3.

THE GROUP of seven paraded through the halls as one unit until they reached the end, where Grayson invited them inside a giant, open ballroom with thirty-foot ceilings, four massive columns holding everything up, the ornate kind with scribed flowery designs residing throughout their circular lengths. The east wall was made entirely of windows, granting a grand view across the moon-slicked bay and the other mansion resting on the cliffs along the waterfront. Marcia was almost drawn to the picturesque nightscape the same way a moth pulls toward blinding lights.

In the distance, lightning flashed behind dark clouds. The sky growled shortly after.

"Murder," Grayson said, shutting the double doors behind them. "Someone in this house has murdered a member of our coven."

Marcia turned around, spotting three new faces in the room. Pale faces. *Vampires.* Two men, one woman. They wore similar attire to Grayson—Victorian outfits that looked very expensive to her untrained eye but were likely cheap costumes purchased secondhand. The woman wore a corset with a poufy dress that gave her the shape of a bell, the botanical green really sticking out, so much so that Marcia was surprised it wasn't the first thing she noticed instead of the gorgeous view. The men wore suit vests, one cow-brown, the other gunmetal gray.

"We are very disturbed by the events of this evening," Grayson continued, his tone darkening as he recited his lines. Marcia was impressed by the showmanship—he delivered the dialogue quite well. Very convincing. "One of us is a murderer. We've invited you six detectives," he pointed to his guests, the participants, "to help us solve the case and bring the offender to justice. You will each be given a clue. You can interview the four of us, ask as many questions as you want about the chain of events leading up to our grandmaster's murder."

"Grandmaster?" asked the dude with the Nirvana T-shirt. "What's a grandmaster?"

At this, Grayson grinned, showing off the pointed tips of those neck-puncturing fangs. "Why, he's our leader. For the last thousand years, the grandmaster, Elvis Tuna—"

"Elvis Tuna?" Chazz blurted out, a harsh, throaty laugh following his initial disruption. "What the hell kind of name is that?"

Grayson shot Chazz a glance that put Marcia's blood on ice. "Please, sir. Do not poke fun. We are in a serious situation here, and if we don't rush to solve the mystery quickly, someone else might also meet their end tonight."

Chazz apologized by covering his mouth with his hand and nodding. He gave his head a quick shake as if that would dry up the laughter. Marcia elbowed him in the ribs, but the pain—if he felt any —didn't seem to register.

"Vivian," Grayson said, turning to the woman in the green dress. "Please hand out the clues to our detectives."

Deliberately taking her sweet time and slowly skipping toward her marks, Vivian approached each one of the guests and handed them an index card. Marcia read hers: *Vivian Redblood likes to drink bad blood.*"

Vivian's eyes glowed at Marcia when Marcia peeked up from the card.

Not understanding, Marcia asked, "What's 'bad blood?' "

"Blood that's not pure," Vivian shot back, using that same faux accent the actor who played Grayson employed.

"Which means?"

"It is the blood of our kin," she said, her smile lasting a beat before she walked away and skipped toward the others, continuing her mission of distributing the clues.

Blood of our kin, Marcia thought, thinking it was too obvious. That their leader had been slain, and this uppity broad enjoyed the forbidden taste of vampire blood. She immediately thought *red herring* because there always was one, wasn't there? And in murder mysteries, there were often more than one—the entire bunch might be red herrings, and more characters might reveal themselves throughout the night.

She'd keep the information handy, though.

Chazz checked his card.

"What does yours say?" Marcia asked him, leaning over.

He moved, blocking her view.

"Hey?" she said, surprised. "We're supposed to be working together. Right?" She looked to Grayson, who clearly heard her but just grinned in response as if to say, *Maybe? Maybe not?*

Chazz shrugged, then must have realized he didn't care very much about the game, didn't give a shit about anything having to do with these neck-biting assholes, and wanted this over and done with ASAP, so why not share the clue? Sharing and teamwork would get him out of there faster and home in time to catch the fourth quarter.

He handed her the card. *Grayson Hook is a liar.*

Interesting. She didn't know what that meant...other than the obvious. Anything that came out of Grayson's mouth was to be considered suspect.

Marcia turned to Katie and Hugo. The four of them traded cards. Katie's read, *Jono Manx is in love with Vivian Redblood.* Hugo's stated, *Elvis Tuna was in love with a human.*

The facts were gathered, though she didn't know who Jono Manx was. She inferred that he was one of the two new vampires who'd entered the room so sneakily. They were huddled in the corner, speaking to each other in low voices so as not to be heard. Occasionally, one looked over at the humans in the room, the chap in the cow-brown coat. His day-old scruff paired well with his blue, almost iridescent eyes. When his eyes caught hers, she felt something electric mingle with her nerves, setting her on edge. As though his eyes were see-through, and the stuff she could see in them was bad. Corrupt. Sick with rot.

She decided she didn't want to stare at them anymore.

"Hello, Earth to Marcia," Katie said, snapping her fingers before her eyes. "You still with us, babe?"

Marcia blinked. Her fiancé, her best friend, and her best friend's new flame were all staring, their eyes eager for the thoughts in her head, thoughts she would not share. "I'm fine," she said, finally. And that seemed good enough, at least for the moment.

She turned her gaze on the other two members of the dinner party, the grungeheads who looked like they just walked off the music video set for "Smells Like Teen Spirit."

"Hey," she said to them, calling their attention. They glanced up from the small, rounded tabletop scattered with pamphlets. Marcia could see the titles of the pamphlets were cute little phrases like *How To Become a Vampire in 2020* and *Are You Getting Enough Fiber in Your Blood Diet?* "What do your clues say?" she asked them. "Wanna share?"

The two exchanged glances, then shrugged. "Sure," the man said, bending the card between his palms.

"Didn't catch your names," Hugo said, working his lips into an amiable smile.

"Oh," the woman said in an accent that was slightly British, or so Marcia thought (she was terrible at placing accents), "I think that's because we didn't throw them." The woman smiled back. "I'm Brittany."

"I'm Foster," the man said. "Pleasure to meet you."

The foursome introduced themselves. After shaking hands and committing names to memory, the group exchanged the available information.

One card read, *Peter Peppermore had a romantic relationship with Elvis Tuna.* Peter Peppermore, Marcia assumed, was the gent in the gunmetal-gray coat.

The other read, *Vivian Redblood hates Peter Peppermore.*

Now that they had all the information they would need for the time being, Grayson clapped his hands together, seeking their undivided attention. "Detectives," he said knowingly, clearly enjoying the performance he was putting on, soaking in every moment, every detail, "you have thirty minutes in this room before we move to the next. Your ultimate mission is to determine who murdered our grandmaster, Elvis Tuna, and correctly identify the killer's motive. Does anyone have any questions before we begin?"

A moment of silence. Then Foster raised his right hand and asked, "Who wrote this story? That's what I want to know."

Chazz chuckled, enjoying the small dose of reality in this fantasy setting the theater company had provided.

Grayson's eyes slimmed as if he wasn't sure he enjoyed that particular question, like he knew Foster was trying to get him to break character by giving credit to the authors of this yarn. "Whatever do you mean?"

Foster slapped the air. "Never mind, sir. Carry on."

"Thank you." Grayson's fingers danced together like he was scheming up something grand. "Unlike other mystery dinners or escape rooms that forbid you to go here or touch that, everything in this mansion is in play and can be trespassed or handled."

Chazz tickled Marcia's neck, whispering, "Oooooh, spooky." She shrugged him off.

"Good luck. Your thirty minutes in this room begins…" Grayson tapped a button on his watch. *"Now."*

4.

SHE'D BINGED ENOUGH *LAW & Order* and *Criminal Minds* over the years to know you always start with the witnesses. In fact, she was positive the actors would give them more information than the books that rested on the extensive bookshelves on the western wall of the ballroom. Old, coffee-stained papers rolled up and neatly tied with string rested on the table next to some other books and periodicals, but she could eye them up later, give them a glance on the way out. It was the interviewing process that was critical.

She started with Vivian Redblood. "Why do you hate Peter Peppermore?" she asked.

Vivan leaned back and laughed. "Peter? Hate him? Hate is a particularly strong word, but that rascal is always trying to slip into my bed. *If* you know what I mean." She winked, smiled.

"Oh?" Marcia jotted this down in the pocket-sized notebook the theater company provided.

"You're really getting into this, babe," Chazz said, sneaking up behind her. He wasn't really doing much except tailing her around, which was becoming annoying. She wished he would conduct his own investigation instead of leeching off her discoveries. "Kinda turns me on—you being all detective-ish. Wanna pick up a pair of handcuffs on the way home? So you can arrest me later?" He *meowed* against her neck, pretended his fingernails were claws, and gently dragged them down her shoulders. "I'll be a bad boy, and you can—"

"Would you go interview someone or look for clues?" Marcia told him, slipping from his touch. "You're wasting time just following me around."

He shot her a pouty-lipped glance, then saluted her. "Yes, captain. Wouldn't want to waste time, would we?" He scrolled through his phone and added, "It's the second quarter, by the way. If you care."

She didn't, and her non-response was enough to force him away, over to the bookcase, where he started scanning the spines. Why, she didn't know—but at least he wasn't on her ass, sucking the fun out of the room.

"Ugh," Marcia said aloud, turning back to Vivian. "Men, right?"

"Oh," the vampire lady said, "you have no idea."

"Actually…you're right. I don't. Tell me—what did you think of the grandmaster? Elvis Tuna—did you like him?"

"He was okay," Vivian said, rolling her eyes. "Not my favorite grandmaster this coven has ever had, but he was serviceable. But then again—I don't trust anyone. Especially Peter. Peter had motive to kill the grandmaster. If it was anyone, it was Peter."

"Interesting."

"She's lying," a voice said from behind Marcia. Marcia expected to turn and see the actor who played Peter standing there, but the voice was soft—a woman's voice. She was surprised when she spun around and saw Brittany standing about ten feet away, fists clenched at her sides. She looked genuinely shaken by the actor's rehearsed lines. "She's lying. That...none of that is true."

Marcia turned back to the actor, and the actor looked just as puzzled. "Excuse me?" Vivian avoided breaking character and kept up with the Dracula accent, but Marcia noticed a slight slip. Brittany's interjection had clearly taken her by surprise.

Foster came up behind his girlfriend or friend, whatever she was to him, and whispered something in her ear. Her face changed suddenly. "I just mean...I thought you loved Elvis Tuna. I thought you were...*friends.*"

The actress paused briefly to compose herself, then delivered a reply: "No, you were mistaken. Whoever told you that...Grayson... he's lying. Grayson always lies."

Foster tugged on the jean jacket tied to Brittany's waist, letting her know there were other actors to (startle) interrogate. The two of them left the immediate area, approaching the actor who played the role of Jono Manx. He stood by himself and faced the massive window, looking out across the moonlit waters.

Marcia rotated back to Vivian, her eyes still fixed on Brittany and Foster. Something about that brief interaction had rattled her. She grabbed the loose threads of her dress and twirled the strand around her forefinger, spending that nervous energy.

"So..." Marcia said, watching the actress's eyes glide back to hers. "Um, so, do you know about this human Elvis was in love with or...?"

It took Vivian almost a full thirty seconds to respond. "No," she said without much enthusiasm, as if Brittany were a vampire herself and she'd feasted on the girl's energy. "No, I never knew their name." And then," Excuse me."

She tore herself away from the conversation, leaving Marica to investigate other leads.

5.

THIRTY MINUTES LATER, Grayson rang the bell, signaling their time had expired. "I hope you all have gathered enough clues. We are heading into the second half of this evening's detective work. I think you've all done a fine job interviewing the suspects—I mean subjects—and I trust we are all one step closer to solving the mystery of who killed Grandmaster Tuna." He sidestepped away from the double doors that led back into the hallway. "Follow me. Right this way."

Marcia gripped Chazz's hand, and he reciprocated by intertwining his fingers with hers. Together, they marched across the room's threshold, following Grayson and the other vampire host's direction. She glanced over at Katie behind her. "Hope you're having fun," she said.

"Um, so much fun. Best birthday ever," Katie said, leaning her head on Hugo's shoulder while sipping from the margarita in her hand.

Once they entered the hall, Grayson stood off to the side while the others continued to their next stations. As she passed Vivian, Marcia noticed something still missing from the girl's eyes: the spark she had earlier, that discernable zest for her performance. The actor's new attitude told Marcia she didn't want to be there, that she'd rather be *anywhere* but this beautiful mansion overlooking the bay, playing her part in this immersive experience. She couldn't see how or why the small interaction with Brittany would dampen her mood so drastically. It was curious, but she didn't let Vivian's peculiar mood change affect her own enjoyment.

Jono Manx and Peter Peppermore headed up the excursion to the next set, a room much smaller than the ballroom, almost a hundred times smaller—the kitchen, even though this kitchen was still bigger than Marcia's first house. Clear containers of red liquid—blood, obviously blood—sat on the stainless-steel counters, a vampire's feast if ever there was one. Marcia assumed there would be no garlic kept back here, almost made that joke aloud, but then opted to keep quiet and let the actors do their thing.

Vivian and Grayson filed into the room last, and Marcia heard them whispering to each other, their tone coming off slightly contentious. She heard Grayson very clearly tell her, "We will talk about this later," and she could tell the man had reached his limit of whatever the two were discussing. However, he cleansed the aggravation from his expression and pressed on with the whole happy host persona, posting a beaming smile for the audience, vamp teeth practically sparkling with cleanliness. "Ah, the kitchen. The place where the body of our grandmaster was found. He was found..." Grayson picked up one of the containers and shook it, the fake blood sloshing around in gluey waves. "...drained of all his blood. A fitting end, some might say, for a vampire."

Marcia couldn't help but watch Foster and Brittany eye each other with a small amount of disgust, like they weren't so keen on the sight of blood, even though it was clearly a prop. Blood wasn't that thick. Nor did it move like pure maple syrup against gravity.

"There are clues in this room," Grayson continued, "clues that will—"

The lights blinked a few times before cutting out. A few gasps sounded in the impenetrable void, one of which might have come from Marcia's mouth, though she didn't realize it until seconds later. She felt someone grab her wrist, someone with cold hands, and she very nearly screamed. Then she realized it was a woman's hands. She could tell by the long—and fake—fingernails that scratched her skin.

It had to be Katie.

There was another noise, a scuffle of sorts, then an utterance: "OH MY GOD!" And a fleshy rip followed that (obviously) scripted line.

When the lights flashed back on, the actor who played the part of Jono Manx was bent over the sink, a jagged latex gash neatly applied to his throat, the phony red dripping from the phony wound.

Marcia took a second to gather her breath before silently applauding the theatrical scare.

But something on Grayson's face told her it might not have been all that fake. He looked worried—*too* worried—and confused. He eased himself back, retreating on his heels, like whatever had happened to the actor could potentially happen to any of them, himself included.

No, Marcia scolded herself, *you're being dumb. This is all part of the show.*

But it didn't feel like that. Did it?

No, certainly not.

"Uh-um," Grayson said, his tongue tripping over his thoughts. "Um, folks—" His accent slipped and was replaced by some north-western inflection, maybe Northern Minnesota. Like he could have been casted in the latest season of *Fargo*.

Vivian spotted the man's ruined throat, that missing hunk of flesh, and then let go of the shrillest scream Marcia had ever heard outside of a horror flick. She launched herself in reverse, backpedaling as far as she could until her spine slammed against one of the six refrigerators. Gasping, she brought her white-gloved hands to her open mouth, muffling the next throat-stripping scream.

Peter Peppermore, seemingly unable to grasp the event that had just transpired, inched his way toward the sink, calling out, "Dean? Dean, you okay?"

Took Marcia all of three seconds to determine that *Dean* was Jono's real name. Peter had broken character.

Suddenly, she realized this might not be an act at all.

Or was it? Could it be an act within an act? Was this somehow part of it? She hadn't known what to expect from the dinner/show. There were no reviews of *Grayson Hook's Vampire Murder Mystery Dinner* on Google, Yelp, or any other site. There was nothing, so there were no expectations, nothing to prepare for, nothing to anticipate— and Marcia Wong had always appreciated foreknowledge of certain future events. It made things…*easier*. Plus, she hated surprises, at least real-life ones. Twists in movies and television shows didn't bother her, but surprise birthday parties and harmless practical jokes really messed with her moods.

Marcia watched her future husband step up to the role of critic. He puffed out his chest, folded his arms, and said in the most unimpressed tone, "Haha, guys. You got us. Funny stuff."

Gravely, Grayson turned on them, his eyes bugging. "We must exit this place swiftly and ordinately."

"Now hold on there, buddy," Foster said, stepping forward, putting his hands up like everyone needed to chill the hell out. "You don't expect us to believe this little charade, do you?"

To sell it further, Vivian rushed out of the kitchen, sprinting through the open door like she needed to find a toilet to hurl into.

"Deena!" Grayson shouted after her, no traces of that Transylvanian accent left.

Marcia felt a slow rush of anxiety forming in her chest, rising like a surf-worthy wave.

"This is bullshit," Chazz said, rolling his eyes. Then he approached the fallen actor, despite the voices in the room shouting their concerns.

Peter Peppermore tried to step in his path, but Chazz forced him aside with an aggravated shove.

Once at the body in question, Chazz bent down for a closer view. His hand went for the neck-job, touching the applied effect.

"What do you see, hon?" Marcia asked, not really wanting to know, fearing the truth of what had taken place in the dark.

He retracted two fingers from the wound, then raised them for the group, showing off the wet red evidence. Then he sniffed his fingertips, taking in a deep breath and holding it. Something changed in his face right there, something Marcia hated with every morsel of her being.

Chazz looked like someone had told him his sweet grandmother had suddenly passed away. His throat bulged with the swallowing of his heavy truth.

It was then that Marcia knew this night would go very differently from how she had anticipated it.

"I think," Chazz said, whatever skeptic energy he had now completely gone, "we should get out of here..."

Marcia still felt compelled to doubt the man was dead, but her fiancé was convincing. He hustled back over to her, grabbed her hand, and started pulling her toward the door.

To the others, Hugo and Katie, he said, "Let's go. Seriously. Fuck this place."

Then the lights went out again.

And everyone screamed.

6.

THOSE TEN SECONDS spent in the pitch black were the worst Marcia could ever recall. Time was funny like that, though. Wasn't it? Ten seconds could feel like an hour under the right circumstances. But an hour could also feel a lot like ten seconds. She tried to cling to the times when the clock went the other way, those moments she wished would last forever but were always gone too soon. Often, those were childhood memories. There weren't too many memorable moments from her twenties—a couple of instances during her college years she wished she could go back to, but not many, and that was because she'd spent most of those years doing what she'd come there to do— study, learn, work hard to earn herself a degree, get a good job after and—

When the lights came back on, she realized that Chazz had stepped in front of her, putting himself between her and whatever potential danger lurked in the inky everywhere. She'd never seen him so protective before, and even though the current situation had her guts tied in inescapable knots, a warmness flooded her heart. At that moment, she could tell he truly loved her in ways he'd never verbally or physically show her because he was *not that kind of guy.*

This moment slashed whatever doubts she had about next April.

A horrible choking sound ripped her from a vision of walking down the aisle and seeing a clean-cut version of the man currently standing guard before her. She followed the noise straight ahead to see Jono Manx standing up now, no longer bent over the sink, eyes staring dead-like, milky-white yet somehow iridescent, eyes that no longer belonged to the living. His eyes were still like that, even though he was up and moving around. He made the sound again as if he needed to clear his throat of some colossal case of post-nasal drip. Then he twitched like his nerves were all shot out, misfiring, unable to adequately respond to the brutal trauma his body had just suffered. Next, he went rigid, leering at the group of living people in front of him. He opened his mouth, and two objects fell from behind his upper lip, hitting the tile floor. Marcia's eyes went directly to where the two tiny pieces scattered, and one bounced close to her feet, giving her a good look—it was a tooth.

Neck hairs on the rise, Marcia glanced back up at Jono Manx. His canines were longer now. Not just long but still growing. The fangs extended past his lower lip and then stopped. Once the teeth were ready to do some damage, Jono crouched, snarled, and emitted a ferocious roar that was wholly inhuman. Marcia noticed the man's fingernails had also grown a few inches. The pallor of his skin matched the tone of wet concrete.

"I think we should run," Hugo said, his voice small, traveling through constricted vocal cords.

"I agree," Chazz said, spinning, immediately pushing the rest of them back toward the doors.

Marcia whipped around, rushing for the exit. But so was everyone else, and the opening quickly became bottlenecked, slowing their escape and bringing them to a halt. She heard the man roar once again, that animal sound echoing off the kitchen's metallic walls.

A human scream followed, and Marcia looked over her shoulder in time to see Hugo fly backward across the room and crash into the low-hanging row of pots and pans. Katie stopped, spun around, and screamed Hugo's name, adding to the room's panic. Even if she wanted to do anything, help in some way, it was already too late. Cat-like, Manx pounced onto Hugo's fallen form that had landed beside some standing shelves full of cutlery. A small puddle of blood began crawling out from under his head. Manx gripped a handful of Hugo's hair, lifting his head from the red puddle. Hugo's pupils were jumping, sliding back beneath his eyelids. One of his legs twitched. Manx applied one hand to Hugo's chin, the other continuing to hold a good clump of wavy-brown hair. Then, the vampiric monster twisted his head in such a way that the movement didn't seem real but more like movie-magic practical effects than anything else. Anger dominated the actor's face as he wrenched the victim's head all the way around. Then, with one last Herculean effort, Manx tore Hugo's head clean off at the throat, the ragged opening spouting a geyser of blood that splashed the vampire's face.

Marcia's entire body went weak, unable to process what she'd just witnessed. Despite seeing the vicious murder take place, she continued to believe this was all a joke. An elaborate gag. A well-played ruse.

But when Grayson Hook screamed like a B-movie queen, that motivated her to accept this new reality.

The bottleneck in the doorway broke loose, and the mad rush into the hallway commenced.

7.

She hadn't committed the route to the mansion's front door to memory, and there were no red "exit" signs (surely a violation of some fire safety code). So, once everyone was out of the kitchen, she followed the herd. Grayson had taken off with remarkable speed, considering his gangly, unathletic form and bulky costume. He was halfway down the hall and rounding the next one before Marcia could firmly plant her feet on the autumn-brown, puke-orange carpet. Chazz was right behind her, checking over his shoulder to see if the thing Manx had become was in pursuit.

For the moment, the coast appeared clear.

They took the next turn, discovering another hallway. Grayson was gone. He had zoomed off and left them to eat his dust. A panic rose in Marcia's chest, swelling like an overinflated balloon, pushing her organs in new directions. Her guts were a twisted mess of anxiety. She faced the turn before her, expecting to see that long-toothed monster that had popped off Hugo's head as easily as a football helmet. Her mind had finally convinced herself they couldn't have faked that, that what she'd witnessed was genuine murder.

"Come on!" Chazz said, grabbing her arm and pulling her down the hall. She nearly tripped over her own feet. In the distance, pots and pans clashed together; the monster in the kitchen was clumsily banging around.

The vampire is coming, she thought, hating how stupid that sounded, hating how *vampire* was a real thing now, no longer a term reserved for movies, books, comics, spooky murder mysteries —*fiction*.

Chazz stopped when they reached the end of the next hall, the mansion's crossroads giving them three lanes to choose from. He spun on Peter Peppermore, grabbing the actor by his collar and shoving him against the wall. "Where the fuck is the exit?"

Peter was practically crying. "I don't know.

Chazz lifted him higher. "Fuck you mean?"

"I've only been here once! I was just hired to perform a week ago! We rehearsed at the Hilton in Seaview!"

Chazz let go of his collar, dropping him back on his feet. "Fuck!"

Marcia glanced over at Katie. Her mind was clearly broken, her blank stare peering into past events, probably re-seeing her new boyfriend's head getting snatched off his shoulders, the gory separation streaming in 4k behind her eyes. With her vacant stare aimed at the antique carpet, her feet took baby steps toward the hallway on the right. Her lips were moving, small sounds escaping that could have been words, fragments of shattered thoughts hitting the airwaves.

"Katie..." Marcia said, approaching her friend, putting a comforting hand on her shoulder. "It's going to be okay." As cliché as that sounded, it was the only solace she could offer, that general phrase people said when things were bad.

Fucked.

Katie whispered, "It's not real. Just a dream..." She repeated the phrase over and over. Her way of coping with the recent past.

Marcia turned to her fiancé and the others. It was just the three of them plus the actor. The two grungeheads, Vivian Redblood, and Grayson Hook had all gone their own ways.

"We have to get out of here," Marcia said to him.

Chazz returned a stare that made her feel ten times smaller. "No fucking shit, Mar. Did you come up with that on your own?"

She wanted to tell him to fuck off, but doing so was useless, wouldn't help them to safety any faster.

"*I'm sorry*," Katie whispered, the clarity of this confession stealing Marcia's attention.

She turned to her friend, offering another comforting shoulder touch. "What's that?"

"I'm sorry," Katie said, "for everything."

"Hey now," Chazz said, rushing over to them. "Let's focus on getting out of here. Okay? We have no idea where that thing is, and we have no—"

"Mar..." Katie said, tears filling her eyes. "Mar, I'm sorry."

"Shush," Marcia said, hugging her friend. "This isn't your fault."

"Yes, it is. It's—"

"Hey!" Chazz interrupted again. "Focus here!"

Marcia turned to him, her lower lip twitching, the nerves in her face alive with unfiltered rage. "Stop!"

"Mar—"

"I don't care. Just stop. Can't you see she's...she's hurting!"

"We're all going to die if we don't get outta here pronto." Chazz spoke slowly and clearly so his tone and the weight of the situation could not be misunderstood. "Does that not matter to you?"

"Have some empathy," she said with a shot of venom.

"Fine," he said, throwing his hands up. "Fine. You want to fuck around here, be my guest. I'm getting out of here. I'm—"

Before he could finish that nasty thought, something behind them bellowed. Everyone spun toward the sound, gasping and shrieking, hoping their worst fears would not be realized. But they were. At the end of the long hallway, the thing that Manx had become stood there, drenched in blood and chunky gore from head to toe. A feral grimace was plastered to the demonic thing's face. It mewled like some cat from Hell.

Manx made for them, taking off with inhuman speed.

A primal scream tore from Marcia's throat, and she turned and ran along with everyone else. They booked it as fast as they could down the hallway to the right, looking for a place to duck into, a door to get behind, anything they could use to barricade themselves from their immediate threat. She located a sturdy-looking wooden door on their right, but it was at least twenty seconds away, and the monster was gaining on them. She snuck a peek over her shoulder, seeing the bloodthirsty creature closing the gap between them.

"Faster!" Chazz shouted as if fear wasn't motivating them enough.

Her legs ached, but Marcia fought through the pain and made it to the door before the others. She cranked the knob and threw her shoulder into the door, the wooden barrier shooting open and slamming against the wall. The three others filed in, and then Chazz shut the door before their pursuer could follow them inside. As soon as the door was closed, a body plowed into it, nearly knocking Chazz backward. He regained his balance and applied his shoulder against the solid oak, giving the unwanted guest a run for his money. The blood-crazy beast on the other side continued to pound on the door, causing the oak shield to rattle on its hinges. Chazz powered the door closed, locked the knob, and threw the additional slide bolt for good measure.

They backed away, as there was nothing more they could do; the door would have to hold. The vampire made a few more attempts, heaving its weight against the barrier, but the barrier did its job and held firm against the violent effort. After about six more tries, the thing gave up. It must have heard one of the other guests or actors and left to pursue them instead.

Marcia took a deep breath, thankful she was alive. Thankful they all were.

She one-eightied and took in the view of the grand library; no windows, just towers of books and more books, ranging from huge volumes to skinny paperbacks, some aligned neatly in perfect rows, others messily stacked on top of each other on cluttered shelves. But it wasn't the books that captured her attention.

It was Grayson Hook. And Vivian Redblood.

Their vampire host was standing over Vivian. She was lying on the ground, holding a throat now generously coated with leaking scarlet. Blood filled the cracks between her fingers, running in hurried rivulets. Her eyes stared up at the vaulted ceiling. It took Marcia about ten seconds to realize she was dead. That those eyes were looking into a world unlike this one.

A dead world.

Then, Marcia's eyes settled on Grayson's, Vivian's obvious murderer. His clothes were soaked with her red.

8.

"It wasn't me," was the first thing out of Grayson's mouth. "Honest!" He stepped back to further separate himself from the mess at his feet. "I found her like this."

"Why's her blood all over your clothes?" Marcia asked, surprised that she had the strength to speak anything at all.

"I was…I found her bleeding. I tried to save her!"

Likely story, she almost said aloud, as if she were still interrogating actors as part of a game. But this wasn't a game anymore, and it didn't matter who killed Vivian Redblood. What mattered was that what happened to Vivian could happen to her, too. And this was no longer a fun evening of cozy murder mysteries but a harrowing night that would test her survival instincts.

"What's going on here?" Chazz marched over to Grayson, getting in the man's face. He was close enough to kiss him. "Tell me right now. Or I'll jam my foot so far up your ass, you'll be shitting my toenails for weeks."

Grayson cowered under the threat, shrinking to a crouch. Defensively, he raised his arms. "I don't know! I swear!"

Chazz grabbed the man by the chin, stuck his fingers in the host's mouth.

Marcia was certain Grayson's next comment was, *"What are you doing!?"* but she couldn't tell for sure because Chazz's fingers blocked most of the words, reducing the sentence to a mumble. When Chazz retracted his fingers, he was holding the man's false teeth, the vampiric add-ons.

"You asshole!" Grayson shouted at him, holding his mouth like the extraction hurt.

Chazz tossed what looked like an orthodontic retainer for the undead on the ground at Marcia's feet. He shot Marcia a look that told her somehow, someway, this was entirely her fault. She hated that look. And, at that moment, *him.*

Her fiancé gripped the host by the neck again and slammed him into a bookcase stacked high with leatherbound hardbacks. Rocked off the shelves, some books tumbled to the floor. "I think you know more than you're letting on," Chazz growled in his ear.

"I swear!" Grayson shouted. "I'm just an actor, man!"

"Who runs this shit?"

Grayson's eyes fell on the long, rolling ladder designed for taller shelves as if he were plotting to ascend and escape somehow. "I...I bought the company last year."

"So you *do* know what's going on."

"This is the first time we've put on this show! When we performed the other story, it was so boring...mobsters and weddings and...recycled storylines, *blah!*"

"So you chose vampires?"

"Exactly!"

"And thought it was a good idea to murder people!" Chazz butted his forehead against Grayson's. "A man literally lost his head tonight, scumbag! You're going to jail for the rest of your life. Just wait until the police get here." As if Chazz remembered they'd forgotten something—"Babe...did you call the cops?"

Marcia hadn't, but she grabbed her phone immediately. She made the call to 911 and gave the woman who answered all the available information—the where, the what.

"This wasn't how it was supposed to happen," Grayson said, his voice breaking. Tears streamed from his eyes, and Marcia felt her heart fold in on itself.

"Put him down," Marcia said to Chazz.

"What? Are you nuts? This motherfucker has to pay." He slammed Grayson against the wall again, harder, shaking more books. Classic literature fell like hail.

"Chazz..." She shook her head, and she knew that *he knew* that headshake. It was the *I'm-right-you're-wrong-and-stop-it* motion that he could not ignore.

"Dammit," he said, slamming the man one last time before letting him go.

"We found a book," Grayson said, the words sounding like a confession. He was feeling various spots around his neck area as if making sure Chazz had left his head attached.

"Well, congrats," Chazz said sarcastically. "You're in a fucking library. I should hope so."

"We thought it was all bullshit."

At this, the room quieted.

Then, understanding that Grayson needed to elaborate, Marcia said, "What was all bullshit?"

"The story. In the book." He said this like she should have known, like he'd told the story and was pissed at her for not following along. But then he relaxed some. Evened out. He sighed, collecting his composure before continuing with the tale they all needed to hear, so this could all make sense. "Deena and I found this book at an estate sale..."

"Who's Deena?" asked Chazz.

"That was Deena," Peter said, pointing to Vivian Redblood's corpse.

Marcia had almost forgotten Peter had been in the room while they were all arguing.

"We always went to estate sales," Grayson continued. "We found this book at some old guy's mansion up in Northern Maine. Started reading the stuff inside, thought it was a hoot, and then thought we could earn some bucks off it. It was a fancy-looking book. Old. Hundreds of years old. It had to be worth something, we thought. It was written like an epistolary novel, the accounts of someone named

Elvis Tuna. He was a grandmaster vampire in charge of this coven and convinced that someone was coming to murder him. It was the ravings of a lunatic, more or less.

"Deena and I…we read it. Saw dollar signs in its pages. Thought we could flip it for a fortune. Thought it was some great literary work, like *Dracula*. It was written in ink, so it was an original manuscript. But…when we researched it…there was no published novel of the sort. This was an original, unpublished work."

"So," Chazz said, "what's that got to with what's happened here tonight?"

Grayson's upper lip twitched. "I'm getting there. See, we had half a mind to take the manuscript and try to get it published. Thought the story was so great, so masterfully told, despite its ravings, that we could publish it under a pseudonym. But…turns out…it ain't that easy to publish a book. So…we tried something else."

"Something else?" Marcia asked.

"We were actors," Grayson said. "Failed actors. Actually, that's how I met Deena. Auditions in New York City. Off-Broadway plays. We won a few bit parts, surely nothing to write home about. Still worked two jobs on the side to pay for our ridiculous rent. When we couldn't sell the book to a publishing house in New York, we opted to turn it into a stage play. But when that didn't work…" He looked at Vivian's corpse quite fondly. "Deena…she worked for a traveling murder mystery theater that put on dinner parties. She said the shows always sold out. It was a gold mine. So…we started one."

"Want to get to the part where you incorporated real fucking vampires into the act?" Chazz demanded. "Or…hired some assholes who *think* they're real fucking vampires."

A grave look glossed over Grayson's face. His eyes couldn't look anywhere but the savaged throat of Vivian Redblood. "Oh…I forgot to tell you—it's real."

Marcia shook her head in disbelief. "Wait? What?"

Grayson found her eyes, and what she saw in them sent a polar rush through her veins, a kind of cold that nearly stopped her beating heart.

"The story…" Grayson said, dreamy-eyed. "It's all real."

9.

"THIS GUY IS FUCKED in the head six ways to Sunday," Chazz said to them.

The three of them—Chazz, Marcia, and Katie—were on the opposite side of the library while Grayson and Peter stood near the corpse of Vivian Redblood. Her skin had taken on a bluish hue that Marcia found sickening, and she couldn't stand being that close to an actual dead body.

The slain bodies on detective TV shows were fine because they weren't real.

"I say we take our chances and get out of here," Chazz said, unable to detach his gaze from the man who'd refused to take off that ridiculous top hat, even under the current circumstances. "We rush out that door and try to find the exit. Find a window to dive through or something."

Katie had barely spoken since her boyfriend's head came off. She remained silent, seemingly uninterested in how to proceed.

Marcia couldn't keep quiet. She said out loud what everyone was likely thinking: "That monster…he's still out there."

"Just one guy, Mar," Chazz reminded her. "We can outrun him. Plus, do the math. He can only take out one of us."

"Oh yeah? Well, what if that one person is *you*?"

"Chance I'm willing to take, babe."

"Oh, of course you are. Because, out of everyone in the room, you're the most likely to survive."

"How's that?" It was a ridiculous question, but she wasn't surprised he asked it. It was like he was asking her to confirm what made him better than everyone else, asking her to feed his ego delicious compliments. *Oh, babe, you're so much faster, stronger. I mean, you do work out every day, several hours a day, while I don't, while I can barely find the time to walk on the treadmill an hour a week…*

Fuck that.

"We can't leave," she said. "The police are coming."

"We don't know that."

"I called them."

"Thirty minutes ago," Chazz said. A humorless laugh followed. "And they're not here yet? Something is wrong."

"Well…" She didn't want to admit that the authorities should have arrived by now. "Fine. We have to escape. *But…*" She tipped her head in Katie's direction. "I don't think all of us are ready to move right now."

Chazz's lips bunched, like he wanted to say something about that, something mean-spirited perhaps, something that would only spark an argument and waste more valuable time rather than come up with a viable solution. So, he stomped his foot and shouted, "Fuck!" Then he grabbed Marcia's elbow, taking her to the side, away from Katie, where she couldn't hear their conversation. "You realize this is life or death, right?"

Marcia couldn't take her eyes off her friend. "You want me to just leave her?"

Biting his lip, Chazz gripped her shoulders. His aggressive touch hurt some. "Mar, please, I need you to listen to me. A man's fucking head came off! Do you not realize there's a fucking psycho running around, killing people?"

"She's my friend. I…I can't."

Chazz leaned close and whispered in her ear, "Is she worth more than your own life?"

Marcia came back with, "She wouldn't leave me."

Eyes smiling, Chazz shook his head. "You don't know that." With that, he walked away, back over to the rest of the group. Before he could get there and round up the others, motivate them to leave the library and make for the exit, there was a knock at the door.

Everyone turned, Marcia included. She fixed her gaze on the sturdy oak slab, wondering how much more abuse the barrier could take. If the psycho had been motivated enough, he could have rammed through it. He must have locked onto easier prey elsewhere, causing him to abandon his pursuit.

Now he was back to finish the job.

But the noise at the door wasn't a shoulder battering but the light tapping of gentle knuckles. "Hello?" a small voice said, one Marcia almost recognized. "Are you guys there?"

Brittany.

Marcia glanced back at Chazz. His face was held hostage by sudden worry. Shaking his head, he telegraphed his opinion on the decision at hand.

"Please, if you're in there," Brittany continued, "I need help. I think the monster killed Foster—I can't find him—and…and I think it's coming back for me."

Marcia felt hollow inside. She imagined *not* letting the girl in and listening to her dying shrieks as her inhuman murderer satisfied their thirst for carnage.

She couldn't do it. Couldn't let the girl go out like that, couldn't live with herself if she left her out there all alone with a bloodthirsty maniac.

"Mar…" she heard Chazz plead, but she was already halfway to the door and committed to the cause. "Mar, let's talk about this. Please."

There was no talking, no swaying her. She reached the door hastily. Gripped the knob. Opened the door just a crack. Just enough to eye the limited opening.

She couldn't see anything save for the hallway. Then she was jolted back, knocked off her feet, and sent tumbling to the ground. She rolled on her back, immediately launching herself to her feet, taking a defensive pose, though clearly outmatched against whatever was coming through the door.

The door swung open, the hinges squealing almost excitedly. As if the anticipation of the intruder was just too much to keep silent about.

Marcia watched them enter. They almost floated into the library, like there were inches between the bottoms of their shoes and the burgundy runner that led into the room.

Foster. Brittany. Both with painted smiles that dripped a runny red.

"Hello again, friends," Brittany said, showing off two rows of teeth, each pointed like the tip of a steak knife.

10.

FOSTER'S NIRVANA T-shirt was splattered with flecks of red, a few chunks of what looked like clotted blood boogers. Their victims' gore also covered most of what Brittany was wearing, like she'd been hosed with the stuff. A metallic perfume defeated the smell of the collection of old books, causing the dinner in Marcia's stomach to churn. Nausea took over, and she felt her gorge defeating gravity.

"What an unexpected surprise," Brittany said, sauntering into the room. Her gaze fixed on Grayson. "Where is it?"

Grayson's eyes diverged from hers, bouncing between the others in the room. "I-I don't know what you mean."

"Surely you jest." Brittany crossed the library, parking herself about six feet away from Grayson and Peter. She glanced at the tragedy on the floor before them. "Her blood is on your hands, Mr. Sandstrom. Everyone who dies here tonight—all your fault."

"Wait a minute. How do you know my name?" Grayson stared on, perplexed. "Who are you people?"

Brittany brightened at the question. "Allow me to formally introduce myself." Marcia hadn't heard it before, but now the woman's accent came through cleanly. She didn't think she was acting. "My name is Vivian Redblood. *Thee* Vivian Redblood. In the flesh."

A stunned silence washed over the room. No one moved, spoke, or even blinked. Marcia could not hear the wind of her own breath.

Then, obnoxious laughter broke the silent spell, echoing throughout the book-laden chamber. Marcia turned and saw Chazz holding his gut, shaking with each hoot and howl. "Oh, man—that's a good one. You all almost had me." He propped himself against a desk in the center of the room as if the laughing had weakened him. Sucking in big breaths of air, he placed a hand over his heart as if measuring out the beats. He then closed his eyes as if that might help center his emotions.

The woman formerly known as Brittany, now known as Vivian Redblood, seemed amused by his reaction. She circled toward him, moving like a lioness stalking easy prey, licking those whittled teeth perfectly designed for shearing through muscle and meat. Unlike the vampire (felt weird using that word in the logical sense) from the kitchen, whose sharp teeth only included the canines, every tooth in Vivian's mouth was a dagger. As Chazz finally got his hilarious outburst under control, Vivian got into position. Marcia was immediately reminded of her childhood cat, Mr. Marbles, who shimmied in place before launching into attack mode at whatever toy/house rodent lay unsuspectingly before him.

Before Marcia could open her mouth to warn her fiancé, Vivian lunged, plunging her hand into Chazz's gut, piercing the shirt, the skin, her appendage disappearing wrist-deep inside him. His eyes opened wide as if they might explode from his head. Vivian pushed a little deeper, her wrist disappearing another few inches. Chazz tried to separate himself, but his strength was outmatched. With her free hand, Vivian kept him where he was by gripping the back of his head, a fistful of his scraggly golden locks. Then she withdrew as if she'd absentmindedly laid her palm on a hot stove, lightning quick. What looked like raw sausages came with the exit. A loop of his intestines dangled out of the blood-filled cavity in his abdomen.

Marcia felt a sick surge of panic leap upon her, nearly knocking her off her feet. She backed away from the madness, the images that couldn't possibly be real, and spun for the doorway.

But Foster was there, his teeth shining with bloody radiance. "Where you going, girly?"

Nowhere, she thought. *I'm going nowhere.*

And she was right.

Chazz fell to the floor, splashing in the inch-thick spread of his own blood. He squirmed and slipped in the muck, trying to find his footing but failing to secure purchase in the soaked carpet. His strength fled from him, and the condition of the floor did not help matters. After a few short moments, he must have realized he was seconds away from meeting his end because he stopped moving altogether and rested his cheek on the wetness beneath him.

"Now..." Vivian said, pointing the finger that had just skewered out some of Chazz's guts, "...where is my goddamn book?"

"Your...book?" Grayson was visibly shaking as he backed himself into a bookcase. "What do you mean by *your* book?"

"I don't know how that rich fuck acquired it, but I want it back. It's mine."

"Ours," Foster said as he approached Peter Peppermore. "Oh, by the way," he told Peter, getting uncomfortably close to the actor, "I'm the real Peter Peppermore. Pleasure to meet the man who planned to burglarize my identity."

Actor Peter's face looked like he wanted to make some sense of what was happening, dial things back, and piece together the information his brain was attempting to process. But things were moving way too fast for him to catch up. He opened his mouth to speak, but the real Peter didn't allow him the opportunity to explore the scenario. The man formerly known as Foster punched his fist into Peter's mouth, grabbing the actor's lower jaw. He took his other hand and inserted his fingers along the top set of teeth, then pulled in opposite directions. The actor's jaw came apart like a wishbone, snapping free. The man's hands immediately went to his ruined head, patting the damage and trying to put himself back together, but that proved useless. In the next instant, the monster wearing the Nirvana tee went for his neck, attacking with his teeth. He sank every tapered tooth into the softness of Actor Peter's neck and bit down, hard, with unstoppable pressure. Blood ejected from the series of punctures. The actor howled through his ruined, deflated hole of a mouth, screams that would die and go indefinitely quiet.

Marcia couldn't watch the murder since she was too busy gagging at the sight of all that blood running from the man she'd gone to bed with almost every night over the last few years.

"Actor man," Vivian said to Grayson, her accent thickening as her ire rose. She snapped her fingers. "Give me the book or more of you will die here tonight."

"The book..." Grayson said as if watching the breaking of his friend's jaw had made him forget all about the thing in the first place. "Oh, right. The book."

"It's location," Peter demanded, tongue-bathing his bloody fingers. "Or I'll keep you alive just long enough for a midnight snack."

"It's..." Grayson pointed toward the desk in the corner of the library, back where the rolling ladder was stationed. "It's in that desk."

"Retrieve it," Vivian commanded.

Grayson did as she asked, hustling over to the desk, opening the drawer, and extracting an old black book, well-worn at the edges. The binding looked loose, separated from the glue that once held it together. Not all the pages appeared to line up with one another. Some were possibly missing. Looked more like a high schooler's messy notebook than a coveted text of well-kept secrets.

"Give it," Vivian demanded once again, holding out her flat palm.

Like a loyal puppy, Grayson brought her the book. He backed

away once it was in her hands, skulking into the shadowy light the room's candles provided.

"At last," she said, flipping through the pages, her eyes soaking in the passing words. "Our history is ours once again."

"History?" Marcia said softly, though she'd meant to keep this to herself.

"Yes, the stories of our past. Where we've been. Passed down from generation to generation. Everything leading up to the murder of our grandmaster, Elvis Tuna."

Marcia wanted to protest this knowledge, tell the woman she was wrong, disturbed, that vampires and covens did not exist. But her intuition spoke to her, telling her this was incorrect.

It was real.

All of it.

And she had witnessed the proof firsthand. It was lying before her in pools of blood.

"If I had known..." Grayson said, his knees quivering as he stood there. "I would have never..."

"Never what?" Vivian asked. "Stolen our story? Our legacy? Do you know how much that hurts? To have our history used and manipulated...for what—local theater? A measly eighty-dollar entry fee?"

Grayson scrambled. "I mean, this was opening night. We were going to charge more, but we thought we'd gain some praise before—"

"SILENCE," the woman bellowed loud enough that Marcia's ears began to ache. "I am not interested in your pathetic excuses, your lies."

"Please..." Grayson dropped to his knees, clasping his hands together—the ultimate pleading position. "We can make this right. With your help, we can make this better than the original—and you can profit from it! Your own story, realized in the theater. Forget murder mystery dinners! We'll be on Broadway!"

Vivian seemed to entertain the thought, smirking at Grayson's proposal. "Peter, love. Show Mr. Sandstrom what we think of his offer."

"My pleasure," Peter said, advancing on Grayson with the quickness of a squirrel finding a winter nut.

Grayson paled. "Wait, nuh—"

Marcia couldn't handle another vicious murder. She turned her cheek on the savage display. No matter how hard she pressed her palms against her ears, she couldn't muffle the sounds of Grayson's tortured screams.

When it was over, there was silence. Marcia snuck a peek, hoping she wouldn't have to suffer more grisly sights, but when she looked, Peter was holding Grayson's head, dangling the rough contour of the hacked neck over his mouth, catching as much of the red drippage as possible.

This time, she puked. Dinner renewed itself without any trouble, a fresh stream of vomit piling up messily on the long carpet.

When it was over, she tried to get up from her knees but couldn't find the strength.

"Come on," Peter said, dancing across the room while holding Grayson's head where it would be if he were dancing with a partner. "It's not that bad." Then he stopped abruptly and tossed the head into the corner of the room like an indignant kiddo *so* done with his toy.

Peter made his way over to Katie, who stood like a stone statue born of Medusa's eyes. Marcia wanted to tell him to leave her alone, back the fuck up, get out of here. Tell them they had what they'd come for, and none of it had anything to do with them. But she couldn't get the words out, her throat burning from the stream of bile that had torn up her esophagus.

"Look at you, pretty thang," Peter said, mimicking some southern accent. "Bet you like your vampires all southern-like, huh? Like *True Blood* or some shit."

"Knock it off, Peter," Vivian warned. She continued flipping through the pages as if making sure every word was accounted for.

"Oh, I know your secrets, pretty thang," Peter said directly into Katie's ear. "Discovered all sorts of things when I drank from your friend over there. You're *just* friends, right?"

Katie seemed mortified by whatever Peter was hinting at. She craned her neck in Marcia's direction.

"Oh," Peter said, "this is juicy. She doesn't know, does she?"

"Peter," Vivian scolded, "stop playing with the humans and come help me."

Peter's eyes glimmered like polished tokens. He ignored Vivian's request and shook his finger at Marcia. "You know, I see some potential in you."

"Peter!" Vivian shouted.

He spun around. "What?"

"Are you going to help or not?"

"What are we going to do with these two?"

Vivian studied them, then checked the bodies on the floor. "Well… we've spilled enough blood today."

"I want her," Peter said, connecting with Marcia's eyes. The longer she stared back, the more distant everything around her seemed. Like the environment was fading. "What do you think? Can I keep her?"

Vivian rolled her eyes, closed the book, and then meandered across the library until she was close enough to kiss Marcia on the cheek. She began inspecting the human specimen before her, measuring her with her eyes, pinching the small bulb of fat on the back of her arms, and gripping her meaty thighs. Then she dragged her hand up her leg, stopping near her vagina. She let her fingertips linger there. If she weren't so afraid, weren't so lost in the daze that Peter's eyes created, she might have tried to dodge this assault. Helpless, she continued to let Vivian Redblood explore her body without resistance.

"She's fine," Vivian said.

"I'm glad she meets your approval," Peter replied with delight.

"Turn her."

"My pleasure."

Before Marcia could protest whatever "turning" entailed—though she'd seen *Interview With The Vampire* enough times to get the gist—Peter was on her, attaching his sharp teeth to the tender spot of her neck, sinking them beneath the surface of her flesh. At first the pain was incredibly overwhelming, a deep, wide ball of agony that seemed to grow several inches per second. But shortly after, there was nothing. No pain. No pressure. A numbing sensation that transcended all other feelings, deadening not just her body's pain receptors but her thoughts as well.

She let the wave take her, sweep her off her feet. It felt like flying high, the lightlessness of the body leaving the earthly surface. She closed her eyes and laughed—actually laughed—succumbing to these shallow sensations that bled through the numbness. All at once, a deluge of happiness fell upon her, and she experienced total euphoria.

She smiled.

Blinked.

Ecstasy ruled over her now, a heavenly flow through her veins.

A second later, she found herself standing next to Peter, watching his bloody smile expand, those sharp teeth stained with her vitality. She couldn't remember ever feeling so good, feeling so free, like she'd just been born. No longer was she concerned about trivial things; the upcoming wedding she'd been stressing over, that desire—no, *need*— to make everything perfect. The daunting task of preparing and ensuring every *i* was dotted and every *t* was crossed—now nothing but a memory of something she was almost certain never happened.

"Feel that?" Peter asked, elated with his work. "It's you... becoming *you*. A new you."

"I'm..." she said, checking her body. Her veins were swollen— pronounced tubes covering the length of her figure. "...hungry."

Peter stepped aside and held out his hands, presenting Katie. "A feast for you. Your first of many."

Katie had been Marcia's best friend, but now, she was nothing more than a sack of blood for the taking.

Marcia didn't hesitate. Her primal focus kicked in, and she lunged at Katie, who only put up her arms and screamed in defense.

Marcia bit into her, drinking from her. The amount of blood that shot from the woman's torn neck was sickening, but Marcia didn't find blood repulsive anymore. Quite the opposite. It was beautiful and flowed like fresh wine from a newly uncorked bottle. She sipped and drank, and images began to flash through her mind. Memories. But not her own. They belonged to someone else, like looking through the eyes of someone else's life, someone else's experiences. Birth. Crawling. Walking. Grade school. Soccer practices. Basketball games. Birthday parties. Some faces she recognized, her own included, taking swings at a piñata in a backyard. Later, high school. Driving lessons. Her first fuck. College. Graduation. First job. First new car. Then...

"Oh yes," Peter said, a new sparkle in his eyes. This one Marcia did not like. "When you drink from someone, you will know them.

Everything they've ever done. Everything they've witnessed. Every single secret they've held onto. Secrets live in the blood."

She looked at Katie. Though the woman wasn't dead yet, she was close. There were tears in her eyes, but not ones that accompanied the knowledge of encroaching death. They were tears of sorrow. Of regret. Of remorse.

"I'm...sorry..." Katie said, the last words that would ever leave her mouth.

Marcia bit into her again, anger fueling this attack. The mess she made was deliberate, tearing through her jugular, shaking her head with fury. Grunting and screaming into the blood that seemed to flow endlessly.

"Marcia will never know," she had said to him, to Chazz. *"She will never know."*

But she knew now. And she had Grayson Hook and his murder mystery dinner to thank. That little black book that led them all here.

"Come on," Vivian said. "Let's get out of here. It smells too human."

As she left, Peter grabbed Marcia by the arm and hoisted her to her feet. "Come, darling," he said before proceeding to the library's exit.

She followed him into that dark, endless twilight.

A TOTALLY NORMAL
AFTERWORD

I'm always curious if anyone reads author's notes, but as an avid fan of single-author collections, I just love it when an author includes behind-the-scenes looks into the stories. Maybe it's the writer part of me that loves them so. I hope there's value in them for the reader, too.

Before I dive into each story in *This is Totally Normal*, I'd like to thank a few people. Firstly, my wife—Ashley—who's been there from the beginning of my publishing journey and continues to be my main source of inspiration. Love you to the moon and back. Also would like to thank editors Kenneth W. Cain and James G. Carlson. Kenneth edited a few of the previously published pieces in here, and James polished the new stories. Both are amazing at what they do, and I can't thank them enough. Lastly, I have to thank you, the reader, because if you're reading this…if you're here with me in this moment…you're awesome. Any writer and publisher will tell you that short story collections are a tough sell (unless you're a household name), so if you're here, then from the bottom of my heart—thank you for taking this weird trip to other worlds with me. Means everything. – **Tim Meyer, 1/20/24**

Okay! Let's get on with the fun stuff!

Trunks – I love a good coming-of-age tale, and they work well in the novella format. *Trunks* came along when I had the idea of a hitman accidentally kidnapping a young kid while taking on contracts for the mob. Thought it might be a novel, but it ended up being a lot shorter, as I mainly focused on the kid instead of the larger cast of characters. Of course, the hitman couldn't be an *ordinary* hitman, could he? No, he could not.

Streaming Live at the Bottom of the World – Social media is weird, isn't it? Honestly, I'm not much of a fan. I see the value in it, of course, but like everything, it has downsides. This one is about obsession and revenge set in a world where social media is not just a hobby or part of life—it *is* life. Reading this one back, I find myself in love with the dark-Twilight-Zone vibes.

Oceans Swallow Our Shores – If you've followed my work, you'll probably know that I love writing stories that take place on the beach or near the shore. I guess that's no accident, as I've lived about 20 minutes from the Atlantic Ocean my entire life. "Oceans Swallow Our Shores" is about a semi-apocalyptic event that drags the Jersey Shore into the water, and a determined investigator exploring the anomaly after her sister goes missing down there. Practically growing up on Jersey Shore boardwalks served as the inspiration for the setting in this one. I also love stories and movies about deep-sea exploration and thought it would be a cool topic to explore in the short story format.

Wolves in the Diamond – I love werewolves and I love baseball. I was invited to an anthology that was suddenly (and sadly) canceled, but this would have been my story. It needed to be coming-of-age, so I decided to combine my two loves for this one story. I feel like it could be expanded into a novel one day…

Gulls – Hungry seagulls can be mean. At least, the ones in this story are. The origins of this story are hazy, but I'm pretty sure I wrote it for my now defunct Patreon page. I remember wanting to write about a woman lost at sea. Madness, her secrets, and the terror in the skies all catch up with her.

Bettor's Edge – I don't live too far from Atlantic City, the backdrop of this tale. I've spent a lot of time in the casinos, playing poker mostly. *A lot* of poker. Not anymore. But for the better part of a year in my early twenties, poker was my main income. Met a lot of interesting characters that served as the inspiration for Dylan McGraw.

Feasting on the Fruits of Forever – I don't think it's much of a secret that my favorite novel of mine is *Malignant Summer.* Hooperstown is based on my hometown of Toms River. It was fun returning to Hooperstown years after the events of the novel. This one is for fans of *Malignant Summer.* And for me.

Attic Girl – I've written a lot about suicide—a super sensitive subject for some, and understandably so—and I can't quite articulate what draws me back to the topic, other than I'm quite familiar with it (in ways I won't get into here). Anyway, this is definitely not the feel-good story of the collection and can't honestly remember why I wrote it.

The Last Great Hot Eating Contest in Northern Mississippi – Who doesn't love a good B-movie? This one was written back when I was writing over-the-top bloodbath horror, like *Kill Hill Carnage* and *Sharkwater Beach.* There's something about genetically mutated animals on a rampage that just tickles me.

The Hag on the Fifth Floor – My wife and I spent over 3 months in the NICU after our kiddo was born. It was one of the worst stretches of my life, in all the ways you can probably imagine. Naturally, I felt compelled to write a horror story about it. And this is it.

White Walpurgis – I'm very familiar with wedding photography, so I wondered what would happen if a photographer showed up to a wedding where the family was into the dark arts. This was the result. And, of course, the goat is my favorite character in the story.

Virescent Sky – I love when fantasy and horror join forces, so this was like what if *Game of Thrones* and *The Thing* had a baby. I wrote it for an anthology invite and doing so reignited my love for high fantasy tales.

Grayson Hook's Vampire Murder Mystery Dinner – A few years back, before COVID, my wife took me to a murder mystery dinner for my birthday. It's a fun experience if you've never been, and I was impressed by the actors who stayed in character for the whole performance, even when interacting with the audience off-stage. I don't know if there is such a thing as a vampire-themed murder mystery dinner—never looked—but there definitely should be, and maybe I just found my next business venture?

ABOUT THE AUTHOR

Tim Meyer dwells in a dark cave near the Jersey Shore. He's the author of more than fifteen novels, including *Malignant Summer*, *The Switch House*, *Dead Daughters*, *Limbs*, and many other titles. When he's not working on the next book, he's usually hanging out with his wife and son, shooting around on the basketball court, playing video games, or messing with a new screenplay. He bleeds coffee and IPAs.

You can learn more about his books at timmeyerwrites.com.

instagram.com/timmmeyer11

tiktok.com/@tim_meyer11

www.ingramcontent.com/pod-product-compliance
Lightning Source LLC
Chambersburg PA
CBHW061240310726
48971CB00007B/2153